THEOPHILUS

A TALE OF ANCIENT ROME

To Mary Ann –
Thanks & God bless!

LEWIS BEN SMITH

eLectio Publishing
Little Elm, TX
www.eLectioPublishing.com

Theophilus: A Tale of Ancient Rome
By Lewis Ben Smith

Cover Design by eLectio Publishing.

ISBN-13: 978-1-63213-272-7

Published by eLectio Publishing, LLC
Little Elm, Texas
http://www.eLectioPublishing.com

Printed in the United States of America

5 4 3 2 1 eLP 21 20 19 18 17

The eLectio Publishing creative team is comprised of: Kaitlyn Campbell, Emily Certain, Lori Draft, Court Dudek, Jim Eccles, Sheldon James, and Christine LePorte.

Publisher's Note

THIS BOOK IS DEDICATED TO:

My daughters, Rachel and Rebecca,
who fill my every day with love and laughter.

My wife, Patty,
who has been my best friend, sweetheart,
and life partner since second grade!

My mom and dad,
whom I love more than I can say.

And, once more, to my favorite pen pal, Ellie,
who read every chapter as I wrote it
and provided me with a ton of constructive criticism.

Ready for the next one?

ALSO BY LEWIS BEN SMITH

The Testimonium

The Redemption of Pontius Pilate

Matthew's Autograph

"It seemed fitting for me as well, having investigated everything carefully from the beginning, to write it out for you in consecutive order, Most Excellent Theophilus."

—Luke 1:3

PROLOGUE
Rome: October, 64 AD

The last of the smoldering embers had been put out weeks before, but the city of Rome still reeked of smoke and death. The Great Fire had swept across the city like a scourge from the gods, destroying three of the fourteen districts of Rome and severely damaging seven others. Tens of thousands were dead, and many others still missing, their charred remains buried beneath the fallen houses and shops that sprawled across the seven hills of the Tiber. The Great Forum had been spared from some of the damage by the frantic demolition of the many wooden buildings that surrounded it, but still two temples had lost their roofs and some of the shops along the far edge of the plaza had burned to the ground.

The Senate of Rome had gathered in the Curia Julia, the meeting hall built for them a century before by order of Gaius Julius Caesar, the *Divus Julius* that many Romans still worshipped as a god. Barely begun before Caesar's life was cut short by treachery, the Curia had been finished by his great-nephew and adopted son, Caesar Augustus, the first true emperor of Rome. The hall was crowded when the Senate was at its full capacity, but the purges and executions carried out by Augustus' three successors had nearly reduced the Senate to its original size of three hundred members.

The mood of the city was ugly, and the Senate's mood reflected that. No one knew for sure how the fire had started, but rumors had swept the city for weeks—and the most persistent rumors involved none other than Nero Claudius Caesar Augustus Germanicus, the *Princeps* and *Imperator* of Rome. Some said that he had set the fires himself, riding out incognito with a gang of young hellions that he enjoyed carousing with. Others said that he had ordered his minions to set the fires, and then stood on the balcony of his villa and played the lyre, singing about the sack of Ilium while Rome burst into flames all round him. The official story was that the emperor had been away from the city, inspecting an aqueduct project in Antium, when the fires broke out. According to his Praetorians, the emperor had rushed back to the city, organizing companies of firefighters and relief efforts for those rendered homeless by the blaze. It was a measure of how much the people had come to despise Nero that very few people believed the official version of events. There were stories that the young emperor had been jeered and even pelted with stones by an angry crowd in the forum when he last showed his face, a month before.

So now this emergency meeting of the Senate had been called, and the Conscript Fathers of Rome waited impatiently for the *Imperator* to make his appearance. Laecenius Bassus, the senior consul, shifted impatiently on his curule chair, glancing at his consular colleague, Licinius Crassus. During the days of the Republic, the consuls had been the highest elected officials of Rome, chief executives who commanded armies and conducted foreign policy during their year in office. But since Augustus' great reforms of Rome's government, the consuls had become senior magistrates who served at the emperor's pleasure. Nero had initially restored some of the Senate's powers when he inherited the purple at the age of sixteen, but in recent years he had become more and more arbitrary and tyrannical, and neither consul dared call the Senate to order without him.

The tramping steps of the Praetorian guards echoed across the Forum, audible through the open doors of the Curia. The murmuring of the crowds in the Forum swelled excitedly, and the members of the Senate turned their gazes to the bronze doors. The marching boots came to a halt, and then the slapping of sandals mounting the marble steps announced the emperor's approach even before he reached the doorway. The Senate stood in respect as he entered the chamber.

Nero, the ruler of a quarter of the world's population, and the last surviving heir of Caesar Augustus, passed through the corridor that bisected the interior of the Curia Julia and took his place behind the two consuls on a raised dais. His marble throne was behind and above the curule chairs of Rome's chief magistrates, but he remained standing for the moment, surveying the chamber nervously. He was not a popular man with the Senate and People of Rome, and he knew it.

Nero was twenty-six years old, and he had ruled over Rome since the death of his great-uncle and adoptive father, Claudius Caesar, ten years before (some said Nero had engineered that death, poisoning Claudius with deadly mushrooms). Once muscular and athletic, his over-indulgence in wine and fine foods had added a sheath of fat to his waist, but he was still taller than the average Roman, and broad-shouldered. His face had grown plump, and his nose was slightly reddened from too much drinking. His toga, once gleaming white and trimmed with the Imperial purple, was stained with soot, ash, and wine spills. His eyes constantly shifted back and forth, as if fearing an assassin's dagger at any moment. His mouth was always in motion, going from a grim, straight line that bespoke determination and cruelty, to a quivering, soft orifice that reeked of fear and a desperate desire for popularity. Nor was he clean shaven, as the previous emperors had been, but grew a short, scruffy beard that swept from his shaggy locks and met under his chin. Only the area immediately surrounding his mouth was devoid of hair. The emperor of Rome was a petulant, angry, fearful, neurotic child, and the Senate and People of Rome paid dearly for his insecurities.

"Conscript Fathers," he said, his booming tenor echoing from the marble walls, "the auguries have been taken and the omens deemed favorable. The pontiffs have given offerings to Vesta and Fortuna, to Jupiter Optimus Maximus, and to the divine emperors past, Julius, Augustus, and Claudius, imploring their blessing on the rebuilding of our great city, and their healing to the wounded hearts and bodies of our citizens."

He shifted his weight from foot to foot, eyeing his audience to measure their response to what he said. Surrounded by slaves, prostitutes, and sycophants for most of his days, he had lost much of the oratorical skills that his tutor, the Stoic philosopher Seneca, had taught him—mainly due to lack of practice. But as he spoke, the words came easier, and he seemed to gain confidence.

"The destruction of the City of Romulus was a great crime, the blackest crime our fair city has known since the foul murder of the *Divus Julius,*" he said. "I realize that there has been much speculation about the cause of the fires since that dreadful day in the month of the Julii when they began. Some of those rumors are simply too ridiculous to merit mention in such an august assembly, but I can assure you that no one has been more eager to find out the truth of this matter than your own emperor. Ever since the last of the fires were extinguished, my agents have been scouring the city, seeking to find the culprits responsible for such massive destruction and bring them to justice."

The senators began to look at one another with interest. Many of them half believed the charges that Nero himself had set the fires, or ordered them set—he was already measuring one badly burned out area to see if it was large enough to contain the massive villa he wanted to build for himself. But, if not the emperor, then who did set the fires? They returned their attention to Nero as he continued. His expression had grown more stern and commanding, as if he were remembering who and what he was.

"You notice that I say culprits, not culprit," he said. "No one man, not even your emperor, could have set so many fires in so many places at once. This was a vast conspiracy involving many evil men, and it very nearly succeeded in destroying our entire city! Who could hate the citizens of Rome so much? Who could possibly wish to destroy our Eternal City? Carthage tried and failed; the Gauls nearly succeeded once, four hundred years ago. The great Italian revolt during the Social Wars dreamed of bringing Rome crashing to the earth. But they failed! They went down into Tartarus with their dreams of our destruction unfulfilled. Even those Romans who have turned our own armies upon us—Lucius Sulla, Gaius Marius, and Julius Caesar himself! They marched on Rome not to destroy it but to capture it and win it over to their causes. So I ask again, who could hate the citizens of Rome so much?"

He cast his gaze around the chamber, his eyes narrowing above his pudgy cheeks. He had the Senate's attention now, and even some of those who had regarded him with contempt as he entered were now watching him with renewed interest. He smiled grimly and continued.

"It took all of my Praetorians, as well as the work of many of my other agents, to ferret out the truth," he declared. "The conspirators were diabolical in their cleverness, walking among us unnoticed. Their fanatical creed had drawn slaves, freedmen, and Roman citizens into its secret rituals. Wealthy plebs and even a few senators and patricians were counted among its members! They did not speak openly of what they had done, but their attitudes and actions in the wake of the fires raised my suspicions, and vigorous interrogation brought out the truth. Now I have come to lay bare their foul plot! For this crime was not just an assault on the Senate and People of Rome, but an attack on our very gods themselves! It was our temples that drew the ire of these animals, and their fanatical desire to blot out the worship of every god whose image can be shaped with men's hands!"

The senators began to whisper among themselves. Could this be true? Could the fires have actually been an attempt by a band of fanatics to destroy Rome's traditional religion? Nero watched their reaction and nodded to himself. He had them now, he thought.

"So who did this thing?" he asked rhetorically. "Who tried, and nearly succeeded, in destroying our city? Who longs to end the worship of our gods? Who resents every sacrifice, every offering, every temple, and every attempt we make to appease our spiritual guardians?"

His voice rang through the chamber, high and clear now, echoing from the marble pillars. Seneca's old lessons on oratory had been remembered, and the emperor was putting on a powerful performance.

"It was the Christians!" he shouted. "Members of a disgusting cult of religious perverts who worship a crucified criminal! It is not enough that they engage in shameful orgies called 'love feasts,' or that they eat and drink the bodies and blood of infants! Those things are despicable enough, but now they seek to destroy the very gods of Rome! So what shall we do with these animals, these monsters, these vile criminals?"

"Death!" cried one senator. "Proscriptions!" cried another. The anger of the house had swung away from Nero and found a new target, and the emperor smiled as he heard their angry cries.

"Conscript Fathers!" He raised his voice, and the angry shouts died down. "I call on you for a measure that has not been taken in a generation. I call on you to pass an Ultimate Decree of the Senate and People of Rome, declaring all Christians to be *hostis*, their lives forfeit, their property confiscated and granted to whoever turns them in. I call on you to name all Christians as enemies of the state!"

Loud shouts of agreement echoed through the chamber. The Senate had become putty in the emperor's hands. Nero's mouth turned in a cruel sneer, and he held up his hands one more time.

"But, it is tradition, before passing such a decree, that I ask if there is anyone here who might object to it. So I put the question before you now—will anyone here speak up for these degenerates? Is there any member of the Senate of Rome who will oppose the permanent criminalization of all Christians?"

Silence fell, and the senators looked at one another for a moment. Nero soaked up his triumph and had opened his mouth to speak again when he was interrupted by a voice from near the back of the chamber.

"I will," said a middle-aged senator as he stepped out from the ranks and into the aisle. He was slim, but his shoulders were broad and he moved with the confidence that came with physical strength and grace. A faded, worn crown of grass was wrapped around his bald scalp. "I will speak for them!"

Nero shook his head and sighed. "Marcus Publius! I might have known," he said.

CHAPTER I

It was a dazzling spring day in the eighth year of the Emperor Tiberius Claudius Caesar Augustus Germanicus—the eight hundred and fourth year since Romulus founded the city that bore his name on the banks of the Tiber. The Great Forum was filled with people, as the new Senate was about to convene following the elections a few days earlier. Priests chanted prayers and took augurs, amateur orators harangued the crowds, and senators, clad in their blinding-white togas with purple trim, slowly walked toward the Curia Julia, discussing matters with their many clients and receiving petitions handed to them by desperate supplicants.

The closer one drew to the curia, the thicker the crowds were, and the slower progress became. The consuls, tribunes, and other senior magistrates had guards assigned to protect them and clear their paths. The senior senators, while not entitled to the professional guards known as lictors, usually hired private muscle men to clear their way through the crowds and fend off potential attackers. But the *pedarii*—the junior senators who lacked the *dignitas* and *arctoritas* that came from a long public career and large clientele—had to struggle through the Roman mob, trying to make headway and keep their togas as clean as possible at the same time.

For the newly elected Marcus Quintus Publius, the day had started as badly as possible. His formal toga had been spattered with mud and dung by a runaway cart only a block from his house; he had been forced to run back home and change into his older toga, which was not as white but was at least clean, and then make his way toward the Forum from his villa near the Ostian gate as fast as he could. But the delay had made him the last senator to enter the plaza, and the crowd between him and the Curia Julia was dense and not at all interested in making way for a thirty-year-old who had barely managed to win election as one of Rome's *quaestors*—the most junior magistracy that still included automatic admission to the Senate of Rome as one of its benefits.

Wrapping his toga firmly about his waist and holding its folds in one hand, Marcus turned sideways and pushed his way through the mob, edging ever closer to the Curia. Finally, he saw the marble steps just a few feet in front of him and lunged past an oncoming vendor's cart, striding quickly up to the bronze doors and slipping inside as the last of the ceremonial prayers was being uttered by the pontiff. He quietly stepped around the outside ring of marble seats until he saw a vacant slot and slid in between two other *pedarii,* one a newly elected magistrate like himself, the other a grizzled old man he did not recognize.

When the last of the invocations were done, Claudius Caesar stepped up to his spot between the two consuls and motioned for the Senate to be seated. For a moment, the Curia was filled with the rustling of cloth as some four hundred togas settled about the forms of their owners. Then silence fell as the emperor of Rome began to speak.

Claudius was fifty-eight years old, and was the great-nephew of Caesar Augustus, the nephew of Augustus' stepson Tiberius, and the uncle of the previous emperor, Gaius Caligula. He was also a grandson of the legendary Marcus Antonius and his wife, Octavia. Despite his grand lineage, no one had expected that Claudius—a shy, stuttering, limping scholar who avoided public life whenever possible—would ever be emperor. But it was his birth defects and his retiring ways that had spared him when many who were closer to Tiberius and Caligula in blood had been executed over the previous twenty years. Good old Uncle Claudius, the limping, stuttering fool, had been a favorite butt of Caligula's cruel jokes, often forced to dance or recite poetry while standing on his bad leg until he lost his balance and fell over.

But Claudius had the last laugh. He knew that the legions and the Praetorian Guard had lost all faith in Caligula's sanity, and his ability to rule. Many thought he had even known about the assassin's plot that had struck down the mad young Caligula after he had served only four years as emperor. Of course, Claudius would not confirm that, but the fact remained that when the Praetorian Guard, fighting a pitched battle with Caligula's German bodyguards after the emperor's murder, found the stammering scholar hiding behind a curtain, they draped a purple robe over his shoulders and hailed him as the new Caesar.

That was eight years past. Claudius now walked without a limp and only stammered when he was startled or excited. He moved with a slow, even step and spoke with care and deliberation, and his keen intellect was evident in the interest that he took even in the most minute affairs of the Empire. No subject was too obscure or common for the emperor to get involved in. From his pen flowed decrees on everything from the proper use of Latin grammar to the importance of detecting fraudulent citizenship claims to the rotation of crops to help preserve the fertility of Rome's public lands.

Many believed that Claudius, enamored as he was of the old Roman Republic, would restore power to the Senate when he became emperor, and gradually release the reins that Tiberius and Augustus had used to keep a tight grip on political power. Indeed, Claudius himself urged the Senate to take more responsibilities on itself and resume its place as the chief source of legislation for the Empire. But the slow removal of so much power by the deft hand of Augustus, followed by the treason trials under Tiberius and the senseless murders and exiles imposed by Caligula, had left the Senate so shy of exercising power that the emperor was constantly forced to do things for himself. On top of that, Claudius knew that his own grip on the *principate* was tenuous at best; twice in the last eight years he had caught members of the Senate conspiring to depose or murder him, and had ordered them tried for treason.

Marcus watched in fascination as the emperor addressed the senators—he had seen Claudius from a distance on a few occasions, and had met him once, briefly, back in the days of Caligula, when Claudius was officially consul. But this was his first time to hear Claudius speak, emperor to senator, and he was determined not to miss a word.

"Conscript Fathers," the emperor began, "it is my pleasure to inaugurate a new session of the Senate of Rome. The auguries are favorable and the heavenly bodies are in alignment; there is no impediment to the business of the House. I should like to begin by welcoming the newest members of the Senate—newly elected Quaestors Gaius Memmius Hortensius, Gnaeus Scribonia Tullius, and Marcus Quintus Publius." Publius looked directly at the emperor as his name was spoken and inclined his head with respect. For a moment, Claudius favored him with an amused look, but then the emperor continued. "Also, newly appointed senators Marcus Quinctilius Rufus, filling the seat of his late father, Marcus Cincinnatus Rufus, and Julius Cassius Strabo, appointed for his loyal service as a military tribune in Syria."

Claudius straightened the crown of laurel leaves on his head—a souvenir of his military campaigns in Britain, which had earned him a triumphal parade upon his return to Rome. When he resumed his speech, a hint of irritation crept into his voice.

"Conscript Fathers, I have been your emperor for eight years. You should know me by now. I am not a tyrant, nor a bloodthirsty madman. I want only fairness and justice for all the citizens of Rome. No honest senator has anything to fear from me because of mere political differences. But when I deliver a proposal to the Senate, no one is willing to debate its merits! The *Princeps Senatus* reads my proposal, calls for a division, and the house votes, without ever once considering that I might have had a bad idea! Such sycophantic behavior does not befit the august title of senator. I beg you, Conscript Fathers, if you dislike my proposal, vote against it! No penalty shall ensue. If you have a better idea, propose it! Debate, argue, compromise, refine each piece of legislation before inscribing it in stone and making it the law of the land!"

A few senators shifted uncomfortably, but most looked bored. From what Marcus had heard, Claudius began every session of the Senate with a similar sermon. The fact was that the Senate was afraid of power, a fear that had been justified for far too long to go away just because the new emperor said it should.

"Now, as to new business," Claudius continued, "there is little I have to present to you. The public works initiated in the last section continue at a good pace, and the new aqueduct in Campania is nearly complete. The treasury is not as full as we might like, but there is more gold in it than there has been in a decade or more, and that is progress from the bankrupt state which I inherited. All in all, the state of our Republic is strong, and the Empire that we rule is well managed. Britain is mostly pacified, and the frontiers are more peaceful than they have been since the reign of the *Divus Augustus*."

Marcus relaxed. It appeared that there might not be any need to cast any votes today, and perhaps they could all get to the inaugural feast sooner than he had hoped. His stomach was already rumbling.

"There is one last matter that I must ask you to take action upon, before our session is dismissed," the emperor said. "There has been much rioting and unrest among the Jewish quarter in recent months, mostly caused by a rabble-rouser by the name of Chrestus, according to my sources. Repeated warnings have proven worthless, so I propose that the Senate issue a decree expelling all Jews from Rome for one year. Let this troublesome race learn that rioting will not be tolerated! Is there any discussion on this matter?"

Quintus Hortensius, a former consul, rose from the front bench. "Most Excellent Caesar," he said, "I number many Jews among my clients, and some of them possess the full Roman citizenship. Surely you do not wish to expel citizens along with the rabble and immigrants from the Jewish quarter, do you?"

Claudius thought for a moment. "Any legal Roman citizen of Jewish blood may be allowed to remain in the city, unless it can be proven that he has taken part in civil disorder. But all other Jews, especially the followers of Chrestus, should be expelled, provided the Senate approves. I thank you for your suggestion, noble Hortensius."

Porcius Antonius, the *Princeps Senatus*, stood and addressed the assembly. "Is there any further debate on the proposal to expel all non-citizen Jews from the city?" he asked in a voice that shook with age. Appointed to the Senate early during the reign of Augustus, he had served for over fifty years, surviving by being as compliant and non-controversial as he could. No one raised any further debate on the issue, and the house divided, the ayes passing to the right side of the consuls' chairs, the nays to the left. The motion carried with only twenty dissenting votes out of three hundred. The Jews had never been a popular minority in Rome—their bizarre invisible god and many cultural taboos made them a difficult people for Romans to understand, and the province of Judea, their homeland, was a perpetual hotbed of rebellion and discontent.

After the vote, the Senate was dismissed to its annual inaugural feast. Marcus watched the toga-clad figures as they filed toward the doors, looking for one face in particular. When he finally saw the man he was looking for, he raised his voice in greeting.

"Uncle Mencius!" he said.

"*Ave,* Marcus!" cried his kinsman in return. "I am glad to see you made it!"

"It was a near thing, thanks to a runaway peddler's cart and a large puddle!" Marcus said. "I had to go home and change, or risk coming to my inaugural session as a senator looking like a stable hand!"

The two fell in together, conversing comfortably as they made their way to the banquet chamber. Mencius Quintus Publius was the oldest brother of Marcus' deceased father, and was nearing sixty years of age. But he was still lithe and well-muscled, moving down the steps of the Curia Julia with the gait of a much younger man.

"So what did you think of your first experience as a senator of Rome?" his uncle asked.

"It seemed routine enough, after the thrill of actually being inside the Curia wore off," said Marcus. "What on earth is this business with the Jews about, anyway? I'd heard rumors of some riots over in the Aventine, but that's across the city from my place, and no one seemed to know any details."

"That is an interesting story, actually," said Mencius. "I heard all about it from a Jewish tentmaker named Aquila last week. Let's find a place at the table and I'll fill you in."

The two *publii* made their way to the banquet table and reclined on the cushions. An attractive Scythian slave brought them a fingerbowl and towel, and they washed and dried their hands. Moments later the first course—a bowl of delicious fresh fruit, including dates—was laid before them. Marcus bit into an orange slice and turned his attention to his uncle.

"So what has the Jews all in an uproar?" he asked.

"Do you remember a senator named Pontius Pilate?" asked his uncle.

"Vaguely. Wasn't he consul when I was little?" Marcus replied.

"Indeed he was," said his uncle. "Although you won't find his name on any consular roll today! Our late, unlamented Emperor Gaius Little Boots had his name stricken from all the records, and his Civic Crown revoked."

"What did poor old Pontius Pilate do to merit such a fate?" Marcus asked. "And what does that have to do with the Jews rioting nearly three decades later?"

"Oh, it's all tied together," his uncle said. "Bear with me, it's an interesting tale." Marcus shrugged and popped a grape into his mouth. His uncle had always been fond of long, convoluted stories, but they were usually entertaining.

"Pilate was a good friend of old Tiberius Caesar, even before Tiberius was emperor," Mencius said.

"I wasn't aware Tiberius ever had any friends," Marcus commented drily. The old emperor's irascibility and loneliness had been legendary when he was a boy.

Mencius laughed. "You are mostly right," he said. "I never knew such a gloomy soul! What's the point in ruling the civilized world if you don't enjoy it? Even our esteemed Claudius knows how to have a good time on occasion, I've heard. But, back to the story, Pilate was thick as thieves with old Tiberius. Earned the Civic Crown fighting under Tiberius in Germany, then came back and served as Tiberius' right-hand man. There are lots of whispered stories about Pilate and the scandal surrounding Germanicus' death, although no one knows what actually happened. Then Pilate served his term as consul, went out to govern Spain, and came back to Rome. Here is where the story begins to get interesting. You see, by that time Tiberius was alienated from his entire family except for his young great-nephew Gaius, whom he had adopted as his heir. Pilate had a young daughter—a beautiful little girl by all accounts—and Tiberius decided that a marriage alliance with his oldest friend was just what was needed to tame young Gaius' wild side."

"He betrothed his daughter to that monster?" Marcus asked in shock. Rome still shuddered at the memory of the mad Caligula, whose four-year reign had been marked by so much violence and perversion, and who had also been responsible for his own father's death.

"Caligula was only twelve at the time," Mencius said. "No one knew about his wild side, although I imagine Tiberius suspected it. I believe they thought that marriage to a high-spirited, kind-hearted virgin would tame him down some."

"I'm guessing it did not work," Marcus speculated with a shudder.

"No. In fact, Pilate's family became the first victims of Gaius' mad cruelty. They went out to visit the emperor on Capri a couple of years after the betrothal, when Gaius was fourteen and Pilate's daughter twelve. The young heir somehow contrived to get the girl alone and brutally raped her. Broke her arm, according to my source."

"I would love to know your source," Marcus said. "But I am guessing he is confidential."

"Of course," his uncle said. "But he was there that week, I can tell you that much. Pilate tried to kill Gaius when he saw what had happened to his daughter, and nearly succeeded. Broke both of his arms and beat his face to a bloody pulp."

"A shame he didn't succeed, but I guess that explains why Caligula hated him so much," Marcus said.

"And it is also why Pilate was sent off to be governor of Judea," his uncle replied.

"Judea!" Marcus exclaimed. "That's not even a consular province! That's a prefect's post!" His new senatorial status had made him very conscious of rank and protocol.

"Indeed," his uncle said. "But it was a punishment, after all. Also, I think that Tiberius might have seen it as a chance to protect Pilate from Caligula's wrath as the boy got older. At any rate, Pilate remained stuck in that gods-forsaken cesspit, trying to keep the Jews and Skenites and Samaritans from killing each other, for the next ten years."

"A pretty awful fate, from what I know of Judea," said Marcus.

"Better than the wrath of Caligula, though," Mencius replied. "But it was there in Judea that this whole Christos business got started."

"I thought it was Chrestus," Marcus said.

"Our beloved emperor does occasionally mispronounce words still," Mencius replied. "Christos is actually a Greek word, of course."

"Doesn't it mean Chosen One or something like that?" Marcus asked.

"Yes, exactly!" Mencius replied. "I'm glad old Demosthenes didn't spend all his time sampling your father's wine collection."

Marcus laughed. His old tutor had been overly fond of drink, and had dozed off during more than one of his student's Greek lessons.

"The actual Jewish word is 'Messiah,' and it means Savior or something like that," Mencius said. "Apparently, the Jews have been looking for this deliverer for centuries, and have a whole set of prophecies that predict his coming. During Pilate's time in Judea, someone claiming to be this Messiah sprang up, and Pilate had to deal with him."

"Did the Messiah lead a rebellion?" Marcus asked.

"That's the thing," Mencius said. "He never once preached armed resistance to Rome or to anyone else. His real name was Iesu, or Yeshu, or something like that. 'Jesus' is the Latin rendering. No, this Jesus told his followers to love one another, but also to love their enemies and do good to those who hated them. He was a carpenter by trade, but his followers said he was a descendant of their ancient King David. There are all sorts of stories, some from reliable sources, that he could heal the sick and even make blind men see. But wherever he went, he told his followers that they must never harm another person, or even be angry with their brethren. He even said that, when it came to taxes, they should render to Caesar what is Caesar's and unto God what is God's."

"If I were Pilate I might have put him on my payroll!" Marcus said.

"I don't think Pilate really wanted to move against him at all," Marcus said. "But the Jewish High Priest, a corrupt old dog named Caiaphas, truly hated this Jesus. He kept hounding Pilate to do something about him, and finally one night an angry mob of Jews, egged on by the priests, showed up at Pilate's doorstep and demanded that this Jesus, whom they had arrested, be crucified. Pilate did his best to wiggle out of it, but when they threatened to report him to Caesar he washed his hands of the affair, and to the cross Jesus went, nailed up like a common criminal."

Marcus shuddered. Crucifixion was the most brutal punishment Rome could inflict, usually reserved for slaves and non-citizens accused of the most grievous crimes.

"But shouldn't that have been the end of the matter?" he asked his uncle.

"You would think so," Mencius said. "But here is the thing. This Jesus refused to stay dead! Three days after he was nailed up and then cut down and buried, there were reports of him being seen alive and well, all over Jerusalem! His followers began proclaiming that he was a god of some sort, and the Jews got very riled up about that—they claimed it was some kind of blasphemy. But this cult that Jesus started—some call them Nazarenes, others call them 'Christians' after their founder—is not only still around, but growing rapidly. That's what all the rioting here in Rome was about. These Christians go around preaching that this Jesus has some strong connection to the God of the Jews, and encouraging men of every religion to convert and become followers of their Christos. The Jews call them blasphemers and idolaters, and the two sides go at it hammer and tongs."

"That is a bizarre story!" Marcus said. "Worshipping a carpenter! That is even stranger than the Egyptians worshipping their cats!"

But about that time the slaves came out with the main course, and the smell of fresh cooked flounder, poultry, and sweetmeats drove thoughts of Jews, religion, and riots out of Marcus' mind. It was a memorable feast, lasting for well over three hours. Etiquette demanded that each dish be sampled, while common sense required each sampling to be a small one. Some said that at Caligula's parties, guests had been required to overeat until they threw up, then forced to eat some more. Marcus could not imagine anything more revolting. He took small portions and small bites of each dish, occasionally looking to see how many courses were left so he could gauge whether or not to get seconds on a particularly tasty dish. Like all Romans, he adored flounder, or "dug-mullets" as they were called. As the meal wound down, the emperor rose from his seat at the head of the table and made his way around, accompanied by two black-clad Praetorian guards and several slaves. Claudius took the time to address each senator by name, if only for a murmured greeting. Eventually he made his way to Marcus' table and greeted the twelve senators clustered around it. His eyes lit up when he saw Mencius.

"I trust you are educating your nephew in the protocols of senatorial service, old friend?" he asked.

"He needs little training from me, Excellency," said Mencius. "His father was a model senator."

"Indeed he was," Claudius said, "and he was ill served by my predecessor. Perhaps I can atone for that in some way. Marcus Quintus Publius, would you call on me at my home tomorrow?"

Marcus swallowed hard. The emperor's words had brought his father's cruel death at the hands of Caligula's Praetorians back to his mind, and he had certainly not expected an Imperial invitation.

"It would be an honor, Your Excellency," he said.

"Very good. I shall expect you around mid-afternoon—I have much business tomorrow morning, little of it pleasant. Good day, sirs."

The portly emperor moved onward, with Marcus staring after him, mouth agape. His uncle laughed at his expression, and the young senator again swallowed hard and looked back at him.

"I wonder what that was all about," he said.

"Claudius Caesar is a just and honorable man," said Mencius, "for all his other faults. He knows that Caligula caused your father's death in a fit of drunken debauchery, and wishes to atone for it. I would not be surprised if our emperor has you in mind for some honorable posting that will increase your *arctoritas* considerably."

Marcus watched as Claudius Caesar made his way around the next table. "I wonder what it might be," he mused.

"Tomorrow will tell that tale," his uncle said. "Now, I am holding a reception for all my clients at my house tonight. I want you to come and be seen at my side. It is time for you to begin enlarging your own clientele. And I, too, have a little gift for you in honor of your elevation to the Senate."

Marcus smiled. "I thank you for it in advance," he said.

CHAPTER II

After leaving the reception dinner, Marcus returned home. To his surprise, he found a small crowd gathered at his door. There were several merchants there, as well as some rather scruffy-looking individuals who appeared to be several steps down the social ladder from the usual Forum frequenters. When they saw him, several began calling him by name. Nearly all of them had small scrolls that they were waving in his direction. Suddenly he realized that these were his first clients as a new member of the Senate of Rome! He stepped past them and up the steps of the portico. His villa was not large, but it was attractive and relatively new, and the front door was several feet above street level.

"*Quirites,*" he said, using the traditional term for a citizen of Rome, "I am honored that you have waited for so long for me to return from the inaugural banquet. While I have an engagement in a few hours, if you will give me a moment to change, I will receive each of you in turn. My steward will attend you shortly. Now excuse me for a moment, and I look forward to meeting each of you."

With that, he stepped into the atrium and clapped his hands to summon his steward, Demetrius. The portly, gray-haired Greek emerged from the library, his tunic clean and his manner fastidious.

"I have clients waiting outside," said Marcus. "I want you to get their names for me and show them into the atrium, in the order in which they arrived, starting in about ten minutes. It's hot outside, so have Lucretia bring them a pitcher of wine—not the nice stuff, but something palatable, lightly watered—and pour them each a goblet. I have some of the less expensive pewter goblets around here somewhere. Now where is Phidias? I need to change clothes!"

"He is in your chambers, *Dominus,*" said Demetrius. "I fear he has dozed off again."

Marcus sighed. Phidias had been a family slave since his father was a teen, and of late he had been less and less useful. He had offered to emancipate the old man on more than one occasion with a generous pension, but the dour old Greek was determined to die in the service of the family that had purchased him fifty years before. He crossed the peristyle to his personal bedchamber, which he shared with no one since his wife had died giving birth to their son three years before. It was a lovely, well-lit room, facing out onto the flower bed that his dear Drusilla had planted while she was still early in her pregnancy and full of hopes for their future. Marcus made sure that the plants she had placed there were painstakingly tended, for they were all he had left of her—the marble bust he had commissioned for the atrium was a very poor resemblance, in his opinion. Here in the roses and lilies she had planted he could still recall her smell, the light in her eyes, and the essence of all she had been—while the sculpture reminded him of nothing except the pallor death had left on her features.

Phidias was sitting in the chair next to the door, his head tilted forward, snoring faintly. Marcus considered him with a smile. It was hard to be angry with the man who had taken a more active part in his upbringing than anyone save his own father. The old Greek was looking frailer of late, Marcus sadly observed. He supposed he would have to buy a replacement at some point, but he hated the noise and stench and aura of hopelessness that hung over Rome's slave markets. Like most educated Romans, he accepted the existence of slavery without question—it was a part of every civilization on earth, after all—but preferred not to be involved in the messy end of it. Even during his brief tenure as a *conturburnalis* under Marcus Tullius, Marcus had let hired agents deal with the thirty or so slaves that were his share of the plunder from their campaign against the Eritreans.

"Phidias, old fellow, help me out of this toga, please!" he finally said.

"What?" The elderly Greek snapped awake. "Of course, *Dominus*, no need to shout. I'm not deaf, you know!"

He bustled around his master, undoing the clasps and folding the bulky garment as he went. "A shame about your dress toga," he said. "We did our best, but it's going to have to go to the fuller's for whitening. Springtime Tiber mud never washes out all the way, you know! Now, what do you wish to wear for the rest of the day?"

"I have several clients waiting for me on the doorstep, and I am going to my uncle's villa this evening for a formal dinner. I'll be dining with important people, so I need to look my best," Marcus said.

"Of course, *Dominus,*" Phidias said. "You are still taking your early steps on the *cursus honorum,* and you must dress to impress! I think that forest green robe with the golden trim, and the dark Corinthian leather belt, perhaps?"

"Just the thing," Marcus said. For all his faults, the old Greek knew his master's tastes perfectly. How would he ever find someone to replace him?

Fifteen minutes later, Marcus was seated in a backless curule chair, similar to those used by Roman magistrates. His posture was ramrod-straight, his right foot slightly in front of his left, and his attention focused on the door as his first client was shown through.

"Vitellius Scribonius," Demetrius whispered in his ear. "Owns a small fleet of grain ships—probably wants an exemption on some custom duty or other."

"My dear Scribonius," said Marcus warmly. "How are the grain harvests this year?"

"Bountiful indeed, Most Excellent Publius," replied the shipping magnate. "But it is wine I have come to talk to you about today. I have obtained a source of the sweetest, darkest wine I have ever tasted, straight from the vineyards of Abyssinia. However, it does seem to cross the boundaries of some ancient and altogether archaic sumptuary law . . ."

Within a few minutes, the merchant had made his request and Publius had given his reply. Even as a *pedarii,* Marcus was reasonably sure that he could grant the man the exemption that he wanted.

Next up was Gaius Antillus, who wanted to open a new *ludus* for gladiators near Marcus' ancestral home of Picenum, but was running into trouble with the neighbors, who objected to a gladiatorial training facility adjoining their property. Marcus didn't know if he could prevail upon them to change their minds, but he promised to try.

And so it went, one client after another, each requesting a favor, a bit of legislation, an exemption, or some post of honor for themselves or their sons. The poorest fellow, Lucius Berettus, needed an advocate to defend him on charges of drunken brawling after he had bitten a man's ear off in a local dive. Marcus listened attentively to each one, nodding sympathetically and speaking to them in a strong, clear voice with perfect modulation. Each favor granted, each matter looked into, wove a thread into the web of *arctoritas* that he was trying to create. The more men who owed you for favors, the more men you could call on, and it was that ring of mutual obligation and personal debt that made Roman government work.

It took him an hour and a half to see them all, and when he was done, Marcus stood and stretched; maintaining the poise required of a Roman aristocrat was tiresome after a while. He went to his study and unrolled the scrolls he had been handed one at a time. He made a few notes on each one—who he would need to see or talk to in order to accommodate his clients' requests—and then filed them into a cupboard. His uncle's dinner began in two hours, but Mencius had told him to arrive early to receive his gift. Once more Marcus wondered what it was his uncle had gotten him. Bidding his steward goodnight, he exited his villa and turned toward the Esquiline district, where Mencius lived. It was a goodly walk from his own home at the south end of the Quirinale, but at least it avoided the slums and stews of the Subura and the Aventine.

"Begging your pardon, sir, but are you traveling afoot tonight?" a voice interrupted his thoughts. He turned to face the speaker, a tall and muscular young man with an angry red scar running up one cheek.

"And what business of yours might that be?" he asked the insolent fellow, whose tunic was threadbare and sandals badly worn.

"Well, a senator should not travel unescorted, sir, if I may be so bold," he said. "The city is full of cutthroats and bandits!"

"How do I know I am not speaking to one of them now?" Marcus asked him with some amusement.

"Well, sir, I was, but I'm trying to quit, and that's a fact. I wanted to join the legions, but they are full up at the moment. Truth be told, I have lived on the wrong side of the law for some years now, and it's not as fun as it used to be. If a certain Numidian's dagger had slipped an inch higher, it would have poked out my eye!" He pointed at the scar on his cheek, which indeed stopped just below his right eye. "I have a sweetheart I want to marry, and that means I need a steady job of some sort. And I got to thinking, why not see if the newly elected quaestor could use a bit of muscle—begging your pardon for my presumption."

Marcus thought of the runaway cart that had nearly run him down that morning, and looked at the fellow's stout arms. Many senators did have private guards that escorted them about the city, he thought. Why not?

"What is your name?" he asked.

"Why, I'm Rufus—Rufus Licinius," the man said. "Born and raised on the Aventine."

"A Roman of the Romans, eh?" he said.

"I don't know about all that, sir," the man said. "Me grandpap was a legionary of the Tenth from back in the Gallic Wars. Lost an arm in the siege of Alesium, he did. Came back to Rome and bought a tavern with his share of the plunder, then bequeathed it to me *pater*, who drank up all the profits when I was a boy—and then he got the crabs disease and died! Been on my own, with only a rented room in an *insula* to call my own, since I was sixteen."

Marcus thought a moment. "Well, I cannot have my escort dressed like a beggar," he said. "I can't pay you too much, but I can certainly keep you in food and drink—as long as you are not too fond of the drink—and give you enough to rent a better place for you and your bride, when the time comes. First things first, though." He walked up the steps and called for Demetrius. The steward came quickly, his always-spotless tunic rustling as he strode toward them.

"Demetrius, this man wishes to be my personal bodyguard. Go and find him a clean tunic and a better pair of sandals, and be quick about it! Rufus, hurry yourself, your first job is to escort me to a dinner party over on the Esquiline."

"Of course, *Dominus*!" the delighted plebeian replied.

"There will be none of that!" snapped Marcus. "You are no slave, but a free citizen of Rome. You may call me Marcus Quintus, or Senator Publius, but you will address me as befits a free Roman!"

"Yes, *Dominus*—I mean, Senator Publius, sir!" Rufus babbled as he disappeared into the house with Demetrius. Less than five minutes later he was at Marcus' side, wearing an old but respectable tunic, a pair of sturdy sandals, and the belt he had worn with his old tunic. A nasty-looking curved blade nearly two feet long was tucked into the right side.

"That looks African," Marcus said. "Where did you come by it?"

"I pulled it out of my face after I sent its former owner to Hades," Rufus said matter-of-factly. "I figured he wouldn't be needing it down there, and my old blade broke off at the hilt when he fell on it. He was a fat fellow, to tell you the truth, but beastly quick for his size. I underestimated him."

"You seem to have led an interesting life, Rufus Licinius," Marcus said as they struck out for his uncle's villa.

"Frankly, sir, I'd be willing to settle for something less interesting and more stable right now, begging your pardon," Rufus replied.

The man did seem to know the streets of Rome quite well, and he was big and menacing enough that Marcus traveled with much greater ease than he had that morning as he rushed to get to the Curia. Maybe this impulsive hire was a good idea, the young senator thought as they made their way across the sprawling city. The late afternoon crowds were pushing their way through the streets—servants bringing goods home from the market district, workers wrapping up their day's labor, and young matrons with children in tow, scrambling to get home and begin preparing supper for the *paterfamilias* when he was done with his daily toil. The odor was overpowering when one left the city for any length of time and returned, but when you lived in Rome, it was simply the smell of everyday life. Marcus loved it—the bustle, the noise, the scent. He was never comfortable away from the city, and always happy to return.

He was still more than an hour early when they arrived at his uncle's house. He thanked Rufus for escorting him, tipped him a denarius, and told him to go to the kitchens and get a bite to eat. Then he mounted the steps to the entryway, where Mencius' steward, Phillipus, awaited him.

"*Dominus* is most eager to see you, young Marcus," said the Greek slave. "And if I may, I would like to offer my congratulations on your election as quaestor."

"My thanks, Phillipus," Marcus said. "Are you keeping well these days?"

"Well enough, sir, thank you," the steward answered. "Your uncle is a good master, and the house runs smoothly most days. Your aunt has not been well for some time, and we try to keep things quiet and soothing for her."

Marcus nodded. His aunt Claudia was a difficult woman and had been such a termagant when she was young that her parents had despaired of ever finding her a husband. Their solution was to offer a huge dowry, but even then, her shrill manner scared off most suitors pretty quickly. Mencius, a charming young rogue in his day, had not only married the shrew but tamed her, and she was devoted to him. But in recent years an illness of the bowels had made her more irritable and prone to drink, and those who had known her for a long time said that she was becoming more and more like her youthful self—except in looks, which had worsened considerably with age. Mencius remained his light, flirtatious attitude with her, but found excuses to be out of the house more often these days.

"Marcus, my lad! So good to see you in my home again!" Mencius boomed as Marcus entered his study.

"Thank you, Uncle," said Marcus. "I am sorry I have not been around more often." Overshadowed by his uncle's political success, Marcus had made up his mind to win office on his own merits rather than family connections, and so he had not visited his uncle's home once during the entire election cycle.

"Think nothing of it, my boy!" Mencius said, beaming. "I suppose I should start calling you Senator Publius now, since you are one of the Conscript Fathers of Rome."

"I'll always be your nevvy, Uncle Mencius," Marcus replied with a smile. He had always looked up to his father's brother, and the man had been a tower of strength to him when Marcus found out about his father's murder and his family's sentence of exile. It was Mencius who had lobbied the new Emperor Claudius to lift the sentence early in his principate.

"I wanted to buy you a gift, to celebrate your election as quaestor and your entry to the Senate," Mencius said. "I thought on it long and hard, and I hope you will be pleased with my choice."

"I'm sure I will be, when I see it," Marcus replied with a smile.

"Very well then!" his uncle said, clapping his hands loudly. "You may enter now, boy!"

The curtains to the back of the room parted, and a young lad, about thirteen years old or so, stepped through. He had dark hair, cropped close, and bright blue eyes that took in his surroundings with a keen interest. He was short in stature but broad-shouldered and muscular. His eyes glinted with intelligence and a hint of mischief.

"What is this, Uncle?" Marcus asked in astonishment.

"We both know that Phidias is too old to be a proper body servant anymore," Mencius said. "But we also know that he would regard any attempt to replace him with an adult slave as a mortal insult. Young Cadius here is the perfect solution. He is too young to be a threat, and too likable to draw the old man's ire. Phidias can begin training him, and by the time the old man crosses Styx, you'll have a young, loyal, well-trained body servant to tend you for many years to come."

"Cadius, eh?" Marcus said. "Odd name. Where are you from, lad?"

"My father was a Greek merchant who did much business at Gades in Spain," the boy replied. "He named me for the place where he met my mother."

"I see," Marcus said. "So how did the son of a merchant become a slave?"

The bright eyes dimmed for a moment, and the boy looked sad. "I was too little to remember," he said. "But my sister said that Papa sold some fish to the palace for one of Caligula's banquets, and part of it spoiled before it was served. Two guests got sick, and Papa was blamed. The emperor had my mother and father cut up and fed to his pet lions, and all of us children sold. I was purchased as a companion for a wealthy banker's son, but he grew into a royal turd and one day I got tired of him pinching and abusing me and gave him a proper punch in the nose. His father marched me down to the slave market, and Senator Mencius bought me. Are you going to be my new *Dominus*?"

Marcus laughed at the story. "It appears to be so," he said. "What do you think about that?"

"Are you going to beat me?" the slave boy asked.

"Only if you earn it," Marcus replied. "But I haven't had to beat a slave in years."

"You're not one of those deviants who like little boys, are you?" Cadius asked.

Marcus laughed out loud. "Emphatically not!" he said. "But what would you do if I said yes?"

Cadius looked at him insolently and replied, "I'd punch you in the nose and take my chances at the slave market again!"

Marcus looked at his uncle. "I like him!" he said.

Mencius grinned. "I thought you might," he said. "He reminds me a good bit of you when you were a lad."

Marcus leaned down and addressed the boy. "Go to the kitchen and you'll find a rather scary-looking fellow named Rufus. He is my new bodyguard. Tell him I said to take you to my house and put you in the charge of my old body servant, Phidias. Tell Phidias that you are his new assistant, and he will find you a place to sleep, and feed you some supper. He's a sweet old man beneath that gruff exterior, and I think you and he will get along just fine. Tell Rufus to come back here when he has dropped you off—I will need him to escort me home. Now off with you! My uncle and I need to talk."

The boy bowed politely and scampered off to the kitchen.

"It's hard to find a boy that age that hasn't had their spirit broken already," his uncle said. "Treat him well, Marcus, and you will have a faithful servant for the rest of your life."

"I'll do that, Uncle," said Marcus. "I really do like him. Thank you for such a generous gift!"

"I know his former master, and the man's son really is a turd," Mencius said. "I think he knows it too—he only gave Cadius a light beating for punching his son, and seemed eager to find a good home for the lad."

"How is Aunt Claudia?" Marcus asked.

"She hurts," his uncle said. "Her stomach aches constantly, and she spits up blood every few days. The physicians can do little for her except milk of the poppy to ease the pain. I fear that her time with us may be limited." He looked sad at the thought, and Marcus realized that, for all his joking about her ill temper, his uncle really was deeply in love with his wife.

"Do you think I could see her before your guests arrive?" he asked.

"She would be delighted," Mencius said. "Or at least, as close as she gets to delight these days. Let's walk back together."

They walked down a corridor to the rear of the house, where the bedroom opened out onto a small garden in the back. A small couch, piled high with cushions, had been carried out into the warm afternoon sun, and Claudia Publius lay on it, looking pale and weary. She was not quite fifty years old, but looked more like seventy—illness had whitened her hair and lined her face. But she smiled at the sight of her husband's nephew, and held her thin hands out for him to kiss.

"It is good to see you again, Marcus!" she said with a strained smile. "You must pardon me if I do not rise—I am not very strong these days. But I am glad to hear of your elevation to the Senate. I hope your career is long and prosperous, even if I am unlikely to see much of it."

"I am sure you will be around for many years to come," Marcus said, gripping her hands gently.

She laughed grimly, but that triggered a coughing spell. She held a white cloth up to her mouth as the coughs racked her frail body, and when she pulled it away there was a red stain amid the spittle. Mencius took a goblet of wine and poured a few drops of whitish liquid into it—milk of the poppy, a powerful drug that numbed pain. He proffered the goblet to his wife.

"Thank you, Mencius," she said and sipped it eagerly. "Your uncle is good to me, Marcus—far better than I deserve. Your family breeds good and decent men, and I think that you are no exception. Sadly, the world doesn't always treat decent men very decently."

"I would argue with you, Aunt Claudia, but my father's fate proves you right," Marcus said.

"I think Marcus is going to restore the fortunes of my brother's family," his uncle said. "He has a private meeting with the emperor tomorrow. I believe Claudius has marked him for some special favor."

"Emperors!" His aunt snorted. "I would plead illness if I were you, nephew! Nothing good comes of hobnobbing with those who rule the Empire."

"Now, dear wife, you know that Emperor Claudius is a good and decent man," said Mencius.

"Since when does that matter?" she asked bitterly. "They all start out as decent people—at least that is what they tell themselves. But power is a bitter drug, Marcus—never forget that! A small dose of it produces euphoria and giddiness, but those who wield it year after year turn into monsters that will destroy all that they love!"

"Now, Auntie, you should not say such things," Marcus said with some alarm. "Augustus was a decent and honest man, and Claudius is much like him."

"You are young, Marcus. Augustus died before you were born," she said. "He was not the patron saint of peace and strength that bards like Virgil and Horace make him out to be. He began his career by proscribing hundreds of wealthy Romans, and cemented his power by crushing his own cousin, Mark Anthony. Only when he was unopposed did he adopt the benevolent mask of the elder statesman. Tiberius was a bitter old man who became a bitter old monster, and Caligula was mad from the beginning. Now we have Claudius, who comes to us in the garb of a scholar and speaks words of gentleness and restraint. But look at the fate of those who oppose him! Power has begun its dark work on his soul, and who knows how far it will take him?"

"If what you say is true, Auntie, then that is all the more reason not to say it," Marcus said.

"Who listens to a crazy old woman?" she said. "Only her husband, who has no choice, and her nephew, who is too polite to tell her to be quiet!"

She coughed again, less violently, into her kerchief and sipped her drugged wine. "I am not fit company for anyone these days," she said sadly. "I don't mean to be a crazed sibylline oracle, but the pain takes me out of my head. Pity your poor uncle, who has to endure me at my worst!"

Mencius smiled. "I had the worst of you years ago," he said fondly. "And that is what made you so fascinating to me, my dear.

Now I have seen the best of you, too, and the fascination is still just as strong. Sip your wine and rest, and I will make sure the servants carry you inside when the evening begins to cool."

"You are too good to me," she said. "Marcus, make sure you find him an adorable sixteen-year-old bride when I am gone. The man deserves some happiness before he dies!"

"I have a fine, well-aged wine, and you want me to gorge on green grapes?" Mencius said. "I do believe you are trying to kill me, my dear!"

"If so, only because I hope to see you on the other side of Styx," she said. "Now go, both of you! I am weary and need to rest."

They walked back to the dining room, where guests would begin arriving shortly. As they walked, Marcus looked over at his uncle and saw a tear rolling down the man's cheek. Without a word, he took Mencius' hand in his own and gave it a squeeze.

Mencius gave him a grateful look. "I am losing her, you see," he said. "I never thought it would happen—she is five years younger than me, after all. But after twenty-five years of marriage, she is slipping away from me. It is more than I can bear."

"You have had more years with her than I had with my Drusilla," Marcus said. "I thought my heart would rip itself out of my chest with grief when she died. But I carried on—and so will you."

"You are wise for one so young," his uncle said. "Let us prepare for our guests."

CHAPTER III

Marcus woke the next morning with an aching head and upset stomach. Although he had tried to temper his intake, the inaugural banquet followed by the private party at his uncle's house had seen him imbibe more wine and rich food than he was accustomed to. He sat up and yawned, and then his bleary eyes registered movement at the curtains that screened Phidias' bedchamber from his own. Moments later the older Greek appeared, bearing a bowl of hot water and a towel. Next to him young Cadius, clad in a fine white tunic, carried a smaller bowl with cold water, mint leaves, and the gold-handled toothbrush Marcus had bought from an Egyptian the year before.

"Good morning, *Dominus*," Phidias said in his usual dry tones. "I am trying to show this young scamp how to perform his duties, but I find him far more interested in devouring every article of food in our kitchen. I was not aware someone could consume more than their body weight in a single morning!"

Cadius rolled his eyes, certain that the older slave would not see him, but Phidias' free hand shot out like lightning and gave him a smack on the back of the head.

"What did I do?" the boy asked plaintively.

"Don't roll your eyes at me when I talk about you, boy!" Phidias said sternly, but there was a hint of affection in his voice.

"How did you know I was rolling my eyes?" the lad asked in astonishment.

"You just told me," Phidias said with a wry grin. "Besides, it was exactly what I would have done at your age."

Marcus laughed despite his aching head, and then splashed and washed his face thoroughly with the warm towel. He brushed his teeth quickly, rinsed his mouth with the cool water, and took a sprig of mint to chew on. The sour taste of last night's wine began to dissipate, and he felt as if he could eat something.

"There is bread and fresh fruit in the next room," Phidias said, "and Demetrius has your daily schedule ready for your perusal."

"Thank you, Phidias. And thank you for taking this lad under your wing," Marcus said.

"I am no fool, master. I am old—not too old to serve, but old nonetheless. If I can show this young scalawag how to take care of you, I'll know that you'll be in good hands when I do get too old to look after you anymore," the slave said.

Cadius looked up at the older man with a glint in his eye. "What's a scalawag?" he asked.

"You are, you foolish boy!" Phidias snapped. "But I will beat the mischief out of you soon enough."

"Not if you can't catch me," Cadius replied, and darted from the chamber. Old Phidias gave a snort of mock anger and wobbled out after him, which made Marcus laugh so hard his head began hurting again.

He slipped some sandals on his feet—it was not yet summer, and the marble floors still had chill to them in the morning—and walked to the small dining nook by the kitchen where he took his meals when he was not entertaining guests.

There was a small, fresh baked roll of bread, a dish of warm olive oil seasoned with cracked garlic, and a bowl of fresh fruit. The smell of the bread stirred his appetite, and he surprised himself by finishing off the entire loaf and a bunch of grapes. Phidias brought him a goblet of fresh squeezed pomegranate juice, and he sipped it as he surveyed his schedule.

At one time, the quaestors had been the sole custodians of the Roman treasury, and had served as tax assessors and accountants. Since the time of Augustus, however, their responsibilities had been diminished and the treasury was under the emperor's direct control. The first emperor had actually appointed people to the office rather than see them elected by the *comitia,* as in the past. But Caligula and Claudius had decreed that the office should become elective again, reserving the right to name their own candidates if they were displeased with the slate. But, while it still qualified its holders as members of the Senate, the office of quaestor no longer had a hard and fast set of responsibilities. Instead, they were assigned duties after taking office by the Senate or by the emperor himself.

Marcus had not yet been given anything to do, so he was continuing to represent clients before the public courts as an advocate. He had a case to plead that morning, set to be heard in the fourth hour. It was a simple enough matter, and he had no doubt he would be done in plenty of time to change before appearing before the emperor.

"Is the fuller done with my dress toga yet?" he asked Demetrius.

"Not until this afternoon," his steward said.

"Bring out the one I wore to the Senate meeting yesterday, then go and stand over the man and make sure that he is done with the other one by noon. I am to meet with the emperor this afternoon, and I want to look my best," he said. "Now, let me get dressed and I shall go over my arguments before heading to the Forum."

He stepped into his bedchamber and shrugged out of the comfortable old tunic he slept in, and then took a moment to wash his body before allowing the slaves to carefully drape his toga around him. The classic garment of a Roman senator was larger than it looked, and had to be wrapped and draped properly in order for its folds to hang just right. The toga was made of fine linen, and kept as spotless as possible. Its wide, loose-hanging sleeves included a pocket on the left side, called the sinus, which could be used to carry scrolls, kerchiefs, and other light sundries. Since his elevation to the Senate, Marcus was eligible to wear purple trim on his toga and a wide sash of purple and gold draped over his shoulders.

Phidias held up a polished bronze mirror so that Marcus could study his appearance. He patted down his stubborn cowlick and made sure that he was clean-shaven, then strode to his study and pulled a scroll from a cubbyhole above his desk. Unrolling it, he rehearsed his arguments, silently at first, and then out loud. He knew that he was taking a chance with this speech, but at the same time, he badly wanted his client to win.

The case was simple enough: a tribune that had been exiled by Caligula's Chief Praetorian, Macro, had returned under Claudius' proclamation of general amnesty to find that the family villa in Rome had changed hands three times while he was gone. While it was evident that the proscription and banishment had been unjust, the senator who had purchased the villa was refusing to vacate, even when offered the full price of the home. The law was somewhat gray regarding the property of those proscribed during the reign of the mad Caligula, so the verdict was probably going to go in favor of whichever advocate could tell the most heartrending story.

Marcus had laid the legal groundwork with the jury two days before, when the court was last convened, and today he and the advocate for the villa's current owner would present their closing arguments. After reading through his planned remarks, he adjusted his toga one last time and headed out the door. Rufus was waiting for him, smartly turned out in a black tunic with gold trim and armed with the wicked dagger at his belt and a smooth, polished cudgel in one hand.

"Good morning, Senator!" he greeted Marcus.

"*Ave,* Rufus Licinius," Marcus responded. "You look very professional this morning."

"Thank you, Your Excellency," said Rufus. "Your man Demetrius has an eye for what looks good—although this thing is a little tight in the arms."

"Of course it is," Marcus said. "He wants my bodyguard to look as muscular as possible."

Rufus laughed. "Well, shall I intimidate a path to the Forum for you?" he asked.

"Indeed," Marcus said. "It is time for us to be going."

With the burly bodyguard shoving people out of the way, they made good progress, and arrived at the Great Forum with no delays—and Marcus was pleased to see his toga was clean and unstained when they got there.

Approximately two hundred jurors were gathered in the Well of the *comitia;* the raised platform at the end of the Well featured a curule chair for the Praetor who would preside over the trial and benches for the defendant, the plaintiff, and the team of advocates. The praetor in Marcus' case was a stiff old patrician by the name of Gnaeus Sempronius; he was a hardnosed senator with years of experience, and a reputation for being tough but fair.

His client, Lucius Hortensius, was waiting for Marcus to arrive. A middle-aged man with a perpetually anxious expression, his bald head gleamed in the morning sun. He greeted the young advocate with a nervous smile.

"*Ave,* Marcus Quintus," he said. "How do you think things will go today?"

"I have prepared a closing argument that would move Pluto himself to tears," Marcus said. "And I used the money you provided to grease a few palms in the jury as well. Our opponent is also bribing, but it doesn't look as if he is outspending us. So it will come down to who makes the better case, and I think the odds are in our favor." Bribing juries was a time-honored Roman tradition; periodically laws against it would be proclaimed, but they were rarely enforced since jury duty did not pay and few people would serve without some form of compensation.

He looked past the judge at his rival advocate, a childhood friend of his named Fabius Ahenobarbus, and gave him a nod. Fabius returned his nod with a smile and a wink, but the defendant, Quintus Africanus, scowled at him. Marcus couldn't really blame him—the man had bought a nice villa at a reasonable price, not knowing its checkered history, and now would be forced to seek a new home if he lost the case. But Marcus' client had lost all his belongings, his parents, and his home to Macro's cruelty and corruption, and Marcus was determined to at least win the man his home back, since his other losses were irretrievable.

By tradition, the defendant's advocate would speak first, so once the auguries were taken and the judge called the session to order, Fabius stood and began to speak. He walked the jury through the facts of the case again, emphasizing the innocence of his client's transaction before coming to a moving conclusion.

"*Quirites,*" he said, "who among us has not purchased property at one time or another? The right to buy, sell, and own property in our fair city is sacred from time immemorial. You know that Quintus Africanus, a descendant of the man who saved Rome from Carthage, a former quaestor, a hero who served bravely in Germania and on the Parthian frontier, was innocent of any wrongdoing when he purchased this villa in the Esquiline. All he wanted was a replacement for his family's old villa, which had been damaged by fire and earthquakes. Now Lucius Hortensius comes along and tells him that he must take his wife and children and pack up and find another place to live. Never mind the improvements he has made on the villa! Never mind the vegetable garden he planted! Never mind the respect in which he is held by his new neighbors. Oh no! None of that matters, because this degenerate who was banished from the city for his family's many crimes must have his old home back, no matter if he ruins poor Quintus in the process. Friends, Romans, *quirites,* do not allow this injustice to stand! I beg of you, permit this hero of Rome, this paragon of citizenship, this defender of our Empire, to enjoy the fruits of his service to Rome. It is the only right and proper thing to do."

With a bow to the jury, the advocate seated himself on the bench next to his client, who took his hand in gratitude. Marcus waited for the praetor to acknowledge him and then stood.

"*Quirites,*" he said, "I agree with my friend and colleague Fabius Ahenobarbus that Quintus Africanus is innocent of any wrongdoing in purchasing this villa. Nor does my client propose to harm him or bring any financial difficulty upon him. We have offered a fair price—indeed, a greater price than Africanus paid for the villa—so that my friend and client Lucius Hortensius can have back at least some small part of what was unjustly taken from him." He paused, surveying the faces of the jurors. They looked intrigued, with only a few faces radiating hostility or boredom. He gave a tiny nod to himself. It was time to hit them with his best shot.

"This case is not really about Quintus Africanus or even about Lucius Hortensius himself, except to the degree that both of these men are part of a larger story, a sadder story, a story that we are all a part of. It is the story of INJUSTICE!" He roared the last word at the top of his lungs, and suddenly the eyes of every juror, as well as the praetor and the defendant, were locked upon him.

"Yes, my friend, my fellow citizens—injustice, something once unthinkable in the days of our noble Republic, now has become part and parcel of the way that our Empire does business—not just with barbarians, but with our own people. No pedigree, no ancient and noble family name, no loyal service to Rome's Senate and People, is so great that injustice cannot overwhelm it, destroy it, and drag its name through the mud. Injustice is that vile monster from which none of us are safe!"

Nods of agreement flickered through the crowd. This advocate was speaking truth, and they knew it.

Marcus lowered his voice and came down from the platform, walking into the front ranks of the crowd. "Do you know me, my fellow Romans? I know you are aware that I am an advocate, and a newly elected quaestor. Some of you—I hope, most of you!—voted for me, and I am grateful for that. But do you know my story? Did you know my father, Senator Marcus Porcius Publius? He was as noble a son of Rome as ever lived. He was a kind man, a good man, a father and a husband that any Roman would do well to emulate. Do you know what happened to him?" He surveyed the crowd. He could see from the somber faces that many of them did know, or at least had heard some version of the events.

"I was just a young man, a *conturburnalis* on my first assignment with the armies of Rome, serving under the command of General Tullius in Eritrea, when disaster struck my family ten years ago. My father, as a member of the Senate, was invited to attend a banquet by our noble emperor, Gaius Julius Caesar Augustus Germanicus. Or should I give him the name we all remember him by—the name by which he will live in infamy forever: Caligula!"

There were groans in the crowd at the mention of the dead emperor's name. Marcus paused, allowing his eyes to moisten at the memory of the story he was about to tell. "My father was instructed to bring his wife and daughter—my dear sister, Marcia—to this imperial banquet, and he did so. How could he refuse? Halfway through the dinner, our great and noble emperor rose and walked around the table, surveying every senator in attendance—and surveying their wives and daughters with even greater care. He paused before my father, and then slid his oily gaze over my mother and sister. My FOURTEEN-YEAR-OLD SISTER!" he roared in anger that was not feigned at all. He was getting caught up in his own memories. "He nodded to his Praetorians, and they seized her and dragged her from the table into a nearby bedchamber. My father leaped up and started after her, but the emperor fixed him with a reptilian gaze and assured him that no harm would come to the girl if he kept his seat. Then Caligula disappeared behind the same curtain that my sister had been dragged behind."

Silence reigned. Every eye was fixed on Marcus Quintus Publius, and stillness reigned over the Forum. His tears were flowing freely now, and he made no effort to hide them.

"The cries that came from behind that curtain were unbearable as the monster Caligula slaked his lust upon a child," Marcus said. "But when she shrieked at the top of her lungs for her *tata* to rescue her, it was too much for my father to stand. He stood and rushed for the curtain, determined to save his daughter from the monster. He never even saw the Praetorian lower his spear, and it ran him through the stomach, driven clean through him by the force of his charge, the force of his love for his daughter, the force of his outrage as a Roman *paterfamilias.* He slumped to the floor, still trying to crawl towards his wailing child, when a second Praetorian ran him through the neck with his *gladius* and finished him. My mother rushed to his side; she was roughly grabbed and hauled behind the curtain, where her shrieks joined those of her daughter moments later. My father lay there in a pool of his own blood, the guests too horrified and fear-stricken to attend him, until finally the emperor returned. Caligula kicked the corpse out of his way, and announced to the other guests that the estate of Senator Marcus Porcius Publius was now confiscated, his titles and citizenship revoked, and his wife and daughter sent to work as permanent staff at the new brothel the emperor was constructing for his Praetorians. By the time I returned to Rome over a year later, my mother had opened her wrists, and my sister had gone mad and stabbed a Praetorian to death—for which crime the emperor fed her to his pet lions."

The jurors were weeping openly now, and to his astonishment Marcus saw that even the crusty old Praetor Gnaeus was wiping his tears away with the sleeve of his toga. Quintus Africanus was staring open-mouthed at his opponent's advocate, and Lucius Hortensius was sobbing as he remembered his own family's fate.

"I am one man, my fellow Romans, who can tell such a tale of injustice. My client's story is different only in the details. His parents, his home, and his fortune were stolen from him by one of the emperor's minions, not by the emperor himself. Macro coveted his wealth and his newly built villa, and concocted false charges of treason against the *paterfamilias* that saw him and his wife executed. Lucius was actually driven into exile, while I was already out of the country when my family's possessions were confiscated. How many of you can tell a similar tale?" Murmurs spread through the crowd. Ever since the death of Augustus, over thirty years before, powerful men had done what they wanted in Rome while cruel autocrats either looked the other way or egged them on to greater excesses.

"I am one man, a *pedari* with a small bit of *dignitas* and limited *arctoritas*. I cannot fix a broken Empire. I applaud our current emperor for his efforts to restore justice and honor to our government, but he too is one man. The work that must be done is as vast as the wrongs that have been committed against the Senate and People of Rome. We cannot fix everything, my brothers. It would not be meet for us to try to fix everything. That is on the lap of the gods."

He swept his gaze across the jurors, trying to make eye contact with as many as possible. "But we CAN fix one thing today!" he shouted. "We can right one wrong, we can restore one man's loss, we can erase one monstrous injustice—the one done to Lucius Hortensius, when Macro took his parents, his family, and his home from him! We cannot bring back his loved ones from Hades, but we can ensure that he is able to live out his remaining days in the peace and comfort he deserves, in the villa he once shared with them. That is what we can do! That is what we must do! Or else we shall let injustice continue to rule Rome, until none of us have anything left that is truly our own."

He slowly walked back over to the bench, his shoulders slumped with exhaustion. He turned and faced the jurors one more time. "Give my client back his home," he said. "For it is the only thing he has left of all he once loved." With that, he sat down, and Lucius Hortensius embraced him gratefully.

"*Quirites*, you have heard the advocates plead their cases before you," Gnaeus Sempronius said. "I charge you in the name of Jupiter Optimus Maximus, of Fortuna and Romulus, to cast your votes now in honesty and fairness to the plaintiff and the defendant, and decide who is right. Are you ready to divide?"

"Wait!" called an excited voice from the defendant's bench. Quintus Africanus stood, leaving Fabius gaping after him. Africanus crossed in front of the praetor's judgment seat and faced Lucius Hortensius.

"There is no need for the jury to vote. I have changed my mind," Africanus said. "My cousins were also killed by Macro's order. It is wrong of me to possess what was rightfully yours, and by holding it, I place myself on the side of those who wreak injustice for a living. Lucius, if your offer still holds, I will accept your proposed payment and vacate the villa tomorrow."

Hortensius rose and embraced his former opponent, and the jurors leaped to their feet as one and cheered wildly. Romans always loved to see the underdog win, and Marcus' argument had shown them all whose side justice was on. Within a few moments, both

Africanus and Hortensius had been carried off on the shoulders of the jurors in the direction of the nearest tavern, where Marcus imagined they would both be congratulated by the crowd and handed enough free drinks to see both of them thoroughly soused within the hour.

Fabius crossed the platform and warmly clasped Marcus by the hand. "That was masterful, my young friend!" he said. "I had no idea you were such a skilled advocate! It's not often that a plaintiff surrenders before the jury even votes."

Marcus shrugged. "I simply spoke from the heart," he said. "The poor man's case struck very close to home with me."

Fabius nodded. "If your uncle's agents had not bought up your father's entire estate at auction, you might have been suing to get your villa back."

Gnaeus Sempronius stood and stretched. "Well, Quaestor Marcus Quintus Publius, that was a neat piece of work. You played that jury like a harp, no doubt. If all advocates were so eloquent, my job would be a good deal more interesting. I doubt Cicero himself could have done better!"

Marcus gave him a salute. "Thank you for that, sir. Praise from a judge who has heard as many cases as you means more to me than that of my peers—no offense, Fabius!" he ended with a laugh.

"Praetor, I believe the honorable advocate just called you an old man," Fabius said.

"That's because I am an old man!" snapped Sempronius. "Now get out of here, both of you! I have another case in a half an hour, and my bowels are restless!"

They ducked off the stage, leaving the Praetor to find a public privy, and Fabius paused as Rufus Licinius joined them, his biceps bulging through the sleeves of his tunic.

"And who is this Hercules?" he asked Marcus.

"This is my new bodyguard, Rufus Licinius," Marcus replied. "His job is to get me safely through the mob to wherever I am going."

"Does he have any brothers?" asked Fabius. "My escort is scrawny by comparison!"

"No brothers, sir, begging your pardon," Rufus said. "But I do have a cousin who is bigger than me. He owns a bar in the Aventine and does pretty well for himself. Not that he ever had a sestercius to spare for me when I was down and out, Pluto take him!"

"Well, Marcus, would you care to come over to my villa for your noon meal?" Fabius said. "I can probably come up with enough food for your hired muscle, too, although I might have to slaughter another pig!"

Marcus shook his head. "I am afraid I have a very important appointment this afternoon," he said. "Otherwise I would be delighted."

"Who are you going to see?" Fabius said. "Or is it some sinister secret?"

"He is going to see the Emperor, Claudius Caesar," a familiar voice cut in, "the same man whose nephew he just slandered for nigh on half an hour!"

"Uncle Mencius!" Marcus turned. "I had no idea you would be in the audience!"

His uncle smiled. "I didn't want you to know," he said. "I was curious to see how you would handle yourself. Fabius, why don't you head off and let me visit with my nephew for a bit?"

Fabius made his farewells, and Marcus set off for his house, turning a curious eye toward his uncle. "Slander, Mencius? Really?" he finally asked. "You know as well as I do that every word I said was true!"

His uncle nodded gravely. "Yes, nevvy," he said, "but some truths should be whispered, not shouted! Caligula was a monster, and I cannot tell you how much I longed to sink my own blade into his flesh when I found out what he had done to my brother! If I had not been in Spain at the time, I might have done it and consequences be damned. But Gaius Little Boots was also the Emperor of Rome, and Claudius, albeit he is a much more decent man, holds that title by virtue of his relationship to Caligula."

"Uncle, I gave great credit to Claudius for his efforts to restore justice," Marcus said.

His uncle nodded. "I heard," he replied. "But it is not your place to give emperors credit—or blame. At least, not as publicly and openly as you did today. Rest assured, if Claudius has not already heard what you said, he will have heard it by the time you go see him this afternoon. His ears are everywhere in this city. If I were you, I would tread very carefully. And be cautious who you take on as your clients in the future!" With that, Mencius Publius turned on his heel and walked away, leaving his nephew deep in thought all the way home.

Marcus found several clients waiting on his steps, and as he tried to sort out what they wanted, he found their number growing. Apparently several who had heard his speech had decided they wanted him to represent them in the future. He looked at the sundial in front of the portico, then climbed the steps and raised his hands.

"My friends," he said, "I deeply regret that I cannot see you this afternoon, but I am to meet the emperor shortly, and that is an appointment I should not be late to! However, I will be available at the third hour tomorrow, and I will be glad to see you all then. Thank you for honoring me with your requests, and I pledge to do what I can to fulfill them!"

Several of the men actually cheered as he mounted the steps and entered his villa, and he thought about how his fortunes had changed so greatly in such a short time. Perhaps, in time, his *arctoritas* and *dignitas* might rival that once held by his father, and now held by his uncle. It was encouraging, after the scare Mencius had given him leaving the forum.

Speaking with such passion had given him a strong appetite, and he wolfed down some roast chicken and a bread roll, then peeled and ate an orange, before retiring to his bathing chamber to change clothes. His dress toga was draped over a clothes horse, gleaming white and spotless.

"Well done, Phidias," he said. "You can't even tell it was stained."

"That's because it wasn't," his butler said. "The fuller couldn't get all the mud out, so I purchased you a brand new one. We owe the tailor next to Livinius' Scribe Services twenty sesterces, by the way. He charged extra for the rush order."

"Good thing Lucius Hortensius paid me up front," said Marcus. "Now help me get ready to go meet with our emperor."

As Marcus shrugged out of the older toga and Phidias draped the new one around his waist and shoulders, he found himself wondering how that interview would go. He said a silent prayer to his father's spirit and the *lares*—household gods that guarded the Publii clan—that it would be favorable. Once he was suitably dressed and shod, he called for Rufus and the two of them set out for the Palatine Hill.

CHAPTER IV

The first emperor, Caesar Augustus, had lived in a modest home on top of the Palatine Hill, wearing clothes woven by his wife and daughter and holding public dinners in the homes of wealthy senators, since his own dining hall was only big enough for a dozen people at most. Augustus had not objected to wealth, per se—he was one of the richest men in Rome—but he wanted to show everyone that he considered himself to be a simple citizen of the Republic. Of course, he was much more than that and everyone knew it—but the illusion helped him maintain his popularity with the common folk and avoid charges of opulence or corruption.

Tiberius, his adopted son, had lived in the Palatine mansion briefly, enlarging it and making some improvements. But the crusty old general was a notorious misanthrope who hated the city of Rome, and only a few years after ascending to the purple he had retired to the Isle of Capri, in the Bay of Neapolis, and lived there for the rest of his life. In his absence, his chief Praetorian and proxy ruler, Lucius Sejanus, had taken up residence in the mansion, which many had taken to calling the "Palace" after its location on the Palatine Hill. Sejanus had enlarged and enriched the traditional residence—all in the name of Tiberius, of course, even though the old man never got to see the place.

Gaius Caligula had bought up two neighboring properties and vastly enlarged the Palace, adding a small orchard and a large dining hall, as well as a private bath and a covered walkway to the nearby temple of Castor and Pollux—the same walkway where Cassius Chaerea and the other Praetorians had stabbed him to death in the fourth year of his reign. It was inside the Palace that poor old Uncle Claudius had been found by the assassins—cowering behind a curtain, according to his enemies; calmly seated at his table, working on one of his many historical essays, according to the emperor himself.

Claudius had not done any building onto the Palace, although he had stripped away some of the more opulent sculptures and the pornographic murals Caligula had favored. Only the Imperial bedchamber remained sumptuously furnished; Claudius kept it that way to please his young bride Messalina, the mother of his two surviving children.

Marcus had heard some very disturbing rumors about Messalina of late, he reflected as he made his way toward the Palace. Of course, the small and unimportant always gossiped about their betters, but still, he couldn't help but think about the stories as he glimpsed the gleaming columns of the emperor's residence across the hill from the Forum. Surely Claudius' wife would not be so insane as to do some of the things whispered about her? He certainly hoped not, for the emperor's sake.

Once they arrived at the palace, Marcus told Rufus to wait for him outside, near the servant's quarters, while he mounted the steps and stepped through the ornate entryway between the enormous columns. A black-clad Praetorian escorted him through the polished marble corridors to a richly appointed library. The walls were adorned with scrolls, each deposited in its own niche, as well as some of the new codices, a stack of single pages bound together with leather thongs inside a thick, rigid cover. Introduced by Julius Caesar himself, this new means of storing information was heavier than a scroll but easier to read, since it did not have to be unrolled.

There were several couches near the center of the room, piled with cushions for comfortable reclining, and a bowl of fresh fruit in the center of the table. Marcus did not feel it proper to be sitting while waiting for the emperor, so he stood and perused the huge collection of scrolls. Each nook was labeled with a small tag of papyrus, listing the number, author, and title of the scrolls it contained. There were many histories, it appeared, both of familiar Roman topics and some places and names that Marcus was altogether unfamiliar with.

"Senator Marcus Quintus Publius," a soft voice echoed across the marble floor. Marcus whirled to see that the emperor had quietly entered the room and stood facing him, dressed in the simple white toga of a Roman senator, with only the Civic Crown decorating his forehead as a reminder of who he was. Once exclusively a military decoration, the emperors since Augustus had worn it as a badge of their rank. At least, Marcus thought, Claudius' crown was actually made of leaves, unlike the golden facsimile the mad Caligula had favored.

Marcus bowed to his host. "Most excellent Caesar," he said. "I apologize for—"

"You need never apologize to me for loving books," Claudius said with a wistful smile. "Please, though, do not call me Caesar. It is indeed a family name—but it has also become a family curse. You may address me as Claudius."

Marcus stiffened. "Uhm, very well then, most excellent Claudius," he finally said. "To what do I owe the honor of this summons?"

The emperor approached him, his calm gray eyes surveying the younger man closely. As he drew near, Marcus was impressed with how exhausted and worn the ruler of the world looked. There were dark circles under his eyes, and an uncontrollable twitch worked one side of his mouth up and down. His gray hair was thinning, and his limp was much more perceptible than it had been the evening before. To his surprise, he saw that there were tears, or at least the remains of tears, running down the emperor's cheeks.

"I am told you gave a most excellent speech before the jury today on behalf of Lucius Hortensius," he said.

"I always try to defend my clients to the best of my ability, sire—I mean, Claudius," Marcus said.

"You made some very critical remarks about my late, lamented nephew," the emperor continued. "Some might say it is unwise to be so critical of an emperor, even one who is no more."

Marcus sighed. "I realize that Gaius Caligula was your nephew, Excellency," he said. "But he was responsible for the deaths of my entire family. I will not sugarcoat my remarks in the name of political expediency."

The emperor nodded sadly. "So you are an honest man," he said. "I thought that was the case, which is why I summoned you today. Your actions this morning confirm that assessment, at least to some degree. But I will ask you directly—are you an honest man, Marcus Quintus?"

"My own words would be the least trustworthy answer to that question, Claudius," Marcus said. "For any liar or scoundrel would answer in the affirmative, while any truly honest man will recognize that duplicity lies in the hearts of us all. Yes, for what it is worth, I strive for honesty and honor in all my dealings. But I am bearing witness of myself. You would do better to ask another who knows me."

"Spoken honestly!" Claudius smiled. "Every word you said about Caligula was true, you know. I was there that night. I was there for all his dinner parties, a buffoon to be ridiculed, and a jester for his corrupt comrades to laugh over. Then the next day he would put me in a formal toga and parade me as his co-consul, pretending to defer to my judgment, but all the while laughing at the pathetic old man he had forced to wear women's clothes and a wig the night before. Every day I was forced to choose between my life and my *dignitas,* and I chose my life every time—to my shame, sir, to my shame."

Claudius sighed and sat down on one of the couches. "Please, join me," he said, popping a ripe plum into his mouth. Marcus sat on the couch across from him.

The emperor continued to study him, and Marcus found his stare disconcerting. Finally, Claudius spoke again.

"No one can wound you as deeply as family," he said. "Caligula was once a darling little boy, the apple of my brother's eye. When they bought him that little centurion's uniform, we all loved to watch him strut and march in it. He would bark orders to the legionaries and they would snap to as if he were a real general. Even crusty old Tiberius' cold heart would melt when Caligula climbed into his lap. But that precious little boy grew up into a monster, and I'm still not sure how. There was a cruel streak in him, even as a child. But most boys have that, and outgrow it. He never did; in fact, he became more and more cruel as he grew older. Then, when he was fourteen, he raped his betrothed bride and broke her arm. Her father, Pontius

Pilate, nearly killed Caligula that day. I sometimes think that the Empire would be better off if he had succeeded."

Marcus listened in fascination, wondering where all this was going.

"But Pilate did not succeed, and the injuries he inflicted on Gaius seemed to reinforce the lad's innate cruelty and insanity. I've been told that Pilate was crucified on Caligula's order shortly after my nephew became emperor, even though the man was a former consul and a full citizen of Rome. Law does not matter to men like my nephew, where vengeance or even personal desires are concerned."

He paused in thought for a while, and then turned to Marcus again. "Are you married, Senator Publius?" he asked.

"I was, once," Marcus replied. "She died bringing my son into this world, and I miss her cruelly."

"You are more blessed than you know, my friend," Claudius said. "I said that no one can hurt you like family, but that is only partly true. There is no hurt that matches being betrayed by the woman you love. Your wife died loving you, and you her. Her love will remain forever unstained in your heart. I, on the other hand, just signed my wife's death warrant."

Marcus paused, shocked, unsure if this was a jest or a metaphor or the horrible truth. He knew that Messalina was thirty years younger than her husband, but such matches were not rare in Rome. Even the great Gaius Julius Caesar had married off his daughter to Pompey the Great when she was still in her teens. Marriage came first, love later—that was the classic advice Roman matrons gave to their daughters.

As he pondered the meaning of the emperor's remark, a horrible scream echoed down one of the corridors, followed by a woman's shrill voice.

"What does this mean? Unhand me, you brute! Let me go!! My husband will have your head for this. Claudius! CLAUDIUS!!!!" The final cry trailed off as Messalina was apparently being dragged outside.

"Forgive me, Senator," Claudius said, and buried his face in his hands.

Marcus sat in awkward silence, having no idea what was going on or why he was even there. Claudius made no sound beyond the muffled sobs that came from behind the sleeves of his toga. Almost a half hour passed, and then a burly Praetorian entered the room and stood before the emperor's couch.

"It is done, Caesar," he finally said.

Claudius looked up, his eyes red and his face streaked with tears. "Did she die well?" he asked.

The Praetorian shrugged. "I gave her the choice of ending her own life," he said. "She took the dagger from me and stared at it for a long time, but she could not seem to bear the thought of using it on her own flesh. So she knelt before me and asked me to make it quick. I took her life with a single thrust to the heart, behind the collarbone and straight down."

Claudius shuddered. "You followed my orders, Vorenus," he said. "I lay one more charge upon you: if I ever marry again, kill me!"

"If you say so, Caesar," replied the guard. "But I will demand confirmation of that order before I carry it out!"

Claudius nodded. "What about Gaius Sillius?" he asked.

"He was arrested and beheaded an hour ago," Vorenus replied.

"Allow his family to sell their property," Claudius said, "and then see to it that they are escorted to Spain. As long as they do not return to Rome, I see no reason to punish them further. As for all those who were on the list, round them up and dispatch them as quickly and quietly as possible, even the slaves. No man who shared her bed, in contempt of me, is to be spared! Now, burn her body and return the ashes to her family. They can take her with them to Antioch."

The Praetorian nodded his head and turned away. Marcus watched him go in wonder, and then looked at Claudius, who was watching him. The emperor looked a thousand years old.

"Caesar—Claudius, I mean," he said. "I am very confused by all this."

The emperor laughed, but there was no joy in the sound.

"She was such a pretty and sweet thing," he said. "Only eighteen when I married her. Caligula ordered me to—he said that I needed a wife from the Julian family, so that my offspring would have a claim to the Imperial throne someday. I wonder if he somehow knew that none of his own children would live?" He gave a long sigh. "She was a virgin when she came to me—I think. She was certainly shy enough, although in retrospect, that may have been more from having to marry a stranger who was much older than her than from innate shyness or innocence. She certainly has not been acting innocent lately."

He stood and began pacing the room. "Infidelity I could have forgiven," he said. "Indeed, considering the difference in our age and personality, I suppose her straying was inevitable. But she did not know the meaning of discretion!" He thumped his fist into his palm in frustration. "She humiliated me, Marcus, but even then, I might merely have divorced her. But when my freedmen brought me reports that she and her latest paramour, Senator Gaius Sillius, were planning to kill me and my son so that they could rule Rome together—well, a man has his limits!"

"Jupiter!" Marcus exclaimed. "There were rumors around town about the Empress for some time, but I thought they were just that."

"Would that they were, my young friend," Claudius said. "You see now why I said that I envy you? Three wives I have had—three!—and not one of them has truly loved me. Urgulanilla was a joke, foisted on me by Augustus' wife Livia so that the granddaughter of her friend and confidant would have a husband. We never loved each other, but we made the best we could of being a pair of outcasts. Me with my stutter and limp, she with her harelip and crooked back—what a pair we made! But she betrayed me anyway, and I had to divorce her. Then there was Aelia Paetina, the cousin of Sejanus. As beautiful as Venus and as cruel as Medusa! She actually beat me, you know, on more than one occasion. I was glad when Sejanus fell from favor so I could be rid of her. Then Caligula asked if I would marry Valeria Messalina, and I thought I had found bliss at last! And, for a while, I guess I did. It certainly felt that way. But we see how that turned out. Now, Marcus, do you see why I envy you?"

"I suppose so, Your Excellency," Marcus said. "But—if I may be so bold—why am I here? Why was I chosen to be a witness to all this?"

"I suppose you must be puzzled," Claudius said. "Let us have a bit of wine, and I will try to collect my wits and explain."

He called for a steward, who brought a pitcher and two fine crystal goblets into the room. "Will you require any food, *Dominus?"* he asked.

"I'm in no mood for a meal now," Claudius replied, "but I would not mind some grilled mushrooms to soothe my stomach. It has been a very stressful day. Marcus, would you like anything?"

Food was the furthest thing from Marcus' mind at the moment.

"I am quite content, sire," he said, sipping his wine. His head was still whirling from all that he had witnessed.

Claudius took a long drink of his wine and dabbed at his face with a kerchief. "I had no idea that this thing with Messalina was going to happen this morning when I spoke to you yesterday," he said. "I had been told by my freedmen that there was a matter of great urgency involving a member of my family and a plot on my life, but I thought it would be one of my cousins, not my bride! I figured I could hear the evidence and order any arrests needed, and then have time to meet with you in the afternoon. When they revealed all the damning evidence against my wife, I was so flummoxed I completely forgot that I had made an appointment with you until you showed up at my door."

"You should have sent me home, Claudius," Marcus said. "I certainly would have understood!"

"I am glad I did not," the emperor replied. "I think this conversation is the only thing keeping me sane right now. The reason

I summoned you is simple. As you may know, I was a historian by choice before I was forced into politics by my family. I am a student of the history of Rome—and of the Etruscans who came before us."

He stood and began to pace. "Rome was a Republic for nearly five hundred years," he said. "I wrote a history of the Republic's fall when I was a young man, but the great Augustus told me it was too soon for a work of that nature, and ordered me to burn it. I had the temerity to relate some rather unpleasant truths about our family, you see. I am a Republican at heart—I would like to see the powers of government balanced once more between consuls, Senate, assemblies, and tribunes. It was a good government for a city of hundreds of thousands, and with some adjustments, I think it could be an effective government for an Empire of millions as well. The principate was created during extraordinary times, for an extraordinary purpose—but I don't think it was ever intended to become permanent!" He paused and took another sip of his wine, wiping his mouth again. Marcus noticed that when the emperor became agitated, a hint of his old stutter returned, and he tended to drool ever so slightly from one side of his mouth.

"The problem, my young friend, is that the Senate of Rome has forgotten how to govern! During the Civic Wars, many of the best and brightest members of the Senate were killed fighting on either side. Most of those who survived were either opportunists who were willing to side with whoever was strongest, or men of limited talent who survived by keeping their heads down and their mouths shut. Then dear old Uncle Octavian seized power and became the Divine Augustus." His voice was laced with sarcasm. "He proscribed some and exiled others, but once he got the Senate filled with men of his own choosing, he could do what he wanted. He could play the part of the virtuous Republican, and even offer to lay down all his titles and powers—only to see the Senate frantically offer them back to him, increased a hundredfold. Oh, how he played them like a harp!"

He flopped back down onto the couch, spilling a few drops of wine on his toga. He leaned forward and fixed Marcus with his intense gaze, the redness in his eyes fading. "Then Augustus finally joined the gods—probably proscribed or exiled a few of them, too, I shouldn't be surprised!—and left all his titles and power to Tiberius. Oh, how I once hated that old man!"

Marcus, not sure how to respond, nodded. "I am told there were few that loved him," he said.

"That is true," the emperor told him. "I don't hate him anymore, though—if anything, I think I understand him now. Tiberius simply understood human nature—and despised it. He recognized that, as emperor, everyone around him would be fundamentally dishonest and self-serving. I think that's why he loved children so much—their affection was perhaps the only honest thing in his life. He was the loneliest soul I ever knew, but even he deserved a better end than the one he was given. Smothered to death with his own pillow at the age of seventy-eight! What an ignoble end for a man who was once a great general, and who could have been a great emperor if fate had been kinder to him in his early years."

The steward brought in a plate of grilled mushrooms, and Claudius paused to eat a few of them. He washed them down with more wine and offered the plate to Marcus, who took a single mushroom and nibbled on it, nodding at the emperor to continue.

"But Tiberius became so paranoid in his later years, he was convinced everyone was conspiring against him," Claudius said. "So he purged the Senate again and again, until very few men of quality were left. Ironically, all the while his own chosen heir was the one plotting to kill him! And when he succeeded, the Empire fell under the rule of my nephew, Gaius Caesar—the same 'Little Boots' whose antics had once set us all to laughter. No one was laughing for long when he became emperor! There was something broken in him by then, some inability to feel compassion or remorse or even genuine affection. Tiberius at least acted logically, striking out against whoever might have become a threat to him. Caligula struck out as his whims dictated, killing some and sparing others. He had no thought for tomorrow, only for what he wanted at the moment. That quality, of course, is what took your family from you. I doubt he had any plans to murder your father or ravage your sister when he invited them to the dinner party. He saw, he wanted, he took—that was Caligula all over! Finally, people sickened of his madness and his own Praetorians cut him down. And so the Empire came to me."

Claudius took a long drink of wine and refilled his goblet. The emperor was becoming quite drunk, Marcus thought, and made up his own mind to stay sober.

"I see a government that has been abused and broken for many years, in many ways," the emperor said. "I know my time is limited, and my son Britannicus is far too young to succeed me yet. What I would like to do, before I die, is see the Republic at least partially restored—to see a Senate worthy of the name, a place where Cicero or Crassus would not be embarrassed to set foot."

"But not Cato?" Marcus asked.

"Gods, no!" exclaimed Claudius. "On that one thing, both Julius Caesar and Octavian were correct—Cato was a sanctimonious turd whose actions did as much as anyone's to destroy the Republic! But he was an honest man, and did have some spine, I'll give him that. We need a Senate that is equal to the task of ruling an Empire, and right now we do not have it. The current Senate is composed of either professional survivors, like your uncle, and worthless sycophants, like that old fool Porcius Antonius. They know how to do nothing except bow and say 'Yes, Caesar!' We need better men. Frankly, young Marcus, we need more men like you."

"I'm flattered, sire, but I am no one special," Marcus said.

"Nonsense!" the emperor replied. "Your speech today shows what stern stuff you are made of. You stood up for truth, even though the consequences could have proven disastrous for you and your client."

"Does the truth really require that much courage?" Marcus said.

"It does these days," Claudius replied. "You remember that Pontius Pilate I mentioned to you earlier?" he asked.

"The father of Caligula's would-be bride?" Marcus asked. "I have heard of him before. He was governor of Judea when that whole Nazarene thing started, wasn't he?"

"That was him," the emperor replied. "But before he went to Judea, he was the closest thing that Tiberius had to a friend. The old emperor once told me that Pontius Pilate was the one man he could count on to tell him the truth, no matter what. I need someone like that. I need someone in the Senate who is not afraid to tell me when I am wrong, who is willing to report truthfully to me about events in the provinces, who will not simply tell me what I want to hear."

"I'm not entirely sure I understand," Marcus said.

Claudius laughed. "What I need you to do is go on being you!" he said. "Don't let politics corrupt you, and don't let me or my successors intimidate you. Stand for truth, tell me the truth, and when I give you a command, carry it out to the best of your ability, or tell me that it can't be done. That is what I want from you—that you continue to be an honest man and a loyal subject."

He rose and swayed on his feet slightly. "I would appreciate your discretion about today's events," the emperor said. "I am sure it will be all over Rome soon enough, but I see no reason our conversation should become public knowledge. I will have a specific assignment for you as quaestor soon enough, but until then, continue to represent your clients and increase your *arctoritas* in Rome. I will let it be known that you are an advocate who enjoys my trust—that should steer quite a few clients your way. Now I bid you good day. I am going to drink myself into oblivion and compose an ode to Messalina."

Marcus bowed, and the steward saw him out. Rufus was waiting for him, but he contained his natural curiosity when he saw the look on the senator's face. Marcus hardly noticed—all the way home, he tried to wrap his head around the afternoon's events. What a bizarre day it had been!

CHAPTER V

For the next few weeks the talk of Rome was the sudden fall of the Empress and her abrupt execution. Over the next few days, some twenty men were put to death—senators, Praetorians, plebs, and slaves—all on the charge of having committed adultery with Messalina. The tales were whirling around the markets and forums and crossroads colleges: that Messalina had secretly married Gaius Sillius; that she had slept with the entire Praetorian Guard in one night; that she had snuck out of the Palace to work for free in a brothel in the Aventine. No one knew which stories were true and which were fabricated, but everyone was talking about them.

The emperor stayed out of sight during this mess, venturing out only at night to visit a few old and trusted friends. Most of Claudius' closest advisors were freemen whose loyalty to him was absolute; he also had a small circle of about a dozen Praetorians that he knew well and trusted fully. Moving within this tiny circle, the emperor was slowly recovering from the emotional ordeal he had been through.

In the meantime, Marcus Publius suddenly found himself one of the most demanded advocates in Rome. He had a line of clients outside his door each day, and his *arctoritas*—the circle of influence which each Roman official worked to build up constantly—was increasing. As he argued cases before Rome's various courts and magistrates, his reputation for eloquence and integrity grew quickly. Soon his court cases were drawing audiences from all over the city, and he even heard one or two people call him "Young Cicero." Being compared to Rome's most famous orator was an enormous compliment, but he also felt it was a bit of a stretch. Still, he thought, he would be lying if he said it didn't make him feel good.

As busy as he was, it was a couple of weeks before Marcus got to have dinner with Mencius again. This time, he invited the older senator to his own home, repaying the man's hospitality in kind. They reclined at the table as Phidias brought out fingerbowls to wash their hands and a tray of fresh fruit to start off with. Young Cadius brought them clean towels and freshened the water in the bowls all evening.

Cadius had apparently adopted the older slave as a father figure; he followed Marcus' body servant everywhere. His attitude wavered between concern for Phidias' health and safety and mischievous pranks that drove the old Greek half mad at times. But in spite of this, he was quickly becoming a capable servant, learning his master's tastes in clothes and food and knowing when to wake him in the morning.

As Marcus and Mencius chatted over the day's events, Cadius entered, bearing a platter of smoked fish and chicken, with a bowl of lentils on the side.

"Well, lad, how are you enjoying your new household?" Mencius asked him.

"It's nice enough," Cadius said. "The food is good, and Phidias is a good teacher. Marcus is a kind master, when he is here. I wish there were other servants my age, though."

"Who's that little urchin I see you playing with in the evenings?" Marcus asked.

Cadius' face brightened. "That's Arnulf, the cooper's boy!" he said. "He and his family are from Germania. His father is a freedman and a client of Senator Gracchus."

"I see," said Marcus. "Is he going to teach you to make barrels?"

"I've watched him and his father at work," Cadius said. "It looks rather hard. I don't see how they get the staves to fit together so smoothly."

"Every slave should learn a trade," Marcus said, "so that if I ever free you, you'll be able to honestly support yourself. I'll tell you what, Cadius—bring a pitcher of wine to the table and go play with your friend. I need to visit with my uncle for a while, and this is more than enough food for us."

"Thank you, *Dominus!*" Cadius replied happily. "I'll tell Phidias that I am going."

He scampered out of the room, and Mencius chuckled. "You are spoiling that boy, Marcus," he said.

"Well, he is mine, after all," said Marcus, "unless you want him back!"

"Not at all!" his uncle replied. "A happy slave is a loyal slave, and those who live in our homes and guard our persons should be treated with kindness. He knows how lucky he is not to be working at a *latifundium* somewhere, or in the tin mines. But now that he is gone, I am dying to know—what happened during your interview with the emperor? Did you have any idea of what was going on in the Palace?"

Marcus nodded. "I arrived right as Messalina was being arrested," he said. "I was there for the whole thing. However, I swore to Claudius that I would not reveal any details to anyone, and I have not, so please don't press me!"

"You were there?" his uncle asked in astonishment.

"Yes, I was," Marcus said, "and that is all I have to say about it."

Mencius shook his head. "Claudius! So you call the emperor by his *cognomen* now? You have risen in the world, nevvy! Still, I know senators who would trade their firstborn to have been inside the Palace when Messalina fell from grace," he exclaimed.

"The emperor entrusted me with his confidence, and I will not betray it," Marcus said.

"That is probably wise," his uncle said. "So tell me about your latest cases. I haven't been able to make it to the Forum this week."

Marcus regaled him with an entertaining tale about Fulvius Atropus, the merchant who was suing a well-known scribe, Marcus Fabricius, for stealing his wife's affections. It was a rather lurid tale of the sort usually worked out in private negotiations rather than in the civil courts, but Fulvius was bound and determined to win back his wife's dowry, if not her affections, from her new lover. He had trotted out many salacious details of the seducer's past exploits in an effort to win the jury's sympathy, but so far, he had succeeded in making most of them envy Fabricius instead, and raunchy graffiti about Fulvius was sprouting on the walls all over the Subura and Aventine districts. Marcus had advised his client to drop the case, but Fulvius was extraordinarily bull-headed, and didn't seem to realize what a fool he was making of himself.

"I think, in my closing arguments, that I am just going to go for the gutter and tell the jury that Fulvius deserves to have the dowry returned as the price of providing them with such rare entertainment," Marcus said, chuckling.

Mencius rolled his eyes. "You know, that strategy just might work, if the court sessions have been as funny as your summary!"

After his uncle left, Marcus sighed and headed for his bedchamber. He was tired, but not sleepy yet, and after Phidias helped him out of his dinner robes, he slipped a pair of sandals on his feet and padded into his study.

It was times like this, he thought, that he missed his wife the most. Her warmth and companionship had made his bedchamber a haven from the cares of the world, but with her gone, the room was simply another place to worry about life. He had thought about marrying again, but could not motivate himself to go questing for another bride—and none of them, he thought, would ever take Drusilla's place in his heart. A few times, when the loneliness was too much to bear, he had sent for Lydia, the slave girl who worked in the kitchen. She was willing enough, but at the end of the day, she was merely a slave doing as she was told, not a companion he could unburden his heart to. He had not summoned her in many weeks, and would not do so tonight, he decided. Instead, he pulled a well-worn scroll of Caesar's *Gallic Wars* from its cubbyhole and immersed himself in the siege of Alesium.

The next day he finished arguing Fulvius' case to the jury. Despite his jest with Mencius, he made no mention of the case's entertainment value, but instead aimed his argument at the jury's emotions.

"Which married man among us does not worry about his wife's fidelity when war or business calls us away from home for months on end?" he asked them. "All of us know someone like Marcus Fabricius—clean-shaven, smooth-talking charmers who never seem to be called away from the business of seduction to earn a living. Wealthy men, most of them, able to employ slaves and stewards to manage their estates while they walk the marketplaces and *insulae* of Rome, trolling for other men's wives. Some of you may have come home from your time serving in the legions, or making a trade voyage to the East, only to find your bride pregnant with another man's child. Even if you have not, I know you have worried about it. We all have! So now we have this perfumed, strutting popinjay who not only has stolen the wife of an honest merchant, but has also taken her dowry, the money her husband was paid by her parents for giving her his name, his trust, and his children! I do not blame Porcia Minor—she is only a weak and feeble woman, after all, prone to the blandishments of seducers like Fabricius! But what Marcus Varrus Fabricius has done to Fulvius Atropus is far worse than simply stealing his wife, and stealing some money along with her. Marcus Fabricius has stolen Atropus' *dignitas,* the respect and public standing without which no Roman nobleman can live. Will you let such an injustice stand? Will you let the bawdy details of this seducer's exploits blind you to the fact that he is a common thief, and Fulvius Atropus a helpless victim? I adjure you in the name of Jupiter Optimus Maximus himself; do not let this injustice stand!"

He sat next to his client, who gave him a curt nod. The truth was, he did not like Fulvius that much and hardly blamed Porcia Minor for wanting to leave the annoying blowhard—but the man was his paying customer, and he had done his best. When the jury divided, he saw to his astonishment that they had decided almost two to one in favor of Fulvius, who shook his hand heartily and thanked him for his services. In addition, he dropped a second bag of gold sesterces into Marcus' hand, almost double the amount Marcus had agreed upon. Marcus grinned as he dropped the purse into the sinus of his toga and joined Rufus for the walk home. The Senate was being convened for another meeting tomorrow, and Marcus was grateful for the bonus, since the meeting would keep him out of the courts for the day.

"You're a silver-tongued devil and no mistake, Senator Publius," said Rufus. "I would have sworn that jury was going to decide for Fabricius going into today's hearing!"

Marcus nodded. As he spent more time with his bodyguard, he had found that the man was surprisingly intelligent, despite his poor background and quaint speech. "I was thinking the same thing," he said. "But one thing I have learned is that Romans have a deep-seated sense of justice, and if you paint a case as an issue of right and wrong, a jury will usually do the right thing."

"Very true, sir!" Rufus said. "No one likes to see the scoundrels win, even if sometimes we can't prevent it! Will we be going home now, sir?"

Marcus stretched and yawned. "I think I want to go to the bathhouse," he said. "I'm tired and stiff and hot water sounds lovely."

They headed toward the Quirinale, where a large *Fermia balnea,* or public hot bathhouse, had recently been erected. Marcus paid the *balneator* with a quadrans, the smallest Roman coin and the price of admission to the baths from time immemorial.

"Shall I wait for you outside, sir?" asked Rufus.

"By no means!" Marcus said, handing the proprietor another coin. "You smell like a horse and the baths would do you good."

Rufus gaped at him. "Begging your pardon, sir, but I've never used a *Fermia* before!" he said. "Our bathhouse in the Aventine is of the old, cold variety, and I only go there once a month—too many thieves about! Last time they nipped four sesterces out of my coin purse while I was washing up!"

Marcus laughed. "This is a respectable establishment," he said, "and your clothes and coin will be safe. Now come on in!"

The *Fermia* was large and clean, with two heated pools, one for men and one for women. In the days of the Republic, the pools would have been in separate rooms, but in recent years, the old moral codes had begun to slip. There was a partition separating the pools, but one could still see people coming and going in various sets of undress.

Marcus, who was a bit of a prude by Roman standards, found it somewhat embarrassing—he knew his own physique left something to be desired—while Rufus gawked openly at the young ladies coming and going from the other pool.

Two hours later, after a delightful hot bath and rubdown, master and servant donned their clothes to head home. Marcus decided to splurge and hire a litter, while a clean, scrubbed Rufus marched proudly ahead of the bearers, urging pedestrians to clear a path for the senator. They arrived at Marcus' *domus* still feeling clean and fresh, as the sun was beginning to move westward and the shadows were lengthening.

"Will you be heading out again this afternoon, Senator?" Rufus asked.

"No, I think I shall spend a quiet evening at home tonight," Marcus said, and tossed him a few denarii. "Why don't you buy your sweetheart a necklace at the marketplace and go home a bit early?"

"Thank you kindly, sir!" Rufus said with delight. "You're a good man to share your day's profit with the likes of me!"

"You're a good man, too, Rufus Licinius—better, I think, than you realize. Now off with you, and enjoy your evening!"

The burly pleb strode off excitedly, and Marcus entered his home, noticing that it was quieter than normal. He strode back to his bedroom, clapping his hands to summon Phidias. Young Cadius appeared in his stead.

"Shall I help you out of your toga, *Dominus*?" he asked.

"Where is Phidias?" Marcus asked with some alarm.

"He is sleeping," Cadius said. "He took a fall earlier today and his knee is hurt."

"Did you send for a physician?" Marcus asked.

"I ran and got one myself," the young slave said. "He looked it over and said that nothing is broken, but Phidias will need about a week to heal. I'll look after you in the meantime."

He was short enough that he had to stand on a stool to undrape Marcus' toga, but he did it quickly and deftly, and already had one of his master's favorite green robes laid out for supper. Marcus was quickly dressed for an evening at home, and told Cadius what he wanted the cook to prepare before going to check on Phidias.

The old Greek was wearing a worn white tunic with his leg wrapped in a poultice and propped up. He tried to sit up a little straighter when Marcus came in.

"Forgive me for not rising properly, *Dominus*," he said. "I just tripped over my own feet this morning!"

"No forgiveness is needed, you old fool!" Marcus said affectionately. "I just want you to be well and on your feet again."

"That is most kind, sir. Did that young scamp take proper care with your toga?" he asked.

"Yes, Phidias, you have trained him well," Marcus said. "Now stay off that leg and do what the *medicus* tells you! Young Cadius will take care of me, and if he is uncertain of anything, he knows to come ask you."

The old man nodded, his rheumy eyes moistening. "I know that I don't have many years left, sir," he said. "But I have served your household since before you were born, and it's all I know. Please don't send me away!"

Marcus felt his own eyes welling up. "Silly old man," he said. "Who else would have you? Believe me, I will never send you away—you'd just come limping back, for one thing. I just wish you would let me send you to Tartarus as a free man. No one should die a slave."

"Master, if I wanted my liberty cap, I would have taken it when you offered it to me the first time, ten years ago," Phidias said. "My wife is dead, I have no children, and you are my family. Slave, free, it matters not to me anymore, as long as I reside in this house."

"You are impossible, you know that?" Marcus said, walking out. He headed to the dining room and reclined at the table, munching on some grapes while he waited for the lamb he had requested for dinner. He could smell it cooking, but before his slaves brought it out, Demetrius entered the room, looking a bit startled.

"*Dominus,*" he said, "there is a Praetorian guard asking to see you."

Marcus rose, but before he could reach the passageway, the black-clad soldier entered the room. Marcus recognized him as the same one who had brought Claudius the news of Messalina's execution.

"*Ave,* Senator Marcus Quintus Publius," he said. "The Emperor Claudius Caesar requests the honor of your presence at his dinner table this evening."

Marcus was startled at the abrupt invitation, but did his best not to show it. "I am, as ever, at the emperor's disposal," he said. "Give me a moment to change into something more suitable for the Palace."

"The emperor is not one to stand on ceremony," the guard said. "Your attire is more than appropriate. He sent a litter after me so that you could be borne in comfort to the Palatine."

"I thank him for the courtesy," Marcus said. "Demetrius, you and the other slaves may have the lamb that Lydia is cooking. Make sure old Phidias gets a good helping—I want him well again soon!" He strapped on his sandals and turned to the Praetorian. "I am ready to go now . . ." He paused, realizing he had never heard the man's name.

"Legionary Titus Sylvanus at your service, sir," he said. "I'll walk ahead of you and clear the way. Shall we go?"

For the second time that day Marcus found himself reclining in a padded litter chair, borne by four strong men across the city. It was a luxury he rarely allowed himself, and resolved not to repeat again soon—he was a Stoic at heart, and such pampering, he was convinced, sapped the character. It took them over a half an hour to reach the Palace, and when they arrived, the sun was dipping below the horizon. Titus led Marcus into the huge building, conducting him to a small dining chamber. The emperor was standing, looking out a window at the sunset.

"*Salve,* Marcus Quintus," Claudius said.

"*Ave,* Caesar," replied Marcus, forgetting that the emperor did not like the name. He studied his host closely. Claudius looked thinner and older than he had two weeks before, but his face was no longer streaked with tears, and his eyes were not red, nor were the bags under them as prominent. "It is my pleasure to be your guest again."

"Did you think I had forgotten you?" Claudius asked with a slight smile.

"Not at all," Marcus replied. "You have had . . . much on your mind, I am sure."

Claudius laughed out loud. "Meaning I have been a broken-hearted, drunken old cuckold?" he said. "Guilty as charged!"

Marcus paled. "Excellency, I would never—"

Claudius waved his hand. "Of course, you would not," he said. "But I am no fool, even if I was a bit blind for a while. The whole city is gossiping about the fate of the Empress and my role in it. But I am pleased to see my trust in you was well-placed, Marcus."

"What do you mean, sire—I mean, Claudius?" Marcus asked.

"You alone, outside my household, were here when events came to a head. I asked you to keep the evening in confidence, and my agents have been listening to all the gossip these last few weeks," the emperor explained. "No one has gotten it right, which means you have kept your mouth shut, as I requested—even to your uncle!"

"How could you possibly know that?" Marcus asked in shock.

"Your uncle loves to talk," Claudius said. "He is harmless, indeed convivial, but the man does not keep secrets well! But after his dinner with you, no juicy tidbits about the details of that awful evening emerged. That's when I knew I was right to trust you."

Marcus bowed. "Your trust honors me," he said. "I would only repay honor with honor."

The emperor inclined his head. "Well said," he replied. "Many Romans say such things, but in this day and age few mean them. I believe you do." He took a small sip of wine. "I hear that your work before the juries is most impressive, by the way. 'Young Cicero,' isn't that what they call you?"

"Only in jest, Claudius," Marcus replied.

"Your humility is a bit overdone, my friend. You're the best advocate Rome has seen in a generation," the emperor replied.

About this time servants arrived carrying plates of steaming hot food—fresh clams and oysters, mushrooms prepared three different ways, and grilled lamb haunches. Marcus, who was starving by now, barely had the willpower to let the emperor fill his plate first before digging in. For a while all was quiet as the two men enjoyed their food together. Finally, after the heaps of food on the platters had become considerably smaller, Marcus took a sip of wine and asked the question that had been on his mind since Titus had arrived at his villa.

"So why did you summon me this evening, Claudius?" he asked.

"I have been thinking about an appropriate assignment for you," the emperor replied, wiping his mouth with a kerchief. "Something that will make good use of your talents, increase your *arctoritas*, and give you an opportunity for advancement and enrichment. When was the last time you traveled outside Rome?"

"It's been a good while, Caesar," Marcus said. "My military service with Legate Tullius, I suppose."

"I am concerned about the state of affairs in the provinces," Claudius told him. "During the latter part of my uncle's reign, things were let slip very badly, and my unfortunate nephew made them even worse, appointing some of the most venal and incompetent governors the Empire has ever seen! On top of that, his lack of sensitivity to regional custom was truly deplorable. I am no admirer of the Jews, but do you know that Gaius Caligula actually wanted to erect a statue of himself as Jupiter inside their Temple in Jerusalem?"

"*Edepol!*" Marcus swore. "That would have been an enormous sacrilege, would it not?"

"Indeed," Claudius replied. "Fortunately, the governor there, Pilate's successor, delayed implementing the order until I came to power and countermanded it. We would still be fighting the Jews—even more so than we normally do, that is. They are a difficult people to govern." He paused for a moment and then continued. "But that is beside the point. I want you to travel to all the imperial provinces over the next three years, gathering information both from the governors and from the locals. My goal is to bring about a more enlightened and less corrupt administration. How are you with financial matters?"

"Columns of figures make my head hurt," Marcus said honestly. "I could never be a banker."

"It is a rare talent," said the emperor. "I am going to send my freedman, Cassius Claudius, with you. He is a skilled banker and accountant, and his job will be to go over the financial records and make sure the governors are being truthful about tax policies and bribery. Both of you will carry an official edict from me, authorizing you to dig as deep as you need to in order to find the truth. I am also empowering you to dismiss any governor, be he prefect or proconsul, if you find him guilty of conduct that is grossly offensive to the *dignitas* of the Senate and People of Rome, and send him back to Rome for trial, or, in extraordinary cases, to administer justice on the spot. You will report back to me in three years' time, or when your tour is complete, at which point I will be ready to honor you with higher office. Is that acceptable?"

"Why yes, sire," Marcus said. "I am much honored. When do I need to set out?"

"I shall announce your commission to the Senate tomorrow, and you can have a week or two to set your affairs in order," Claudius said. "But I do not want any great delays. I need this task completed in the allotted time—I do not know how long the gods will spare me, but I want to redeem the days as well as I can."

He crossed over to the table in the corner and picked up a small scroll. "You will be entitled to one lictor, and any additional muscle you want to hire, to serve as your protectors. Cassius Claudius is also a sturdy fellow in a scrap."

"I have a very good man I recently hired as my bodyguard," Marcus said. "I will see if he would be willing to come along."

The emperor smiled. "Very good! If he serves you well, perhaps he would like to be appointed to the College of Lictors upon his return?" he asked.

Marcus tried to imagine how Rufus would react to being appointed as one of Rome's most elite public protectors. "I imagine he would be delighted, sir," he said.

"It's done then!" Claudius said. "I shall announce your appointment to the rest of the Senate tomorrow. Thank you, Marcus, for helping me return good government to Rome's provinces."

"Thank me when I return," Marcus said. "This is no small task, and it may prove to be beyond me."

"I doubt that," the emperor said. "I believe you will succeed at whatever you set your hand to. Now, before you go, I want to talk to you about one governor in particular . . ."

CHAPTER VI

Five weeks had elapsed since that interview, and Marcus was hanging on for dear life as his ship wallowed its way through a fierce Mediterranean storm. The pouring rain drenched every corner of the deck, and water ran and seeped through the wood into every compartment—there was not a place on the vessel that was completely dry, and even the fires in the galley were struggling to remain lit. At least, he thought, hanging onto the rail for dear life and watching his breakfast as it came hurling out of his mouth to vanish into the rough waters, the wind was pushing them in the right direction, to the west. Hopefully, in the next day or two, the coast of Tarraconensis would come into view, and this hellish voyage would be over.

There were nearly thirty Imperial provinces in the Empire by the time of Claudius; this total did not include the thirteen provinces administered by the Senate. Allowing for brief stays and quick travel time, Marcus had figured that it would take him at least two years, and maybe longer, to visit each of them. Of course, he would be sending regular letters back to Claudius informing him of conditions in each province, as well as a more detailed personal travel journal that he would keep with him.

"Are you all right, *Dominus*?" came a voice at his elbow.

He turned and saw young Cadius, hanging onto the rigging to keep from being pitched overboard, but still registering concern for his master.

"Just seasick," he said.

"You haven't kept any food down in two days," the boy said. "That can't be good."

"It's not, but I'm tougher than I look," Marcus said.

"Begging your pardon, sir, but shouldn't you go below? These decks ain't safe in such a blow, and that's no lie!" Rufus added. He had followed the boy onto the deck and was standing there, solidly planted as an oak, not holding onto anything. Marcus found that to be a bit much—he felt as if the wind would pick him up and blow him away at any moment—but Rufus looked completely unconcerned for his own safety.

"I can't stand the stench down there another minute," Marcus said. "This air is wet and cool, but at least it doesn't reek of dung and puke."

The *Venus Vitrix* was carrying about two hundred sheep and twelve horses as well as a hold full of wine jars, wheat baskets, and about twenty other passengers, most of whom were at least as sick as Marcus. He had boarded her in Ostia three weeks before, hoping for a smooth late summer voyage to Rome's westernmost provinces. The first few days had lived up to that hope, but after their brief stop in Sicily, the seas had grown steadily rougher, and for the last week they had simply run ahead of the rare east wind, hoping it would deposit them somewhere near their goal.

Phidias had been bitterly disappointed that he could not accompany his master on the voyage, but at his age and with his injury, a pitching deck was the last place he needed to be. He had spent several days rigorously training young Cadius on how to care for Marcus on the road, warning him that their master's welfare was strictly up to him.

"And I don't care how old I am or how bad my legs are, if I hear that you have tried to run away from him, I will hunt you down and kick your little *podex* clear back to Rome!" the old man warned him as the group set forth.

"Don't worry, Phidias," Cadius said. "Why would I run away when our *dominus* is such a good man? I have no intention of taking my chances with Fortuna twice in a row!"

Marcus had listened to the exchange with interest—as Cadius well knew. He still wasn't sure if the boy had come to regard him as a surrogate father, or if he was just saying what Marcus and Phidias wanted to hear. That was the problem with slaves, thought Marcus—you never really knew what they were thinking.

Marcus' uncle had been happy to see his nephew honored by the emperor, and had given him several useful bits of advice on how to get to the truth of what was happening in the provinces.

"Listen to what the local proconsul tells you, and then ignore virtually all of it," Mencius had said. "Every provincial governor is convinced that they are the most enlightened, efficient, and honest administrator ever placed in charge of a province—at least, as far as you know! The people that will give you the real picture of how things are going are folks like stewards, local merchants, the native rulers, and even prostitutes. Talk to them all, take everything they say with a grain of salt, then add all the accounts together and see if a consistent narrative emerges. Between that and the emperor's scribe poring over their books, you should get a pretty good idea of how things are being run. Might I add—don't stay too long in one place! Arrive, investigate, and move on—before they have time to decide if you should be bribed or assassinated!"

Mencius was half joking, but Marcus was still glad he had Rufus along. Any assassin would have a hard time getting at him with the bulky bodyguard at his side! Rufus, on the other hand, regarded Marcus as a near demigod—the man who had lifted him out of poverty and made him respectable. When Marcus had mentioned a possible appointment to the College of Lictors, Rufus had been as giddy as a thirteen-year-old boy who had just been kissed by a girl for the first time.

"You are too good to me, sir!" he had said. "A real lictor? I'd never dreamed of being such! I'll not forget this honor, sir, and that's no lie!"

Marcus laughed. "Well, we have to make this journey and survive it first," he said.

"Don't you worry your head about that, sir!" Rufus said. "No harm will come to you as long as I am around!"

He seemed determined to keep that pledge too, Marcus thought as the heavy boat heaved through the waves. Rufus had stayed within a couple of yards of him constantly, ready to do battle with

Neptune himself if need be to keep his master safe. Marcus said a mental prayer of thanks to Fortuna, the goddess of luck, for sending the big Roman his way. Then, after wiping his mouth and dashing the salt spray out of his eyes, he headed back down below, hoping to catch a few winks of sleep if the constant stench and motion would permit it.

Late that afternoon the storm finally passed them by, fading to a black line on the western horizon by sunset. The east wind remained, however, steadily pushing them across *Mare Nostrum* toward the Pillars of Hercules. Marcus and the other passengers all came topside, enjoying the warm sunshine and the relatively calm progress. Now that the boat wasn't bucking like an unbroken maverick, he found his sea legs and discovered he had a prodigious appetite. The sailors celebrated the end of the storm by breaking out some salt fish and leeks from the forward hold and cooking them on the open deck. A few even threw lines overboard, hoping to haul in some fresh fish that could be grilled.

Just before sunset a sizable island hove into view off the starboard bow. The captain surveyed it through his Greek telescope, and then turned to Marcus and the others with a grin.

"That's Formentera!" he said. "We're only a couple of days out from Nueva Carthage now!"

Marcus breathed a sigh of relief. Despite the storm, they were not only on track but actually ahead of schedule. New Carthage was the main seaport of Tarraconensis, the largest of the Spanish provinces, and in the summers the governor resided there, usually decamping in October for the highlands around Toletum, where the largest iron mines were located. Tarraconensis was the first province on Marcus' itinerary, followed by Lusitania and the two North African provinces of Mauretania. Then he would cut northward into Gaul, visiting Aquitania, Lugdunensis, Belgica, and the newly established province of Britannia. That, he thought, would see him through to the end of the year. He finished his supper and asked Rufus to bring his bedding topside and spread it out on the ship's deck, away from the sailor's watch stations, so he could sleep under the stars that night.

Two days later the *Venus Vitrix* docked at Nueva Carthage, and Marcus traveled to the local bank to withdraw some gold from the sizable expense account Claudius had set up for his mission. The emperor had cautioned him against carrying too much coin with him, and had given him a letter of credit instantly redeemable for as much gold as he needed almost anywhere in the Empire.

"I know that travel for five people is expensive, and you will need to purchase horses and other conveyances along the way," he said. "Use this letter responsibly and I will make sure the credit is good for as long as it takes you to return home. Guard it carefully, however! Many men would love to get their hands on it!"

Next Marcus, Cassius Claudius, and their three companions traveled to the local stable to purchase five good horses to use in their travels. The governor's residence was several miles outside of town, and Marcus did not want to give the man warning of his approach. The emperor had received several disturbing reports about Titus Granicus, the proconsul of Tarraconensis, and Marcus wanted to drop in on the man without warning.

Once they were mounted, the five travelers spurred their horses toward the distant fortress. Ever since Claudius had shared the reports about Granicus with him, Marcus had been weighing how to approach this assignment. He knew that his first inspection would set the standard for the entire trip, and he intended to make a memorable first impression. Given what he had heard, he knew that he could not afford to show weakness in front of this particular proconsul.

As they neared the fortress, he spotted several crosses beside the road. Some of the bodies had obviously been up there for months, with little more than skeletons remaining, while others were bloated and reeking. Nearer the gates, three victims were still alive, heads lolling, gasping for breath. Marcus read some of the placards over the heads of the unfortunate victims: "Assaulting a Legionary," "Insulting the Governor," "Stealing from the Empire," and one that he had to read twice to actually digest: "Refusing the Governor's Desires." Clearly, something was seriously wrong in this province!

Two tall legionaries lounged at the fort's gate, looking slovenly and distinctly unmilitary. Marcus dismounted his horse and approached. One of the men spat at the ground and looked at him with disdain.

"And who might you be?" he said.

"Quaestor Marcus Quintus Publius, Senator of Rome, on a confidential mission to see the Proconsul Titus Granicus!" he snapped. "Now stand aside, Legionary!"

The man slowly slouched to attention. "A real quaestor, eh?" he grunted. "Well, the governor is busy now, but I will let him know you are here. He may get to you sometime tomorrow."

Marcus sighed. "I am afraid that is not how the game is going to be played," he said, giving Rufus a nod. The bulky bodyguard leaped forward, slamming the legionary against the wall and yanking the man's *gladius* from its scabbard before the shocked soldier could react. As he placed the point of the blade at the man's throat, the other legionary tried to draw his own weapon. Seconds later, he went slumping to the ground as Cassius' lictor smashed him over the head with his *fasces*.

Marcus spoke to the man who was still conscious. "Now then, soldier of Rome, my companions and I are going to present ourselves to the governor. I have full *imperium mais* from Claudius Caesar himself to speak to any proconsul at any time and demand to review any records of their administration, and to dismiss and arrest any governor who I deem incompetent. I intend to use that *imperium.* The emperor has also decreed that I and my companions are under his personal protection, and that any who seek to harm us will be arrested by Praetorian guards and crucified, so don't even think about picking up that blade and coming after us. Now Rufus—return the man's sword to him and let's go." Marcus watched the shock on the man's face with satisfaction as he and his men marched into the fortress.

The governor's personal quarters were in the largest and most secure keep of the sprawling facility, and as Marcus walked through the huge wooden doors, he could hear screams coming from the audience chamber. When he entered, the scene that unfolded before his eyes stunned him for a moment.

A beautiful, dark-haired woman was chained to a pillar, stripped nude and bleeding copiously from multiple whip wounds on her back. A legionary was drawing back the cat-o-nine-tails for another stroke, while seated on a high stone chair, a morbidly obese figure in a toga watched, sipping a glass of wine, with two seminude serving girls standing behind him. Several locals, judging by their garb, were standing with their backs to the far wall, horror, anger, and grief written on their features, while four legionaries stood on either side of them, weapons drawn.

"WHAT IS THE MEANING OF THIS?" Marcus roared at the top of his lungs.

The legionary froze, his arm in mid-swing. The flayed woman at the pillar turned her head to look at Marcus, and then slowly slumped, unconscious. The crowd of Spaniards looked at him with a dawning of something that might have been hope in their eyes. The huge figure rose from his stone chair, his toga stained with wine and food.

"Who the bloody hell are you?" he asked.

"I am Quaestor Marcus Quintus Publius, Senator of Rome and special legate of the emperor, Claudius Caesar," Marcus said. "I have been commissioned by the Senate and the emperor to tour the provinces and report back to Rome on the conduct of our provincial governors, and your name was near the top of our list. I can see why."

The proconsul glared at Marcus, his pig-like eyes narrowing. "Well, aren't you special?" he sneered. "You think because old Claudius gives you a scrap of paper you can come here and spoil my fun? You think you have the right to question my authority and challenge my system of justice?"

"I don't think any of those things," Marcus replied calmly. "I know them to be true. The emperor requested that his *imperium mais* be transferred to me during this inspection tour, and the Senate has approved it."

"The bloody emperor?" sneered Titus Granicus. "I remember that fat, stuttering fool from when I was a guest at Gaius Caligula's dinner parties. The real emperor used to make Claudius dress in women's clothes and dance for us! You think I am afraid of that old man?"

"You think I am impressed when you drop the name of Caligula?" Marcus replied. "Who is your senior legate?"

"None of your damned business!" snapped Granicus.

"Very well, if that is the way you wish to play this," Marcus said, turning to the legionaries. "Do any of you men recall that you work for the Senate and People of Rome, and not for this pig?"

A centurion stepped forward, relief written on his face. "It's about time you arrived," he said. "I wrote to the emperor months ago. I am Ambrosius Pullo. Legate Maximus Crassus has been confined to his quarters for insubordination—he questioned some of the judicial sentences that the proconsul has handed down recently. He wrote the emperor, too, although his letters were intercepted and burned."

Marcus nodded. "Tell your men to bring the legate here," he said. "Now, why is this woman being whipped?"

"She refused to crawl into Titus' bed when he commanded it," the centurion replied.

"That is a lie!" roared the proconsul. "She insulted the *dignitas* of the Senate and People of Rome! I was defending the honor of the Empire!"

"He lies, Quaestor!" said one of the locals. "Hylia is my daughter. We are Roman citizens, and the governor demanded that I deliver her to him as if she were a common prostitute! When I refused, he ordered his guards to shut down my business, and then arrested us for being behind on our taxes. He said he would release us and allow my shops to reopen if I would give Hylia to him, all the while trying to pull her into his lap and grope her! She spat in his face, and I don't blame her!"

"Will you listen to the whining of this provincial over the word of a proconsul of Rome?" Titus Granicus demanded.

"Ex-proconsul," Marcus said calmly. "By the *imperium* granted to me, I strip you of all your rank and titles. You are herewith arrested on charges of corruption and abuse of Roman citizens and subjects. I will collect all the evidence I need to convict you in the next three days, and then you will be sent back to Rome in chains, and tried before the Corruption Courts. While the normal sentence in such cases is exile for life, I am going to personally recommend that the sentence in your case be elevated to death by flogging and decapitation—to serve as a warning and example to the governors in other provinces. Now Rufus and Cassius, would you take Titus Granicus into custody?"

"Legionaries! Kill the first man who touches me!" screamed Granicus, genuinely terrified now. The servant girls who had attended him were slowly backing toward the walls of the room, leaving him alone.

"You no longer give orders here, Titus Granicus," a new voice interjected.

Marcus turned to see a tall, spare man, dressed in the soiled garb of an officer, stepping into the room behind two legionaries. He had a bloody bandage across his forehead, and one of his eyes was bruised black and swollen nearly shut.

"Jupiter!" Marcus exclaimed. "Lucius Maximus Crassus—is that you?"

"Marcus Publius?" the pale man replied. "What are you doing here?"

"Promoting you to Prefect, and Acting Governor of Tarraconenis," Marcus replied. "Since you promoted me to military tribune ten years ago, I figured it was time to return the favor."

The legate broke out in a huge smile. "You are the emperor's emissary?" he said. "That is rich! I remember you as the young junior legate who paled at the sight of blood! By all the gods of Rome, it is good to see you again, Marcus!"

The old friends embraced, and Maximus turned to the legionaries. "Chain the former governor and throw him in the lowest dungeon!" he snapped.

"But sir, that dungeon is full of men he imprisoned!" one of the legionaries said.

"You think I don't know that?" Maximus asked. "Tell the other prisoners that they cannot kill him, or mortally injure him. He will stand trial in Rome, I am sure. But do remind them that all those who are able may journey to Rome to testify against him. Otherwise—well, tell them not to leave too many marks."

By now Titus Granicus was gibbering with fear, pleading and begging for a sword to fall on. The legionaries looked at one another, then at Maximus, and grabbed Titus by the arms and hauled him out of the audience room.

"Rufus, follow them and make sure that the former proconsul does not persuade them to do anything that would keep him from standing trial in Rome," said Marcus. "Now, for you citizens of Nuevo Carthage, I would ask that you carefully gather any evidence you can that would aid in the prosecution of Titus Granicus and present it here tomorrow. Cut Hylia free and get her to that couch for now! Cadius, you go and see if you can find a *medicus* who will tend this poor woman's hurts. Cassius Claudius, summon the stewards and accountants and survey all of Granicus' financial dealings."

He watched as the people he had spoken to scurried to do his bidding, wondering at the power a simple letter from the emperor had invested him with. He could almost feel it flowing through him, as if he were a living conduit of the majesty of the Roman Empire. He turned to Maximus.

"I hereby decree, by the *imperium* granted to me by the Senate and People of Rome, that you are promoted to prefect and granted governance of this province until an appropriate replacement is found," he said, "or until you are confirmed in the office by the Senate. Now, can you find an old friend an appropriate place to sleep tonight, and perhaps offer us some food?"

That night, as Cadius handed him a comfortable old tunic to sleep in, Marcus reflected on all he had heard since dinner. The depths of squalor and corruption that Titus Granicus had sunk to were truly amazing. Lulled into believing that Rome no longer cared about events in the provinces, he had turned all of Tarraconensis into his own private domain, reveling in luxuries that would put an Eastern potentate to shame. He demanded the favors of every pretty woman that caught his eye, but once he grew bored with them, he turned them over to his legionaries before setting them free. Several decent, virginal daughters of local families had committed suicide rather than submit to his attentions—or after suffering from them. While details were sketchy, apparently, some of the governor's tastes had been absolutely disgusting.

But sexual abuse of free women, both citizens and subjects, was only the beginning. While Cassius Claudius' work was far from complete, he had whispered to Marcus after supper that it appeared that Titus was embezzling on a grand scale, perhaps as many as twenty million gold sesterces. Marcus had no doubt that the Senate would be merciless to the former proconsul—abusing young women was bad enough, especially if they were citizens, but stealing from the Senate and People of Rome was accorded much less tolerance! Word had spread quickly since the afternoon, and Marcus heard that there would be over a hundred local citizens lined up at the door, waiting to give evidence, the next morning.

He seated himself at a small writing table and asked Cadius to bring him a quill and scroll, so he could begin his report to Claudius. The young slave returned moments later, handing the implements to Marcus.

"So what did you think of today's events, young Cadius?" he asked.

The boy began talking rapidly, excitement in his voice. "I've never seen anything like that before!" he said. "That proconsul was a very bad man, and you totally destroyed him in a matter of minutes! He kept turning redder and redder, and I thought he was going to fall over when the legate walked in and told the soldiers not to defend him! I just wish—" He paused for a moment, and the enthusiasm faded from his voice.

"What is it, lad?" asked Marcus.

"This is wicked, I know, but I wish someone had done the same thing to Caligula—before my father and mother—" His voice trailed off.

"I lost my family to Gaius Caligula, too," Marcus said. "I have often wished the same thing."

"I've always heard of heroes," Cadius said. "My *tata* told me the stories of Romulus and Remus, of Hector and Achilles, when I was little. But today I saw a hero with my own eyes. I am very glad you are my *dominus*, Marcus Publius."

Marcus bowed his head over the parchment for a moment, so the boy would not see the tears starting to form in his eyes. If only he were truly the man that the young slave imagined him to be! The fact was that he had been terrified for most of that confrontation, exhilaration only kicking in when he realized that his authority was going to be respected and his *imperium* obeyed. At any moment, he had expected the proconsul to order the legionaries to attack, and them to obey.

"That will be all for now, Cadius," he said. "Why don't you go down to the kitchens and get something to eat?"

"I am already full, *Dominus*," the boy said.

"Then go on to your chambers and go to bed," Marcus said. "I want to be able to concentrate on this letter."

"Yes, *Dominus*, I will!" the lad replied. "I can't wait to hear all the witnesses tomorrow!" he added before scampering off.

Marcus wrote for about a half hour, describing the situation as he found it, when there came a gentle knock on the door.

"Enter!" he said. Rufus poked his head through the opening.

"Begging your pardon, sir, but there is a young lady asking to see you. She said her father is a prominent merchant in town," the bodyguard said.

"Tell her I will hear testimony about Titus Granicus tomorrow," Marcus said. He was weary and ready for bed.

"Well sir, she says—" Rufus began, before a feminine voice interrupted him.

"I have nothing to say about the pig Granicus," it said, and the owner of the voice pushed past Rufus into the room. She was a tall, dark-haired Spanish beauty, clad in a long, forest-green gown. Marcus surveyed her with interest.

"Well," he said as she looked him over, "what do you have to say?"

"I wanted to thank you," she replied. "My name is Ardelia, and the woman you rescued from the whip was my younger sister."

Marcus stood and took her hand. "I am only sorry that I didn't arrive sooner," he said. "How is she faring?"

Close up, he saw the woman's cheeks were streaked with recent tears. "She will bear the scars for the rest of her life," she said. "But at least she had not yet been turned over to the legionaries for their entertainment, or suffered from that pig's disgusting embraces. Many of our girls have died after a single night in the Guards' barracks."

Marcus shook his head. "Soldiers are simple creatures by nature," he said. "They ape the behavior of their commanders. Soldiers who are taught to conduct themselves with strength and honor will usually act like honorable men. Soldiers who are commanded by lecherous boors become lecherous boors. I cannot punish an entire legion, but I can hope that, with a change of command, there will be a change in behavior. The Senate and People of Rome deserve better representatives than these men."

"A week ago, I would have told you that I hated the very name of Rome," she said. "But you at least have shown me that all Romans are not pigs. Granicus left my family with little to our names, but I would like to show my gratitude."

"Your thanks are all I need—indeed, more than I need," Marcus said.

"I had something more personal in mind," she said, reaching for the ties of her gown.

"No!" Marcus exclaimed, putting his hand over hers.

"Why not?" she asked. "I freely offer you that which Granicus would have stolen from me."

"Because if I take it," Marcus said, "I am no better than him."

She looked at him in amazement. "You truly are an honorable man!" she said. "Are there many like you in Rome?"

"There are," he said. "Sadly, there are also some like Granicus. Romans are like all other men—some are good, some are wicked, and most fall somewhere in between."

"That may be true," she said. "But there is one great difference between Romans and other men."

"What would that be?" he asked.

"Romans rule the world," she said, then turned and left the room, leaving a faint aroma of Spanish roses in her wake. He thought long and hard about what she had said before he returned to his letter.

CHAPTER VII

Letter from Marcus to Claudius Caesar, The Kalends of February, 49 AD

Quaestor Marcus Quintus Publius, Senator of Rome, to Tiberius Claudius Caesar Augustus Germanicus, Princeps and Imperator of Rome, Greetings!

While the enclosed reports will give you a detailed account of my findings in Lusitania, Aquetania, and the two provinces of Mauretania, I thought that a quick summary of my impressions might relieve some of your concerns and save you some time. After seeing the disastrous results of Titus Granicus' mismanagement of Tarraconensis, I was apprehensive that such abusive practices might have become rampant throughout the provinces. It is with some relief that I can report to you that this is not so.

Porcius Masigius, the Proconsul of Lusitania, received us with hospitality and presented to us a province well run and accounts that were balanced and carefully managed. At first I thought that he was forewarned of our arrival and was simply presenting us with a manufactured show of confidence. But Cassius dug deeply into the province's financial records, and I spoke with numerous locals both high and low, and found nothing but praise for the man's probity and sensitivity to local issues, both political and religious. Masigius appears to be a Roman of the old school, a strong Stoic with a powerful sense of duty. He has garnered some personal wealth during his tenure as governor, primarily by raiding pirate strongholds and crushing a powerful bandit ring that had amassed considerable treasure. However, he lives simply and modestly, his soldiers respect him, and his servants are competent and not given to venality. We were treated with every respect and consideration, and he expressed great relief that Tarraconensis would be better governed in the future. If I may be so bold, I think that Porcius Masigius is a trustworthy and highly competent administrator that Your Excellency may wish to mark for future advancement.

After a week in Lusitania, we made the voyage south to visit Mauretania Tingitana and Mauretania Caesariensis, the two newest provinces in

Africa. Both are fairly poor provinces. Gaius Bibulus, Prefect of Tingitana, is a mediocre administrator, somewhat given to strong drink and the company of prostitutes, but does a decent enough job of running the place. Some of the locals express concern that he does not to do enough to stop the depredations of the pirates who infest the coast, but Roman governors have been trying to end piracy on the African coast since the days of Scipio, and it still endures. It would not surprise me if African pirates are still plying their trade long after Rome has passed into antiquity!

At any rate, Bibulus' books were fairly well balanced, and corruption in the province seemed to be within normal levels—enough to make some locals unhappy, but not enough to inspire widespread rebellion or grumbling. Bibulus has a freedman named Octavius who does a great deal of the day-to-day work of governing for him. A sharp fellow, this Octavius, seeking to advance himself at every opportunity, but generally staying within the law to do so. I would predict that if Your Excellency orders anything to be done in the province, Octavius will be the one who does it, even if the governor takes the credit.

We stayed about six days in Tingitana and then made our way eastward to Mauretania Caesariensis. The governor here was a sharp young fellow by the name of Lucius Numidicus, only recently elevated to prefect. He mentioned that he once served Your Excellency as a personal secretary, when you were co-consul with Gaius Caligula. Numidicus struck me as highly intelligent, very ambitious, and eager to advance his arctoritas at every opportunity. While the accounts of the province were in excellent order, I found that there was a good deal of resentment towards the Prefect's rule. His eagerness to please his superiors has turned him into a martinet, intolerant of the least failings in his soldiers, and very demanding of the people he governs. He is so intolerant of corruption that practices which are almost universally winked at throughout the Empire draw heavy punishments here, and several tribal leaders grumbled that they were better off before the Romans came.

He is also very stingy in sharing the benefits of Roman citizenship and Latin rights, which are universally competed for and recognized as one of the chief benefits of Rome's rule. I believe most of his mistakes are due to his youth and his lack of a senior legate to help him govern. If it were up to me,

I would send an experienced soldier and administrator with some seniority here to serve as his assistant and perhaps to educate him a bit better on the way the world actually works! Rigid idealists can be so tiresome at times.

We spent about ten days here, and then chartered a ship to make the short hop north to Narborensis, whence we shall travel by horseback to Lusitania. There is a merchant ship here at the harbor that is bound for Ostia; I have entrusted my reports to the captain, who has promised to send them to you by the fastest courier he can find as soon as he docks. I hope that this letter finds you safe and well, Claudius! You may forward your reply to Britannia, for that is where I will most likely be by the time it could reach me. Give my regards to my uncle, when you see him. Hail Caesar!

Letter from Claudius Caesar to Marcus, the Ides of April, 49 AD:

Tiberius Claudius Caesar Augustus Germanicus, Princeps and Imperator of Rome, to Quaestor Marcus Quintus Publius, Senator and special envoy to the provinces,

Greetings, my young friend! Your reports confirm the wisdom of my choice in sending you to the provinces to report on their administration. Between you and Cassius Claudius, my freedman, I am finally getting an accurate account of how things are run away from Rome. It does no good for me, as emperor, to tour the provinces, as the governors are always warned of my coming and put together a mime's farce, which they try to pass off as the status quo. If I were like the Divus Julius, able to ride fifty miles in a day and speak two dozen languages, perhaps I could sweep in unannounced and get a better idea of how things are really done. But despite our common name, I am not much like my illustrious ancestor. Indeed, I think that no one, not even Augustus of divine memory, was quite like Gaius Julius Caesar!

But I digress. My purpose in writing is to give you news of Rome, and some further instructions for your journey. First of all, it grieves me to inform you that your aunt Claudia has crossed the river Styx. I know you were aware of her long illness; it finally took her a fortnight ago. Your uncle is mourning her deeply, but privately. I knew Claudia for many years; some called her a shrew, but I always admired the intelligence and fiery spirit she carried so unashamedly. That she should fall in love with your uncle, and he with her, is a remarkable statement of his character. I do not know that he will ever wed again; it is so rare for a man and woman to love each other to the end that I doubt he will find another love like hers.

While we are on the topic of marriage, you will be surprised to learn that I have chosen to wed again. I know, I know—I told the Praetorians to kill me if I ever did anything so foolish! But the Senate would not quit worrying me about it, pointing out that my son Britannicus is still of tender age, and that an emperor needed "an heir and a spare" to ensure the succession. My choice is the lovely Julia Agrippina Minor. While she has a woeful reputation, my own experience of her is that she is a lonely and misunderstood woman, whose sole focus in life is the protection and advancement of her son, Nero Claudius. He is a bright lad of eleven, highly intelligent and very promising. It is time that Britannicus had a brother close to his own age, and I am hoping they will be great friends. As for Agrippina, once she understood that my purpose was to protect her and hers, she was more than enthusiastic about my offer of marriage. Suffice it to say that I am personally happier than I have been in years.

Now, as to your ongoing mission—by the time you receive this, you will probably be in Britannia. While the province is newly conquered and may still be somewhat unsettled, I have great confidence in Vespasian, the general I left in charge there. He is young—at least compared to me, he is young!—but I look for him to accomplish great things in the future. For the moment, however, his military skills are needed in Egypt. Please inform him to set affairs in order for his successor, who should arrive with or shortly after this letter.

After you leave Britannia, pay especial attention to the German provinces, and to Raetia. The Alpine provinces you may pass over; they are close enough to Italy that I have agents who report to me regularly on the state of affairs there, and in Noricum as well. However, I have received disturbing reports of the conduct of Rufus Aelius in Dalmatia, and no reports at all in the last six months from the two regions of Pannonia to the north. While they are not yet full provinces, several veterans' colonies have been set up there in recent years—and a legion posted to protect them. All have fallen silent. Hasten thence, and let me know what state of affairs you find. Your imperium mais over the provinces I hereby confirm once more; do what you need to do to set things right in Germania and the Balkans, and thence to the East!

Best regards, and stay safe on the roads. Your services are too valuable to the Empire, and to me, to be dispensed with. May the gods of Rome protect you on your journey, and hasten your return!

It was nearly midsummer in Britannia when the message caught up with its recipient. After reading it, Marcus set the letter down and let out a low whistle. The emperor, married to Agrippina? He still could not understand how a person who seemed as wise and experienced as Claudius could be such a poor judge of character when it came to women. Even as he was reflecting on it, his tent flap parted and Cassius Claudius entered, as upset as Marcus had ever seen him.

"Did he tell you?" the angry freedman said without even uttering a greeting, his shadow wavering in the candlelight.

"About his marriage?" Marcus asked. "Yes, he did. I am still trying to figure out what he could have been thinking."

Cassius let out a long sigh and flopped down on Marcus' couch. "He doesn't think—that's his problem!" he said. "Don't get me wrong, Claudius Caesar is a decent and wise man. He is temperate, honest to a fault, and generous to those who earn his trust. I was given to him as a present for his twentieth birthday and have been in his service ever since, first as a slave and then as his freedman and client. But when it comes to women—well, gods, the man has no common sense!"

Marcus nodded. He had gotten to know Cassius better and better during their months on the road, and found the freedman to be good company, highly intelligent and devoted to his former master.

"Well, it's not like we can do anything about it up here on the dreary roof of the Empire," he said. Britannia had not impressed him much—the natives were strange barbarians and the Roman presence obviously new and painfully unwelcome.

Cassius nodded. "He wouldn't listen in any case," he said. "I advised him against his marriage to that wicked little minx Messalina, for all the good it did! We had been telling him for years that she was cuckolding him behind his back, and he didn't listen until three senators and two Praetorians confirmed our warnings."

"How can such a wise man be so naïve?" Marcus wondered aloud.

"Claudius Caesar is a kind-hearted soul," Cassius replied, "but he has never been loved or appreciated by his family. Augustus was ashamed of him, Tiberius ignored him, and Caligula ridiculed him. Old Livia, the widow of Augustus, absolutely despised him and I never could figure out why! Perhaps she saw his physical defects as an insult to the family's *dignitas*. At any rate, Claudius has been starved for love his whole life, and seeks to find it through marriage, no matter how many times he fails."

"Something I've wondered about," Marcus said. "Claudius carries himself with such great dignity and speaks very well, yet all the old stories referred to him as a slobbering, clubfooted idiot."

"He has worked very hard to overcome his handicaps," Cassius said. "He wears specially made sandals that disguise his limp by making his legs more equal in length, and he practiced his speech with the aid of a Greek tutor named Pyronius for many years. Pyronius was the one who showed him that he did not stutter when he sang. That was the breakthrough for Claudius—for months he stumped around the house singing his orations. Over time, he gradually made them sound less and less like songs, although you will still hear echoes of musical rhythm in his addresses if you listen closely enough when he is speaking to the Senate. He told me that he still hears the music in his head when he speaks, and that is what keeps him from tripping over his words."

"Fascinating!" said Marcus. "Now tell me, what do you know of Agrippina Minor?"

"Well, she is the sister of Gaius Caligula and the daughter of Germanicus," said Cassius. "She is descended from both Augustus and Marcus Antonius, and does not seem to display the insanity that her brother was so well known for. She is quite lovely and knows how to display her attributes to her advantage without seeming wanton or lewd. But—and mark my words well on this—everything I have observed tells me that she is highly intelligent, utterly ruthless, and endlessly ambitious. I'm sure she set her sights on dear old Uncle Claudius the minute the Praetorians cut down Messalina. Poor Claudius! Messalina was wicked but stupid—I knew it was only a matter of time before she would encompass her own downfall. Agrippina—she will not make Messalina's mistakes, and Claudius will never suspect what she really intends."

"What do you think she intends?" Marcus asked, startled at the man's vehemence.

"Why, to make her son emperor, most likely!" said Cassius.

"Everyone knows that Britannicus is his father's favorite," said Marcus. "I doubt young Nero will take his place."

"Never underestimate the powers of a ruthless woman," Cassius said. "After all, Britannicus is the son of a woman executed for adultery and treason. No one has ever called his paternity into question—he does resemble Claudius pretty strongly after all—but I have no doubt that Agrippina is already trying to poison Claudius' mind against him."

"This is just too depressing!" Marcus said. "But Rome is over a thousand miles away, and we have a mission to fulfill. I need to go see Vespasian and carry a message to him. Good night, my friend!"

He stepped out into the starlit night and looked at the sky. The miserable British weather, which seemed to mainly rotate between actually raining and looking like it was about to rain, had finally given way to a sunny afternoon, and a clear night thereafter. Isca Dumnoniorum, the main Roman city in Britannia, was still partly made of tents, although new wooden houses were going up every day. Marcus and Cassius had chosen to stay in a well-appointed centurion's tent, but the commanding general and acting governor, Titus Flavius Vespasian, dwelt in a sturdy log house in the center of the growing settlement. Two legionaries stood guard outside the tent.

"Good evening, Senator," said one of them.

"Good evening, men!" Marcus replied. "Is the general still up?"

"That one?" one of the guards replied. "He rarely sleeps more than three hours a night! He is listening to scout reports at the moment."

"I'll step in and await his pleasure," Marcus said.

The plank floor was still somewhat rough, but the walls were hung with oil lamps and tapestries, and there was a comfortable couch for visitors to recline on. The door to the legate's receiving room was open, and two very young centurions stood before the general, deep in conversation about Pictish incursions into Roman territory. The balding general listened carefully and issued curt orders to his men, then dismissed them. As they walked out, he saw Marcus reclining on the couch.

"Good evening, Quaestor!" he said. "To what do I owe this honor?"

Marcus liked Vespasian better than any of the governors he had encountered thus far. The man was polite but not fawning, respectful but not obsequious, and overwhelmingly competent. He was slightly below average height, but massively muscled and nimble on his feet. Despite his premature baldness, he spoke and moved with the energy of a man ten years younger than his forty years.

"News from Rome," Marcus replied. "The emperor enclosed this letter for you along with his message to me. It appears as if you are headed for warmer climes, General!"

"Thanks be to the gods!" Vespasian exclaimed. "Three years in this gods-forsaken wasteland and I don't think I have ever seen the sun shine for more than a few days in a row. I am from Spain, and this climate seems like Hades by comparison!"

"Well, perhaps Egypt will be more to your liking," Marcus said. "Caesar said that was where he was sending you. He has great confidence in your abilities, General."

"Egypt, eh?" Vespasian said, scratching his scalp through his thin fringe of hair. "From one extreme to the other, it seems! Well, perhaps my orders will give me time to stop in Spain and see my boys again. I have missed them both, and my wife as well, in this land of fog and rain. I assume my replacement is en route?"

"That is what Claudius said, although I am sure his letter to you is more detailed," Marcus replied.

"I see," said the legate, breaking the seal and opening the short scroll. He scanned its lines quickly, nodding once or twice, and then looked up at Marcus.

"It appears that he is replacing a soldier with a politician," he said. "Do you know Fabius Ahenobarbus?"

Marcus grinned. "He and I have sparred in the courts as advocates on several occasions," he said. "But he has also done his time in the legions, and was a competent military tribune under General Tullius when I was quartermaster. He will do well here, in peace or in war."

Vespasian nodded. "Good," he said. "We have pacified the native resistance for the moment, but we are not loved here. But when have any people ever loved their conquerors?"

"In time, as they see the benefits of Roman rule, that will change," Marcus said. "Look at Gaul today, and think where it was a century ago."

"Point well taken," said Vespasian, "but it will take good governance to win loyalty. In the meantime, as my old commander Aulus Platius said, 'Let them hate us, as long as they fear.'"

Marcus nodded. "Wasn't he the one who also said that he would 'make a desert, and call it peace' if the Britons did not cease resisting him?" he asked.

"He didn't say it, but it was said about him," replied Vespasian. "However, I don't know that he would disagree with that assessment!"

"Well, Titus Flavius Vespasian," Marcus said, "my assessment of you corresponds with the emperor's. You are one of the most efficient governors I have encountered in my travels, and a fine soldier as well. If the Empire produced more men like you, the provinces would be less troubled!"

The military governor laughed, a short bark of amusement. "I'm just a simple soldier, doing his duty to the Senate and People of Rome," he said. "It's the politicians that give the Empire a bad name! Men like Titus Granicus should not be put in charge of public toilets, much less major provinces! May the gods spare me from a political career!"

"I do not know that your prayer will be granted," Marcus said. "Caesar has his eye on you!"

Vespasian shrugged. "Caesar's wish is my command," he said. "But for now, he seems to prefer me to be a soldier—and that is what I wish for as well! So, are you moving on also?" he asked Marcus.

"I have many provinces to tour before I can return to Rome," Marcus said. "But at least I am heading south now. I, too, have missed seeing the sun in the sky."

"Well, safe journeys, Quaestor," said Vespasian. "I shall begin preparing for the arrival of your friend Fabius."

Marcus returned to his tent, and did not see Vespasian again for many years.

The next morning, Marcus, Cassius, and their companions set out for the coast. A ship from Gaul had just anchored, and the captain was eager to get back across the stormy channel that separated Britannia from the mainland. Marcus saw Fabius Ahenobarbus disembarking, and had a chance to exchange a few words with his old friend before Fabius headed toward Dumnoniorum. Then he and Cassius and the others boarded the ship and headed toward Gaul.

The crossing was uneventful enough, and their horses were still waiting at the stable where they had left them when they crossed over to Britannia. The five men mounted up and headed westward, towards the two German provinces that marked the northwest boundary of the Roman Empire. Although the nights were cool, the midsummer days were warm, and they seemed to have left the rain in Britannia. It took them three hard days of riding through the pastoral countryside of Belgica to reach the borders of Germania Inferior, the smaller of the two German provinces recently organized by the Senate. The Colonia Agrippina, named for the wife of Germanicus, was the major Roman settlement there, and it took another day of riding for Marcus and Cassius to reach it.

The official governor's residence was still under construction, so Varus Marius, the prefect in charge of the small province, was living inside the fortress constructed for the legions a generation earlier. He was a thin, scrawny person with a perpetually nervous air; he kept tugging at the sleeves of his tunic as he spoke to Marcus.

"It is always good to have guests from Rome," he said, "but I did not know you would be here so soon. My senior legate, Maxentius, is still in the field with his men—we've had some raids from across the Rhine lately, and he was hoping to track the rebels back to their village and repay them for their depredations. I don't really have adequate quarters for guests of such importance—"

"It is quite all right," Marcus told him. "We slept in tents in Britannia; we can sleep in the inn here—it looks fairly well kept."

"It is," the governor said. "Maxentius' men favor the place, so he makes sure that it serves good wine and food, and has an adequate number of girls employed."

Marcus wrinkled his brow. A senior legate running a tavern? Something about that, and about his host's attitude, did not ring true. Nor did Cadius' report that, as soon as they left the prefect's company, a swift rider left town and headed east. Cassius and his lictor, Arminius, went to visit the *publicani* who collected the taxes for the province, while Marcus ate a quick meal at the tavern and then returned to the prefect's quarters for another attempt to find out what was going on.

He left that evening more puzzled than when he arrived. Marius was polite to a fault, and answered every question that Marcus asked—yet everything he said seemed scripted and rehearsed, and when Marcus pressed him for details, he found a way to change the subject. Periodically he would glance out his window, as if looking for someone to arrive. It took Marcus a while to pin down exactly what was wrong with the man, but eventually he realized that Varus Marius was afraid—more than afraid, the man was downright terrified. But of what? That was the question Marcus could not answer.

He returned to his room that evening and retired early. He was seated at the small table in his room, composing a letter to his uncle, when Cadius entered and said that one of the girls from the inn wanted to see him. He nodded and asked Cadius to show the girl in.

She was a buxom blonde German, somewhere between sixteen and twenty, wearing a white shift that was somewhat translucent in the lamplight.

"My name is Cardixa," she said, "and I was asked to make sure that your stay here was comfortable and enjoyable." There was a gleam in her eye that left little doubt as to what she meant.

"And who asked you to do that?" Marcus inquired.

"Well, old Dragox, the innkeeper," she said. "He gives all us girls our assignments."

"And who gives him his assignments?" Marcus asked.

"Well, um—that's not really for me to say," the wench replied, obviously uncomfortable with the question.

Marcus pulled a couple of gold sesterces from his purse. "Now, girl, listen to me," he said. "I know there is something odd going on around here. I am willing to bet that you, being in the hospitality business, probably know more about the way things are done around here than the average legionary. So here is my offer: I will pay you triple what you get for your usual—services, shall we say?—

if you can tell me who is really running this outpost and why the prefect seems like such a frightened rabbit. And you won't have to earn your gold on your back for a change."

Her eyes gleamed with greed at the sight of the coins, but she still looked wary. "If anyone finds out that I told you–" she started to say.

"Don't worry, lass, no one will know," he said. "If anyone asks, just tell them I was as insatiable as a satyr and kept you busy for hours."

She gave him a smile. "That sounds more fun than just talking," she said.

He sighed. "Just give me some information," he said. "I'm tired of being in the dark."

"All right, then," she said. "Here is the gist of it: the prefect is a pansy, the senior legate knows he is a pansy and threatens to report him to Rome as a deviant, and thus the legate runs the fort, the legion, and the town while the prefect minces about his quarters jumping at shadows."

Marcus nodded. It all made sense now—the prefect's strange attitude and his obvious desire to say nothing of substance until his subordinate was there to tell him what to say.

"If that is the case, it sounds as if Maxentius should be governing, instead of Marius," he said.

"Gods forbid!" the girl exclaimed in obvious fright. "The man is a brute!"

"Really?" Marcus asked. "How so?"

"He is corrupt, sadistic, greedy, and incompetent!" Cardixa said. "The soldiers only obey him because he caters to their every whim, the locals hate him, and the prefect is terrified of him."

"Who else here could run the place?" Marcus mused aloud.

"The senior centurion is a good soldier and an honest man," she said. "He has stood up to Maxentius repeatedly, but Maxentius has a couple of hired thugs who have managed to beat him into silence—for the moment. Most of the soldiers would jump to his command if he would give them the word. But he respects Maxentius' rank and position, even if he has no respect for the man himself."

"And does this paragon of Roman virtue have a name?" Marcus asked her.

"His name is Sergius Paulus," she said. "If Rome produced more men like him, my people would not hate Rome as much as they do."

Marcus nodded. "I'll tell you what, girl," he said, handing her another sestercius, "I'll have another of these for you if you will go and get Centurion Paulus and bring him here without anyone seeing."

Her eyes lit up. "I will be glad to, sir," she said, "as long as you promise me no harm will come to him."

"Does he mean something to you?" Marcus asked.

She hung her head. "Before Maxentius forced me to work here as a whore, Sergius and I were lovers," she said. "He even said he wanted to marry me once. I don't know if he still has feelings for me—he avoids this place like the plague—but I know he will come if I ask him to."

"Then go and bring him," Marcus said. "Cadius can show you out. And tell him to bring Cassius Claudius in to see me."

Cassius entered moments later, his eyes wide. "It seems we've stumbled on quite the nest of corruption here," he said. "Not on the part of the governor this time! Apparently, his senior legate runs the province. He has some hold over the prefect, the publican I talked to doesn't know what it is—but he uses it to get his way in everything, and he is running the province as his own personal empire."

"The governor is—shall we say, enamored of the Greek way of love," Marcus said. "Maxentius knows about it and holds it over his head like a club."

"I've never understood why the Romans are so prudish about love between men," Cassius said. "I am Greek by birth, and it's a part of human experience—some do it for a while, before they marry, some never try it, and others never learn to love women. We don't look down on anyone for who they sleep with."

Marcus nodded. What he wanted to say was that was probably the reason why Athens was an impoverished shadow of its former greatness while Rome ruled the world, but he had no desire to offend the Greek freedman. Instead he said: "It doesn't carry the stigma in Rome that it once did, but it's still frowned upon in the senatorial classes. I can see how Maxentius exploits it."

"So what shall we do?" Cassius asked him.

"Maxentius has to go," Marcus said, "but we will need someone to replace him. We are about to meet the most likely candidate."

"Who told you about this alternative legate?" Cassius asked in surprise.

"No one knows men better than a whore," Marcus replied. "The girl said that Sergius Paulus is an excellent soldier and an honest man. But I want to talk us to him in person and see what we make of him."

"From centurion to legate—that would be quite a jump!" Cassius said.

Marcus nodded. "Caesar told me he wanted men of ability to govern his provinces, regardless of their origins," he said. "I intend to obey that order."

There was a knock at the door moments later, and Cadius came in, followed by a middle-aged man with iron-gray hair and a muscular build.

"I am Sergius Paulus," he said. "You sent for me, sir?"

"Yes, I did," Marcus replied. "I am Quaestor Marcus Quintus Publius, Senator of Rome and special agent for Emperor Claudius Caesar. I have been sent on a mission by Caesar to make sure that his provinces are properly run. It seems to me that there is a great deal amiss here in Germania, and I would like to set things right. You have a reputation as a good soldier of Rome and an honest man. Tell me, if you will, where you think the problem lies."

"Speaking your mind is not a healthy habit in this province," the soldier said. "Last time I opened my mouth it cost me a broken nose and arm."

"Maxentius has no hold over me," Marcus said. "I have *imperium mais* to raise up and cast down whoever I see fit. I've replaced one proconsul already. A senior legate means nothing to me. Now tell me, in your opinion, what is wrong with this province and how it can be fixed."

Sergius Paulus looked at the senator with a new respect. "The place was not that bad before Maxentius arrived," he said. "The prefect is not a bad fellow, apart from his fondness for young men. Personally, I find that distasteful, but if a man is competent at his post, what he does in his bedchamber is not my concern. The old legate, Rufus Florentius, was of the same mind. He and the prefect got along, and the province was very well run. But then Rufus returned to Rome to run for Praetor, and Maxentius was sent out to replace him. Within a fortnight, he had found out the governor's little secret, arrested his lover, and was threatening to expose him to the entire Senate of Rome. To his credit, Marius tried to stand up to him at first, but he is not a physically strong man, and Maxentius is a great big brute—and he had the governor's favorite pretty boy in his dungeons! In no time, the governor simply abdicated his *imperium* and Maxentius set himself up as acting prefect. He does what he pleases, terrorizes and extorts the locals, and squeezes the province for every sestercius he can get—and I'll guarantee you damned little of it makes its way to the treasury in Rome!"

"The *publicani* told me the same thing," Cassius said. "He said that Maxentius actually had the senior tax collector flogged and beheaded for threatening to report his corruption to Rome, and the rest of them fear him like he was Pluto himself!"

"How do you think Maxentius would respond to being stripped of command?" Marcus asked.

"Violently," said Sergius. "Most of the legionaries despise him, but there are always those who thrive on corruption and cruelty, and he has them acting as his personal Praetorian guard—in fact, I was

Primipilus Centurion until he replaced me with one of those blackguards! But there are really only a half dozen or so of his bully boys that would be so foolhardy as to attack an emissary from Rome."

Marcus nodded. "I imagine we will be seeing Maxentius sometime tomorrow," he said. "As soon as he arrives, I am going to call a hearing with him and the prefect. I'll have my man by my side, and Cassius here has a very capable lictor. But I want you to gather a dozen men you can trust and be waiting outside the audience chamber. If things get ugly, I'll need you to step in quickly. Is that understood?"

Sergius Paulus nodded. "I'd love to see this place set to rights," he said. "It's not a bad little province—or at least it wasn't, until that *mentula* took control of it. But who will take his place as senior legate?"

Marcus looked at him. "Well, it would need to be someone who has the respect of the legion, who knows the locals, and is familiar with the province," he said.

"Where in Rome would you find such a person?" Sergius asked. "And how long would it take him to get here?"

"I was actually thinking you might be up for the job," Marcus said.

The big centurion paled. "Me?" he asked in shock. "I'm just a plain old pleb, sir—a loyal soldier of Rome, but not a politician at all."

"You already have a politician," Marcus said. "What the province needs is an administrator. That I think you could do quite well."

"Well, sir, I'll do my best," he said. "But it's beyond my station in life."

"Your station is where the emperor places you," Marcus said, "and I speak with the voice of Caesar."

Sergius snapped to attention and rendered a legionary's salute. "Then I shall obey orders to the best of my ability," he said.

"Very well," said Marcus. "I'll send my lad Cadius for you when the time comes."

Sure enough, as Marcus and Cassius sat down to breakfast the next morning, the doors of the tavern banged open and a tall, burly man stepped in wearing the scarlet cape of a senior legate of the Roman legions. Marcus noted how the two or three girls working in the tavern subtly edged away from him. Dragox, the innkeeper, nodded toward their table, and the big man strode over, all smiles.

"Gentlemen! I am sorry I was not here to greet you yesterday," he said. "I am Lucius Maxentius, Senior Legate in the service of Rome, and of Prefect Marius. I trust the accommodations were to your liking?"

"They were most excellent, *Legatus,*" said Marcus. "How did your expedition against the bandits go?"

"Slippery buggers," said Maxentius. "We caught three of them and nailed them up as a warning to the others, but we didn't find their hideout. We'll get them next time, though!"

"It sounds like the province is in good hands," Marcus said. "But my auditor here did notice some odd discrepancies on the tax rolls. Could we have a little meeting with you and the prefect in about an hour? Just a formality, of course."

The smile vanished and the craggy brows drew together. "I see no need to involve the prefect," he said. "Come on up to my quarters and I am sure we can hash things out together."

Marcus laughed. "Oh, come on now!" he said. "I know who really runs this province, but we do have to preserve appearances for the poor old pansy's sake!"

The smile returned. "Well, when you put it that way," he said, "I suppose you are right. I'll see you in an hour." Maxentius turned and stalked out of the inn, pausing to pinch one of the serving wenches on his way out.

"That," Marcus said after he was out the door, "is a very dangerous man. Much more so than Titus Granicus, if I am not mistaken. We need to tell Rufus and Arminius to be on their toes during this interview, because Maxentius is not going to like the way it ends. And if I were you, I'd tuck a dagger in the sleeve of my toga."

One hour later, Marcus and Cassius, with their two bodyguards in tow, appeared in the governor's audience chamber. Cadius had been dispatched to find Paulus and tell him to bring his men up and wait outside. Marcus entered the huge double doors and saw that the legionaries who had guarded the prefect the day before had been replaced by two burly, scowling guards. Two more stood behind the platform where Varus Marius sat in his curule chair, with Lucius Maxentius standing directly behind him.

"Well, *Quirites,* I hope you enjoyed your night's stay," Varus said.

"Your tavern's hospitality was first rate," Marcus said. "And we had a chance to acquaint ourselves first hand with conditions in your lovely province."

"I hope that everything meets with Rome's approval," the prefect said nervously.

"Actually, we have found evidence of fraud on a massive scale, mismanagement of the legions, and brutality to local civilians," Cassius said.

"As well as the illegal execution of a publican," Marcus added. "Not to mention the disgusting blackmail of a prefect by his senior legate!"

"You cockroach!" Maxentius roared at the prefect. "How dare you tell them?"

"I swear, Maxentius, I didn't say a word!" Marius wailed.

"Then how could they know such details?" the legate demanded.

"Honest men are always ready to expose evildoers," Marcus said. "In twenty-four hours, we have found no fewer than six individuals who bore witness to your corruption and cruelty. If your intelligence only matched your greed, you might have been a little more discreet and less brutal. As it is, we have more than enough evidence to satisfy us as to your utter ineptitude. You are unfit to supervise the sewers of Rome, much less the affairs of an entire province."

"Maggot!" yelled the legate. "I am a god in this province! I'll see you both dead before nightfall!"

Marcus stood his ground and spoke with a calmness he did not feel: "By the *imperium mais* invested in me by Claudius Caesar, and confirmed by the Senate and People of Rome, I hereby strip you of all offices and titles, and arrest you on charges of corruption and murder."

"Never!" Maxentius said emphatically, drawing his sword and advancing on Marcus. "Take him, boys!"

The four legionaries drew their blades and closed in on Marcus and his companions. Rufus drew his wicked curved sword, while Arminius wielded his *fasces* like a cudgel. Marcus and Cassius drew their daggers from their sleeves, and for a moment, the opposing sides froze, taking each other's measure.

Then two of the legionaries charged, and frenzied action replaced the momentary lull. Rufus spun in place and gutted one of the men with a single slash, while Cassius planted his dagger in another man's throat. Marcus found himself borne backwards by the force of Maxentius' charge, grappling frantically at the man's wrists to keep the *gladius* the legate held from ripping through his toga and into his flesh. It took all his strength to hold that blade at bay, so he could not bring his own dagger into play. Arminius was dodging and weaving from the blade of a third legionary, waiting for a clear shot to bash the man's head in with his *fasces.* Rufus was frantically fencing with another legionary, while the man he had slashed across the abdomen tried to pull himself clear of the melee with one hand while holding his intestines in with the other.

Maxentius was a huge man and full of rage. Marcus found himself on his back, using both hands to keep the man's sword from running him through, and losing his grip on his dagger altogether. The legionary Rufus was fighting was doing his best to keep himself between Marcus's bodyguard and Maxentius, to Rufus' obvious dismay.

Suddenly Rufus shifted his blade to a one-handed grip, dipping his other hand into the bosom of his tunic and drawing it back all in one smooth motion. A short but razor-sharp throwing knife flew across the room and buried itself in the small of Maxentius' back. The big man let out a roar of pain and grabbed for the blade with one hand, his concentration broken for the moment. Marcus seized his chance—and his dagger, which had fallen to the ground next to his head. Keeping his right hand locked around his opponent's wrist, he snatched up his blade and drove it deep into his enemy's throat. The legate's eyes bugged out for a moment, and then he slowly slumped to the ground, his life blood spurting out around the edges of the dagger in his throat.

Marcus stood and dusted himself off. Rufus' opponent had thrown down his blade and raised his hands when he saw his commander fall dead, and the legionary Arminius had been fighting fled to the front of the room.

"Well, that was more interesting than I thought it would be," said Marcus.

"Help!" Marius cried in a strangled voice. The last of the fleeing legionaries had grabbed him in a chokehold and had a dagger to his throat.

"Now this is what is going to happen," the man said. "I am going to back very slowly out of the room, and walk the prefect to the gate of the fortress. You will bring me a horse, and I will release Marius, mount up, and ride out of town for good."

"No," said Sergius Paulus from the back of the room. "That is not what is going to happen at all." He and six legionaries had burst into the room just as the fight ended. One of his men had a crossbow trained on the soldier who was holding the prefect hostage.

"I am getting out of this alive!" the man snapped. "Or the prefect dies!"

Paulus looked at the man with the crossbow, who gave him a curt nod. "Take him," he said.

The bowstring twanged, and the quarrel shot across the room faster than the eye could follow. The legionary let out a strangled scream and reached for the bolt, which was protruding from his eye socket. Before he could grasp it, his remaining eye lost its focus. His hand dropped to his side, and he swayed on his feet for a moment before collapsing like a sack of flour with its bottom ripped out.

Varus Marius stood and looked down at the legionary, then walked over to where Marcus stood. He picked up the *gladius* that Maxentius had dropped, and suddenly his face went purple with rage.

"Rot in Hades, you filthy pig!" he shouted, and swung the blade over his head with all his strength at the fallen legate. It took him three strokes to sever the big man's head, which he then kicked across the room as hard as he could. Finally, he looked up at Marcus, breathing hard, his toga stained with blood.

"I don't really care what you think of me, Quaestor," he said. "I know I am finished as prefect here. But for the opportunity to slice that bastard's head off, I will always be grateful."

"Your status as prefect remains unchanged," Marcus said. "I am sorry for what this man put you through, but prior to his arrival, your official conduct was blameless. I am promoting Sergius Paulus to senior legate to help you administer the province."

The man's face went through an astonishing series of expressions—disbelief, shock, and delight—one after the other.

"But don't you know that I am—" he began.

"What you are on your own time is no concern of mine, or Caesar's," Marcus said. "What matters is that this province be set to rights. Do that, and no one outside this room need ever know of whatever private foibles you may have."

Varus Marius nodded. "I am more grateful than I can say," he told Marcus. "I will be delighted to work with Centurion—I mean, Legate Paulus. I have always respected his abilities." He turned to look at the new legate. "Could you please send one of your men to Maxentius' dungeons and see if—" He looked at Marcus, then back at his new second in command, and lowered his voice to a whisper. "Just see if he is still alive," he finished.

Marcus looked at the prefect sadly. "I wondered how Maxentius managed to gain such a hold on you," he said. "Now I know. It wasn't just the loss of *dignitas* you feared."

"Of course not!" Marius said. "I value my reputation as much as the next man, but not to the extent that I would sell my province for it. That vile man found out who was dearest to my heart, and took him as a hostage for my cooperation. When I protested"—he paled for a moment—"the bastard sent me one of Lintanius' fingers!"

Marcus sighed and turned to his companions. "I think we have seen enough here," he said. "Let us return to our quarters, and get ready to head south tomorrow."

As they headed out, Sergius Paulus caught up with them.

"A word with you, if I may?" he asked.

"Of course, *Legatus,*" Marcus said.

"That title is going to take some getting used to!" Paulus said. "But my girl, Cardixa—she was a good girl before that *mentula* Maxentius forced her into whoredom. I know that I am an officer and a gentleman now, but do you think it would be acceptable if I were to marry her in a year or two's time?"

Marcus smiled at the earnest officer.

"If you love her, make her your bride," he said. "No one in Rome need ever know about her past."

"Thank you, Quaestor—for everything!" Paulus said as they reached the tavern. Marcus nodded, returned to his room, and finished his letter to Claudius.

CHAPTER VIII

Letter from Marcus Publius to Claudius Caesar, the Ides of November, 49 AD

Quaestor Marcus Quintus Publius, Senator of Rome, to Tiberius Claudius Caesar Augustus Germanicus, Princeps and Imperator of Rome, Greetings!

I am writing to you from Salonae in Dalmatia, as I make my way eastward toward Moesia. It has been a most eventful autumn, and the full report attached will include all the dreary financial and legal details of our findings. All five of us are still alive and well, despite some difficulties along the way. Since I last wrote to you, I have passed through the provinces of Germania Superior, Raetia, Noricum, and the Pannonian region before winding up here in Dalmatia. We are about to head out once more, passing through Dacia, both Moesian provinces, and Thracia. I plan to be in Ephesus by next May, if the gods are kind, and you can forward your next letter to me there—it is a regular shipping hub, and it will be easy for me to reply to you. Now, let me sum up our adventures and findings since my last missive:

After leaving Germania Inferior, we passed through the larger German province and found things well run and settled under the wise governance of Lucas Amelius. Cassius Claudius could find no evidence of graft or fraud in the tax rolls, and the locals seemed quite content—a marked contrast to the hornet's nest of discontent we had dealt with just to the north!

Raetia was another matter. Quintus Ambrosius, the proconsul there, was an arrogant, boring senator who is obviously past his prime. He spent over an hour of our first audience with him describing his service with Tiberius Caesar and Pontius Pilate in Germania more than twenty years ago, and his glorious Senate career during the rule of Augustus. He seemingly had no clue as to what was going on in his province, allowing his personal steward to see to all "that accursed administrative ***cacat****" as he put it. We finally managed to escape his presence after two hours, still having no idea what was going on in the province. So Cassius began speaking to the publicani and local officials, while I hung around the barracks, bought drinks for the soldiers, and listened to their gossip. I also* *was treated to an hour-long rant from the senior centurion about the general crookedness and corruption of Greeks in general, and of the steward Democles in particular.*

After three days of investigating, it became obvious that this Greek freedman was taking advantage of his patron's indifference to the welfare of the province and the details of governing to feather his own nest—and with the most expensive feathers imaginable. Cassius and I presented our findings to Ambrosius, who went from arrogance to anger in the space of a moment! Democles, the steward, was stripped of his freedom, flogged, and sold to some Gallic merchants who were passing through. Cassius recommended one of the publicani he had picked out to run the province's finances in the future, but frankly, I think Quintus Ambrosius is long overdue for honorable retirement. That decision, of course, I leave in your hands.

As you recommended, I bypassed the three small Alpine provinces and traversed Noricum without conducting any inquiries there—from all I could see, the people appeared happy and the province well run. However, as we neared the border with Pannonia Superior, we began to hear disquieting rumors of war and rebellion ahead. Clumps of refugees wandered the roads, and while many had no Latin or Greek, the phrases we picked up indicated that there had been unrest in Pannonia Inferior that had spilled across the border into the larger territory.

Once we crossed into Pannonia Superior, the trickle of refugees fleeing the insurrection became a flood. We encountered a number of Roman colonists who were able to tell us in greater detail what was happening. A massive tribe of barbarians they called the Osterlings had come pouring out of Sarmatia, apparently seeking to relocate from their far-off homeland—no one knows why. The legate stationed in Pannonia Inferior had taken his single legion out to stop them, convinced that he had all the military talent he needed due to his descent from Scipio Africanus. The Osterlings relieved him of that conceit, and of his head and half his legion. The survivors escaped, fleeing to the west into the larger Pannonian territory. The retired proconsul who ran the colony there, Titus Andronicus, an older man, recognized that he did not have the forces needed to overcome the massive incursion. However, before he could send for aid, he and his household were cut off and surrounded at the small fortress of Carnuntum. The legions tried to cut their way through the Osterlings and rescue him, but they were turned aside and forced to retreat, losing their commander and his second in command in the process.

Two more days of hard riding and we found what was left of the three legions that once occupied this territory. There were enough healthy men to make up one legion and four or five cohorts from a second one. They were badly demoralized and had built a decent camp, but were unwilling to take the field against the enemy without a commander. I realized that there was actually an opportunity to strike back, for according to the refugees I had talked to, the Osterlings had spread across the province in order to pillage and loot, believing that all organized resistance had been broken.

At this point I did what any senator of Rome in my place would have done—I assumed command. I am no great military strategist, but I did serve under one in the person of Legate Tullius, and took advantage of that opportunity to see how an army should be run. I've also studied the campaigns of the Divus Julius for many years, so I had some fair idea what to do. First, I sent out quartermasters in all directions to gather as much food and weapons as they could find, and I reorganized the surviving troops, placing the green recruits under the command of seasoned veterans, and finding out from the remaining centurions which men had shown themselves deserving of promotion. I put them to drilling and training the men daily, restoring a measure of confidence and pride to them.

I also set patrols out to safely escort refugees to our rear, and interviewed as many of those fleeing from the enemy as I could. Within a few days, I heard of a force of some twelve hundred Osterlings that had split off from the main body in order to loot a nearby district known for its rich farms. I immediately ordered the men on a forced march under cover of darkness and caught the enemy just after dawn. The barbarians were mostly still sleeping as we stormed the camp and put 600 of them to the sword, taking about 400 captive. Only a tithe of them escaped our wrath. My patrols reported that they had fled to a larger force that was coming up behind them, and that the Osterlings had sped up their advance when word of the defeat reached them.

I just had time to arrange my forces for a classic ambush when the vanguard arrived. I had posted my cavalry in a small copse of trees to the right rear of the main legion, and ordered most of my veterans to conceal themselves in the ruins of a burnt-out village to my rear. Facing the enemy, bowed toward his ranks, I placed five cohorts, anchoring their flanks with some of my most experienced legionaries and their centurions.

I'm sure you recognize by my description what I had planned—the same kind of double envelopment made famous by Hannibal at the battle of Cannae. Fortunately, the Osterlings had never heard of the Punic Wars! They fell into my trap beautifully, and my front ranks retreated steadily, luring them into the pocket that was being formed around them before they ever noticed that only the center was retreating! Upon my signal, the legionaries stopped their retreat, turned, and launched a volley of pila at them. The enemy's front ranks paused and staggered as the spears took their toll, and at the same time, my men who had hidden among the burnt-out houses came charging at the enemy. The two veteran legions on either end of the line, which had not retreated a step, came piling in on the Osterling's flanks even as my cavalry crashed into the rear of their line. The organized resistance failed in the amount of time it took me to write these lines, and my legionaries dispatched them all. Having marched through the shattered villages and bloated bodies of the innocent colonists, they were in no mood to take prisoners, and some three thousand Osterlings were felled before they were done.

You never would have guessed that these grim, bloody-handed soldiers were the same demoralized, shattered troops I had found just ten days earlier! The cheeky fellows even tried to hail me as imperator on the field, but I would have none of it. I wanted to keep pressing our advantage and try to find the leader of this massive band of nomads. We marched east for two hours to get away from the stench of the battlefield and of the pyre we burned their dead upon, and then set up camp. I then sent out some scouts under cover of darkness to try and locate the enemy's main force, and they came back two days later, as we were still slowly advancing, with the report that there was a massive Osterling force camped by the river at the foot of the mountains, about two leagues away.

At this point I ordered the men to halt and rode my horse to the top of a small outcrop where they could all see and hear me. I reminded them of the misery and woe that the Osterlings had brought upon them, and of the deaths of their proconsul and many of their comrades. I called on them, in the name of the Senate and People of Rome, and of their emperor, to avenge these atrocities upon the barbarian host.

"Two leagues?" I said. "What is two leagues? The Divus Julius could march his men that far in a single morning and still conquer half of Gaul before sunset. Are you any less men than the men of the Tenth Legion? Will you stand embarrassed before your grandsire's shades when they ask why you were too tired to fight at the end of a holiday stroll?"

Of course, that got their blood up, and we covered the distance at a regular trot. The enemy became aware of us, but too late—by the time we burst out of the trees and fell upon them, they were just beginning to form ranks. It was a bloody good fight, all told—the Osterlings were desperate to defend their chief, and put up a furious resistance. But I swear the Pannonian legions were possessed by the spirit of the Tenth that day—they cut through enemy ranks like butter!

I'll admit I got carried away. I rode into the center of the enemy, looking for their chieftain, with only a few legionaries and my trusty man Rufus at my side. The ling of the Osterlings—his name was Beorn or Bjorn or some such barbarian nonsense—took a look at me and charged with a frightening bellow. I grabbed a pilum from one of my legionaries and launched it at him with all my strength as he came tearing at me—and can you believe I caught him square in the throat! I who could not hit the ring one time out of five when I was a lad training at the Campus Martius!

That pretty much put an end to it. The remaining Osterlings either threw down their weapons and cried mercy, or flung themselves into the swift river and tried to swim to safety. Very few of them made it across that I could see. Another four thousand of the enemy lay dead by sunset, and five thousand were now our captives. I stayed in the province for a month, crushing the small bands of raiders that had not got word of the defeat, and returning colonists to their ruined homes. We did rescue one junior legate from the enemy camp, and after some medical attention and rest, he assumed command of the legionaries. You will need to dispatch a new governor to the region, although I recommend that the line of settlement be pulled back some distance—there are too many remote farms here, and the area is too lightly populated to really be a proper province.

One last thing, although it embarrasses me a bit to admit it—the men hailed me as imperator on the field a second time after we destroyed the main Osterling host. When I do eventually return to Rome, I would like some recognition, not so much for myself as for these brave boys who risked so much for Rome that day. Maybe not something so elaborate as a triumph, but an ovation from the Senate would certainly be in order for such a display of bravery as the men gave that day.

After such a lively time in Pannonia, the tour of Dalmatia was matter-of-fact to the point of boredom. The governor had been dipping too deeply into the public till, and was squeezing the locals far beyond their ability to pay. It took us three days to gather enough evidence to charge him with extortion and corruption. Since it is such a short hop across the sea to Italia, I took the liberty of arresting him and sending him to Rome by the same ship that is bearing this letter to you.

I had my doubts about undertaking this long and arduous mission when you first gave it to me, but I find myself having a marvelous time, despite the dangers we have faced. There is something wonderfully fulfilling about seeing a problem and having both the ability and the imperium to fix it. I find myself looking forward to our trip to the East, where I imagine there will be more provinces in need of shaking up. I thank you, Most Excellent Claudius, for this opportunity to serve both Rome and you, and I pray that my services do not disappoint. Yours in the service of the Senate and People of Rome, Marcus Quintus Publius

Letter from Claudius Caesar to Marcus Publius, The Kalends of January 50 AD

Tiberius Claudius Caesar Augustus Germanicus, Princeps and Imperator of Rome, to Quaestor Marcus Quintus Publius, Senator and special envoy to the provinces,

My dear Marcus, how splendid it was to receive the news of your crushing the invasion of Pannonia! I had just received a desperate letter from one of the settlers, begging for five legions of troops to come and save what was left of Rome's foothold there. I had already budgeted the money and appointed a legate to command the expedition when your missive arrived, bearing word that the invaders were already defeated. What a relief to inform the Senate that the enormous and expensive military expedition they had authorized was no longer needed! Fifteen days of public thanksgiving were ordained for your victory, and you will be granted a triumph upon your return to the city. The shiploads of slaves have already arrived from the province; once they are auctioned off, the proceeds will be set aside to reward you and your soldiers for their service to the Empire.

I am sending this letter to Ephesus, as you requested. I hope it will arrive before you, for there are several matters that need your attention in the East. Judea continues to be a running sore—the Jews are more and more restive under Roman rule, and the Zealot revolutionaries, so thoroughly crushed by Pontius Pilate, have flourished again during the troubled terms of his successors. Of course, my deranged nephew did not help matters when he tried to have a statue of himself erected in the holiest precinct of the Jewish temple!

The rest of Syria is also experiencing difficulty, and Galatia and Bithynia will always bear some watching. I have heard some stories of graft and corruption, as well as some disturbing rumblings from the Parthians. Augustus may have made peace with them, but great Empires are seldom good neighbors. Even though Gaius Caligula is more than eight years in his grave now, his neglect of the Eastern provinces generated problems that still require dealing with. I will admit, my young friend, that I sleep better at night knowing that I have appointed a wise and competent quaestor to sort out the provinces.

I do have one last request to make of you, and this has little to do with the governance of the provinces—at least not yet. But it began in the region you are moving towards, and continues to spread outward to this day, like some strange plague. That may not be a very good metaphor—but I don't know how else to refer to this movement. I am not sure if it bodes good or ill for the future of Rome.

Are you a religious man, Marcus Quintus? I have held several priesthoods in my time, but I am at my heart a Stoic and a skeptic. While I certainly believe that there is some divine force that guides our destinies, I think that the traditional gods of Rome are our attempt to impose some sort of recognizable face on the unknown. I highly doubt that Jupiter Optimus

Maximus resembles the ancient statue that adorns his temple—if he even acknowledges the name that we mortals have given him!

The reason I ask about your beliefs is because the matter I want you to look into is a religious one. A new cult sprang up in Judea during the Prefecture of Pontius Pilate, almost twenty years ago. It was built around the teachings of a Galilean mystic named Jesus, whose followers call him the "Christos"—not "Crestus," as I mistakenly referred to him during your first meeting with the Senate. This fellow had acquired a huge following during the time of Pilate, and so provoked the High Priest of the Jews that he persuaded Pilate to crucify the man. However, for some reason that did not end the matter. There are all manner of stories about how this Jesus lives on in one form or another, and none of them make much sense—partly because I have heard them all at the second or third hand.

The Nazarene sect, as they are called, has spread far beyond Judea, even claiming some followers in Rome itself. If you have the chance, I would like to hear a detailed account of who these people are and what they believe—as well as your assessment as to whether or not this movement represents any sort of threat to Rome. Thus far, it has been treated as a sect of Judaism, which is a recognized and legal religion throughout the Empire. The Jews, however, insist that the Nazarenes are heretics and revolutionaries, and disavow all association with them—which is odd, since most of the Nazarenes come from the Jewish faith.

At any rate, find out what you can for me and include as many details as you can in your next report. I pray to whatever gods inhabit the cosmos to guide you on your journey and bring you back safely to Rome. You can rest assured that your loyal service will earn you further advancement in the Senate when you come home. Be safe, my young friend.—Claudius Caesar

Postscript: I failed to include any news of your family, or of events in Rome. All goes well for your uncle—his mourning has ended and he is thinking about standing for Censor in the next election. I think he would grace that office well, and of course it is a great honor to your family. I am happy enough in my new marriage, although Agrippina is a temperamental woman at times. Give Cassius Claudius my express greetings, and tell him that his brother has recently entered my service as a scribe and accountant of public records.

"Do you believe in the gods, Cadius?" Marcus asked his slave as the boy helped him remove his sandals.

"Which ones, *Dominus*?" the teenager asked. He had grown nearly a foot since Mencius had gifted him to Marcus nearly two years before. His black hair had thickened, and he was becoming quite muscular, but he still had a little boy's mischievous twinkle in his eyes—something that the young girls they encountered never failed to notice. Marcus feared that the lad would leave a string of broken hearts from Armenia to Rome by the time their expedition was done.

"Well, any of them," Marcus replied. "What gods did your parents worship?"

"My mother was devoted to the Bona Dea," said the young lad, "but my father was a worshiper of Apis. Not that either god lifted a finger to help them when Caligula cut them down. I pray to Jupiter Optimus Maximus, when I pray at all, but I don't think he listens very well."

"What makes you say that?" Marcus said.

The boy shrugged. "I'm still a slave," he said. "Understand, I am grateful to have a kind *dominus* like you, and to have survived all the scrapes we have come through—but I'd like to be a free man someday."

"You'll have to become a man first," Marcus said, ruffling his hair.

"I am fourteen now!" the boy protested. "I even killed a man in that big battle we were in!"

"That you did," Marcus said. A huge Osterling had gotten past the guards into the baggage train near the end of the battle, and Cadius had put three arrows into him before he finally collapsed, barely two yards in front of the lad. "But that doesn't really touch on our conversation about the gods."

"I guess the answer, then, is that I would be happy to find a god I could actually believe in," the lad finally said. "A god that actually loved men, without hedging them in with demands and threats. What about you, *Dominus*? What gods do you pray to at night?"

Marcus thought a moment. "Well, Cadius, I think you and I are in the same boat. I've sacrificed to the gods of Rome my whole life, and I think the rituals of religion have an important place in binding the people of the Empire together. But I am a Stoic at heart, and while I do believe that Plato's Prime Mover is out there somewhere, I do not know who he is, or what name he wishes to be called by."

"Maybe we will encounter the gods before our journey is over," the boy said.

Marcus laughed. "I doubt it—but maybe so. What do you know about the cult of the Nazarenes?" he asked.

"You mean the Christians?" Cadius asked. "My friend Arnulf, the cooper's boy, comes from a Christian family. His parents were in Jerusalem and got to hear Jesus preach years ago, and they are convinced that the Galilean was the Son of God. It's all he talks about when we get together."

"Really?" Marcus said. "I had heard that some of the cult's members had come to Rome, but I know little about them."

"Arnulf's family are the only ones I have met, but they are the kindest people I know—except for you, *Dominus*," the lad corrected himself.

"Cadius, you don't have to be afraid of me," Marcus said. "You're a solid, dependable body servant, and I am not going to order you flogged if you observe that one of your friends is kinder to you than I am."

The boy shook his head. "*Dominus*, to be a slave is to be afraid," he said. "Not that I am necessarily afraid of you—although I know that you have the power to sell me to another owner at the drop of a hat, or to have me flogged anytime you feel like it. I don't believe you are going to do those things, but knowing that you could do so is a part of my life every day. And what if something should happen to you? Who knows what kind of master my next *dominus* would be!"

Marcus paused, a bit surprised at how open the boy was. Every Roman accepted that slavery was a natural part of the social order, and the dictum was that no master ever trusts his slaves completely, and vice versa. One of the laws added to the Twelve Tables after the Spartacani Revolt was that, if any slave in a household raised his hand against his master, every slave in the house would be crucified. It was a draconian measure, but Rome had not had a slave revolt since Marcus Crassus had crushed Spartacus and his rebels over a century before, so Marcus thought it was effective, even if it was not terribly fair.

"You're a good lad, Cadius, and I shall add a clause to my will stating that if anything happens to me, you will be freed and given a stipend from my estate. Will that at least relieve one worry from your mind?" he asked.

The lad beamed. "That's why I said you are kinder than Arnulf's family!" he said. "I am happy to be your slave—I just don't want to be anyone else's!"

Marcus smiled. He had never had a son of his own, and he found himself thinking of Cadius more as a family member than a servant sometimes. "Well, go fetch Cassius Claudius for me," he said. "I'm anxious to see what Ephesus is like outside this tavern."

Ephesus was a senatorial province, and therefore not officially part of Marcus' inspection tour, but at the same time, he was ready to stretch his legs after weeks at sea, and the town had looked very interesting as glimpsed from the sea the evening before. The great temple of Artemis was built on the lowlands outside the city, and Marcus was anxious to see this much-vaunted wonder of the world. When Cassius Claudius joined him, they set out, with Rufus and Arminius in tow, to see what the great city of Ephesus was like.

CHAPTER IX

Marcus enjoyed his stay in Ephesus, but despite the large Jewish community there, he had no luck in finding any who belonged to the Nazarene sect. The more religious Jews were reluctant to speak to him at all about matters of faith, since he was a pagan, or "Gentile" as they put it. Some of the Alexandrian Jews, however, who had a Greek education, were less fussy about tradition and regaled him on the topic of the Christian movement.

"It was that Caiaphas, the High Priest, who fueled it," commented Eleazar ben Mosche, a cultured merchant from Egypt. "When he had the Nazarene put to death, he turned him into a martyr. If he had just let that Jesus fellow live, the crowds would have eventually seen through his trickery—and recognized him as just another charlatan."

"What trickery do you refer to?" asked Marcus.

"Why, the so-called miracles and healings this Jesus performed!" said the Jew with a sneer. "You can only sustain that kind of fraud for so long before someone who is really sick comes to you. When you can't cure them, the people realize that all the other so-called sick people you healed weren't really sick at all—and the game is done! If Caiaphas had left Jesus alone, the people would have turned on him, and his little movement would have ended. Instead, now you have Nazarenes going throughout the Empire proclaiming that this Jesus was the Messiah and the Son of God!"

"So you think all the stories about Jesus healing the sick were false?" Marcus said.

"Of course!" snapped Eleazar. "Such things are impossible!"

"Do you not believe in your God, then?" Marcus asked him.

"Of course I believe in God," said the merchant. "Every Jew does—after all, somebody is out to get us!" With a harsh laugh, he turned away and left Marcus and Cadius staring after him.

"Why do the Jews worship a God if they believe he is out to get them?" Cadius asked.

"You are asking the wrong person," Marcus said. "I don't know any Roman who claims to understand the Jews."

"I don't think he knew what he was talking about," observed Cadius. "Arnulf's father told me he and his wife saw Jesus heal dozens of people, including a leper, in one day!"

"That seems improbable to say the least," Marcus said. "Let's see if we can find someone else to ask."

Several other interviews produced similar results—the Roman and Greek inhabitants of Ephesus were mostly unfamiliar with the new religion, and the Jews were universally scornful about it. After a couple of days, Marcus gave up and decided to proceed with their journey to the Eastern provinces. It was only a few days' ride from Ephesus to the small twin province of Lycia and Pamphylia, where Marcus found that the prefect, Antonius Lycenus, was an old friend of his uncle's. The small province had enjoyed a string of effective and honest governors, and the people, from the natives to the Greek merchants who had moved there in great numbers, seemed happy and proud to be part of the Empire. Marcus was sad to take his leave of Antonius, who had been very welcoming. The old man left them a stern warning regarding the nearby province of Galatia, however.

"Phillipus Acro has been up to no good there, I think!" he said. "Merchants are fleeing the province left and right, saying they can no longer afford to do business there. I don't know what his game is, but there are some ugly rumors floating about."

Marcus thanked the prefect for his trouble and headed northward to Galatia. The provincial capital was Ancyra, but he and Cassius Claudius took their time, traveling incognito and watching the legionaries and tax collectors at work in the villages they passed through. The *publicani* were all fat, either literally or metaphorically speaking—they strutted through the streets, stayed in the best lodgings, paid for the prettiest women, and lorded it over the locals at every opportunity. Each one was accompanied by at least a half dozen legionaries at all times, and the complaints and curses leveled against them were the same in every town.

"We never paid taxes like this under the old prefect," one innkeeper groused to Marcus. "Acro claims that the emperor has doubled the rate on all the provinces, but my cousin in Cilicia says they've never heard of such."

"My uncle was friends with a senator in Rome," chimed in a customer. "He tried to write a letter protesting the taxes, and the governor had him imprisoned for it!"

Cassius Claudius took careful notes of every violation of Roman law he heard of, and by the time they arrived in Ancyra, he had a good-sized scroll filled with irregularities that needed investigating. Marcus focused on the legions, gathering information on their commanders from both locals and individual legionaries that he bought drinks for in the taverns.

"This is going to be harder than the last few," he told Cassius the night before they arrived in Ancyra. "The senior legate is assisting the governor in fleecing the locals, and there doesn't seem to be a competent subordinate that we can call on to step up and rein him in. At least, not one these legionaries know of."

"What do we do, then?" Cassius said.

"I'm going to demand to see the legate privately, let him know that the jig is up, and try to persuade him that his only chance to salvage his reputation is to side with us," Marcus said. "Then I will try to find an honest centurion in the capital if I can."

"You'll need to be careful," commented Cassius.

Once they were set up at the local inn, Marcus located a patrol and asked one of the legionaries who their centurion was.

"Cornelius Cinna," he said. "Transferred in from the Italian Cohort in Caesarea a couple of months ago."

"What sort of fellow is he?" Marcus asked.

"Honest as the day is long, and very professional," said the legionary, "but a bit strange when it comes to his religion. He is one of these Nazarenes, you see. Talks about some Jewish god named Jesus all the time."

"And he hates our governor!" chimed in another one. "He says that Acro is a crook and a fraud."

Marcus nodded. "I am Marcus Quintus Publius," he said, "*Triumphator* and Quaestor of Rome, and emissary from Claudius Caesar. I have a mission for you men. You will go and tell Cornelius Cinna to report to me immediately, and not breathe a word of this to anyone, do you understand?"

The legionaries saluted. "Yes, sir!" they said, and scurried off. Marcus smiled at their alacrity—technically, he would not be a *triumphator* until after his parade, but Rome's supreme honor had been voted to him, and he knew that it would carry great weight among the legions.

Within the hour, the doors of the tavern opened, and a white-haired Roman centurion stepped through. Marcus raised an eyebrow—this man was at least fifty, a decade older than the oldest centurion he had yet met. Apparently, his reputed honesty had not helped his career much.

"Are you Marcus Publius?" the centurion asked.

"I am," Marcus replied. "You must be Cornelius Cinna, recently from the Italian Cohort at Ephesus."

"Indeed, I am, sir," the man said.

"I need your help, Centurion," Marcus said. "Something is rotten in this province, and I am here to set things right."

The old soldier looked at him and gave a long sigh. "You've got your work cut out for you, sir," he said, "but I'll help any way I can. I've hated this place since I set foot here. The proconsul is a snake, and my superior, Legate Marcus Amelius, is no better. Most of the men imitate what they see in their superiors, and the result is one of the most lazy, corrupt, abusive set of soldiers I've ever served with. My faith prizes honesty and kindness, and I have thought about leaving the legions permanently ever since I came here—but then who would there be to try and undo the damage these evil men have caused?"

"Your faith sounds interesting, Cornelius," said Marcus, "but let's focus on fixing things here first. Is Legate Amelius a strong man, or is he a follower?"

Cornelius laughed. "He's a worm," he replied. "A coward on the battlefield, and a sycophant in the governor's court."

"It sounds like he can be turned, then," Marcus said.

"He'll turn whichever way the wind blows," Cornelius agreed, "but he'll turn again the minute your back is to him. Use him if you must, but don't trust him."

"That's where I will depend on you," Marcus said. "I plan to relieve Acro and send to Rome for a replacement, but you will need to keep Amelius on the right path till that replacement gets here."

"I'm just a centurion," Cornelius said. "I'm not even *Primipilus* here, although I was in Judea."

"I have *imperium mais* from Claudius Caesar himself," said Marcus. "I will appoint you as acting military tribune, so that you can veto the legate if necessary."

"You do me too much honor, Quaestor," Cornelius said.

"That remains to be seen," Marcus replied. "Go and bring me your legate, and we'll give him a good shake and see which way he falls!"

It was too easy, Marcus bitterly thought in retrospect two days later. He had been lulled into false complacency by the open confrontations of his last few stops, and forgot how devious desperate men could be. Marcus Amelius had blustered, threatened, and then collapsed like a wet tent with its ridge pole cut. He promised to do exactly as the quaestor told him, and to help them take down Phillipus Acro that very day. Without giving the legate time to sneak a warning to the proconsul, the five travelers had gone straight to the governor's court and Marcus had rolled out his most threatening indictment of Acro's corruption and cupidity. The proconsul, a scrawny man with a weasel-like face, had growled and threatened the group, but in a matter of moments he, too, knuckled under and allowed himself to be taken into custody.

Marcus ordered five legionaries that Cornelius recommended to escort the proconsul southward into Pamphylia, where Lycenus could take custody of him and ship him off to Rome for trial in the Provincial Corruption Courts that Claudius had recently established. The five companions were walking toward the inn where they had purchased rooms, talking among themselves about how easy this particular assignment had proven to be. Cadius was walking behind Marcus, strutting with happiness as he listened in on the conversation his master was having with Cassius Claudius. If he had not seen the blurry shadow rushing in from behind, Marcus thought, the mission to the provinces might have come to a sudden and bloody end.

"*Dominus!!*" the boy shouted. "Look out!"

Marcus whirled, drawing the *gladius* he had worn ever since the battles in Pannonia. A burly legionary was withdrawing his blade from the slave boy's stomach as Cadius collapsed to the ground, blood welling from his wound. With an inchoate cry of rage, Marcus slashed the soldier's throat with a wild swing. But then a half dozen more legionaries came charging up, blades drawn. Rufus pitched into them, his scimitar whirling, while Marcus and Cassius covered his flanks and Armenius the lictor watched their backs. Marcus had never felt such white-hot anger before—he slashed and stabbed in fury, cutting down two more attackers in the short but intense skirmish.

The legionaries had been expecting little resistance and were totally unprepared for the furious defense the group mounted. Five of the six were cut down, and the last one dropped his blade and fled for dear life—until Rufus' throwing knife buried itself between his shoulders. With a cry, the final assailant fell on his face, grabbing at the wound but unable to grasp the hilt of the blade.

"Cassius—see to the boy!" snapped Marcus. He walked to the fallen foe and yanked his head back by the hair. "DOG!!" he roared. "Who put you up to this?"

The legionary was still very much alive, and obviously terrified. "My legs!" he shrieked. "I can't move my legs!"

"Listen to me," Marcus said, his voice going very quiet. "You are going to die—you have attacked a personal emissary of the emperor of Rome. There is only one choice you have left: the manner of your death. I will see you nailed up shrieking to a cross and left for the birds, or I can make it quick and clean right here and now. So I will ask again: who put you up to this?"

"It was the Proconsul and Legate Amelius!" the man said. "They knew you was coming—Amelius has a cousin in the Senate who wrote him a letter, told him about your cleaning house up in Germania and all. They pretended to go along meekly, planning to kill all of you as soon as you left the governor's castle. They picked us because we helped them protect the *publicani* and shake down the locals. Six of us to kill you, six more to rescue the governor, and six to arrest Cornelius and lock him up."

Marcus nodded grimly. "Thank you for your honesty, soldier," he said, and slashed the man's throat. The eyes bugged out for a moment, then went dull with death. He turned to Rufus, Cassius, and Armenius.

"Our group is really too small for this sort of thing," he said. "Before we leave here, we will hire some mercenaries to ride with us from this point forward. But, at the moment, it sounds as if Marcus Amelius may be alone in the fortress, with all his minions off on errands. I suggest we pay him a visit before that changes."

He knelt beside Cassius Claudius, who was cradling Cadius in his arms. The boy was pale but conscious, holding both hands over the oozing wound in his stomach.

"You won again, *Dominus,*" the lad said.

Marcus felt tears well up in his eyes. He leaned forward and kissed the faithful slave's forehead. "A victory that may have cost me far more than it was worth," he said. "Listen to me, Cadius my boy—you need to hold on. Hold on, at all costs. Cassius is going to take you to the tavern and summon a *medicus* to treat your wound. I have to go finish dealing with the bad people who did this to you, but I need you to make me a promise. Can you do that?"

The slave boy nodded.

"Promise me to stay awake until I get back to the tavern. Stay awake until I speak to you again. Do you promise?" Marcus asked softly.

"Yes, *Dominus*," the boy said.

Marcus smiled and squeezed his shoulder. "You saved my life today, Cadius. You saved all of us. For better or for worse, as of this moment you are a free man. Do you understand me? I am officially emancipating you, in the presence of all these witnesses."

A tear rolled down the boy's cheek. "Don't send me away," he said. "I'd rather be a slave by your side than a freeman away from you."

Marcus choked back a sob. "You have nothing to fear," he said. "We are together through thick and thin from this day forward."

He stood and dusted off his robes, then wiped the blood from his blade onto the tunic of one of the fallen legionaries.

"Rufus, Armenius," he said. "Come with me. We are going to be hard, fast, and ruthless!"

The guards at the entrance of the fortress where the governor resided were not alarmed at all to see Marcus approach.

"Back so soon?" one of them said.

Marcus fixed him with a furious glare. "Who do you serve, legionary?" he demanded.

"Why, the Senate and People of Rome," the puzzled man replied. "And the Emperor Claudius Caesar!"

"What about Legate Marcus Amelius?" Marcus asked.

"Well, sir, we are under his command, but you are his superior," the legionary said.

"That answer just saved your life," Marcus told him. "Your legate just tried to have me and my companions assassinated. Needless to say, he failed. We are going to pay him a visit. I order you to join us, and, if necessary, fight at my command. Am I clear?"

The two legionaries snapped to attention and saluted. "Yes sir!" they barked in unison.

"Let's go then," Marcus told them. "And keep your *pila* in your hands!"

The guard outside the audience chamber had a completely different reaction when they rounded the corner of the hallway and went striding toward the door. His eyes widened in shock, and he turned and tried to run into the chamber.

"Kill him!" Marcus snapped, and two *pila* flew through the air and skewered the man, one through the shoulder, the other through the chest. He collapsed to the ground, his warning cry giving way to a death rattle.

"Retrieve your spears quickly, then throw the door open and come in behind me," he said softly to the two legionaries. They complied quickly and quietly.

Marcus Amelius was lounging on the governor's *bema* seat, but leaped to his feet when he saw the emperor's envoys striding into the room. He read his doom in Marcus' eyes, and did not even try to put up a fight.

"It was Acro's idea!" he wailed. "I told him it was foolish to attack an emissary from the emperor! I warned him that his corruption was getting out of hand! You have to believe me!"

Marcus could not keep the contempt out of his voice. "It was your cousin that warned you we were coming—and you warned the governor!" he snapped. The widening of the legate's eyes showed the truth of the charge. "Marcus Amelius, you are guilty of high treason and attempted murder. By the *imperium mais* granted to me by Claudius Caesar, and confirmed by the Senate and People of

Rome, I sentence you to death by flogging and beheading. You are a coward, a thief, and a traitor, and will die as such."

"NO!!" shrieked the legate. "At least let me fall on my sword like a soldier!"

"What would you know about being a soldier?" sneered Marcus. "Now, before these honest legionaries clap you in irons, tell me—where is Cornelius Cinna?"

"I had him locked in the dungeons—he put up a tremendous fight when my boys arrested him! I can have him released and brought to you, if you will spare me the flogging!" Amelius begged.

Marcus sighed. With only five men, he did not have the necessary forces to hold the receiving hall and make a raid on the dungeons. "Do it!" he snapped. "Legionaries, keep the point of your *pilum* against his back, and bring him straight back here to me. Do you understand?"

"Yes, sir!" they said. They marched Legate Amelius to the doors on the far side of the chamber, and he leaned out long enough to bark some orders, then was hustled back to stand before Marcus. Moments later, three legionaries entered the room, with Cornelius between them. His nose was bleeding, and one of his eyes was swelling rapidly. They beheld the scene in the audience chamber and looked at one another, eyes narrowing.

"You three are guilty of treason," Marcus said. "However, you were following your legate's orders—even though you knew those orders were illegal. I will let you live if you surrender now, but your days as soldiers are now done."

The tallest legionary shouted his defiance, drew his *gladius*, and tried to charge at Marcus—but quick as a snake, Cornelius shot his foot out and tripped the man. He fell on his own blade, and screamed as the *gladius* cut into his stomach. Marcus drew his own blade, marched over, and dispatched the burly soldier with a quick thrust through the neck. Then he looked at the other two, his blade still dripping with their companion's blood.

"So are you going to try and resist?" he said.

Their swords fell to the floor, and they stepped back.

"Good!" Marcus said. "Now get out of this town by sunset, and never let my eyes fall upon you again." He used his bloody blade to cut the ropes that pinioned Cornelius. The old centurion rubbed his hands to restore the circulation.

"Thank you, sir," he said. "I tried to get a warning to you, but Amelius had six of his bully boys jump me the minute you left."

"I notice only three brought you here," said Marcus. "What of the others?"

"One is dead, and two wounded badly enough that they had to be taken away," Cornelius replied.

"Summon the entire garrison to the courtyard," Marcus said. "I want all those who took part in the attack on me, or were privy to it, arrested."

"There weren't that many," Cornelius said. "No more than thirty, all told. Six were sent to kill you, six arrested me, and six went to retrieve Acro. The other twelve were told to return to the barracks and await orders."

"You know who you can trust, I hope!" Marcus said.

"The boys in my century are pretty reliable," Cornelius replied. "I'll get them first."

Within a half hour, some six hundred soldiers were assembled in the courtyard. Marcus paced back and forth, waiting for the final act of the drama to unfold. Moments after the last group of soldiers assumed their positions, it happened—Proconsul Phillipus Acro strode into the courtyard with four legionaries at his back. The smugness on his face vanished as he surveyed the cohort and the grim quaestor who stood at its head.

"Phillipus Acro, in the name of Emperor Claudius Caesar, and of the Senate and People of Rome, I strip you of your citizenship, and the title of proconsul. I find you guilty of high treason and attempted murder. You are sentenced to death by flogging and beheading, said sentence to be carried out immediately, in the presence of these legionaries!" Marcus thundered.

The four guards who were escorting the former proconsul saw the folly of resistance and surrendered their weapons right away. Acro pleaded and begged for his life, but Marcus steeled his will and stopped his ears. He had been assured by Claudius Caesar that his authority would be backed up if he should ever have to resort to such a step, but the execution of a member of the Senate, a proconsul of Rome, was a staggering responsibility. But when he remembered Cadius' pale face, and the blood welling from the boy's stomach, all hesitation fled.

Acro and Amelius were forced to their knees before the legion, and Marcus spoke once more.

"Former Legate Amelius made some amends for his crimes by helping me rescue Legate Cornelius Cinna from the dungeons," he said. "For this small act of atonement, I have rescinded the sentence of flogging and have granted him a quick death. Rufus, carry out the sentence."

Marcus' burly bodyguard stepped forward. "It'll be quicker if you don't try to duck the blade," he told Amelius, who dutifully hung his head forward. The scimitar flashed, the body spasmed, and the head rolled.

"No such boon will be granted to you, Phillipus Acro," he said. "Legionary Lucius Parthenius, administer a hundred lashes to this man!"

Thirty-nine was the legal limit, but Marcus was so furious at this cowardly wretch he did not care. The former governor was tied to the whipping post, and for the next fifteen minutes the cat-o-nine tails reduced his flesh to bloody strips from his thighs to his shoulders. Acro screamed at first, then gibbered, then lost consciousness. When the final lash fell, two legionaries dragged him to a blacksmith's block, where Rufus took his head as well. From the time the attack in the streets had occurred until the former proconsul's head hit the ground, less than two hours had passed.

Marcus Quintus Publius climbed onto a platform at the end of the courtyard, where all the soldiers could see him. He projected his voice, and his anger, over the assembled crowd.

"Soldiers of Rome," he said, "you have been abominably led. Your proconsul and your legate despoiled and extorted the people of this province, and many of you aided and abetted them. That time has come to an end. Tax rates are officially reverted to normal levels. Extorted funds will be returned, those unjustly imprisoned will be released, and a new proconsul from Rome will be sent to lead you shortly. Until then, I am promoting Centurion Cornelius Cinna to legate, and he will lead this legion and govern this province until his new superior arrives. You are to obey his orders unconditionally. IS THAT CLEAR?"

The shouted reply shook the walls of the fortress: "Yes, Quaestor!"

"Then you are dismissed!" Marcus said. "And someone burn the bodies from today's needless carnage."

The soldiers dispersed, and he turned to Cornelius. "I am giving you one simple order," he told the man. "Clean house! I want this province to be impeccably run by the time the new proconsul arrives."

Cornelius smiled. "That's the most welcome set of orders I have ever received," he said. "Fear not, Marcus Publius, I will do all I can to restore peace and order here. I may have to lean pretty hard on some of the *publicani*. Can you help me?"

Marcus sighed. "Right now, I must return to the tavern. Someone very dear to me was grievously wounded in the attack. I don't even know if he is still alive."

"Let me come with you," Cornelius said. He turned and barked orders at two of the centurions standing nearby, and then he followed Marcus back to the tavern.

Cadius lay on one of the beds. His midsection was swathed in fresh bandages, but blood was already seeping through them. An earnest young Greek was pouring a potion down his throat. Cassius Claudius stood when they entered.

"Thank the gods!" he said. "I feared there would be legionaries coming to arrest us if you had failed. What about Acro and Amelius?" he asked.

"Both dead!" Marcus snapped. "I'll explain, but I need to ask this *medicus* a few questions first."

He pulled the Greek aside. "How is the boy?" he asked.

"He was stabbed through the entrails," the man said. "I have sewn up the wound, but there is no way to prevent it from becoming gangrenous. He may live three days, possibly a week, but there is no recovery from such an injury."

Marcus bowed his head and wept. "What can I do then?" he asked.

"Poppyseed milk will numb the pain," the man said. "But if it were me, I would wait till he is sleeping and make a quick end of it. Such wounds make for a very slow and agonizing death."

Marcus dropped a couple of *denarii* in the man's hand and thanked him, then went to Cadius' bedside. The boy saw him and tried to smile.

"I stayed awake, just like I promised," he said. "Am I going to die, *Dominus*?"

Marcus shook his head. "You'll be on your feet in no time," he said.

The lad looked up at him sadly. "You are too honest a man to be a good liar, *Dominus*," he said. "It is all right. I am not afraid to die, for I have served the greatest man in Rome."

Marcus could not stand to look at the boy one moment longer. He stepped out of the tavern into the night air. After he left, Cornelius walked over to the bedside. He placed his hands on Cadius' forehead, closed his eyes, and muttered under his breath for a few moments. Then he stepped outside and found Marcus.

"I believe the boy can be saved," he told the quaestor.

"The *medicus* said otherwise," Marcus told him grimly.

"Listen to me, Marcus Quintus," said Cornelius. "I know that it seems impossible, but with God all things are possible. I serve Jesus Christ, the Son of the Living God. Do you know of him?"

"He was a carpenter and a religious teacher, executed by Pontius Pilate nearly twenty years ago," Marcus said. "I fail to see how he can help us now."

"He rose from the dead," Cornelius replied, "and He reigns in heaven to this day. Have you heard of His powers of healing?"

Marcus nodded.

"That power was passed on to his disciples," Cornelius said. "About a week's ride south of here is the city of Antioch. Go there and ask for the Christian leaders. A man named Paul of Tarsus should be there—the Jews call him Saul ben Issachar. He has been given great power by God, and is known to heal the sick and crippled by his touch. I have prayed over your boy, and the Holy Spirit has promised me that he will survive the journey if you leave this very day. If this child's life is as valuable to you as you say, go now! I will send twenty of my most trusted men to escort you, and they will prepare a litter to carry the boy in. If you wish to save his life, you must go!"

Marcus looked at him. "I don't understand," he said. "Can your god not heal him here?"

Cornelius nodded. "He could," he told Marcus, "but He wants you to go to Antioch—I am not sure why, but the message from the Spirit was very clear."

"I need to know more about your god," Marcus told him.

"I will send a legionary named Titus Afarensus with you," said Cornelius. "He is a member of my household, and a fellow follower of Jesus. He can answer some of your questions along the way."

Marcus nodded, and returned to the tavern. "Load your gear," he told Cassius and the others. "We leave for Antioch within the hour."

CHAPTER X

The ride to Antioch was a nightmare. They moved swiftly, stopping for three or four hours at a time to snatch some desperately needed sleep. Every few days they would pause for eight hours, to rest the horses and switch them out and give the men a decent rest. The legionaries that Cornelius had dispatched to protect them were professional and courteous to a fault; partly out of their respect for their centurion, partly out of fear of the quaestor. Any man who had the authority to flog and behead a proconsul was obviously not someone to be trifled with.

The litter they had contrived to carry Cadius in was really just a glorified stretcher with a canopy—it was lightweight, and the boy's small size made him a negligible burden. The legionaries took turns carrying him, four at a time, and they rolled down the ancient Persian road from Ancyra to Antioch at a swift pace.

For the first day or two, Cadius was alert and conscious. He was weak, but his eyes took in the strange sights, and he asked Marcus and the soldiers who were carrying him questions about the region and its people. But after the second day, the wound began to suppurate. Instead of red, the stain on his bandages turned brown and then black; the wound emitted a foul stench when the dressings were changed. Fever racked the lad's body, and he passed in and out of consciousness, crying at times for his mother or father. Those cries tore at Marcus' heart. By the fifth day, Cadius lost consciousness altogether. As his wound continued to fester, he wandered in a deep sleep, his body shedding weight and his face growing paler and paler. He would sip water if it was put to his lips, but not a bite of food or a sip of broth would he take. At times, his countenance looked so deathlike that Marcus held a piece of polished silver to his lips to see if he still breathed.

Yet, miraculously, he held onto life. He sank to a point at death's door and seemed to pause there, unwilling to pass through until the party arrived at their destination. Marcus recalled the words

Cornelius had spoken and prayed they were true, even though he had no idea who he was praying to.

They were two days away from Antioch, eating dried fish and dates on a quick rest stop, when one of the legionaries approached Marcus. He was obviously nervous, but determined to speak. Marcus nodded at him, and he asked his question.

"Sir, no disrespect intended, but the lads and I were wondering something," he said.

"What would that be?" Marcus replied.

"Well, sir, what's the point?" the soldier asked, nodding at the litter, which they had set down under the shade of a cedar tree. "The boy is a goner. Even if he lives until we reach Antioch, no *medicus* on earth can save him. His guts are already rotting."

Marcus sighed, running his hands through his thinning hair. Funny, he thought, it had been full and shaggy when he left Rome. He looked at the soldier and replied.

"Legionary, that fourteen-year-old boy saved my life. He took a blade that was meant for me. He was never meant to be a slave—his parents were free Romans who fell victim to the cruelty of a madman, and he wound up in the slave markets. He's been by my side for two years, serving faithfully and never complaining. My wife died trying to bring my first child into the world. I've never remarried and have no children of my own. Cadius is the closest thing I have ever had to a son." He paused a moment, fighting back tears. "Your centurion, Cornelius, has assured me that this Paul of Tarsus can save him. I don't know if he can or not—frankly, I don't know what to believe about any of this Nazarene nonsense. But if there is even the smallest chance that this boy's life can be saved, I'm going to do all I can. And so will you. Once we arrive at Antioch, you and your men are free of my command and can return to Ancyra at your leisure, with my thanks and with my gold in your purses. But till then, we press on every single day until we reach our goal—or until the boy dies. Is that clear?"

The legionary nodded. "Aye, sir!" he said. "I was not in Judea when the Nazarene sect started, but I have heard strange things. Cornelius is a good centurion, and the Nazarene carpenter seems to be god enough for him. Mayhap one of the disciples of this Jesus can do something no *medicus* can accomplish."

"Mayhap," Marcus agreed. "Are the men rested enough?" The soldier nodded. "Then let's move," he said, and they set out again.

As the soldiers marched along the dusty road, Marcus rode his horse up next to the litter for a moment and surveyed Cadius' face. The boy was just as thin and pale as he had been for the last three days, but the pained expression had slowly given way to some semblance of peace. Marcus hoped it was an indication of improvement, but feared that it was the hand of death cutting off the ties that bound the boy to the world of the living.

One of the soldiers carrying the litter looked up at the quaestor.

"I've been praying for him since we left Ancyra, sir," he said. "The boy will still be alive when we reach Antioch."

Marcus looked at the legionary. The man was a veteran, nearing forty years of age. His skin was deeply tanned and there were crinkles around his eyes, but there was an air of kindness about him. Suddenly Marcus realized who he was talking to.

"You must be Titus Afarensus," he said.

"That is me, sir. Cornelius asked me to stay close to the boy and lift him up in prayer throughout our journey," the man said.

Desperate to take his mind off of Cadius' pale, wax-like face, Marcus hopped off his horse and took one corner of the litter from the legionary walking behind Titus. "Why don't you ride ahead and look for water," he told the man.

"Aye, sir, and thanks!" the man said, swinging onto the horse and riding off.

"So you are a Nazarene, too?" he asked Titus.

"Yes, sir, although most of us call ourselves Christians now. Cornelius and I served together under Pontius Pilate, and both of us were in Jerusalem the week it all started," he said.

"Tell me all about it," Marcus said, his curiosity temporarily overriding his concern for Cadius.

For the next two hours, he listened, enthralled, as Titus told him the story of a Passover week nearly twenty years before.

"I was a young replacement, just arrived in Judea from Rome. That was when old Tiberius was still emperor, and Pontius Pilate was prefect," he explained.

"What manner of man was he?" Marcus asked.

"A good commander, very competent, and by all accounts a brave soldier and general," said the legionary. "But he carried some deep personal grief or grudge that made him very temperamental. He had taken an arrow through the knee in a raid on a Zealot stronghold some time before, and still walked with a bit of a limp. They said he was a regular bear for a year or so afterward. I barely knew him, you understand—he was a former consul and provincial prefect, and I was a green recruit. I went out of my way not to be noticed by him, truth be told."

"Like any good soldier, I suppose," said Marcus.

"Like any new soldier is more like," the legionary said with a chuckle. "We had a first-rate centurion, name of Cassius Longinus, who was thick as thieves with the governor. He had taken a Jewish wife, and understood the local culture very well—he'd even taken to worshipping the Jew's invisible god. He and the prefect were keeping a very close eye on this mystical preacher and healer named Jesus, from a town in Galilee called Nazareth—hence, Nazarene, you see."

"So I do," Marcus said. "Go on."

"Well, the Jewish priests were terribly upset with this Jesus. They had been after the prefect to arrest him for some time, but Pilate was about sick of them and told them to do their own dirty work. During the Passover feast, they managed to pay off one of Jesus' disciples—

a shifty fellow by the name of Judas—to betray his whereabouts at night, when he didn't have a huge throng all around him. They arrested him in a garden outside the city, dragged him before the High Priest, and roughed him up pretty good, then declared him guilty of blasphemy. Under their law, that merited a death penalty. However, their right to administer the ultimate punishment had been rescinded by the Senate and entrusted to the governor of the Province. So, shortly after midnight, here they came, a huge, screaming mob of angry Jews, dragging this bedraggled prophet before them, and hollering for Pilate to have him crucified," the man said. "That's where I come into the story. I was a guard in the Praetorium at the time. I saw the whole trial—and I will tell you something, old Pilate was in the hot seat that night! He wanted no part of killing Jesus—he was convinced of the man's innocence. But he was in bad light with the emperor then, and the Jews knew it. They'd reported him to Caesar a few years before, I heard. Eventually, he washed his hands of the whole affair, and told Longinus to take some of us and nail Jesus up outside the city walls."

"You were there when he was crucified?" Marcus asked.

"Yes I was, and it was the worst thing I ever did—the worst thing I ever saw!" the main said with deep emotion. "He never cursed us, and only screamed once—when we drove the nails into his hands and feet. After we dropped the cross into its shaft, he cried out to his Father to forgive us. Sir, I've done many things I'm not proud of in my life, but hearing that Galilean ask God to forgive us after what we had done to him—I'll be honest, I didn't want to be forgiven at that point. All I wanted was to be drunk so I could forget that awful day. I swilled wine all afternoon, and the others did too. But an ocean of wine couldn't drown out the memories. The sky turned black—no clouds, no eclipse, nothing like that. But the sun went out for a while, as if it had turned its back on us. Claps of thunder sounded, even though there was not a cloud to be seen. Then, when he finally breathed his last, about three hours past noon, the earth shook beneath our feet. It was the worst quake I ever felt in my life. Then, just as suddenly, the sun came out again, the earth was still, the thunder ceased, and all you could hear was the weeping of these women who had come to stand by Jesus as he died. Old Longinus looked at the cross—some Jewish scribe was trying to tell him something, I couldn't make it out—and he turned on the man and shouted, 'This was the Son of God, surely—and we've killed him! We murdered a god today!'"

Titus gave a long sigh. "Some of Jesus' folks wanted to take his body down from the cross and bury it before dark, but Longinus, as rattled as he was, wouldn't let them do it until we made sure. He grabbed my lance and drove it through Jesus' chest, right into his heart. I was standing there, sir, I saw it. Blood and water flowed from the wound, but Jesus never so much as twitched. On my life, sir, he was as dead as any man was ever killed. Then his friends cut his body down and took it away. Their weeping was something to behold! They knew that this was no ordinary man we had crucified that day, but there was something so hopeless about their cries I could barely listen. Not long after that, we finished off the other two that we crucified—broke their legs to hasten the end, since the Jews didn't want dead bodies hanging outside the city walls during their Passover."

He paused a moment. "Now, I wasn't out there at the tomb that Sunday morning, but I talked to the three legionaries who were. Carmello Antonius told me himself what happened. The tomb was sealed, and there were about twenty of the Jews' temple guards standing watch over it. Carmello, Decius, and Tiberius were watching them from a distance. It was as quiet and still as could be, when suddenly a blinding light came down from the sky right before dawn and hovered in the air over the tomb. The Jews fell down like dead men, and Carmello and the others were trying to get closer to see what was happening. He told me the last thing he saw was the light splitting in half, and two manlike forms beginning to solidify next to the tomb—then one of them looked at the three legionaries, and they collapsed too. Next thing you know, it's daylight, the tomb is wide open, the huge stone they'd rolled across the entrance was lying several yards away, and the body of Jesus was nowhere to be found."

"You believe this?" Marcus asked him. "It sounds like a spectacular myth of some sort."

"Sir, Carmello Antonius was as tough and steady a soldier as I have ever known, and he was terrified when he got back to the fortress of Antonia," Titus said. "If you had seen and heard him, you would believe it too. By the next morning, the city was full of reports that Jesus had been seen alive, walking with his disciples on a road outside the city. He even appeared to one of his own brothers, a fellow named James, and to his closest disciple, Simon Peter—a man who had run out on him and denied him the night he was arrested."

Marcus shook his head. "Titus Afarensis, you know that dead men stay dead!" he said.

"Aye," said Titus, "that they usually do. But this Jesus was no ordinary man. I was skeptical, too—then Longinus saw Him!"

"He appeared to a Roman centurion?" Marcus asked incredulously.

"Not just any centurion, sir, but the same man who led His crucifixion detail!" Titus said. "Longinus was eaten up with guilt over the whole affair, and determined that he would fall on his sword not long after the crucifixion. He sent his wife and servants away, and made ready to end his life—and suddenly, inside his locked bedroom, Jesus was standing there. He asked Longinus to become one of His disciples, and so he did. Left the legions that same day, and never looked back."

"And you followed him?" Marcus asked.

"No, sir, I stayed on, although I thought long and hard about what all of it meant," Titus said. "They promoted Cornelius to centurion not long after that, and I was assigned to his century. We served together for several more years—then one day, Cornelius had a dream in which he was commanded to send a messenger to Joppa to find a man named Simon Peter. He sent me and another legionary to go and bring this man to him, and we did. Peter came along willingly, and when we got back to Caesarea, Cornelius asked us to stay and listen to the Galilean. Peter got up before us and explained how he, too, had a vision right before we arrived, directing him to come with us peacefully and share the truth with us. Then he told us all about Jesus, why He came when He did, why He had to die, and why He rose again."

"And why was that?" Marcus asked.

"Why, to save us," the man said. "This whole world is broken by human sin and wickedness, and none of us are fit to stand before God. Jesus gave His life on that cross in order to make atonement for us—a sacrifice to God for the sins of the whole world! That's why we call him the Lamb of God. Every single one of us was baptized that night, and I've been a believer in Jesus the Christ ever since."

Marcus looked at him with considerable wonder. This was the first time he had knowingly met someone who belonged to this new religion, supposedly a refuge for all kinds of foreign fanatics, and the man was a fellow Roman, a solid soldier, and seemingly as sane as he could be! Perhaps there was something to this new faith, after all. This train of thought led him to another question.

"What do you know about this Saul of Tarsus we are going to see?" he asked.

"Well now, there is a story in itself," said the legionary. "He was the youngest member of the Jews' Sanhedrin—that's their version of our Senate, a supreme legal counsel. He was abroad when Jesus was tried before them, but got back just in time to see the Apostles—that's what we call those who were personally appointed by Jesus to lead our movement—preaching and healing in Jerusalem. At first, the Jews were so flummoxed when Jesus returned from the dead they had no clue what to do. It was Saul who began to stiffen their resolve, and soon great persecutions broke out. Herod Antipas, the tetrarch, had one of the Apostles beheaded—James, the son of Zebedee. Then one of the church's leaders, a fellow named Stephen, was stoned to death by an angry mob of Jews for preaching about Jesus. Saul, he held their cloaks while they threw the rocks!"

"Wait a minute!" Marcus said. "I thought this Saul was a leader of the Nazarenes—I mean, the Christians!"

"So he is, now," Titus said. "How he got there—it's a long story! You see, he got warrants from the High Priest to travel to every city in Judea and even up into Samaria and Galilee and arrest any believers he could find, and bring them back to Jerusalem for trial. Old Caiaphas, he was a happy man—he thought he'd finally found an agent to root out and destroy the Way of Jesus. Saul was breathing threats and murder as he and his lackeys rode up towards Damascus. That's when it happened."

"What happened?" Marcus asked.

"Apparently, God had His eye on old Saul the whole time. He and his men were just outside Damascus when a blinding light shone down upon them and they were all knocked flat. Then Jesus spoke to Saul from the sky, informing him that he had been chosen by God to be one of the Apostles, and to carry the name of Jesus Christ to places where it had not yet been heard," Titus explained. "When the light faded and the voice stopped speaking, Saul stood up and found himself to be completely blinded! They guided him into the city, and he spent three days fasting and praying, trying to sort out what had happened to him. On the third day, a follower of Jesus by the name of Ananias came and prayed over Saul, and laid hands on him—and suddenly he could see again!"

"Very dramatic," Marcus said.

"I don't know about that," Titus replied, "but Saul has been an outspoken champion of Christianity ever since. He has debated the Jewish scribes and elders in their own synagogues, showing them from the Scriptures that Jesus is, in fact, the very Messiah they have waited a thousand years for! When the Jews rejected him, he took his message out to the wider world, and has traveled all over the Eastern provinces, preaching the gospel to any who will listen. He just got back from one long journey, and they say he is about to undertake another."

"But don't the other—what do you call them, Apostles?—resent him as an interloper?" Marcus asked.

"They were frightened of him at first," Titus replied. "They thought he was lying about being a believer in order to get in their confidence, and then betray them. But he has endured enough persecution in the name of Jesus that they all accept him as a brother and an equal now."

"Persecution?" Marcus asked. "From who?"

"The Jews, mainly," said Titus. "They can't abide the thought that they may have murdered their own promised Messiah, and a group of them follow Paul around wherever he goes, trying to stir up the people against him. He's been whipped, beaten with rods, even stoned and left for dead on one occasion."

They spent the afternoon talking, and as it drew toward evening, Marcus relinquished his end of the litter to another legionary, reflecting on all he had heard and trying to make sense of it all. There was a deep well alongside the road, and they paused there, drawing water for the weary men and horses. One of the legionaries who had gone ahead to scout came back and reported that they were now only a day away from Antioch. Marcus summoned Titus and asked him a favor.

"You know these people," he said, "and you are known by them. Would you ride ahead of us into Antioch and try to find this Saul or Paul or whatever it is he goes by? I fear Cadius may not last too much longer."

"He will last as long as God wills," said Titus, "but Jesus also said not to tempt God to wrath! I will ride like the wind and be back with you by dawn."

Marcus gave the legionary a swift mare that he had purchased in Ancyra before leaving, and watched as the soldier rode off into the twilight. Jesus, he thought, if you are truly out there watching and listening, speed him safe on his way and bring him back with good news!

The soldiers were tired, and Cadius seemed more fragile than ever, so Marcus ordered the men to spread out their bedrolls and get in a good rest. He told the watch to wake them three hours before dawn, so they could make good use of the coolest hours to travel. He lay down and closed his eyes, and in his dreams, he saw three crucified men on a hill, silhouetted against a dark sky. Soldiers stood at the foot of each cross, and a handful of men and women watched the center cross with devastated expressions. The tortured figure hanging there suddenly arched, straining every muscle against the nails that held him to the rough wood, and a voice cried out in a language that Marcus could not understand: *"Eli, Eli, Lama sabactani!"* Then the figure slumped, and a final whispered phrase escaped his lips. The earth began to shake, and the shaking continued until Marcus realized it was the night watch shaking him awake.

He stumbled upright and rinsed his mouth out with water, then ate a quick bite of bread and dried fish. His knees groaned in protest as he mounted his horse, but in a matter of minutes he and the others were underway again, four legionaries carrying the litter with Cadius' limp but still breathing form inside..They marched and rode in silence for a while, and eventually the sky began to grow lighter, and the first rays of the sun eased over the distant hills. A half hour or so later, they saw a rider approaching from the south. Marcus shaded his eyes and recognized the horse he had loaned Titus the night before. A few minutes later, the exhausted legionary rode up to him.

"A good thing you sent me, sir—Paul was supposed to board ship this morning, along with several other believers, on another voyage," he told the quaestor.

"Will he wait for us to arrive?" Marcus asked anxiously.

"Wait?" the man chuckled. "Paul is not much for waiting. He and several others are coming out to meet you. They are only a few hours behind me. God is good, Marcus Quintus—one of the men who was in Antioch to see Paul and his friends off is none other than John, the son of Zebedee. He was one of the original twelve disciples of Jesus, and God has given him great powers to heal sickness and grievous wounds."

Marcus bowed his head in gratitude for a moment, and then turned to the legionaries. "Well, men, you have been steadfast and uncomplaining," he said. "It seems to me that our journey is nearly done. Give me one last good burst of speed, and I shall reward you well in Antioch!"

The legionaries gave a hoarse cheer and picked up their pace. Marcus rode out ahead of the group, anxiously surveying the road ahead to see if he could make out the group Titus spoke of. It was still two hours short of noon when he spotted the group, all on foot, making their way north toward him. He looked over at Titus for confirmation, and the soldier gave him a quick nod. Marcus then spurred his horse, riding out ahead of the group to meet the man he had heard so much of.

There were eight of them, six men and two women, walking rapidly up the road to meet Marcus' party. They stopped when they saw him approach. He rode up to them and dismounted, walking forward. Three older men stood in front to greet him, and three younger men held back. The two women brought up the rear.

Marcus surveyed the three leaders. One was perhaps in his fifties; he was bald and had a beetling brow and a slight hunch to his back. His face was seamed with scars, but his eyes held a piercing intelligence, and his mouth seemed that it would be equally quick to smile or scowl. His nose was a sharp, hooked rudder that steered a middle course between the two. The other man was taller and more slender; he was in his forties and wore a full beard. His expression was serene, his eyes such a dark shade of brown they appeared black, and a slight smile played upon his lips. The third man was clean-shaven and had the olive complexion and blue eyes of a Greek; he wore a simple tunic with a threadbare robe draped over his shoulders.

Both of the men seemed to defer to the balding man in the middle, so Marcus made a guess. "Are you Paul?" he asked.

"I am," the man answered. "Paul, a son of Israel of the tribe of Benjamin, also known as Saul ben Issachar, a citizen of Rome and a native of Tarsus in Cilicia."

"I am Quaestor Marcus Quintus Publius, a senator of Rome, and emissary of the Emperor Claudius Caesar," Marcus replied with equal formality. "I thank you for coming. I have heard that you have the power to heal, and my young companion has great need of your help."

"It is God who has the power to heal, Marcus Quintus," said the bearded man. "We only have the honor to be his vessels in this world. I am John, the Son of Zebedee, called to be an Apostle of Jesus Christ."

"I meant no offense," Marcus said. "I have only the slightest familiarity with your beliefs."

Paul smiled, and his scarred, creased face lit up. "No offense taken, my friend," he said. "Titus has told me of the situation. Introductions to the others can wait for the moment. Please, show us to the lad."

Marcus' companions had by now nearly caught up to them, and so he led Paul and John to the litter, tossing the reins of his horse to one of the legionaries. His heart dropped when he looked at Cadius—the face was turning gray, and the breath was so faint he could not hear it. For a moment, he despaired of the boy's life. But then the lips parted, and a faint sigh escaped from the blue-gray lips. Life lingered still.

"Can you help him?" he asked.

John looked for a long time at the limp figure, then at Paul, and finally at Marcus.

"He is beyond all human aid," he said. "But God can accomplish anything for those that love Him. Are you a lover of God, Marcus?"

Marcus did not know how to answer the question. Finally, he said, "I do not even know your God. But I will love anyone who can restore this boy to life and health."

"Then let us pray for him, that God's will might be done," the Apostle told him.

Marcus retreated a few steps and watched, and the two men stepped up on either side of the litter. John laid one hand on the child's brow, and Paul laid a hand upon the stained, malodorous bandage that covered his midriff. Their eyes met for a moment, and each raised their free hand to the heavens. Paul closed his eyes and prayed silently, while John stared straight into the sun and spoke softly, but distinctly.

"Lamb of God, you told us once, long ago, that wherever two or more gathered in your name you would be with us. You said that if we agreed on earth, then the heavens themselves would respond to our prayers. Dear Jesus, my friend and Messiah, heal this wound and restore this boy's life, I pray, that your name may be glorified in him from this day forward," the Apostle said.

Marcus watched, torn between skepticism and awe. But as he looked at the boy's face, he saw a flush of color return to his cheeks. The chest began to rise and fall more regularly, and the pallor of death began to recede. The stench of infection was replaced with a faint aroma of roses, seemingly borne across a long distance by a sweet, warm breeze. Paul and John grew visibly paler for a moment, tensing and then relaxing as some invisible power welled up in them, then passed through them and into the boy's body. Finally, they lowered their arms and removed their hands from him, and Cadius opened his eyes and sat up.

His eyes roamed aimlessly for a moment, then fixed on Marcus.

"Dominus?" he asked. "Where am I? And who put these stinking rags around my middle?"

Marcus strode to the boy's side and wrapped him in a warm embrace, not caring who saw him weep.

CHAPTER XI

Marcus sat across the table from the Cadius and watched in astonishment as the teen finished his third bowl of soup. The bones of a roasted chicken lay on the plate next to him, and the rind of a loaf of bread that had been devoured along with it. The teenage boy had been eating for nearly an hour straight, ever since they had arrived at the inn on the edge of Antioch. Other than a matching pair of white scars on his back and belly where the blade of the *gladius* had passed clean through his abdomen, he bore no trace of the wound that he had sustained, or of the infection that had nearly killed him. He had no memory of anything that had transpired since the moment of the attack.

The small band of Christians sat at the next table, talking among themselves as they dug into the meal Marcus had bought them—the only reward their leaders would accept for saving the boy's life. John and Paul were watching Marcus with obvious amusement as he continued to stare at Cadius in disbelief. Their other companion, Silas, whispered something and John threw back his head and laughed.

On the other side of the tavern, most of the legionaries who had escorted Marcus to Antioch were clustered around three tables, talking quietly among themselves. The miraculous healing of a boy whom they had all given up for dead had shaken them badly; Titus was explaining to them how God had used Jesus to make such things possible. On the way down, most of the soldiers had been dismissive and even mocking of their companion's embrace of this new religion; now they were listening intently, and some were nodding.

Marcus was still unsure what to think about the whole thing. There was no doubt in his mind that Cadius would have died before sunset, but how his badly wounded and deeply infected body could have been restored to health and wholeness so rapidly was beyond the quaestor's understanding. He had tried to urge Cadius to slow down in his feeding a time or two, but the looks he got in return were so mournful that he gave up and told the innkeeper to continue bringing food until the boy was full. Recognizing that might be a while yet, he left Cadius to his meal and walked over to the small group of Christians.

"Join us, Your Excellency!" said Paul, scooting down to make room on the bench.

"Please, just call me Marcus," the Roman replied as he took a seat.

"I'm not even going to ask how you did whatever it was you just did," Marcus said, "but I want you to know how grateful I am."

"We did nothing," said John. "God healed the boy. We were merely vessels for His glory."

"I had been planning to leave with Silas here for the last week," Paul said, "but contrary winds kept our ship in port until today. I see now why God delayed our departure."

"I just want you to know, Paul of Tarsus—and you, also, John of Galilee—that if either of you ever need anything from me, I am at your service. I am an advocate, a senator, and I have the honor to be a good friend of our emperor, Claudius Caesar. I hope that you will someday do me the honor of letting me repay the debt I owe you for this boy's life," Marcus told them.

"Any service you render should be rendered to God," Paul said. "It is in Him we live and move and have our being."

"I do not know your God," Marcus said. "But I do find myself wanting to know more about Him. A God who heals children is a God that I could learn to love."

"It will be my delight to tell you more about Him," said John.

"I want to know everything you can tell me," said Marcus. "But first, I must apologize. I have been rude in not learning the names of your companions."

"That is easily remedied," John said. "Paul and Silas and me you have already met. The younger of these two ladies is my wife, Miriam. The lady next to her is her older sister, Naomi. The younger men are Naomi's son, Gaius, and the man on the end is Joseph, although most of us call him Barnabas. His young companion is named John Mark."

Marcus studied the group with interest. Miriam was a lovely woman of perhaps thirty-five, beautiful in the classic Semitic fashion: long, gently curled black hair, a sharp aquiline nose, and dark eyes. However, the woman John called her sister did not resemble her at all—her hair was dark, but her complexion much lighter, and her eyes blue. She was nearing fifty years of age or so, but had obviously been a great beauty in her day. Marcus thought she looked far more Roman than Jewish. Curious, he said to her in Latin:

"I do not think you two ladies really shared the same mother!"

She answered him in the same tongue: "Actually, we did, but—" Then she laughed out loud as she realized her mistake. "Well done, sir!" she said. "You have detected our small subterfuge. Miriam is indeed my dear sister in Christ, but we are not related by blood."

"Nor by nationality," Marcus said. "I know the accents of the Capitoline Hill when I hear them! You are a highborn lady of Rome, unless I mistake myself greatly."

She nodded. "In another life, I was named Procula Porcia," she said. "I am the widow of—"

"Pontius Pilate!" Marcus exclaimed. "Of course! And I would guess that this young man is his son?"

Gaius looked at Marcus with suspicion. "And if I am?" he said.

"Then we both lost our fathers to the cruelty of Gaius Caligula," Marcus said. "Believe me, son, I am no enemy to you or your mother, or anyone at this table."

"My father told me to take the name Gaius right before he died," the young man said. He was tall and slender, but was well-muscled. "I was born Decimus Pontius Pilate."

"Your father is still well spoken of in Rome by those who remember him," Marcus said. "I am surprised to find the two of you among the followers of the man your father crucified, however."

"Forgiveness is part of our creed," John said. "Jesus said if we do not forgive one another, then neither can the Father in Heaven forgive our sins. Pilate himself sought refuge among us after Caligula became emperor, and we gave it readily. He died believing in the name of Christ."

"Pilate died as a Christian?" Marcus said. "That is the most remarkable thing I have heard yet!"

Porcia smiled sadly. "He fought against it very hard," she said. "He was a good man, but there was a ruthless streak in him—he could be cruel at times, although never to those he loved. It took a great deal for him to humble himself before our Savior."

John nodded. "I baptized him myself," he said. "But he did not want it to be known that he had become a believer. He said he did not deserve to be forgiven at all, and would rather be remembered as the man who sent our Master to the cross rather than as a man who became a disciple when he ran out of other options. But when Caligula's Praetorians came after us, it was Pilate who sacrificed himself so that Miriam, Naomi, Gaius, and I could escape. The master said, 'Greater love has no man than this—that a man lay down his life for his friends.' Pilate lived out those words."

Marcus nodded again, and then he looked at Porcia with renewed respect. "Madam," he said, "our emperor, Claudius, has devoted much of his energy and attention to righting the wrongs perpetrated by Caligula. I have no doubt that if you wished to return to Rome, he would most assuredly do justice for you and your son."

Porcia looked at him sadly. "There was a time when I longed for that more than you can know," she said, "but that time is past. This is my home now, and the disciples of Jesus are my family. I serve, I teach other women about the Gospel, and I enjoy being a mother to my son."

Marcus nodded. "Of course I will honor your choice," he said. "But I am curious—I have heard this world 'gospel' used in reference to Christianity several times. I know my Greek, and the literal meaning is plain—but what is its significance to you followers of Jesus?"

"The teachings of Jesus are good news for all of mankind," said John. "That word has become our brief way of referring to our entire message, that Jesus was the Son of God who died and rose again in order to take away the sins of the world."

"Marcus Quintus, I asked you a question when we first met you outside the city," Paul said. "Now that your lad is whole and safe, I will pose it to you again. Are you a lover of God, my friend?"

Marcus thought long and hard on that question. "Your God gave life back to this young man, who is like a son to me," he said. "How can I not love Him?"

Paul nodded. "In time, you will come to love God for who He is, not for what He has done for you," he said. "That has been my path, at least. Now, are you willing to be baptized in the name of Jesus, and accept him as your Lord?"

"My friend, I am not quite ready to take that step yet," Marcus said. "I will confess I wish to learn more about your Jesus before I commit myself to believe in Him as a God."

"I hope God grants you as much time as you need to make your decision," Paul said. "But be aware—none of us is guaranteed so much as another day. We are all like the desert flowers that bloom in the morning, then wilt in the heat of the sun. Do not delay too long."

"When you see me again, Paul, I will gladly accept baptism from you," Marcus said. "I just need time to think about all of this."

"Well, then, Lover of God, until we meet again, may His hand guide you and His will make itself known to you," Paul said. "Grace and peace be with you all, in the name of the Father and His Son Jesus Christ." With that, he excused himself and Silas, and they made their way out the door toward the docks. John and the others remained at the tavern, and after chatting with Marcus for a few moments longer, they made their way across the room to the legionaries seated there. Titus and John spoke for a moment, and then all of them traipsed outside together.

Marcus followed them, curious as to where they were going. They passed through the city gates and headed down toward the Orontes River, upstream from the busy docks. As Marcus watched, six of the legionaries followed John into the swift muddy waters. One by one, he took each of them by the hand and raised his free hand to the sky, intoning a prayer or invocation to Jesus, and then ducked them into the stream, immersing their heads and bodies completely. When they came up out of the water, each of the men embraced the Apostle and walked to the bank. Finally, John himself waded ashore and spoke to the men, then turned and walked toward the sycamore tree Marcus was standing under.

"So that is your baptism?" he said.

"Yes," said John. "It is an outward symbol of what our Lord called being 'born again'—dying to our old sinful self and becoming a new creature in Him."

"Interesting," Marcus said. "In Rome, the followers of Apis are baptized in the blood of a bull when they join the faith."

"The Jews sacrifice vast numbers of animals in their temple every year," John said. "But Jesus was our final sacrifice. His blood, shed on the cross, takes away the sins of the whole world. There is no need for the blood of lambs and calves to appease God's anger anymore—Jesus was the propitiation for all our sins. All the other sacrifices were a portrait of what He would do for us."

Marcus nodded. "I suppose that makes sense," he said. "A God who was willing to sacrifice Himself would not require further sacrifices."

"Paul says that we are a living sacrifice," John replied. "We serve God not with our deaths, but with our lives."

Marcus nodded. "You have given me a great deal to think over today," he said. "I hope that, at some point, I, too, may be of some service to your God."

The Apostle looked at him and smiled again. Marcus could not help but think that there was something majestic about this soft-spoken Galilean who had walked with Jesus. His robes were cheap and frayed, and although his Greek was quite proficient, his accent was purely rural—yet somehow, he radiated a quality that reminded Marcus of the *dignitas* and *arctoritas* associated with the most respected members of Roman society.

Something occurred to him as he stood there. "How many of Jesus' original Apostles are left?" he asked. "It has been nearly twenty years since He was crucified."

"There are nine of us out of the first twelve," he said. "My brother James was the first of us to perish, and Philip was killed in Arabia, trying to preach the Gospel among the Skenites last year. We also reckon Brother Paul, and James the Lord's brother, as Apostles, even though they were called years after us."

"Have you given any thought to how you will preserve your Gospel when all of you are gone?" Marcus asked.

"At first, we truly expected our Master to return for us at any moment," John said. "To this day, I wake up each morning expecting to hear Him summon us home. But I begin to think that it may be a long time yet before He returns for all of those who believe in Him. I know that my road is still long—that much has been revealed to me—but I intend to write down my own account of Jesus before I am taken from this world."

"That would be wise," Marcus said. "I would hate for the words of Jesus to die with you."

"They will not," John said. "The Master told us, while he yet walked among us, that His words would endure forever and ever."

"I have only heard a few bits and pieces of what Jesus taught," Marcus said, "but there is a timelessness about His words that tells me you may be right."

He stood and looked back at the city gates. "I need to go and see how Cadius is doing," he replied. "Then my companions and I have a mission to finish. The emperor has sent me to investigate the governance of the provinces, and I still have long miles to travel."

"I will be in town for another day or two," John said, "And then I am going to return to Jerusalem. Peter and James are waiting to hear that Paul is safely underway. But if you wish to speak further while you remain here in Antioch, you can find me in the Jewish Quarter at the house of a blacksmith named Asher."

Marcus bade him farewell and returned through the city gates to the inn. Cadius was still seated at the table, staring at the wreckage of the six or so meals' worth of food he had devoured since returning from death's door. Rufus was beside him, and Cassius Claudius sat across the table from him, staring in disbelief. The boy smiled when Marcus walked in.

"Hello, *Dominus*!" he said. "I think I may be full now, but I am going to wait a moment and see."

Rufus ruffled the boy's hair. Like everyone in Marcus' entourage, he had grown very fond of Cadius and had been as grieved as Marcus to see him stricken down. Even Cassius, who was more reserved, was grinning widely. The innkeeper came bustling up, wiping his hands on a greasy apron.

"Would you care for anything else, lad?" he asked. "I've got some nice hens I could throw on a spit, and half a rack of lamb that was left from last night's dinner."

Cadius opened his mouth to answer and an enormous yawn split his countenance. "I don't think I can eat anymore right now," he said. "In fact, I am getting rather sleepy!" He yawned again, and like a large tree being sawed by a very lazy woodsman, he slowly toppled over to one side, his face planting onto Rufus' muscular shoulder. In a matter of moments, he was snoring.

Marcus turned to the innkeeper. "It appears as if we shall be needing a couple of rooms," he said. "Rufus, will you carry him off to bed?"

"Gladly, Quaestor!" the big man replied. He lifted the boy on his shoulders as lightly as if Cadius were a five-year-old, and the innkeeper showed them to a set of rooms at the far end of the tavern, behind the stairs. He closed the door behind them, and then came back shaking his head.

"That lad just ate enough for five men!" he said. "Normally I include meals in the cost of a room, Your Excellency, but I am afraid I will have to charge a little extra in your case."

Marcus laughed. "That will not be a problem," he said. "The food smelled excellent, even though I was too upset to eat earlier. I'll take a cup of your best wine and that half rack of lamb you mentioned earlier, and here is something for your trouble!" He tossed the man a few denarii.

"Thank you, Your Excellency. Why on earth did that boy eat so much? Have you been starving him?" he asked.

"He's been through a tough ordeal," Marcus said. "He's been mostly dead for three days!"

The man looked puzzled. "Mostly dead?" he asked.

"I can't think of any other way to describe it," Marcus said. "He was run through with a legionary's *gladius,* right through the gut, just a week ago. We were rushing to get him down here, but the wound was infected and I thought the lad would die for sure!"

"You're having me on!" the man said. "That boy is as healthy as a horse!"

"If you'd seen him a couple of hours ago, you would have been preparing a funeral pyre," Cassius cut in. "I am still not sure how those Nazarenes healed him!"

"Nazarenes—Christians—trouble is what I call them!" the innkeeper said. "Everywhere they go, telling folks that our old gods are no good, and that the only true god is a crucified Galilean tinker! Begging your pardon, Your Excellency, but you'd do better not associating yourself with such folk!"

"Well, they—or their God, I suppose—just pulled my boy back from death's door," Marcus said, "so I am inclined to give them the benefit of the doubt right now."

"If you say so, sir," the man replied, bustling off to the kitchen. He returned a few moments later with the promised lamb, grilled to perfection and basted with a sweet sauce of garlic and honey. It had been expertly seared on both sides to hold in the natural juices, and Marcus was surprised at how vigorous his appetite was after the first bite. He did not pause to talk or take a drink until the last shreds of meat were stripped from the bones. Then he drank his full cup of wine and took a few bites of bread before heaving a deep sigh. His companions looked at him with amusement.

"What?" he finally asked.

"It's good to see you enjoy something again," Cassius said. "Rufus and I were almost as worried about you as we were about young Cadius."

"I was in a very dark place for this last week," Marcus said. "I've grown very attached to that boy. He is like a son to me."

"What did those Nazarenes do?" Cassius said. "I have never seen anything like it. I thought the child was as good as dead!"

"So did I," Marcus said. "But all they did was pray for him. One laid his hand on the boy's head, the other placed it over the wound, and John asked their God to heal him. I've never seen anything like it."

Cassius nodded. "Nor have I," he said. "I've always believed in the gods of Greece, even though many people consider the Olympian deities to be a faded cult from antiquity. But I have never seen Zeus or Apollo respond to a prayer that swiftly or that completely. It makes me wonder if I have been putting my trust in the wrong place all this time!"

"I've racked my brain for the last two hours, trying to come up with a natural explanation for what I saw," Marcus said, "and there isn't one. The God of the Christians healed Cadius—that's the only logical conclusion. For that, He has my gratitude from this day forward. I want to learn as much as I can about Him, and then I intend to join His followers myself."

"I wonder what the emperor will say about your decision," Cassius mused.

"Well, he asked me to find out as much as I could about the Christians," Marcus said. "What better way than to become one?"

"I don't know if that is what he had in mind," Cassius commented.

"Well, I need to sit and write him a long letter," Marcus said. "I have been so preoccupied that I haven't even explained our actions in Ancyra!"

"I dashed off a quick note just before we left," said Cassius, "explaining what had happened and why you acted as you did. But I am sure he is eager to hear a more complete explanation."

Rufus rejoined him about that time, pulling back the bench and seating himself at the table. Marcus always hated eating at taverns and inns—having to sit straight up while consuming food was so barbaric! He missed his dining couches at home, where a man could recline in comfort, and he also missed the lavish dinners he had hosted for friends and clients.

"How is the boy?" he asked his burly bodyguard.

"Snoring like a congested ox," said Rufus. "He didn't even stir when I dumped him onto the bed."

"You don't think he's relapsing, do you?" Marcus asked.

"Oh, no, sir!" the big man replied. "His color is good and his flesh filling out again. I think his body is just repairing itself, finishing the process those Christians started. That's why he consumed so much food—he needed to fuel the fires inside, so his flesh could finish knitting together."

"We were talking about the healing," Cassius said. "Have you ever seen anything like that in your travels?"

"No, sir, and that's a fact!" said Rufus. "That boy was all but dead, and those Jews somehow called him back to life. It would be spooky if it weren't so wonderful, if you take my meaning!"

"They are not Jews, they are Christians!" Marcus said.

"They all looked pretty Jewish to me, except for that older woman and her son," Rufus replied. "Those two looked Roman born and bred!"

"Well, they are all Jews by birth, I suppose," Marcus said, "but not in their religion. They are starting something new in the world of faith, and unless I miss my guess, it will still be around long after they—and we—are gone!"

"You may be right," said the lictor Armenius, joining them at the table. "I have spent the last hour listening to that Titus fellow instruct the legionaries that John baptized. I am halfway thinking about joining them!"

"As am I," Marcus said. "But right now, I am going to write a long letter to the emperor, and then I think I am going to sleep for three days!"

CHAPTER XII

Letter from Claudius Caesar to Marcus Publius, The Ides of July, 50 AD

Tiberius Claudius Caesar Augustus Germanicus, Princeps and Imperator of Rome, to Quaestor Marcus Quintus Publius, Senator and special envoy to the provinces,

Well my young friend, it sounds as if your journey has taken you down some dangerous paths of late! First of all, let me set your mind at ease regarding the actions that you were forced to take during your visit to Ancyra in Galatia. Attempting to murder one of my personal envoys is Great Treason—no different than if Acro and Amelius had tried to assassinate me. I have issued a decree declaring your actions to be legal and proper and in keeping with Rome's ***mos maorum****, and Amelius' cousin, who warned him of your mission, has been voted into exile by the Senate. I appreciate your taking the time to give me a full and detailed account of events, however—knowing exactly what happened, as seen by both you and Cassius, gives me ammunition to reply to those who have tried to tell me that my quaestor has gone too far. A fair warning, however—you may find when you return that your actions have earned you a few enemies in the Senate. The Amelii are an old and powerful patrician family; and all those senators who have engaged or plan to engage in graft and corruption when they govern a province are alarmed that their conduct can draw such swift and severe punishment. That being said, there are many good and decent senators who will now be more likely to ally themselves with you, since you have shown yourself to be such a scourge to the corrupt! That is what they are calling you in the Senate, you know—"the Scourge of the Provinces." I rather like it, don't you?*

The remarkable story of your young servant and his healing is fascinating to me. Does he continue in good health? Does he remember any of what he saw during his time at the brink of death? Do you have any idea how these Christians could possibly be capable of performing such wonders? I'll admit I am more interested than ever in this new faith now. I do not think that the Christians pose any danger to Rome, but any God that can confer such powers on mortal men is a God that I have no desire to offend. If you choose to embrace this new religion, I certainly have no objection. But I do expect your personal loyalty to me and to the Senate and People of Rome to be unimpeded by such a measure. If you find that you cannot be a good Christian and a good Roman at the same time, then please do me the courtesy of telling me so. I would rather remain on good personal terms with you and recruit another agent than have someone whose service to me was compromised by their religion, but unwilling to say so. In the meantime, I would appreciate any further information you can provide on this movement, certainly the most significant religious development I've seen in my lifetime.

Your uncle was elected to the office of Censor this spring by a handy majority; I think he will do the office great credit. His health is good, although he shows his years more now than he did when you left—as we all do, once we pass fifty summers. I have urged him to marry again—there is nothing like a sweet young wife warming the bed to make a man feel young again—but he has no interest in taking another wife, so far as I can tell. I do think that you ought to marry again, however, upon your return to Rome. You have not yet reached forty, and you have a long life ahead of you—too long to spend alone!

I do have a considerable alteration in my instructions to you: I realize now that touring and inspecting all the provinces was too great a task for one small group of men. I have dispatched another young senator, Tiberius Falco, with a similar level of **imperium** *to yours, to inspect the provinces of Arabia and Egypt, and am forwarding this letter to our legate's office in Jerusalem, where I hope you will be by the time it finds you. The incidents along our border with Parthia have been increasing of late and I find myself fearful that Rome may be dragged into another ruinously expensive war in the East. So I am enclosing a personal letter from myself, signed and endorsed by the Senate, offering to make a peaceful settlement. I wish you to personally deliver this message to the Parthian king and bear me back his reply, along with any other message he wishes to convey but does not wish to entrust to paper. If there are any provinces on your itinerary that you have not toured by the time this reaches you, send a letter to Egypt and order*

Falco to complete their inspection. This message to the king of the Parthians trumps all other considerations, and I know that I am entrusting it to a worthy and honest envoy. Vonones, the new king of the Parthians, is by all accounts a seasoned veteran of the intrigues and assassinations that dog the Eastern courts, so be wary of him. Observe him carefully, and inquire of those around him as discreetly as you can as regards his intentions toward Rome. Once you have completed this mission, return to Rome straightaway, where honors and accolades await one who has served his emperor, and the Senate and People of Rome, so well. I hope to see you by next spring, or midsummer at the latest. Till then, my warmest regards and gratitude for your loyal service.

Marcus read the missive carefully, and then looked at the embossed scroll, bearing the emperor's seal and the Great Seal of the Senate, which accompanied it. A mission to inspect and discipline provincial governors was one thing, but to be entrusted with a diplomatic mission to the most powerful Empire in the world other than Rome itself was an honor far beyond anything he had ever imagined. This was the kind of mission that Mark Anthony and Lucius Cornelius Sulla had undertaken in the past! The idea that his name might be mentioned in the same context as theirs was truly breathtaking!

He carried the letter to the room where Cassius Claudius was staying. The freedman was perusing his own scroll from the emperor, but he looked up when Marcus entered and gestured him to sit down while he finished reading. When he was done, he rolled the scroll back up with a flip of his wrist and smiled.

"Well, one more journey, and we can return home, it seems," he said.

"Indeed," replied Marcus. "To Parthia! That is further than I ever thought to go. Have you ever been there?"

"No," said Cassius, "but I did read the account left by Lucius Decimus Brutus, who traveled to Ecbatana during the reign of Augustus. He described the capital in some detail, as well as his travails in reaching it. We will be traveling through some very forbidding country on our way."

"I know that Vonones is now the king, according to Caesar's letter, but last I heard, Vardanes was ruler. Do you know what has transpired since his death?" Marcus asked.

"It's complicated," said the freedman, "but fortunately Herod Agrippa, the son of the old Jewish King Antipas, sent a scroll along with the emperor's giving me a complete description of the current situation. I've already read it—would you prefer to read it yourself, or let me summarize it for you?"

"Both, please," said Marcus. "You have a knack for summing things up, but I would also like to go over the more full information afterward."

"That's an intelligent way to go about it," said Cassius. "I can see why my master favors you so highly. Vardanes was Rome's choice to rule over Parthia after the death of Artabanus III, but his brother Gotarzes thought he had a better claim, and the two fought one another tooth and nail until finally Gotarzes managed to arrange for his brother's 'accidental' death on a hunting expedition. Gotarzes took over, but he was such a bloodthirsty tyrant that the Parthian nobility sent a secret expedition to Rome to ask for the release of the crown prince, Meherdates, who had lived in Rome since he was a teen. They thought that Gotarzes was so hated that the people would rally to any challenger with a blood claim to the crown. Apparently Gotarzes thought the same thing; he arranged for two provincial governors to kidnap Meherdates and bring him to Ecbatana in chains. Once he had the poor prince there, Gotarzes blinded him and cut off his ears. That mutilation disqualified the prince from ever becoming king."

"Goodness!" said Marcus. "And I thought we Romans could be a bloodthirsty bunch!"

"Nothing matches an Eastern potentate for sheer, wanton cruelty," Cassius said. "Romans kill when they have to; these Asians don't just kill—they mutilate and humiliate for both policy and amusement. They said that Gotarzes kept poor Meherdates on a gold chain, like a dog, forcing him to go on all fours and eat out of a bowl on the floor. Apparently, that was too much; Gotarzes was poisoned this spring—some say that it was an illness, but Herod seems to think that his uncle Vonones may have had a hand in it. At any rate, Vonones, the old king's brother, is ruling now, although he has yet to be formally crowned."

"What manner of man is he?" Marcus asked.

"Cautious and sensible, by all accounts," said Cassius. "He has spent most of his life ruling the small kingdom of Media Atropatene as a vassal of his brother, and his nephews. He is in his sixties, and that alone says something—members of the Parthian royal family have notoriously short life spans. If I were to guess, I'd call him a trimmer—one who has always managed to stand with those left standing."

"Interesting," said Marcus. "Many say the same about my uncle, although I don't think the situation in Rome was quite as dire as it sounds like Parthia has been for the last half century or so. Still, Mencius has lived as long as he has by knowing which way the winds of fortune were blowing. This Vonones has apparently done the same thing."

He yawned, and looked at the scroll Cassius was holding. "Did the emperor send you any further instructions?"

The Greek freedman laughed. "Just to watch your back and keep you safe!" he said. "He has become quite fond of you. He recommends we take a full century of soldiers with us to Ecbatana—enough to hold off any bandit raids, but not so many as to appear a threat to the Parthians. He also told you to hire another seven lictors—appearance will be more important than speed on this trip."

"Eight lictors!" Marcus said. "That's a proconsul's escort!"

"You are a personal emissary of the emperor of Rome," said Cassius. "That is the equivalent of proconsular status. Your *dignitas* reflects that of Claudius Caesar himself."

"Well, I suppose you're right," said Marcus. "I will go talk to the prefect at the Praetorium and see about getting some lictors and a century of legionaries."

Ventidius Cumanus was a harried, impatient, and disagreeable man. Nonetheless, he had gone out of his way to accommodate Marcus' inspection of his province. He was not particularly corrupt or incompetent, but he neither understood nor liked the Jewish people he had been sent to govern. He was insensitive to their customs, contemptuous of their religion, and ignorant of their language.

"They say old Pontius Pilate tamed this province," he had told Marcus the previous day, "but gods take me if I know how he did it! There was never a more contrary, ungovernable bunch in all the *gens humana* than these Jews!"

Between the resurgence of the Zealot rebels, the constant persecution of the Christian community in Jerusalem, and the increasingly tense relations between the Jews and the neighboring Samaritans, the prefect of Judea definitely had his hands full. But Marcus' status caused the governor to give him instant access and grudging respect, so now he was quickly shown to the governor's private quarters in the Fortress of Antonia.

"Parthia, eh?" he asked when Marcus explained his change of orders. "Better you than me, I suppose. That's a bloody long way off, through some awfully rough country. Lictors are no problem; I have more than I need at the moment, and I understand the need for appearances. Giving up a century of good troops, though—that is going to hurt, I won't deny it. I have a legion here and another in Caesarea, but both are pretty badly under strength. I don't know how Pilate and the others managed this province with just one legion! Talk about a nightmare!"

"I am sorry to make your life more difficult, Prefect," said Marcus, "but I think that if I tried to cross that desert with a single squad, the vultures would be picking my bones in no time! The bandits are numerous and bold, according to the tales I have heard."

"Merchants have told me horror stories, too," the prefect said. "I am going to give you a century and a half, even though it will weaken our presence here. The last thing Rome needs is another war with Parthia—and I have no desire to be in the path of an invading army! They've penetrated this far before, and left fire and ruin in their wake. I'll ask Manlius Hortensius to command them—he is one of my sharpest centurions, and has an ear for languages. How soon do you need them?"

"I need to write several letters this evening," Marcus said, "and find riders to deliver them. I'll say we leave the day after tomorrow."

"I'll send Manlius to talk to you this evening," the prefect said. "He's a solid soldier and a plainspoken fellow; the two of you should hit if off quite well."

"My thanks, Prefect," said Marcus. "Your cooperation will be reported to the emperor."

"I appreciate it," said Cumanus. "Goodness knows he has probably heard enough bad things about me from the High Priest and his cronies!"

Marcus left the overworked governor behind and returned to his quarters. He dropped by the barracks where the lictors resided and explained that he needed the services of seven of them for the next several months; the chief lictor told him that they would report first thing on the morrow. Returning to his quarters, he drafted a quick letter to Tiberius Falco, explaining his findings in the provinces he had visited and ordering the young senator to pay a quick visit to Mesopotamia and Assyria, two provinces that Marcus had not yet inspected. He would actually cross through both of them on his way to Parthia, but the emperor's new mission did not allow him any time for delay. He also prepared a more formal reply to the emperor's letter, and a third letter to his uncle Mencius, informing him that he should be returning to Rome the following spring or summer.

By the time he was done, the sun was westering in the sky, and Cadius came to his door to see if Marcus wanted to eat in the common room of the tavern, or have something brought up to him.

"Tell the innkeeper to send up two racks of lamb," he said, "and then I want all five of us to eat together. I have some information to share."

"Very well, *Dominus,*" the boy replied. "I'll order supper and then fetch them straightaway. Are we changing our travel plans?"

Marcus laughed. The boy showed absolutely no ill effects from his ordeal in Galatia, and seemed to have grown another two inches that summer. He was now an inch taller than Marcus, and would top Rufus soon if he kept growing.

"Cadius, you are a free man now," he said. "You can quit calling me your master!"

"Well, sir, 'Marcus' seems too familiar, and 'Quaestor' seems too formal," he said. "You were my *dominus* for a good while, and I still feel comfortable calling you that."

"You're incorrigible," Marcus said. "Now go order our supper and bring the others up."

The innkeeper came back up with the boy and told Marcus that he was too important a guest to have to dine with his companions in the small bedroom. He showed them to an upper room at the end of the hallway, far from the tavern's common area, where they could dine in privacy and comfort.

"It's a fine room, this, with room for a group twice as big as yours," he said. "As a matter of fact, have you ever heard of Jesus of Nazareth?"

"I am familiar with the name," Marcus said drily.

"The night before he was crucified, he and those disciples of his ate their last Passover together in this very room!" the man said. "My pap was running the place then, but I brought them their food and cleaned up after them. Do you know that famous rabbi actually dismissed the house slave and washed the feet of his disciples himself? Strangest thing I ever saw. He told them that he wanted them to be servants to each other if they wanted to become great kings, or something like that. Some of his followers are still around—

they rent the room from time to time to hold their meetings. But tonight, you and your friends have it all to yourself."

Marcus looked around. The room had a lovely, low table, and best of all, no beastly chairs anywhere—there were proper couches and cushions to recline on, with one side of the table clear so servants could bring in the food and wine. What a relief to eat like civilized people again!

Within a few minutes, Cassius, Rufus, Cadius, and Armenius had joined him, and they all washed their hands and reclined at the table. Marcus took the center spot, with Cadius at his left hand and Cassius at his right. As he leaned back on the cushions, he briefly wished that he could have been a fly on the wall seventeen years before, when Jesus and his disciples had broken bread in this very room. Then he grinned cynically and wondered how many other innkeepers in the city might regale their guests with tales of how Jesus and his disciples had eaten their last supper at their establishment. He reminded himself to ask John, if he ever saw him again, if this was indeed the place.

The lamb was passable, if not as good as what they had enjoyed at Antioch, but the wine was first-rate, and the fish was grilled fresh. There were hot loaves of bread with olive oil for dipping, and some sort of lentils cooked into a savory stew. The company dug in with gusto, for they had only arrived in Jerusalem two days before, and the road there had featured many hard miles of walking and pretty lean fare. Conversation waited until they were done, by general agreement.

After they were done eating, Marcus poured wine for all four of his companions, and then addressed them.

"I don't know if Cassius has shared anything with you yet or not," he said, "but there has been a change of plans. The day after we arrived in the city, I received a letter from the emperor, bidding me to carry a message from him to the king of the Parthians. Our inspection tour is done, my friends. Once we deliver Claudius' message to Ecbatana and receive the reply of King Vonones, we will return straightaway to Rome. It's been three years and more since we left—I for one will be glad to get back!"

Cadius smiled, but his eyes were wide. "Parthia!" he exclaimed. "Isn't that on the far side of the world?"

"It is beyond the borders of our Empire," Marcus said, "about four hundred miles to the city of Ecbatana, where Vonones rules as king. However, compared to the distance from here to Britannia, it is a mere stroll!"

"That's bandit country, sir," said Rufus. "I don't know if Armenius and I—and Cadius, begging your pardon, lad!—are going to be protection enough."

"That has been addressed," Marcus said. "There will be seven more lictors and a century and a half of legionaries making the trip with us. Bandits will think twice about assaulting such a large party."

"Won't the Parthians think we're invading?" Cadius asked.

"One does not invade an Empire of millions with less than two hundred men!" Marcus said. "I doubt that the *Divus Julius* himself could have pulled that one off. What we have is sufficient protection from brigands and Zealots, but not enough to seem like a hostile force. It's nearly December, so it may well be the end of January before we arrive. But once our errand there is done, home we will go at last—and there will be rewards for each of you when we get there!"

"When do we leave then, sir?" asked Rufus.

"The day after tomorrow," said Marcus. "Here is our purse, Rufus. I want you and Cadius to go down to the stables and buy us some good, swift horses—this is going to be a fast trip!"

The innkeeper came into the room, bowing politely. "Begging your pardon, Quaestor, but there is a centurion here, asking to see you," he said.

"That would be Manlius," said Marcus. "Show him in."

Moments later, a burly centurion about thirty years old walked into the room and gave Marcus the legions' salute. "Hail *Imperator*

Marcus Quintus Publius!" he said. "It is an honor to meet the hero of Pannonia!"

Marcus returned the salute. "I haven't had my triumph yet," he said, "so please don't call me that!"

"Very well, Excellency," said the officer. "But I want you to know you have my highest respect and gratitude for your services to my family. My men and I will get you safely to wherever you wish to go, or die trying!"

"Wait a minute," said Marcus. "What service did I render to your family?"

"You helped my brother Lucius get his home back, by arguing his case in court so well," the man said. "I was in the crowd that day, listening to your oration. Brilliant, sir, simply brilliant!"

Marcus laughed. "It's a long way from the Forum, isn't it, Centurion?" he said. "But we have a long way to travel yet. Do your men know our destination?"

"Ecbatana in Parthia," the man said. "Quite a long haul—it will take us two or three months, depending on the weather. I am anxious to see the place—my grandfather's oldest brother was hauled there as a prisoner after Crassus' defeat at Carrhae. I've often wondered if he survived and made a life there for himself."

"Perhaps we will have a chance to find out," Marcus said. "At any rate, how many of your men will be mounted?"

"We will have half a century of cavalry, and a full century of infantry," he said. "But don't worry. My boys can make fifteen miles a day in good weather and ten when it's bad. We will get there soon enough."

"Most excellent," said Marcus. "I look forward to traveling with you."

"And I likewise, sir," said Manlius, bowing before he made his exit.

"You appear to have gained quite the reputation on this trip, my friend," said Cassius.

"Let's hope this last excursion doesn't ruin it!" Marcus replied with a laugh.

The next day they all visited the markets and shops of Jerusalem, buying up clothes and supplies for the long trip. Winter was coming, and the plains of Parthia could become brutally cold, so Marcus made sure they had fur-lined boots and heavy cloaks in addition to the summer tunics and robes they were wearing. He also took a moment to go and see the Gentiles' Court in Herod's great temple, the epicenter of Jewish worship. As he walked around the vast building, the smell of burning animals filling the air, he heard a familiar voice speaking from the steps of the temple.

"Then Jesus told him: 'Unless a man be born again, he cannot enter the Kingdom of Heaven,'" John was addressing the crowd. "This puzzled Nicodemus mightily, for he had never heard such a saying before. 'How can this be?' he asked. 'Can a man enter his mother's womb a second time, and be born?'"

Marcus stood to one side and listened as John described the conversation between Jesus and a Jewish rabbi, holding the crowd's rapt attention. Only when the Apostle was finished speaking did Marcus approach and make himself known. The Galilean smiled broadly when he saw the quaestor approach.

"Marcus Quintus," he said. "It is good to see you again. Welcome to Jerusalem. Come with me a moment, I'd like to introduce you to someone."

Leaving a disappointed crowd of listeners, he led Marcus out of the temple precincts to the Merchants' Quarter. There stood a large guild hall, and people were standing at the doors and peering in the windows. They had to wait a good while before the crowd began to disperse, and then John led Marcus in.

Standing at the head of the room was a huge, burly Galilean whose shaggy black hair was turning gray. He wore an expression of calm and humility, offset by an aura of underlying strength. John went up and spoke to him, and he smiled broadly and came to greet their visitor.

"Marcus Publius," he said, "I am Simon son of Jonah, but most call me Peter. That was the name our Master gave me. It is an honor to meet you."

"And I am honored to meet one who walked with Jesus," said Marcus, taking his hand.

Something passed between them as their hands met—something Marcus had never experienced before and never would again. There was a rush of images, too fast for him to make sense of, and some sort of current or connection between their minds. It passed in a second or less, but it left the Roman gasping sharply.

"What was that?" he asked, startled.

Peter looked at him intently. "It was the voice of prophecy," he said. "I have heard it before, but seldom so clearly. You will return to Rome with honor, Marcus Publius, and do a great service to God there. But that service to God will cost you your favor with the emperor, and you will fall from your high place. In the end, you will share the Word of God with the whole world, and generations yet unborn will honor your name as a true lover of God."

Marcus was shaken to his core. He had never been the subject of a prophecy before, and did not know what to make of it.

"If your God calls me, I will serve," he said. "I can do no other."

"The call has already been made," Peter said. "You just have not heard it yet. But you will. And one other thing—I will see you again, before my own journey ends, in Rome itself. Now go and fulfill your errand, and return to your emperor. But I fear your time with him will be brief."

CHAPTER XIII

The winter sun was not hot, but it was phenomenally bright, Marcus thought. High overhead, it illuminated the desert landscape harshly, casting black shadows and making the scrub grass and sandy flats so bright one had to squint. Colors were muted, and the whole landscape looked barren. They had left Zeugma behind just a few days before, and in the distance Marcus could make out a small cluster of clay and brick buildings rising out of the plain.

"Is that it?" he asked.

"It is," Manlius Hortensius replied. "Carrhae, the graveyard of Crassus' legions."

Marcus looked across the innocent-looking plains with a shudder. A hundred years before, Marcus Licinius Crassus had led an army over 40,000 strong across this desert in a campaign designed to destroy the Parthian Empire and replenish the public coffers of Rome, drained by years of civil strife—some said that Crassus also hoped to enhance his own fortune, but since he was already the richest man in Rome, Marcus had always doubted that. According to his grandfather, who had briefly known Julius Caesar when he was a young man and Caesar was dictator, Crassus was simply jealous of the great fame that Caesar and Pompey had enjoyed as generals. Pompey had defeated the great rebellion of Sertorius in Spain, and crushed the pirate kingdoms that harassed Roman shipping throughout the Mediterranean. Caesar was winning a string of battles in Gaul that were earning him a fame that exceeded even Pompey's. Of course, Crassus had led the forces that crushed the great slave revolt under Spartacus, but no one remembered that fact twenty years later—or, if they did, they pointed out that crushing an army of runaway slaves was hardly the same thing as conquering three new provinces in Gaul!

So Crassus, sixty years old and hard of hearing, had arranged for his son Publius to detach himself from Caesar's command and join his father on the campaign that would show all of Rome that Crassus was just as great a general as his fellow *triumvirs.* But bad luck had dogged his expedition from the start—one of the tribunes of the plebs had cursed Crassus as he and his legions left Rome, damning him for planning an illegal war of aggression. Then Crassus ignored the advice of the Armenian king, Artavasdes, who had counseled him to take his army by a longer route, through the Caucasus Mountains, and avoid the dry deserts of the Mesopotamian plateau. Despite the king's offer of 16,000 additional troops, Crassus had listened to his advisor, Ariamnes, and led his men straight into the forbidding desert, the shortest possible route to Ecbatana. Unknown to Crassus or his son, Ariamnes was in the pay of the Parthian King Orodes II and was leading the Romans into a trap.

In the plains that Marcus now rode over, a combined cavalry force of cataphracts—the fearful armored horses and riders that could cut right through a shield wall without harm—along with hundreds of mounted archers, had attacked Crassus' numerically superior force. Crassus and his men endured a brutal rain of arrows that never seemed to run out, and were unable to defend themselves from the cataphracts and attack the archers at the same time. Publius Crassus had led a force of Roman and Gallic cavalry to attack the mounted bowmen, but he and his men were cut off and isolated by the cataphracts, and Marcus Crassus, the richest man in Rome, had been forced to endure the sight of his son's head on the end of a spear before sunset. That had broken him. He asked for terms from the Parthians the next day, and during the meeting between him and the emissaries of General Surena, the Parthian commander, a scuffle had broken out, and Rome's *triumvir* had died from a Parthian sword driven through his belly. Of all his mighty legions, only 10,000 men had escaped death or captivity, and all seven of their eagle standards were captured by the Parthian army.

Cadius came and stood by Marcus' side. About a hundred yards in front of them, a dry gulch wound through the sand and scrub. Marcus pointed it out.

"I imagine that is what is left of the stream where Crassus and his men paused before the battle began," he said. "Most of the fighting would have been on the far side."

With that, the party mounted and began riding forward again. Behind them, the infantry legion resumed its march, while the cavalrymen rode out ahead, scouting the way to the village.

"I heard when I was a lad that the Parthians killed Crassus by pouring molten gold down his throat," Rufus said.

"The survivors who came back to Rome years later said he was already dead when they did that," Marcus replied. "They also said that there was a fat centurion in the legion who looked a good deal like Crassus. The Parthians dressed him up in Crassus' best suit of armor, paraded him through the streets of Ecbatana, then stripped him and put him in a woman's dress before cutting him to pieces in front of a screaming mob."

"Barbarians!" said Cadius. "That is no way to treat a vanquished hero!"

"It is certainly not the Roman way," Marcus said. In a Roman triumphal parade, the conquered kings of the enemy marched in full royal regalia behind the general who had bested them, with all the trophies of war on display on wagons and rolling platforms behind them, followed by the victorious legions. After the parade was over, the captive chiefs could be released and enrolled as client kings under Rome's dominion, or, if they were regarded as a continued threat, they could be taken into the Tullarium, the ancient Roman temple of war, and strangled privately—but they would never be publicly humiliated. Rome wanted its citizens to see that their champion had vanquished a worthy foe, not a disgraced vagabond.

"What's that?" Cadius asked, pointing at the ground. A metallic gleam was shining up from the sand.

Marcus slid off his horse and knelt in the sand, brushing it aside with his hand. The gleam of gold was unmistakable—as were the dried-out leather and steel rings it was attached to. A Roman centurion's cuirass lay buried in the desert floor before them. Marcus cleared away enough sand to grab it by the collar, and when he heaved on it, he was able to lift it free of the sand and gravel that had covered it. He saw that it was still occupied—a bare skull was protruding from the depression it had left in the sand, and he could see the dull white vertebrae and ribs inside the armor as the sand poured out of it. There was a single hole in the leather, just below the shoulder blade, with the broken shaft of an arrow protruding from it. He let the remains go with a shudder.

"He must have tried to flee when he saw the battle was lost," Marcus said. "Or perhaps he was a courier, sent to ride back towards Syria for reinforcements. But whether he was a hero or a coward, or just a man desperate to survive, death found him nonetheless. And now this wasteland is his grave."

He turned to the legionaries behind him. "Collect these bones," he said, "and any other Roman remains we find. They have lain here as spoil for the beasts too long. When we make our camp tonight, we will give them a proper Roman funeral pyre, so that their spirits can rest in peace. Now let us move on, and leave this accursed place behind us!"

They marched as quickly as they could through the harsh desert that lay between them and the village of Carrhae, where Crassus had spent his last night alive after his son's death. Marcus had no desire to stay at that ill-fated place, so when a local informed the Romans that there was a spring five miles ahead, he led the century onward. Despite their hurry, though, the men spotted and collected another dozen or so skeletons, all wearing the remains of Roman armor. They were respectfully loaded into the wagons and carried along. Two hours before dark, they halted by the banks of the small stream. A cluster of palm trees grew around it, and the water was sweet and clear.

Marcus was loath to cut any living wood when there were so few trees growing there, but a quick search located two dead trees, felled by age or wind some time before. He ordered the men to cut the wood up and stack it neatly, and then they arranged the bones of Crassus' legionaries on top of the pile, still clad in the remnants of their armor. The legionaries, both cavalry and infantry, formed up before the pyre. Marcus lit a torch and stood next to it, before the assembled men.

He hesitated for a moment. In his heart, he had already embraced the God of the Christians, but these men were Romans, citizens of the old Republic, steeped in the worship of the ancient gods of Rome. Surely, he thought, a God who chose to incarnate Himself in the form of a gentle carpenter would not be offended if he honored these brave, fallen souls in the way that they would have wanted? He hoped that was the case, at least.

"Legionaries and citizens," he began, "we have gathered here the bones of brave men, who fell serving their general and the Senate and People of Rome to the very end of their lives. Long have their bones lain here, parched by the desert, their flesh food for scavengers, their restless spirits unable to pass into eternity. In the name of the gods of Rome, of the gods they worshipped, of Jupiter Optimus Maximus and Mars Invictus, and of the goddesses of hearth and home, of Juno and Vesta, I commit their mortal remains to the flames. May their spirits find rest, and may their ashes be returned home at last, where I shall erect a tomb to house them, that all of Rome may know that these legionaries, who died at Carrhae in the service of Marcus Licinius Crassus, have come home at last!"

With that, he thrust the torch into the dry wood, which caught right away. The desiccated bones burned quickly, and in less than a half hour, the pyre and its long-dead occupants were consumed. Marcus then dismissed the men to pitch their tents. The centurion Manlius approached him as the legionaries went about their business.

"That was well done, sir," he said. "The men have been grumbling ever since they knew that we would be passing over that accursed spot, but now they are bursting with pride at the thought that we will be bringing some of Crassus' men home."

Marcus nodded. "It was the least I could do," he said. "The minute I saw the bones, I realized what was needed."

Rufus had been standing there listening, but after Marcus was done, he spoke up.

"One thing you will learn about Marcus Quintus Publius, Centurion," he said. "He has a knack for understanding what needs to be done—and doing it!"

Manlius laughed. "So I have heard," he said. "Do you know what they call you behind your back, Quaestor?"

"What would that be?" Marcus asked.

"The scourge of the provinces!" the centurion replied. "They mean it in a good way, though, I think."

Marcus raised an eyebrow. "The scourge of the provinces, eh? The emperor told me the same thing," he said. "I rather like it."

Cadius came trotting up as the three men conversed. "Your tent is ready, *Dominus*," he said. "The cooks are preparing supper. Will you be dining with Cassius Claudius and the rest of us?"

Marcus thought a moment. "No," he said. "Not yet, at least. I want to walk among the legionaries and visit with them a bit. I will join you in an hour or so—if I go much longer, come and find me."

The century did not build a fortified camp, as a full legion would. Instead, each squad of ten carried a tent big enough for all its members to sleep in, and now fifteen such tents were scattered across the desert along the edge of the tree line. The soldiers had taken the time to fill their water bottles completely, and many were already going back for seconds—in this terrain, no one knew where the next fresh water source might be found. Marcus circulated among them, thanking them for their service, answering their questions, and listening to their comments. He was pleasantly surprised at how highly they had come to regard him. They had been riding and marching together for ten days now, but his choice to pause and pay proper respect to the fallen of Carrhae, after a full century, had endeared him to these hard-bitten veterans.

"My father was a cremator for one of the *mortis collegia* in Rome," said a young legionary named Decimus Octavius. "When the fires have burned out, I will gather the ashes into an urn and deliver them to you."

"I thank you," Marcus said. "I was going to ask someone to do that. Perhaps your father can help us purchase a plot to erect their tomb upon?"

"He would have loved to," the man said, "but he died four years ago, just before I left for Judea. My uncle still works for the *collegia,* though, and would be glad to find a plot and build the tomb for you."

"Then you shall furnish me with a letter of introduction before I sail for Rome," Marcus said.

"Gladly, sir!" the soldier replied.

Marcus wandered through the camp for another hour, making sure that he was seen by every legionary, and spoke to all those who seemed interested in talking to him. When he headed back to his tent an hour later, he reflected on how important personal connections were. When the expedition set forth a few days before, he was just another aristocrat in a toga to these men, a bloviating non-entity they were tasked to escort across the desert. Now the men looked up to him with respect and admiration. The discovery of the skeletal remains of Crassus' men could have dogged the mission with worry and fears of the restless dead—but now the men carried themselves with pride, knowing that, thanks to the quaestor, their predecessors in the legions would finally be coming home to the rest that their sacrifice had earned.

Inside the tent, he found Rufus, Cassius Claudius, and Cadius waiting for him. The meal was simple—some bread loaves that were not entirely stale yet, a bowl of figs and dates, and fresh roasted chicken from the village of Carrhae. The quartermaster had purchased enough meat from the tiny town for every soldier to have some fresh food that evening—the dried fish and mutton would have to last them for the next three weeks as they journeyed to Ecbatana.

Marcus thanked them for holding up the meal for him, and fell to with a vengeance. Back in Rome, he had been an indifferent eater, surrounded by plenty and trying to eat sparingly so as to avoid the obesity that was becoming more and more common as Epicureanism replaced the traditional Stoic values of Rome. But nearly three years on the road had worn away any hints of a middle-aged belly, and he had done without food often enough to cease taking good meals for granted.

"I never thought that I would stand on the battlefield where Crassus died," Cadius told him. "This journey of ours has taught me so much!"

"Experience is a good teacher, lad, but you need to learn your letters, and have some schooling in logic and rhetoric as well," Marcus said. "When we get back to Rome, I am going to hire a tutor for you."

"I don't understand," Cadius said. "I know you have freed me from slavery, but I am still a simple pleb, a son of slaves. Why bother to educate me when you might have children of your own someday?"

"Cadius, Rome is not what it was a hundred years ago. Freedmen can serve on juries and hold important offices," Marcus said. "You saved my life in Ancyra, and I intend to repay that debt by helping you make something of yourself. You have the brains and the gumption—all you need is the education now."

"Don't look a gift horse in the mouth, my boy," said Rufus. "You and I have been blessed with a generous employer who is rapidly climbing the *cursus honorum.* If he wants to pull us up behind him, who are we to question his judgment?"

Marcus laughed. "You two have been good companions," he said. "I am delighted to do what I can for you." His own secret plans he had not spoken to either of them yet—indeed, he was still debating in his mind whether or not to follow through with the impulse that had first occurred to him as he watched the miraculously healed Cadius gulping down enough food for a small army at the inn of Antioch. But it was there, nonetheless—the impulse had, in fact, gained force and clarity in the days since then. Marcus did not know if he would ever remarry or not, but even if he did, there was no guarantee that he would ever sire a natural son. Why not adopt this boy he had come to love as his own? It would not be the first time a Roman had adopted a former slave. Indeed, Cato the Censor, that immutable symbol of the Old Republic, had married one of his slaves—to the shock and chagrin of the children he had by his first wife! Marcus would have a much easier path than that, since he had no living children.

"So what's cooking in that head of yours?" Cassius Claudius asked him. Marcus started, realizing he had been sitting there silent for some time.

"Just thinking about home," he said. "It will be three full years since we set out, by the time we get back."

"Indeed," Cassius said. "It will be good to see my master again."

"I do hope the emperor is well," Marcus replied. "He is a good man, and I think the Empire has flourished under him."

"I am worried about his successors," Cassius replied. "In his last few letters, he has said less and less about his own son, Britannicus, and goes on and on about what a genius Agrippina's boy Nero is."

"Such thoughts are above our station," Marcus replied. "emperors do what they do, and we live or die as a consequence of their decisions."

"Indeed, we do," Cassius said. "All the more reason to pray to the gods that they make good ones!"

"Or to one God," Marcus replied.

"Going on about that again, are you?" the Greek freedman said. "Well, I have had enough religious talk for a lifetime on this trip. I am going to bed."

"I think I will turn in as well," Marcus replied. "We have a long day ahead of us, and another long day after that one is done!"

Cadius followed him to his bed—a simple hammock supported by the tent poles—and helped him out of his robe and sandals. Marcus stripped out of his tunic and used a bowl of warm water to wash himself. How he longed for a proper oil bath, followed by a good swim and a rubdown! But such luxuries were in Rome, half a world away. He shrugged into the light tunic he slept in and pulled the linen sheet up to his chin. Through half-shut eyes he saw Cadius preparing his own bedroll, and then he let his dreams take him far away from the harsh sands of Parthia.

It was still dark when voices woke him. He shook his head, sat up, and rolled out of his bed. A figure holding a torch stood in the tent's main chamber, with Rufus' solid form standing firmly between Marcus and the new arrival.

"What is it?" he asked.

"Sorry to disturb your rest, sir," the legionary said. "But Parthian soldiers have surrounded our camp, and they wish to speak to you. Manlius says you'd better come quick."

"Cadius—my dress toga—now!" Marcus snapped. He grabbed a tortoiseshell comb and brushed his thinning locks into place, then washed his face and mouth. He looked in the bronze mirror and did not like the fact that his face was stubbly, but there was no time to shave.

"Rufus!" he said. "Fetch my lictors, and have them formed up outside my tent in five minutes! I will greet them as an emissary of the emperor of Rome, with all the appropriate ceremony!"

Moments later, Marcus came striding out of his tent. His toga gleamed solid white in the moonlight, and the ornate scroll with its gold and teakwood carrying case was tucked under his arm. Eight lictors formed in perfect ranks, four on each side, with the senior man bearing the *fasces* that represented Marcus' *imperium* gripped upright before him.

They walked through the camp, past the light of the dying campfires and the smoldering embers of the funeral pyre from the night before. The neighing of horses carried loudly through the night, and he could see that their small force was surrounded by a Parthian army at least ten times as large. Well, he thought, we did not come to start a war, so the numbers should not matter.

On the open ground beyond their tents, a group of Parthian soldiers stood, facing Manlius Hortensius and a squad of legionaries who had been on watch. One of the Parthians had the sash and plumed helmet of an officer; he saw Marcus approach and stepped forward to meet him.

"I always heard that the Romans were bold to the point of foolhardiness," he said in fluent Latin. "But to invade my master's Empire with only a hundred and fifty men goes beyond foolishness and into the realm of insanity!"

"This is no invasion," Marcus said. "I am an envoy of the Emperor Tiberius Claudius Caesar Augustus Germanicus. My name is Marcus Quintus Publius, and I am an elected Quaestor of Rome, with *imperium maiis* over all the provinces. I come to the realm of the King of Kings, Eueregetes and Dikaios, Vonones II Epiphanes Philhellen, bearing the express greetings of one great ruler to another. If you claim to serve your King Vonones, then you must escort us to him and allow us to fulfill our embassy. Otherwise, you will be committing an act of betrayal to your royal master as well as an act of war against Rome."

"Well, you certainly said a mouthful there, Roman!" the Parthian officer said. "And you took the time to remember all of our king's titles and honors, no doubt! However, I fear I cannot take you to see King Vonones." His deeply tanned face lit up with a smile. "I could possibly send you to him, however."

Marcus furrowed his brow. "I have no doubt you stand high in the service of the king," he said. "But I stand equally high, if not higher, in the service of my great emperor, the conqueror of Britannia and the *Princeps* of Rome. Such riddling ill becomes you, Captain. Speak plainly! Why would you send Vonones to us but not take us to him?"

By now many of the Parthian soldiers were snickering to themselves, and Marcus guessed the truth before the officer spoke it.

"Because old Vonones is in Hades, Roman!" the captain said. "His son Vologases rules in Ecbatana now, and he is young and strong and unafraid of your crumbling, effete Empire!"

"He does not know Rome if he does not fear her," Marcus said. "But if he is now the king, then bear me to him. I would carry

Caesar's message to him directly, not to his underlings, no matter how important they think they may be."

"And if I slay you and your paltry force instead?" the Parthian captain sneered.

"Then Ecbatana will be in flames, and your king dead by this time next year," Marcus replied. "And your force will return to Ecbatana much smaller than it is now. I am no Crassus! I cannot stop you if you would run to battle with me, but I can arrange for you to limp on your homeward journey!"

The captain scowled at Marcus, searching his face for signs that he was bluffing. Then he threw back his head and laughed.

"You have stones, Roman, I will give you that!" he said. "Fine, then, I shall escort you to Vologases. But be warned—your bravado will not endear you to him."

"I did not intend bravado," Marcus said. "I am a representative of the emperor, Senate, and People of Rome—no more, no less."

"That is why I will take you to my king," the captain replied. "I am called Ventularia. You have my word that you and your men will stand safe and unharmed at the gates of Ecbatana in three weeks' time."

"I will hold you to it," Marcus said.

CHAPTER XIV

It was some six hundred miles from Carrhae to Ecbatana. Much of the distance was across desert and savannah, and even though it was the coolest season of the year, it was still a hot, dry journey. In order to make the distance in the time promised, the century of dismounted legionaries were given horses by the Parthians. Despite the hot, dry weather, they were able to make over fifteen miles a day most days, pausing every three or four days to rest the horses and appropriate fresh mounts from the cities and villages they passed.

Ventularia proved to be a courteous and talkative guide, to Marcus' surprise. It seemed as if the Parthian were attempting to make up for his earlier rudeness—or, perhaps, to throw the Romans' guard off. Marcus returned the courteous conversation in kind, but still slept surrounded by his own legionaries, with Rufus and his deadly scimitar only a few yards away and the faithful Cadius' bedroll on the floor besides his hammock. However, the Parthians showed no sign of treachery—only a desire to make haste.

The procession followed a southerly course, staying in the foothills of the Parthian plateau, where there was grass for the horses and trees for firewood when they made camp at night. They would make a sharp turn north on the final leg of the voyage, covering the last hundred miles or so to Ecbatana in a few days. That stretch was pretty desolate, according to their Parthian guide.

"They say that it was more green and fertile when Ecbatana was built over five hundred years ago," Ventularia told them. "But the long drought has slowly killed the grass and dried up the springs, and every year Ecbatana has a harder time feeding its population. I would not be surprised if the capital is moved to Persepolis soon—the kings spend as much time there as they do at Ecbatana now."

"I hope that we catch Vologases there," Marcus said. "I am anxious to complete my embassy and return home. It has been more than three years now since I gazed upon my own house."

The Parthian looked at him sympathetically. "Duty is a hard mistress," he said. "Does your wife wait for you in Rome?"

"She waits for me in the afterlife," Marcus said with such grimness that his escort changed the topic.

That night they camped at the foot of a long, sloping hill crowned with trees. Marcus was restless, sitting by the brazier they had lit and trying to focus on Caesar's *Anti-Cato*. Many Romans still looked back at the famous senator and orator as something of a hero, the last-ditch defender of the Republic against the man who destroyed it, but Marcus found the man's fanaticism completely off-putting. He often wondered how different Roman history would be if Cato had simply allowed Caesar to come home from Gaul and run for consul rather than accusing him of war crimes and demanding he be banished from Rome forever. Marcus had read most of Caesar's surviving works, but the level of invective the great Roman hurled at Cato never ceased to amaze him. As renowned as Caesar was for his clemency toward his opponents, Cato must have wounded him deeply to merit such a posthumous flaying.

He saw someone approaching, and looked up to see Manlius coming toward the fire. He stood and greeted the centurion warmly.

"We are making good time," Marcus said. "In two more days, we will turn north and make straight for Ecbatana."

"These Parthians know how to move swiftly across this gods-forsaken territory, I'll give them that," Manlius said. "But I still don't trust them."

"I trust them to act in their own best interest," Marcus said. "Right now, I just hope that war is not in their best interest."

"Powerful empires make for uneasy neighbors," the centurion replied. "I feel sorry for the people of Armenia and Syria, caught between the two of us!"

"Indeed," Marcus said. "I wonder what manner of man this new king is."

"He is young," Manlius says. "That rarely bodes well."

"Our own experience shows that to be true," Marcus said. "Caligula was a spoiled brat who grew into a monster. Even the *Divus Augustus* was much less benevolent in his early years than he later became."

"Vologases is young indeed," the voice of Ventularia came from the darkness. The Parthian officer stepped into the circle of firelight. "He is proud and independent, but he is not foolish. I cannot speak for him, but I can tell you that he respects honesty. If you show him due respect and listen to his proposals, he will most likely return the favor. But as I said, he is proud. Any affront to his honor he will not take kindly."

"It is kind of you to offer advice," said Marcus. "I know where your loyalty lies, as a Parthian officer and nobleman. But within the confines of your loyalty, any additional information you can offer about your new king would be greatly appreciated."

Ventularia sat down between Marcus and Manlius, his expression serious. "Your presence here puts me in an awkward position," he said. "I was a companion of Vologases from his youth, and at one time I enjoyed great favor in his eyes. Since he became king a few months ago, he has disassociated himself from many of us who were once his friends. I like to think it is because he wishes to devote himself more closely to affairs of state, but there are many professional courtiers bending his ear. He wants to prove himself a great leader, like Mithridates of old, and the time-honored way to do that is to measure one's strength against our traditional enemies—and Rome heads that list."

"Why should that be awkward for you?" Marcus asked.

"I have traveled through the Roman provinces," said the Parthian. "I have watched your legions in action, and I have seen how your men conduct themselves. A war with Rome is a very dangerous undertaking. While I displayed the necessary belligerence in front of my men when I met you, I would not look forward to a clash with the full might and fury of Rome. Even if we were victorious, the cost would be huge, and if the effort failed, Parthia itself could be destroyed. But the king no longer seeks my counsel. Your Emperor Claudius—does he desire peace?"

Marcus nodded. "I certainly think so," he said.

"Be careful how you articulate that desire before Vologases," the Parthian told him. "If Claudius seems too eager for peace, our king might take that as a sign of weakness. The result would not be good for Rome or Parthia."

Marcus nodded again. "Thank you, Ventularia, for your advice," he said. "I will take all you said into consideration."

The Parthian captain rose, gave a bow, and strode off into the darkness. Marcus looked at Manlius Hortensius and pointed toward his tent. They stepped inside, and he quietly told Rufus Licinius to step outside and watch for eavesdroppers.

"So what did you think about that?" he asked when he was sure they were alone.

"I'm not sure, Quaestor," the soldier replied.

"He seemed sincere enough," Marcus said, "but it's always hard to be certain with Easterners. They play their game of thrones, poisoning and stabbing their own siblings in order to promote their claim to the crown, and bathe in so much falsehood their whole lives it is impossible to know when they speak the truth."

"You mean that our host might actually want war with Rome?" asked Manlius.

"He might," Marcus said, "or he might be telling the unvarnished truth. He could be pressuring me to come across as more belligerent than I originally intended, in hopes it will stir the king to war, or he may be genuinely afraid of a war with Rome and be sincerely trying to avoid it."

"So what will you do?" the centurion asked.

"Carry out my embassy," Marcus replied. "I will watch Vologases very closely when I am introduced, and try to tailor my remarks to suit his mood."

Manlius yawned and stretched. "I am glad to be a soldier and not a politician," he said. "All I need know is who the enemy is, and what his weaknesses are."

Marcus laughed. "It's not that much different from politics," he said. "Except that our weapons, more often than not, are words."

"Give me a *gladius* and a *pilum* any day," the centurion said. "With those, you know when you hit your mark!"

After he left, Marcus slipped out of his robes and into his bed, pulling the blankets up to his chin, as the nights in the foothills were chilly. The last thing he heard before fading off to sleep was a tiger off in the woods, roaring over its prey. He hoped it was not a sign of things to come.

Two days later, the mounted column of Romans, escorted by the Parthian cohort, turned northward, across the dry limestone hills interspersed with alkali desert, thundering along a wide, hardened cobblestone road toward the ancient capital city. All day long they rode, stirring up a huge cloud of white dust behind them that marked their passage from miles away. About an hour before sunset, they spotted a clump of trees and buildings in the distance and spurred their horses on to one final burst. As they drew closer, they saw that the settlement was larger than it appeared from a distance, and was in fact a good-sized village.

"Where are we?" Marcus asked Ventularia.

"That is the city of Alexandretta Helios," his escort said. "Founded by the conqueror himself shortly after he occupied Babylon. Apparently, Alexander envisioned it as a major hub of Greek learning and culture, but it never was more than a mid-sized farming community guarding an olive grove and a fresh-flowing stream. The town's elders, however, pride themselves on being descendants of Macedonian and Greek soldiers, and can recite their pedigree back for five hundred years or more!"

The elders were apparently expecting a large group, because they had laid out a feast for the Parthian soldiers and the Roman delegation as well. Marcus and his small team, as well as the centurion Manlius Hortensius, were seated at the head table next to Ventularia and his officers. The dishes were huge and varied, including everything from poached peacock's eggs and glazed hummingbird tongues to various salted or grilled meats and fruits. Marcus enjoyed the food thoroughly, although some of the exotic dishes were a bit harsh on the tongue. Cadius, however, partook of everything with vigor, polishing off huge amounts of food without ever seeming to fill up. Ever since his near-death experience, the lad's appetite had been insatiable. Even Cassius, a parsimonious eater most of the time, applied himself to the food with unaccustomed enthusiasm.

The village headman, Demetrius Stephanos, gave a flowery speech of welcome to the visitors, and then a long-winded tribute to the heroism and courage of Parthia's soldiers, winding up with an hour-long oration in praise of the new ruler Vologases, whose reign would surely bring Parthia and Rome into a new age of cooperation and friendship.

When he finally concluded, Marcus made a few brief and noncommittal remarks, thanking the village for its hospitality and echoing Demetrius' hopes for a peaceful future. He was applauded more vigorously than the headman had been when he sat down, although Marcus thought that was more for his brevity than for the eloquence of his speech.

Demetrius and the council of elders would not hear of their Roman guests sleeping in tents, and offered a large house with multiple bedrooms for their lodging. Marcus was a bit embarrassed to find that the native hospitality also included a comely slave girl in each bedchamber, but for once he was too lonely to send the girl away. Indeed, as he fell asleep with his arm around her waist, he reflected that perhaps Claudius was right, and he should take another wife when he returned to Rome. Life was too short to sleep alone every night, he thought.

They were now some fifty miles from Ecbatana, but the hills were becoming steeper and the flat stretches of desert fewer, so the going was slower the next day. But the moon was full and rose early, so the party continued to ride on through the cool night for several hours after sunset, and Marcus retired to his tent that evening knowing that the next day would see him arrive at his destination.

They got underway shortly after sunrise, heading almost due north along a cobblestone road that threaded the crests of the hills. Despite the rough terrain, the road had been shored up in the valleys, and the hilltops scraped level where it passed, and they made good time, pausing around noon to rest the horses, drink some water, and eat a hasty meal. An hour later they took to the road again, and not long after that, Marcus caught the first glimpse of white walls in the distance, gleaming between the hills. All through the afternoon, the walls loomed ahead, taller and brighter with each glimpse, until finally the road rounded one last hilltop and emerged on a long straightaway toward the towering city gates.

The city had been built by the first king of the Medes some five hundred years before, and Herodotus, the famous Greek historian and serial exaggerator, had described it as an enormous metropolis of seven walls, each taller than the one before it, covering hundreds of acres. The truth was a bit more modest, Marcus thought as he beheld the legendary Parthian capital. There was one white limestone wall, about twenty-five feet tall, encircling the entire city, with enormous gate towers standing some fifty feet above the main entrance, guarded by colorfully clad sentries. Some distance back from the wall, a single enormous tower stood, with six levels, each higher and narrower than the one below it, until the final level which consisted only of the tower, eighty feet in diameter. Marcus had seen a number of these towers scattered throughout the territory of the ancient Median Empire; one of the locals had told him they were built over a thousand years before and were called *ziggurats*. The Medes had chosen to make this tower the centerpiece of their great capital, blending ancient architecture with their own. This was the first *ziggurat* Marcus had seen that was intact.

As the cavalcade came thundering down the causeway, the city gates opened and a hundred or so armed guards emerged, scarlet and yellow sashes flapping in the afternoon breeze, and formed up in neat ranks along either side of the road. Ventularia and his guards rode ahead, smartly saluting the guards with upraised fists, then parting to either side of the road to allow Marcus and his Roman legionaries to ride forward between their ranks. As they approached the gate, a delegation of richly dressed courtiers came to meet them, led by a tall, heavyset Parthian with a shaved head and large golden earrings. Marcus held up his hand as they approached, and the legionaries halted. He dismounted his horse, followed by Cassius Claudius, Cadius, and Manlius Hortensius. His lictors formed up ahead of them, bearing the *fasces* that was the symbol of Marcus' *imperium.* Rufus took position behind the party, but still close enough to Marcus that he could intervene if things turned ugly.

The bald courtier stepped forward and made an elaborate bow. "To the emissaries of the illustrious Emperor Tiberius Claudius Caesar Augustus Germanicus I bear express greetings," he said obsequiously. "I am Perseus Democritus, Grand Vizier to the High King Vologases, the First of his Name, son of Vonones II, Ruler of Parthia, Babylon, and all the dominions of the East, King of Kings, and God of Mesopotamia. His Majesty has instructed me to lead you to his palace, where he will see you as soon as his duties permit."

"From the Emperor Tiberius Claudius Caesar Augustus Germanicus to the high king I bear greetings in return," Marcus said, "and the emperor's condolences upon the death of his noble father, King Vonones the Second. To which, I might add, my own condolences are heartily appended. I realize the duties of the king are many, but I pray that he will not long delay our audience, for there are grave matters of state at hand that must be dealt with sooner rather than later. Lead us on, by all means, that we may await the high king's pleasure."

"Your soldiers will be accommodated in the Royal Barracks, alongside the warriors of the high king," Perseus said smoothly. "They are welcome in all the inns, taverns, and brothels that the king's soldiers are allowed to frequent, and I have ordered a Parthian soldier assigned to each squad so that he may show them the areas in which they are welcome, and which areas are reserved for the nobility. You, your companions, and the officers will be staying in the Royal Palace, where special guest quarters will be provided."

"My lictors must attend me and be quartered near me," Marcus said. "Their presence is the visual token of my *imperium*."

"Of course," the unctuous Greek replied. "And this burly fellow whom I imagine to be your bodyguard will share quarters with you as well. We certainly do not want any emissary from the great Claudius Caesar to feel unwelcome or imposed upon during his visit with us."

"Your hospitality is much appreciated," Marcus said.

"Then let us proceed," said the Vizier. "Your men may dismount; your horses shall be well attended in the royal stables until you are ready to depart."

The hundred and sixty Romans dismounted and grooms emerged from the gates, taking the reins and leading their horses down a side road that led to the royal stables, which were outside the city walls about a hundred yards distant. Then the entire party marched through the towering gates and into the ancient city of Ecbatana.

The streets were cobblestoned, with deeply cut drainage ditches to either side, and the shops were mostly built of the reddish sandstone of the surrounding hills, although some of the older and more elaborate structures were made of the same white limestone blocks as the wall and the ancient tower. The people gathered, curious, along the sides of the road to watch the procession go by. Marcus imagined that most of them had never seen a Roman before. The last war with Parthia had been over twenty years before, during the reign of Augustus, and not many Romans had fallen into their hands that time—unlike the disastrous enslavement of thousands that had followed Crassus' defeat at Carrhae.

The base of the enormous tower was perhaps a half mile or more from the gates, and the houses and shops grew larger and more ornate as they drew nearer to it. Fewer people lined the streets here, although Marcus did see several well-dressed Parthians watching them from windows and balconies. The gates of the tower were nearly twenty feet tall and covered with hammered bronze that had been polished till it gleamed in the setting sun; fantastic reliefs of sphinxes, manticores, and satyrs danced across its surface. The guards here were the most ornately dressed yet; their armor was trimmed in gold and silver and their sashes were scarlet, red, and yellow, while the rich leather was dyed the deepest black. The enormous doors swung open, and Marcus entered a wide, marble floored corridor whose polished tiles were arranged in a checkerboard pattern. Down either side of the hallway stood ranks of palace slaves. Men and women alike were scantily clad and bowed deeply as the Romans went by. Marcus noted with amusement that young Cadius was taking in the view most appreciatively.

"Your quarters are on the second level of the tower," said Perseus. "There are four bedchambers and a communal dining area where your evening meal will be served shortly. You have nothing to fear here; you are under the roof of the high king of Parthia. To harm the king's guests is treason, punishable by being boiled alive in a vat of oil. As long as you are here, your persons are sacrosanct."

They climbed a flight of limestone steps and a pair of wide wooden doors opened before them. A fair-sized table was spread out, groaning with a sumptuous feast, while servants clad in sheer white robes waited with basins and pitchers to wash their road-stained hands and feet. Marcus saw with pleasure that the table was set in the Roman style—a curved surface with couches along its outer side, piled high with cushions for reclining, while the inside of the curve was open to the center of the room, enabling the servants to come and go with ease, bringing new dishes as they came.

"Enjoy your meal, and let the servants know if there is anything you desire—more food, wine, male or female companionship—all will be provided upon request. I go now to confer with my royal master, and will see you again ere you go to your beds," Perseus told them.

"Where is the privy?" Cassius Claudius asked.

"Through the doors across from your bedchambers," answered their host. "Pull the golden cord when you are done, and flowing water will flush everything away. I shall see you in about two hours."

Cassius waited until he was gone, then turned to the others. "With me, all of you!" he whispered, and the entire party followed him to the privy. It was a large affair, mostly marble, with four seats as well as a long marble urinary basin with a bronze drain at the end.

"Begging your pardon, sir, but I don't really have to go right now—" Rufus began to say.

Cassius interrupted him with a laugh. "Neither do I, you oaf!" he said. "But I wanted to share a word before we begin our supper. We need to keep our wits about us—all of us—so I would counsel you to go very light on the wine this evening. And while I am sure the young ladies—and boys—the Parthians might offer us are both beautiful and accomplished in the arts of love, I would urge you to wait until we return to friendly lands to slake any urges you might feel at the moment. This is the home of Rome's greatest living rival, and every word and deed will be reported back to him within an hour of your utterance. I know none of you would knowingly give our enemy any intelligence that might harm the Empire, but you have no way of knowing what he does or does not already know. The slightest tidbit of information could influence his behavior towards us, so let us not give him anything more than we absolutely must."

"I concur wholeheartedly," Marcus said. "It was probably foolish of us to accept the women offered to us at Alexandretta Helios, but we should definitely not repeat that error here. Am I clear?"

Rufus and Cadius could not disguise their disappointment, but Manlius gave a quick nod of affirmation, as did the lictors. Marcus looked all of them in the eye, and then gave a curt nod. "Now let us eat," he said. "I am famished!"

"I'll join you in a moment," Cadius said, looking anxious.

"Are you all right?" Marcus asked him.

"Yes, *Dominus*!" he said. "But I really do have to go!"

The meal was excellent, and after each of them had drunk a single glass of the excellent wine that was provided, Marcus asked one of the waiters to bring them pitchers of fresh squeezed fruit juice. The man returned with juice from oranges, grapes, and pomegranates. Marcus enjoyed the chilled pomegranate juice and the roasted quail especially, as well as the delicious dates that were fresh plucked from the trees in the high king's garden. Dinner conversation was kept to a minimum, and when the Romans did talk, it was to discuss the things they had seen on their way to Parthia, and the curious plants and animals they had encountered in Asia. Occasionally, they would ask the servants about similar topics, trying to see what they could learn. The Parthian slaves were fairly tight-mouthed, although one of them did volunteer that the king would be glad to give them a tour of his menagerie, since they loved animals so much.

As they finished off the last of the fruit and sweet cakes that the servants had brought out for dessert, Perseus entered the guest quarters again, with two royal guards trailing him. The Greek vizier was all smiles.

"Fortuna herself favors your errand," he said. "My Lord the high king is so eager to see you that he has deferred meeting with his satraps until afternoon. You will be ushered into the king's presence at the third hour of the morrow. Until then, may you rest from your journey, and enjoy pleasant dreams."

"Thank you, Perseus Democritus," Marcus said. "You do your office well. I look forward to seeing your master tomorrow, and bearing the message from Caesar to him. If I may be so bold, let your slave girls and boys retire from our quarters with you. We are all wearied from our journey, and are not in need of sport or distraction this evening."

The Grand Vizier nodded knowingly. "Of course," he said. "Once the table is cleared, you will have the guest chambers to yourselves. I will have the butler leave pitchers of fresh, cold water and fruit juice for you, as well as some wine."

"Then we shall see you in the morning," Marcus said, and with that, Romans and Parthians parted company for the evening.

CHAPTER XV

At the third hour from dawn, on the Kalends of January in the eleventh year in the reign of Claudius Caesar, which was some eight hundred and four years after the founding of Rome, Quaestor Marcus Quintus Publius found himself standing at the doorway to the court of the high king of Parthia, Vologases I. An impressive doorway it was, he thought—about twelve feet tall and covered in gold leaf, which had been hammered into ornate reliefs depicting the exploits of past kings of the great empire. One panel, he noted with some sadness, depicted the defeat of Crassus at Carrhae, with the portly Roman being led in chains through the gates of the city, the legion's Eagle standards reversed and dragging through the dirt behind him.

Marcus stood, clad in his best and cleanest toga, gleaming white with the purple trim of a member of the Senate, as well as the broad stripe on his sleeve that symbolized his status as an elected Quaestor of the Senate and People of Rome. His lictors kept perfect formation ahead of him, each dressed in the short, gold-bordered tunic and black leggings that were the uniform of their office. Behind him came Cassius Claudius, wearing a long, formal green robe trimmed in purple, marking his status as a personal servant of Rome's emperor, with his own lictor Armenius beside him. Behind them stood the muscular form of Rufus, wearing a black leather cuirass with gold trim, and Cadius, who was now wearing a fine-tooled leather hauberk that Marcus had bought for him in Jerusalem. As he glanced at his companions, he thought that they were a good visual representation of the Empire's citizens.

Then the doors swung open, and the throne room of Vologases I, High King of Parthia, loomed ahead of them. The floor was made of solid, polished jade that brilliantly reflected the morning sunlight coming in through the tall, colonnaded windows. Ranks of courtiers stood on either side of the door, forming a human wall from the entrance to the throne. Some were obviously servants, others soldiers and bodyguards, as well as magicians, advisors, and satraps. On the far side of the room, nearly a hundred feet away, was a raised dais on which sat an ornately carved throne, made of black teakwood with golden trim, surmounted by the tusks of two massive elephants that curved inward and met nearly ten feet above the floor. The tusks were elaborately carved and engraved, with gold bands encircling them every foot or so. At the right side of the foot of the throne sat a leopard cub with a golden collar and on the opposite side a lion cub was dozing with its head on its paws. Two concubines, wearing only flowing white skirts and gold necklaces, stood a pace behind the throne, holding ostrich feather fans with handles of gold and teakwood.

Vologases I was seated on the throne, but as Marcus and his party entered, he stood to greet them. His garb was simple but carefully chosen—tall, polished leather boots with golden toes, black leather breeches stitched with red, yellow, and gold threads in elaborate patterns, and a long scarlet cloak that hung from his shoulders, also trimmed in gold. His bare chest was crossed by two black leather bands studded with golden crescents and stars, and on his head was a golden circlet with a ruby the size of a hen's egg in the middle of the forehead. His scalp was shaved and polished till it gleamed, and his eyebrows were jet-black, as was the finely trimmed beard that started at his ears and ran in a single, solid line down his jaw to come to a tapered point on his chin. He had a hawk-like nose and piercing green eyes, with high cheekbones and a broad forehead. His torso was heavily muscled without a trace of fat, and he wore a gem-encrusted scimitar at his side.

Marcus and his escort advanced until they stood about twenty feet from the throne, then the lictors halted, as he had ordered them to, and parted into two ranks, facing toward the center, allowing him to advance until he stood ten feet from the high king of the Parthian Empire. There he stood, poised like a statue, right foot slightly ahead of the left, his toga gleaming in the morning light, and waited for his host to speak first.

Vologases looked at him long and hard, advancing until he was only a couple of feet in front of Marcus, taking his measure with those calculating green eyes. Marcus met his gaze fearlessly, surveying the high king with a cool, detached interest. The pomp and splendor of Eastern monarchs was always impressive, but no match for the simple Republican dignity of a servant of Rome, he thought. All the colors of the rainbow were not as powerful as the brilliance of pure white.

After a silence that seemed to last an hour, although Marcus realized it was more like a minute or so, the high king threw back his head and laughed, a booming sound that echoed in the silence of the gleaming court.

"Now here is how a representative of a mighty Empire should conduct himself!" he said to his assorted sycophants. "Say what you like about Romans, but they understand the concept of dignity and honor! To bow his head or bend the knee would sully the honor of his mighty emperor, but to speak first would impinge upon my royal prerogative. So he keeps his silence, and allows me to speak first—and preserves his own *dignitas* and that of his emperor equally. Marcus Quintus Publius, you are welcome in my court!"

Marcus spoke and tried to keep the relief out of his voice. "To the mighty high king, Vologases the First of His Name, I bring greetings in the name of the *Princeps* and *Imperator* of Rome, Tiberius Claudius Caesar Augustus Germanicus. I was dispatched to carry a personal letter from my emperor to your august father, the former High King Vonones, Second of His Name. It was not until I arrived within the borders of your kingdom that I learned of his passing over Styx, and so I bring you the letter that my emperor addressed to him, and will gladly answer any questions you have and bear any message you wish to deliver in return, for I will travel straightaway to Rome when I leave your fair city." With that, he extended the scroll to the Parthian king, who accepted it and tucked it under his cloak.

"I will read it with great interest, I promise you, Marcus Publius," he said, "and after I have met with my satraps and counselors this afternoon, I would invite you to a private dinner and a stroll in my gardens. There you will have my answer to your emperor in full, and I will send him a letter which I will entrust you to deliver."

"I thank you for seeing us so quickly, and for the hospitality which you have offered to me and my men, Your Highness," Marcus said. "I certainly look forward to sharing a meal with you."

"News from Rome travels slowly," the high king said. "Your Claudius has ruled for several years now, and I have heard that he is a wise man. What would you have me know of him, ere I take counsel with my court—speaking as his emissary, of course?"

Marcus thought for only a moment. He had anticipated a question like this, and had rehearsed how he might answer it.

"He is a man of considerable intellect, with a remarkable sense of justice," Marcus said. "He also is a person of unexpected strengths. For many years, he was underestimated and ignored, and rather than take offense, he bided his time until his moment came—and then seized it. The great Julius Caesar invaded Britain but could not hold it; Claudius Caesar conquered it and made it a province of Rome. Other rulers stripped power away from the Senate and elected officials of the Empire, but Claudius Caesar restored them. He is a man who is confident of himself and comfortable in his role as emperor. He is a loyal and steadfast friend, but a subtle and deadly enemy. He has brought back a dignity and honor to Rome that it has not seen in years."

The high king nodded. "An interesting man, by all accounts," he said. "Indeed, the picture you paint is not unlike that compiled by my own confidential agents in Rome and elsewhere. What of his predecessor, Gaius Caligula? We hear many stories, most of them unpleasant. What manner of man was this young ruler?"

Marcus hesitated much longer this time. He had not anticipated this question at all! But he had no wish to offend his host, and remembered what Ventularia had told him about Vologases' love of honesty.

"I am not an unbiased source for information about Caligula," he finally said.

"Unbiased source?" The high king threw back his head and laughed a second time. "If there is such a thing in the world, I have never heard of it! I do not ask for an unbiased opinion of your late and apparently unlamented emperor. I ask for your opinion, Marcus Publius!"

Marcus smiled grimly. "Then you shall have it," he said. "Gaius Caligula was a loathsome, obnoxious boy who was drunk with power and cruelty long before he ever succeeded to the purple. He reveled in inflicting pain for no other purpose than his own pleasure, and he especially savored the pain of the innocent. He took the lives of my father, my mother, and my precious sister when they were guests at his table. If Cassius Chaerea had not killed him, I might well have done the deed myself."

Vologases nodded, eyeing Marcus curiously.

"Was he mad, do you think?" he asked.

"Not always," Marcus said. "He was quite calculating as a young man. But, although I was away from Rome at the time, I think that he did become insane before the end. He did things that were so irrational, so monstrous, that all of Rome came to despise him. A good leader should always be feared—but it is a grave error to give your own people too much reason to hate you."

"You are a wise man, Marcus Quintus Publius, and you serve your emperor well," Vologases said. "My satraps and advisors now await me, but I look forward to meeting you again this afternoon, in a less formal setting."

"And I likewise," Marcus said, inclining his head. The high king nodded brusquely and returned to his throne, and Marcus stepped back until his lictors were between him and the high king. When he stopped, they turned on their heels and marched out of the chamber. Marcus gave one last polite half-bow, and then turned on his heel and left the throne room last.

He did not speak a word until they had returned to their living quarters, where he shed the immaculate toga and donned a simpler robe over his tunic. Cadius poured him a cup of wine, and he reclined on the couch with a sigh. Moments later Cassius Claudius joined him, and the other members of the original party stood close by, while the lictors posted themselves at the doors and windows and shooed the palace slaves out of the chamber.

"I thought you handled yourself very well, Marcus," said Cassius Claudius. "The new high king is a formidable man, but you stood your ground before him!"

"To be sure, sir, I wouldn't have been in your shoes for all the gold in Egypt!" Rufus said. "But you were as cool as a March morning the whole time!"

Marcus laughed. "I did not feel particularly cool," he said. "But I did not want the man to see me sweat. That question about Caligula caught me totally off guard, however. I wonder if someone told him of my family's fate?"

"It wouldn't surprise me," Cassius said. "The kings of Parthia have long maintained clients among the more impoverished—or greedy—senators of Rome."

"Sometimes I wonder why embassies like this are even necessary," Marcus said. "Why not just let the Parthians Rome has bought talk to the high king while the Romans the Parthians have bought talk to Caesar?"

Cassius laughed. "Because we have to preserve appearances!" he said. "Not to mention, neither the high king nor Caesar want the other to know which of their people are on each other's payrolls."

Marcus gave a wry grin. "I suppose you are right," he said.

After a light luncheon, he sat down at a desk with pen and papyrus and began drafting a lengthy account of the morning's audience with the high king. He did his best to recall every word, every expression, and to give the most accurate possible description of Vologases' throne room. He was beginning to describe the appearance and dress of the courtiers in attendance when a voice distracted him from his writing.

"The high king requests that you attend him in his gardens," a richly dressed steward told him. "The freedman Cassius Claudius is also invited to attend, although Vologases asks, as a gesture of trust, that you leave your guards behind. He personally guarantees your safety."

Marcus rose and stretched. "Give us a few moments to prepare," he said, "and you may conduct us to him."

The butler bowed out, and Rufus immediately made his way to Marcus' side. "I don't like this, not one bit, sir!" he said. "I don't trust that bald king any further than I could throw a sweet cake underwater!"

Marcus smiled. "I think that, if Vologases wished us any harm, it would have been accomplished by now," he said. "But I appreciate your concern for my safety."

"Be careful, *Dominus*!" said Cadius. "We are a long way from Rome."

"I'll be fine," Marcus said. "Now help me into my toga."

Moments later, he and Cassius Claudius were both attired as they had been for the morning's audience, and the butler led them past the bronze doors of the throne room, deep into the tower, and finally out through an ornate marble door into a beautiful garden. It was perhaps a hundred and fifty feet in depth, stretching from the back wall of the ziggurat to the city wall, and separated from the streets on either side by two stone walls that ran from the corners of the tower's base straight outward to the walls of the city. However, the city wall was barely visible over the tops of the beautiful trees that stood throughout the garden, with paved walkways in between. At the foot of the steps was a small patio, where stone benches had been padded with cushions before a small table. Reclining on one of the benches was Vologases the Second, attended by the same female slaves that had fanned him in the throne room. He rose as they descended the steps.

"Welcome, my friends, to the high king's garden. This is where I cast aside my burdens and come to relax. You are the first foreigners I have ever entertained here."

Marcus and Cassius bowed deeply. "We are honored by your hospitality, Great King," Marcus said.

"You did not bow to me in the throne room, Marcus Quintus Publius," the high king observed. "But here you did not hesitate. Why?"

"In your throne room, I stood as the representative and embodiment of the Senate and People of Rome," Marcus said. "Rome bows to none. Here, I am simply Marcus Quintus, the guest of Vologases, and I bow to show my gratitude for your friendship and hospitality, just as if I were at a friend's house on the banks of the Tiber."

The high king nodded, his shaved pate gleaming in the sun. "Even so," he said, "I set aside my crown in this place. Now have a glass of wine, and let me show you my collection!"

The two slaves stepped forward and each poured a goblet of wine for Vologases' guests, and then they stepped back. The high king started down one of the paved pathways, and Marcus and Cassius followed him. The path meandered through the trees until it came to a low wall, from which high iron bars curved up and back, away from the curious Romans. On the other side of the wall were a series of recessed chambers, each one walled and barred from the other, but quite spacious.

In the first chamber, the largest lion Marcus had ever seen paced back and forth, roaring at the visitors, while two lionesses sprawled, watching the big male as he stalked about.

"The great cats have fascinated me since I was a boy," said Vologases. "I began building a collection of them long before I became king, but these are my most splendid specimens. Leo Magnus here was a notorious man-eater from the far-off land of Ethiopia. He was captured by the Queen's royal consort there, who believed that he was possessed of some demonic spirit. The royal court was quite relieved when my agents offered to purchase the beast."

He walked down to the next cage, where three spotted cats, smaller than the lion but still quite large, were calmly seated on the rocks observing them.

"These are my leopards," the king said. "I named them Alexander, Antigonus, and Ptolemy. You should see how they fight over their food! Actually, in a moment, you will see." He nodded in the direction of the wall, and a door at the back of the chamber opened, and a terrified man, stripped naked, was shoved into the cage with the great cats. Seeing them, he raced toward the wall, begging for help—but too slowly! One of the leopards pounced on him and dragged him down, sinking its fangs into his neck. The other two joined the fray, one grabbing an arm, the other a foot, snarling and tearing at the screaming man until the screams stopped.

Marcus was appalled, but dared not show it. Cassius, on the other hand, turned slightly green around the cheeks and neck. Watching gladiators fight each other, or even wild beasts, in the arena, was one thing. They were armed and had a chance to defend themselves. But seeing a defenseless man devoured even as he begged for his life was a depth to which Rome had not sunk—at least, not yet, reflected Marcus.

"Do you think me barbaric?" the high king said. "The man was a common criminal, found guilty of robbery and murder. His death served a nobler purpose than his life, for my majestic pets are more worthy to breathe than he was."

"I suppose so," Marcus said. Cassius merely nodded, still looking a bit sick.

They walked to the last enclosure in the row, where two large tigers were tearing and biting at a dismembered body.

"By the gods, I told the handler not to feed them until we were watching!" snapped Vologases. Then he looked more closely at the ravaged corpse. "Oh—never mind, that is their handler. See his bracelet with the seal of my house? I've warned him about being careless around those two. They are sneaky. Oh well, that's why I have three handlers per beast. We'll just have to train another."

"How many handlers have you lost?" Marcus asked.

"Maybe one or two a month," said the high king. "I pay them well, but it is dangerous work."

With that, he turned and walked away from the row of enclosures, across the garden to the opposite wall. Marcus and Cassius trailed behind, casting curious glances at each other.

"Now I will show you the prize of my collection," the high king said. He led them to the back corner of his garden, where another pit, deeper, wider, and larger than the first two, had been dug out. A pool of clear water lay at one end, fed by a trickling spring, and a large pile of boulders had been artfully arranged to form a cave at the opposite corner. The enclosure was nearly a hundred feet across, and its floor was covered with green grass, although there were several well-trampled trails crisscrossing it. There was no sign of any occupant, although a pungent musk hung in the air as they leaned over the wall, holding onto the bars and trying to see.

"He sleeps by day, most of the time," said the high king. "But he always wakes up for his meals." He nodded toward the back wall of the cage, and another carefully concealed door opened. A burly man with a shaved head and bushy beard was shoved through, cursing and swearing at the unseen figures beyond the wall in several different languages. Spotting the three spectators, he stepped toward the wall, hurling invective at them.

Suddenly a deafening roar came from the artificial cave, and something from a nightmare stepped out, licking its chops. It was a cat, but what a cat! A beast nearly twice as big as the lion in the first cage, its yellow eyes took in the scene with quick, darting glances. It had a short tail like a lynx, but its body was massively muscled, especially the neck, and its forelegs were twice as large as its hindquarters, causing its back to slope sharply downward from its bulging shoulders. Two enormous yellow fangs, each about a cubit in length, drooped from its upper jaw and protruded straight down, past the lower jaw, with saliva dripping from them. It gave a low growl that was deeper and more menacing than any sound Marcus had ever heard. The prisoner took one look at the monstrosity and began to scream like a ravaged maiden.

The monstrous cat crossed the distance between them in two leaps, grabbing the hapless wretch in its front paws and bearing him to the ground. The bearded prisoner was gibbering in fright now. The mighty head reared back, and the lower jaw gaped wide open, flat against the furry breast of the monster. Then with a single powerful swoop, the beast drove its fangs clean through the prisoner's torso—they were so long that each fang came out of the man's back and pinned him to the soft earth. The prisoner's scream trailed off into a gurgling death rattle, and the great beast planted its front paws on the victim's chest and slowly wrenched its fangs free, tossing its huge head back and forth. Then the great cat grabbed the corpse by the head and pulled it into the cave. In the stillness that followed, the sounds of crunching bones and tearing flesh could be clearly heard by the two Romans.

"What in the name of Hades was that?" Marcus finally asked.

Vologases grinned. "He is, so far as I know, the last of his kind. We call them speartooth tigers, and they figured largely into the legends of our land for many centuries. I thought they were an old wives' tale until some shepherds reported seeing this one in the mountains to the south and east of here about three years ago. I offered a million sesterces to the man who could bring him to me alive, and after several failed attempts, one of my father's satraps succeeded."

Marcus thought of those enormous fangs and shuddered. "He is most assuredly the deadliest beast I have ever seen," he said. "Without meaning to give offense, I do hope he is the last of his kind!"

"Thank you," said the high king. "I named him Caesar."

The two guests were silent as Vologases guided them through the rest of the garden, showing his rare plants and flowers, and a pit full of the biggest crocodiles Marcus had seen outside Egypt. Finally, they wound up back at the table where they had begun, and the high king gestured for them to recline as the concubines refilled their wine goblets.

"I know you are a long way from home and doubtless are eager to return," Vologases said. "So let me give my reply to your emperor, and tomorrow you can be on your way. Here is a scroll bearing my personal message to Claudius Caesar, sealed with my own ring. But I will tell you the gist of my message here and now: if Rome truly desires to live in peace with Parthia, that peace will come at a cost. My price is simple, and not outrageous: I want Armenia returned to the Parthian Empire!"

Marcus swallowed hard. "Armenia has been under Roman rule for seventy years," he said. "I doubt that the Senate, or the emperor, will countenance giving it up."

"That's not entirely true and you know it!" Vologases replied. "Orodes was the king there less than fifteen years ago, and he was a loyal subject of Parthia!"

"He was installed while Rome was distracted by the death of Tiberius and the tyranny of Caligula," Marcus replied. "As soon as Claudius took the throne, Roman control of Armenia was reestablished under Mithridates."

"Mithridates is old, and his nephew Rhadamistus longs to take the throne from him," Vologases said. "If that happens, we will seize Armenia easily during the confusion. Why not save all the havoc of war and simply cede Armenia to us now? Rome has an abundance of provinces, and Armenia is more trouble than it is worth. Parthia will possess it one way or another, so why not make the transfer easier?"

Marcus sighed. "It is not my place to make war or peace," he said. "I will bear your message to Claudius, but I would urge you to make a different demand. He will not do this, and to ask for something that cannot be granted is to guarantee war!"

Vologases shrugged. "Then war it will be," he said. "But the choice is Rome's, not mine. I have offered other concessions in return for Armenia, outlined in my letter. I will return all the standards we took from Crassus, as well as his bones. I will renounce all claims to the lands of the Skenites, and grant Rome the most favored trade status I can offer. But Armenia I must have. It is a matter of pride."

Marcus stood and bowed to his royal host. "I shall convey your offer to my emperor," he said. "I hope we can meet again in peace, high king. But your demands render that unlikely. Take a good long look at your pet Caesar. Reflect on why you gave him that name, and think on the wisdom of stirring such a great beast to wrath unnecessarily."

Vologases grinned. "You are a brave man, Marcus Quintus," he said. "Not many would speak so to me here in my own gardens. But I would ask you to reflect on this—as mighty as Caesar is, I keep him in a cage!"

"Fair enough," Marcus said. "I speak bluntly to you because to be dishonest would be discourteous. And you have shown us great courtesy during our stay, for which I thank you. Now my comrades and I must prepare for our return journey." He stood, and with Cassius following him, made his way back toward the palace.

"Fare thee well, Marcus Quintus Publius," said the high king of Parthia.

CHAPTER XVI

Marcus leaned on the rails of the ship, watching the beautiful blue waters of the Mediterranean slide by. Gulls shrieked and dove in the bireme's wake, and dolphins leaped out of the water periodically. It was early summer, and the ocean breeze was warm. Although he was still saddened by the answer that Vologases had returned to Rome, he was nonetheless pleased with the result of his three-year provincial tour. He had earned a reputation as a scourge of corruption, enlarged his own *dignitas* and *arctoritas,* and most importantly, he had rendered good service to his emperor and to the Senate and People of Rome. In the end, he reflected, being useful to one's fellow man was perhaps life's highest achievement.

The journey back from Ecbatana had been largely uneventful, although a sandstorm had trapped them in Carrhae for several days. After it passed over, several dozen more Roman skeletons had been exposed in the desert flats to the west of the ancient village. Marcus repeated his earlier performance, gathering them all up and cremating them once the party reached the end of the desert and found an area with sufficient timber to make a fire. Their ashes were gathered in empty wine jugs, which were exchanged for traditional burial urns once they reached Roman territory. Marcus had already drawn up the epitaph he wanted inscribed on their tomb in Rome.

Once they were clear of Parthian territory, he had cut south toward Judea, returning the legionaries who had escorted him back to the Prefect Ventidius Cumanus. Cumanus was up in arms because the Jews had launched another wave of persecution at the Christian community in Jerusalem.

"I don't understand this conflict at all!" he said sharply. "Aren't they all Jews anyway? All this fuss over whether or not some carpenter was a holy man or not—it's such a stupid thing to shed blood over!"

"There is a bit more to it than that," Marcus said. "The Nazarenes—or Christians as they call themselves now—believe that Jesus was actually God in the flesh. To the Jews, that is the worst sort of blasphemy."

"I don't know which side to take," Cumanus said. "All I want is peace and order!"

"This province has long been short on both," Marcus said, "but having had some experience with the Christians, I would say that they pose no threat to Rome. Don't let the Jews be too hard on them."

"Easy for you to say," the prefect replied. "You are headed back to the comforts of Rome, while I am stuck here in this miserable province!"

"Rest assured I shall put in a good word for Caesar with you. Your legionaries were very helpful," Marcus said.

The next day the five of them had boarded ship at Caesarea and were bound for Rome. There had been a bundle of letters awaiting them upon arrival, although nothing from the emperor this time. Marcus read his missives with interest, especially the one from his uncle.

To Marcus Quintus Publius, Quaestor of Rome and beloved nephew, from Mencius Quintus Publius, Censor of Rome, and irritable uncle,

Well, lad, I have followed your exploits with great interest since you departed our fair city nearly three years ago. What a remarkable odyssey you have been on! You have disciplined governors, set whole provinces in order, led troops, won battles, witnessed a miracle, and seemingly found a new faith. I begin to think I may not even know you when you return home!

I appreciate your occasional letters; the emperor has also been kind enough to share some of the information that you have forwarded to him, so I have a pretty fair idea of what you have seen and done—although I will admit I can't wait to hear all the juicy details from your own lips, especially regarding your visit to Parthia! So few Romans have ever actually been there, and our relations with that empire have always been so hostile that almost any fantastic tale about the place is likely to be believed.

As you may have heard, I was elected Censor last year, and have enjoyed the office a great deal. The Senate has been badly disrupted in recent years, what with purges and plots and treason trials, and is far below the membership of five hundred that the Divus Julius enlarged it to some eighty years ago. The only positive thing about this entire woeful situation is that most of the posers are gone—Tiberius in particular was ruthless in purging the Senate of ineligible members. With the help of the emperor, I am actually trying to enlarge the Senate's membership, making appointments from honorable families whose path up the cursus honorum has been blocked by false accusations or unexpected reversals of fortune. While the Senate may not reach five hundred in our lifetime, I do think the membership shall be restored to at least some three hundred and fifty by the end of the year.

As far as personal news goes, after living as a widower for two years, I am seriously considering marrying again. However, I am NOT interested in a sixteen-year-old bride, as my dear Claudia suggested on her death bed—at my age that would be pure foolishness, and an open invitation for some young swell to put cuckold's horns on me! I have been seeing a respectable widow named Tertia Livilla, once the wife of my old friend Marcus Livillus. She is forty years old, pleasingly proportioned, and makes me laugh. Her sons are grown and married, and while she continues to live with her eldest, his wife is not fond of her, so she is looking for a new husband. We have not announced our intentions yet, but we probably will do so as soon as you are safely back in Rome. It would be an honor to have you stand with me on the day of our nuptials!

The emperor tells me you should be home by the end of spring, so I look forward to hearing your reply in person rather than reading it. Stay safe, my dear nephew, until I can embrace you again. Lucius Hortensius sends you greetings; he has never forgotten the day you won him his home back. May the gods guard you on your journey!

Marcus smiled at the thought of seeing Mencius happily wed—his uncle surely deserved to spend his last years with a companion who would bring him joy and make his house a true home again. On that note, he began reflecting on his own situation. He was now in his mid-thirties, with a record of honors and accomplishments that should make him a very eligible bachelor once he returned to Rome. Did he really want to remarry? After much debate, he had decided that he did. The thought of spending the next thirty years of his life alone, or only enjoying the occasional company of a slave girl in bed, was not something he looked forward to. But how to go about finding a bride? His first marriage had been arranged by his parents, and they had chosen well. But now that he was truly on his own, he had no idea how to court a woman. Perhaps, he thought, if he was as good a catch as he imagined himself to be, his next bride would find him.

Rufus Licinius joined him at the rail, looking uncharacteristically troubled. He was clutching a sheet of papyrus which he glanced at from time to time. Marcus had noticed that ever since the letters from Rome had arrived, Rufus had been downcast, but Marcus had lacked the opportunity to ask him about it before now.

"What's troubling you, my friend?" he asked. "You've been glum for the last week!"

The burly bodyguard sighed. "Well, Your Excellency, I hate to bother you with my troubles, you being such an important fellow and all."

"My dear Rufus," Marcus said, "you are not just some bit of hired muscle to me! We've been through enough together that I count you as one of my closest friends, and I would not be alive to make this voyage home were it not for your bravery and loyalty. When you are troubled, I am troubled with you. So out with it—what's weighing so heavily on you?"

"It's this!" the big man said miserably, thrusting the letter at Marcus. "Read it yourself—I can't stand to look at it again."

Marcus took the letter and studied it closely. The handwriting was feminine, but very crude, and the spelling was creative to say the least. But the message was still crystal clear:

Deer Rufus, it read.

Pleez don't be angry when you reed this. I waited fer you as long as a good girl shood, but you been gone fer nigh on three yeers now when you sed it wood only be fer two. I thank you fer the gold you sent me, but a few danaryus don't warm my bed at nite, or keep the scoundrels in our neyberhood from groping at me when I goes to the well every morning. I have took up with the blacksmith who lives down the street; he sez will be maryed as soon as he can make enuff money to pay the pontiff fer a servis. I am happy now; I loved you fer awhile and enjoyed our time together, but it's done. Don't you come sniffing around trying to get me back neither; Janus sez he'll knock your hed in with his smith's hammer iffen you make any trouble. I am sorry to tell you like this, but I figger it's better than you coming home and finding me gone. Yer brother has all yer stuff that you left in the insula. No longer yers truly, Flavia

Marcus looked at the big man, whose eyes were red with tears. "Ouch!" he said. "I'm sorry your true love wasn't true, my friend."

"Better to find out now, I guess, sir," said Rufus, balling up the letter and throwing it into the sea. "But here's the rub—I really did love her! I wanted her to be my wife and mother to my children. Now what do I have to come home to?"

"My dear Rufus," Marcus said, "for one thing, you have the friendship and patronage of a rising star in the Roman Senate. I am going to secure you that spot in the Lictor's College and request that you be permanently assigned as the head of my detail. I am also going to see about finding you a decent house instead of a room in some flea-infested insula in the Aventine. Between your lictor's salary and a nice home, you will have young girls falling at your feet by the end of summer, and you can take your pick of the lot!"

"Begging your pardon, sir, but why would you want to go and do all of that?" Rufus said.

"Because you're my friend, you oaf, and you've saved my life more times than I can count!" said Marcus. "Now wipe that frown off your face—you have a whole new life waiting for you in Rome."

Overcome with emotion, Rufus caught Marcus in a bear hug that lifted the quaestor clean off the deck of the ship and squeezed the wind out of him.

"Gods bless ya, sir!" he said. "I've never had such a friend! I'm ashamed of myself for moping around when you have been so good to me. Let Flavia have her smelly blacksmith! I've seen the fellow she's taken up with, and he is bald, fat, and only has six teeth in his whole head!"

Marcus tried to laugh, but he couldn't draw in enough air. "Put me down, man!" he said. "My friendship does you no good if you squeeze the life out of me before we get home!"

"Sorry, sir, I was just a bit overcome!" Rufus said. "I'll leave you to your thoughts." He walked down the deck whistling a merry tune, leaving Marcus smiling and rubbing his bruised ribs.

Cadius came running up from the stern, where he had cast out a trolling line in the ship's wake, trying to catch a fish.

"What was that all about, *Dominus*?" he asked with some concern. "I thought Rufus was going to throw you overboard!"

"No," Marcus said, "he was actually being affectionate. Did you hear about his news from home?"

"He wouldn't tell me, but I guessed. His girl left him for another, is that it?" Cadius asked.

"That's what happened, all right," said Marcus. "He was feeling pretty glum, but I think I may have helped him some. Are you ready to be back home, lad?"

"I think so—but it's been so long since we left Rome, it will take me awhile to get used to not traveling everywhere," Cadius replied.

"I agree," Marcus said. "I've also gotten used to being on the move all the time."

"What are you going to do with me, *Dominus*?" Cadius asked. "I'm no longer your slave, so what will become of me? Will I still be able to live with you and work for you?"

Marcus looked up and down the deck to make sure no one was too close. He had been thinking about the lad's fate for a long time, and now his mind was made up. He figured it was time to let Cadius in on his plans.

"I think it's high time I hired a pedagogue for you so you can learn your letters and the rudiments of public speaking," he said. "You are behind where you should be on your education, but as intelligent as you are, I think you can catch up quickly enough if you set your mind to it."

"A pedagogue?" Cadius asked, puzzled. "Why on earth would you want to send me to school? That's a lot of money, and I'm only a simple freedman."

"Do you want to continue to live in my household, Cadius?" Marcus asked him.

"Of course, *Dominus*!" the boy said. "I have no idea how to live on my own. You have been so kind to me, I don't want to leave your—your service."

"You started to say something else there, lad," Marcus said. "What was it?"

"Well, I didn't want to be presumptuous," Cadius said.

"You weren't," Marcus replied. "I just want to know what word you started to say before you changed your mind."

"Well, I was going to say that I didn't want to leave your family," Cadius finally said.

"Is that what I am to you?" Marcus asked.

"Forgive me, *Dominus*, I didn't mean to insult you!" the boy said. Despite his physical growth and quick wits, the look in his eyes was that of a frightened orphan. "It's just that you have been so kind to me, I've come to look up to you as if you were—well, as if . . ."

"Are you trying to tell me that you see me as a father?" Marcus asked.

Cadius nodded. "You've been the closest thing I have had to a father since Caligula took my own father from me," he said.

"And I have come to love you as a son," Marcus replied. "So I think the most obvious solution for both of us is to make it official. I would like to adopt you, Cadius. Would you like to become my legal son?"

The teen's eyes lit up, and he gave Marcus a smile of overwhelming joy. "You would do that for me?" he said. "You would make me your own son, your heir, part of your family? Really? Oh, *Dominus*, that is more than I could ever have hoped for!"

"On one condition!" Marcus said sharply.

"Of course, sir, anything you say!" the boy replied.

"Never call me *dominus* again!" Marcus told him with a mock scowl. "You may call me by my name, or you may call me *Pater.* But I want every last trace of the master-slave relationship to end here and now!"

For the second time that morning, Marcus found himself the recipient of an enthusiastic hug—although this one was not nearly as bone-crushing as the one Rufus had inflicted on him. He had made two men very happy this morning, he thought. He hoped that some Roman woman he had not yet met would be as overjoyed to share his name as this young man was.

"Thank you so much, *Pater,*" said Cadius.

"I have been contemplating this ever since you took that *gladius* that was meant for me," Marcus said. "But I figured since we were on our way home, this would be the time to tell you what was in my heart. Now, have you caught any fish this morning?"

"No," Cadius said. "They have stolen my bait several times, and once I set the hook, but the confounded thing broke my line!"

"Well, let's go see if we can haul in a nice big one for our dinner," Marcus replied, and they made their way to the stern of the ship.

The rest of the voyage passed uneventfully—the winds were favorable, the seas were occasionally choppy but never terribly rough, and the crew went about their duties cheerfully. Marcus discovered that, among the dozen or so other passengers, there was another Christian—a friend of Paul's named Andronicus. He took the time to sit with the man and listen to him relate many of the stories about Jesus, and even committed some of Jesus' wonderful stories to memory. The more he learned, thought Marcus, the more sense the Nazarene religion made to him. He looked forward to seeing Paul again at some point, so he could fulfill his promise to be baptized into the new faith.

It was on a fine morning during the first week of Juno when the harbor of Brundisium finally came into view. Marcus, Cassius, and their companions, as well as the other passengers, all stood topside to watch the Italian coastline slowly grow closer. It was a perfect day in early summer, and the ship's sails crackled in the wind as they neared the harbor. As the crew began to scramble down from the rigging and make preparations to tie up to the pier, Marcus went below decks to gather up all his personal effects. It was surprising, he thought, how little he had left with and how little he had returned with. One medium-sized trunk, a large pack full of clothes, and two saddlebags had seen him to the edge of the Roman world and back.

His companions likewise gathered their gear, and in a less than two hours from the time they first glimpsed the shoreline on the horizon, they were standing on the pier, back on Italian soil for the first time in almost three full years. It was nearly five hundred miles from Brundisium to Rome, however, and there were several things to attend to before they could begin the final leg of their journey. Marcus turned to the others and began going over what was needed.

"Rufus, if you and Arminius would please go find the nearest stable and purchase us five swift horses and a nice strong pack mule, I need for Cassius to act as my witness in a matter I need to take care of before the local magistrate," he said.

"I know what you're going to do," Rufus said, "and while I'll be glad to hire us some horses, I would like to be present also."

"And I!" said Arminius. "I would like to see some good come from us having to tote that boy from Ancyra to Antioch!"

Marcus looked at the two men, and at Cadius, whose eyes were dancing with excitement. He had forgotten for a moment that these two men had come to love the boy as much as he did.

"Fine!" he said. "Another hour more or less on the way to Rome will not matter that much!"

And so it was on a fine June day, in the presence of a grumpy old magistrate named Janicus Frumentius, that Cadius the orphan boy became Cadius Quintus Publius, the son and heir of Senator Marcus Quintus Publius, Quaestor of Rome. Their three companions acted as the principle witnesses of the ceremony, while four professional witnesses were hired from the group that usually congregated around a magistrate's office, in order to bring the number up to the seven required by Roman law.

The *Agrodatio,* or adoption of an adult or near adult, was normally a complex ritual. However, since Cadius had no father, the first half of the ceremony, in which Marcus would have paid Cadius' father three times for his son, and then seen him bought back twice, could be skipped. Instead, the magistrate questioned the three principle witnesses, who all verified that Cadius was a freeborn Roman who had been orphaned, and then the magistrate pronounced that Cadius, from that day forward, fell under the *patria potestas* of Marcus Quintus Publius, and that he would legally remain a son of house Publii from that day forward until the day he died. After the papers were signed and the necessary vows uttered, Marcus paid the professional witnesses and retired with his new son and their three companions to a nearby tavern, where they celebrated the occasion with wine and a roasted kid, as well as some stewed vegetables and fresh fruit just brought over from Carthage.

"I must say, Marcus," Cassius Claudius commented in between sips of wine, "this is not the outcome I expected when we commenced this voyage. Even when you brought it up to me earlier, I never thought you would actually follow through with it!"

"I've thought about it ever since the day that legionary tried to kill us and Cadius took a blade that was meant for me," Marcus said. "I was already fond of the lad, but his heroism deserved a greater reward than merely freeing him. I have watched him grow up over these last few years, and I have found in him every quality that I would hope to find in a son of my blood. Life is short, and I have no wife. Even if I change that, who knows if God will ever bless me with another boy? Here I have before me all the son any man could ever want!"

Cadius looked up at his new father with adoration in his eyes, and then he stood and spoke also.

"And I must say that, although my mother and father were as good and kind a set of parents as any boy could wish for, my *pater* Marcus Quintus has been a kind and loving master, and I know he will be my kind and loving father from this day forward!" he exclaimed. "Long live the Publii!"

The people in the tavern were all listening in, and when Marcus embraced his boy, there was much cheering and thumping on tables. By the time they were done feasting and drinking, it was past mid-afternoon, and Marcus decided that they should spend the night and light out for Rome first thing the next morning. Rufus and Arminius set out to hire horses for them, swaying a bit from too much wine, and Marcus rented them a large pair of rooms on the top story of the tavern in which to sleep.

Dawn came far too early the next day, and with much grumbling and harrumphing Marcus managed to get everyone up and ready to go. Their bags and trunks were loaded, and by the third hour, the party of five that had set out from Rome almost three years before were mounted up and riding hard north and east along a well-cobbled Roman road. They were going home at last.

CHAPTER XVII

"Armenia!" Claudius Caesar exclaimed. "Is the man mad?"

The emperor was reclining on a couch in the rented villa outside Rome where Marcus and Cadius were staying. They had hired it as soon as they arrived two days before, since, by ancient tradition, Marcus could not cross the *pomerium* and enter the city until after he had celebrated his triumph, something that might not happen for several months. Indeed, in past times, many *triumphators* had waited years outside the city until some crisis had passed, or the political landscape had changed, so that they could celebrate their moment of supreme martial glory. Marcus' household slaves had quickly made the trek from his villa in the city to attend to their master, whose fairness and kindness had earned their loyalty long ago.

Claudius had been busy drawing up legislation for the Senate, which would convene in a few days, but Marcus had sent the freedman Cassius Claudius straight to him, bearing the letter from Vologases to the emperor of Rome. Cassius had returned later that evening, bringing word that Claudius would join Marcus at the villa for the noontide meal in two days. Marcus had set his slaves to work cleaning the place up, and old Phidias, leaning on a cane but as spry and irascible as ever, pressed the cooks to come up with a meal worthy of the empire's ruler.

It was an excellent meal, Marcus reflected, but a wasted one. The emperor arrived shortly before noon, with the muscular, stocky form of his adopted son Nero trailing him closely behind. Marcus had raised an eyebrow at that, but Cassius had told him that Nero was neck-deep in all the emperor's councils these days, even though he was not quite fifteen yet. Claudius had only taken time to pop a couple of grilled mushrooms into his mouth before he began to speak, posing his outraged question to his host.

"He is most assuredly not mad, Most Excellent Claudius," Marcus said. "He is ruthless, ambitious, cruel, and highly intelligent, but he is completely sane."

"Cassius told me of your interviews with him," the emperor said, "but I want to hear it all from your own lips. Act as if I had never read this letter or spoken to my freedman, and tell me everything that transpired."

Marcus related the entire story of his mission to Parthia, from the moment he received the emperor's letter until his arrival at Brundisium. Of course, he focused primarily on his time in Ecbatana and his interviews with the high king. The emperor listened intently, nodding from time to time and periodically interrupting with piercing questions. Nero looked bored for the most part, although his eyes lit up when Marcus described the emperor's menagerie of great cats, especially his description of the fearful speartooth tiger. He actually interrupted Marcus' tale at that point.

"What a monster!" he said. "Surely there must be more than one of them left in the wild somewhere? Uncle Claudius, could you find me one? I would love to have it ever so much!"

"I'm sure you would love to have a basilisk and a gorgon while I was at it!" the emperor said with some affection. "How about I bring you Medusa as well? Perhaps her gaze would turn you to a statue and I could finish this important conference without further interruption!"

The burly youth hung his head for a moment and then gave a hangdog smile. For just a second Marcus thought he saw a flash of anger in those muddy brown eyes, but it came and went so quickly he could not be sure.

"Cadius!" he said. "Why don't you take our guest out and show him the horse I bought for you yesterday?"

"Of course, *Pater*," the teenager replied. "Would you like to come and see my horse, Nero?"

The emperor's heir snorted. "I'd rather hear the rest of the story about Vologases," he said, "but my esteemed father has decided otherwise. By all means, show me your horse."

Emperor and Quaestor watched as the two young men, only a few months apart in age, left the couches and headed outside.

"So you actually adopted the slave boy your uncle bought you?" the emperor said. "I have freed many of my slaves, and slept with a few of them, but I never thought to make one of them my heir!"

"The boy was born a free Roman," Marcus said. "It was only through ill fortune and the madness of Caligula that he became a slave."

"You're a kind soul, Marcus Quintus," the emperor said. "That was well done. Now, finish telling me about your second interview with Vologases."

Marcus related the end of his time with the high king and then briefly described his homeward voyage, pausing to mention the woes of the current prefect of Judea, Ventidius Cumanus. Claudius shook his head.

"That is such a difficult province to govern," he said, "and the empire rarely has competent governors to spare for such a poor region. I had hoped he would be more successful at keeping the peace. It seems as though the introduction of this new faith you seem so fascinated with has complicated things even further!" He sighed, taking a sip of wine, and finally began to focus his attention on the table. He selected a few pieces of grilled chicken and fish to put on his plate, and Marcus did likewise.

"Retrieving the bones of Crassus' men was a stroke of genius," he said. "I have already spoken to the *Pontifex Maximus* about holding a public funeral for them, with games to honor their memory. Would you be willing to speak to the people?"

"Of course, Claudius," said Marcus. "I would rather not offer the sacrifices, however, since I have come to a parting of ways with the gods of Rome. Traditions I will continue to honor, but actual worship—I find myself increasingly uncomfortable with the idea."

The emperor nodded. "You are the first highborn Roman I know of to actually embrace this new faith," he said. "When time allows, I wish to learn more of it from you. For now, I am going to mull over what you have told me of Vologases, and how to reply. I am asking the Senate to expedite your triumph as quickly as possible—I want you to stand for Tribune of the Plebs this fall. I will be serving as consul, with Nero as my colleague. It may take both of us to keep him reined in properly."

"Consul at fifteen?" Marcus asked in astonishment. "That seems frightfully young for such a responsibility!"

Claudius nodded. "Indeed, it is," he said. "But I am past sixty, and the *medicus* says that my heart is growing weak. I must give thought to who will succeed me. Nero is the older of my two sons, but I do not think he has the makings of a capable emperor. No doubt his mother will offer him some guidance—but I would rather live long enough to see my Britannicus succeed me! Agrippina has done her best to make me forget the son of my blood, but I will not see him shunted aside so easily. Nero is intelligent, and has some skill in logic and rhetoric, but he tends to let his passions run away with him. Caligula demonstrated those are not good qualities in an emperor! But Nero is also beloved of the people as a descendant of Augustus and a grandson of Germanicus. I think a disastrous turn as consul might show the people the wisdom of my decision to replace him in the succession. Your judicious use of the veto could save the Republic, my friend!"

Marcus swallowed hard. He was proud to be a friend of the current emperor, but he did not wish to make an enemy of the new one. Still, he was grateful to Claudius for all he had done, and wanted to repay the emperor's trust to the best of his ability.

"You honor me," he said finally. "If you wish me to stand for Tribune of the Plebs, I will gladly do so."

"If Rome produced more men like you, Marcus, it would have suffered less turmoil over the last century," Claudius told him. "Or perhaps not. There were many good, decent Romans in the Senate during the Civic Wars, and some sided with Cato and Pompey, while others sided with the *Divus Julius.* My noble uncle Augustus proscribed some of the most capable members of the Senate when he was dividing power with Anthony. Virtue, sadly, is no guarantee of reward—but in your case, I will try to make sure that you receive the rewards your loyalty and competence have earned!"

"To enjoy your confidence and friendship is reward enough," Marcus said.

The emperor laughed. "My confidence has been well placed!" he said. "And, in lieu of future rewards, I would like to give you a gift. I have a lovely villa in Pompeii that I rarely use. I grant it to you and your heirs in perpetuity. May it be your refuge from the worries of Rome and the burdens of office!"

Marcus bowed deeply. He was truly grateful for all Claudius had done for him, but his worries about the future still lingered. Some of his apprehension must have shown on his face, for the bushy-haired emperor smiled and gave him a wink.

"I know you are concerned about what may happen if I raise you up as a tool against Nero's succession and he winds up following me to the purple anyway," he said. "Fear not! What I intend to do is make you so indispensable to the governing of the empire that my heir and his mother are both convinced that they cannot do without you. You will still be around, and honored above all councilors, long after I go to join my predecessors."

"You don't miss much, Excellency," Marcus said. "I'll admit the thought had crossed my mind."

After that they settled down to dinner, and Nero and Cadius rejoined them. The two boys seemed to get along well enough, but Marcus could tell that Cadius was less than thrilled with the company he'd been forced to keep. Later that night, after the emperor and his entourage had left, he called the teen to his side.

"Well, son," he said, "tell me what you think of the emperor's heir."

Cadius looked at him warily. He was still adjusting to his new role as Marcus' son and heir, instead of merely a loyal servant. Finally, he spoke.

"He's a bright fellow," he told his adoptive father. "He knew a great deal about horses and showed me a thing or two about riding."

"He's had a wonderful education," Marcus said, "but what do you think of him? That is what I asked. Do you find him trustworthy and honorable, or not?"

The boy's face darkened. "No," he said sharply. "He's a bully. I dealt with enough like him when I was a slave. He'll be as kind as you please until no one is watching, and then he will beat you just to hear you cry. He reminds me of the son of my old master—the one I was sold for punching in the nose!"

Marcus laughed. "Do me a favor and don't punch Nero!" he said. "He may well be emperor one day, and I have no desire to wind up as another Pontius Pilate!"

The next month passed in a blur of preparation. Marcus' clients wasted no time reestablishing their relationship with their patron, and every morning found a line of them standing outside the villa, even though he was not able to enter the city and argue cases yet. Colleagues from the Senate, some he remembered and some he could not recall meeting at all, came out to congratulate him on his impending triumph and to solicit his opinions. One of them was none other than Quintus Africanus, the defendant in the first case Marcus had prosecuted as a senator. Even though he had volunteered to relinquish his villa to Lucius Hortensius, Marcus was still a bit surprised to see him.

"I'm one of the senior *pontiffs* now," he said. "I am to preside over the burial service for the ashes of Crassus' men that you brought back to Rome."

"I am happy that your fortunes are on the rise," said Marcus. "I understand now why you have come to see me."

"I do wish to discuss the funeral rites," said Quintus, "but there is something else I would talk with you about."

Marcus looked at the older man with curiosity. Africanus was nearing fifty, and other than the case over the villa he had purchased during Caligula's proscriptions, Marcus had never had any dealings with the man. He certainly did not appear to be the sort who would wish to become the client of a junior senator, however powerful.

"You have filled me with curiosity," he said. "What else do you want with me?"

"It's rather delicate," said Quintus. "But if you would consent to come and dine with me at my villa the night after your triumph, all will be explained."

"A mystery!" Marcus said. "How can I refuse?"

"Then I shall see you in a few weeks' time," Quintus said. "In the meantime, let us discuss your funeral oration for the lost legionaries of Crassus."

Not long after that the legion that Marcus had commanded in the recapture of Pannonia arrived in Rome, having been relieved of their post so they could come to the capital and celebrate their victory. Of the ten thousand Osterlings that had been sent to Rome as prisoners, all the warriors—some six thousand—were still being held back from sale as slaves until after the procession; they would march behind the wagons holding their weapons and the armor and crown of their king in Marcus' triumph. Afterward, they would be auctioned off at the slave markets and a third of the proceeds would go to the treasury of Rome. The remainder Marcus would divide with the men of the Pannonian Legion; he had resolved to keep a third for himself and give them two thirds, instead of the traditional halfway split—after all, he had been an interloper arriving on the scene, not their regular commander.

However, no one would have guessed that by the way the legionaries hailed Marcus when he went riding into their camp. Huge cheers split the air, and cries of "*Imperator*" greeted him as he rode along, leaning down to clasp hands with some of the centurions he remembered. The temporary legate he had appointed, Antonius Corbulus, was now fully healed of his ordeal as a captive of the Osterlings and eager to share dinner with the man who had rescued him.

"The Senate confirmed your appointment of me as legate and made it permanent," he said. "We've had a few incursions by smaller bands of Osterlings here and there along the frontier, but you taught them to give our legions a wide berth, and I destroyed one band of about five hundred three or four months ago, right before we came back to Rome. The prisoners we took have said that most of their people have moved northward, into Germania. Let the Cherusci deal with them! They deserve each other."

Marcus laughed, imagining the fierce head hunters of the black forests of Germania locked in mortal combat with the Osterling horde. Was it possible they could both lose? he wondered. A man could only hope.

"The men look well," he said. "Victory agrees with them!"

"Does it disagree with anyone?" Antonius said. "Speaking of which, the men would like to invite you to inspect them after we eat. They are forming up even now."

"An odd invitation!" Marcus said. "But I will be delighted to review them when we are done."

The luncheon was spare but wholesome—roasted fowl, leeks, and steamed mussels, along with bread and olive oil. When they finished, Marcus stood up from the couch and stretched.

"You'll need your military uniform to inspect the men," Corbulus told him. "I took the liberty of having your man Rufus bring it from your villa."

Marcus raised an eyebrow. "Is there something you are not telling me, Legate?" he asked.

"I have no idea what you are talking about, *Triumphator!*" he said.

Marcus donned his cuirass and leggings with the help of the legate's manservant, then strapped on his *gladius*. Rufus came into the tent and joined them, wearing the uniform of a centurion, since the legion had voted to make him an honorary officer after the campaign in Pannonia. The burly Roman was grinning at Marcus, who felt increasingly as if he was being set up for something.

"The reviewing stand is this way," said Legate Corbulus, walking out of the tent. A platform had been erected at one end of the Campus Martius, and the legion was formed up before it. As

Marcus climbed the steps, he was astonished to see the emperor standing there, in full military regalia.

"Hail Marcus Quintus Publius, *Imperator* and soon to be *Triumphator!*" he said with a smile.

"Your Excellency!" Marcus said. "What on earth are you doing here?"

"The soldiers of the Pannonian Legion, newly designated as *Legio XIX*, have asked me to come and be their witness today as they honor you," Claudius replied, "to which I have gladly assented."

"They have already hailed me as *Imperator* on the field," Marcus said. "I will be the first of my family to ever celebrate a triumph. What more can they do?"

"I shall let them tell you," the emperor said.

A group of thirty centurions formed up on the field and marched toward the reviewing stand, then mounted the steps three abreast. Their leader, the *Primipilus* Centurion Decimus Meridius, stepped forward, his decorations gleaming on his finely tooled black leather cuirass.

"After you left our province, I met with all the centurions and senior veterans that you led in battle against the Osterlings," he said. "We all agreed that our legion was doomed before your arrival. Beaten, over half our number slain, bereft of leadership, and driven into a fortified camp, there is no doubt among us that had the Osterlings attacked us before you arrived, we should have been slaughtered to the last man. You rallied us, reorganized us, reminded us that we were Romans, and led us to destroy our enemies even as they would have destroyed us. You single-handedly saved our legion from destruction, and slew the king of the Osterlings with your own hand. So after our meeting, I went with ten of the veterans of the battle, and we wove this for you!"

He gestured, and the centurions parted ranks to reveal one of their number bearing a cushion of scarlet cloth, upon which rested a simple crown woven of Pannonian grass and flowers. Marcus stood astonished, unable to speak.

"Upon behalf of the Nineteenth Legion, with the permission and approval of the Senate of Rome, let all the chronicles show that the men of the legion have bestowed upon their legate, Marcus Quintus Publius, the *Corona Granicus,* the Grass Crown, the highest military decoration that the Roman Republic may offer one of its sons," the emperor proclaimed.

Marcus knelt before Decimus Meridius, who placed the Grass Crown upon his head. Marcus stood, and the entire legion rendered a closed fist salute, and then shouted with a roar that made the walls of Rome tremble: "Hail *Imperator*! Hail to Marcus, the winner of the Grass Crown! Hail Victory!"

One week later, Marcus wore the Grass Crown upon his head, as well as the traditional laurel wreath that was held above him by a slave while he stood, ramrod straight, in the ancient Triumphator's chariot. His face was painted scarlet, his officers and legionaries were marching before him, and the spoils of his brief campaign were piled in wagons behind him. Last of all, six thousand Osterling prisoners marched, chained together, jeered by the crowd and pelted with vegetables and rotten fruit. As was tradition, the legionaries chanted bawdy songs praising their victorious commander and poking fun at him all at once:

Who was Quintus Publius? Old Claudius' right-hand man,

He toured the provinces of Rome, and how those crooks all ran!

He came to Pannonia, found our legions in a bind,

But once he took command we left our woes all far behind!

He was short and bald and his voice was far too soft,

A hero of the empire should be made of sterner stuff!

But you can ask the Osterlings whom he sent straight to Hades,

Who had plundered our whole province, and murdered wives and babies,

If this simple Roman senator is truly made of steel,

And with their slain king they'll tell you Marcus Quintus is for real!

The heavy red makeup that covered Marcus' face was prone to crack easily, but it was hard for him not to smile was he heard those lyrics shouted to the crowds, who soon took up the cry themselves. It was enough to go to one's head straightaway, he thought—which was why there was another age-old tradition regarding Roman triumphs: the slave who stood behind the *triumphator* in the carriage, whispering an ancient Latin phrase in his ear: *"Respice post te—homenum te memento!"* Look behind you, and remember you are but a man!

The procession wound through the city of Rome, winding up at the Great Forum on Capitoline Hill, where the laurel wreath was returned to the Temple of Mars Invictus, while the armor and crown of the Osterling king were laid by Marcus' men before the altar of Jupiter Optimus Maximus, the chief deity and protector of Rome. Marcus felt rather ambiguous about the religious overtones of all of this, given his secret loyalty to his new god, Jesus, but he had promised the emperor that he would observe all the niceties of the occasion without protest. Besides, he thought, in many ways, Jupiter Ops—Jupiter the Greatest and Highest—was the closest thing the Romans had to the single God of Israel. Immortal, invisible, and majestic, Jupiter was represented by an ancient statue in his temple, but even the Pontifex Maximus acknowledged that his true names, and true form, were unknown to mortal men. Perhaps Jupiter the Best and Greatest was simply the form in which the true God had made himself known to Rome long before. Marcus made up his mind to ask Paul about that if he ever saw him again.

After the offerings were concluded, Marcus was able to wash the red *stibium* from his face and don his dress toga in place of his military gear, although the Grass Crown would remain on his head for the remainder of the day. After that, he would place it carefully in the cabinet where he kept his family's *imagio*, the wax memorial masks of notable ancestors that were worn during funeral processions. The Grass Crown might fade and wither, but it could never be replaced with another, and when Marcus died, it would be placed on his brow before his body was committed to his funeral pyre.

The entire Roman Senate rose and applauded, led by the emperor himself, as Marcus entered the chamber and took his seat. Although he had never been elected consul, he was no longer a *pedarius*, a back bencher who would speak only when addressed by the *Princeps Senatus* or the emperor. He was now a respected senior member, a Conscript Father of Rome, whose voice would be heard in debate only after the consuls and former holders of that rank had spoken. Marcus delivered copies of his written reports on the Pannonian Campaign, his tour of the provinces, and his interview with Vologases, high king of Parthia, to the emperor and the *Princeps Senatus*. The Senate voted their thanks for his services, and Claudius gave a speech praising Marcus' service to himself and to the Senate and People of Rome. After a prayer of thanksgiving by the *Pontifex Maximus,* the senators were dismissed to the feast that had been prepared to honor the newest hero of the Republic, Marcus Quintus Publius.

CHAPTER XVIII

The mystery of Quintus Africanus' invitation was cleared up for Marcus the night after his triumph. After a comfortable night back in his own home, he answered the summons to dinner the next evening, wondering what his former legal opponent might have in store for him. The villa was luxurious, not large but well appointed, with a lovely atrium in the center, its reflecting pool open to the sky. The main dining chamber featured a series of curved couches, facing inward to a nice-sized table. The furniture could easily be rearranged to accommodate more guests, but this evening the room was set for a small group—one couch for the men, another for the women, but placed closely enough that the two groups could converse easily. In the Republic, men and women only dined from the same couch when the family was alone.

Marcus reclined at the couch with his host, Quintus, and Quintus' eldest son, Titus, who was seventeen and had just donned his *toga virilis*. He was a bit wide-eyed at the thought of sharing the table with a *triumphator* of the Republic. After fending off several inquiries, Marcus finally regaled him with a much abbreviated account of the battles in Pannonia, trying to de-emphasize his own role as much as possible and talk about the bravery of the legions. It was no use, however; by the end of his narrative, Marcus found that father and son alike were staring at him with admiration, joined by the three women at the next couch.

The ladies were Antonia Claudia Africanus, Quintus' wife, and his oldest daughter, Antonia Minor, who was twenty-two, and finally his youngest child, thirteen-year-old Lucretia. Antonia the elder was in her early forties and still a handsome woman, a bit plump but pleasant of disposition and of considerable intelligence. Antonia Minor was another story—red-haired and green-eyed, she had a complexion of pure cream and surveyed Marcus with an appraising eye that he found rather unnerving.

After some further conversation, in which Marcus was pressed to do far more of the talking than he was comfortable with, family slaves brought in the dinner. The food was delicious—Marcus had to discipline himself not to overeat; he still had not adjusted to the bounty of Rome's tables after three years of touring the provinces! But the feast yesterday had been so generous he still had not recovered his appetite, so refraining was easier than it might have been. Quintus and his family were perfect hosts; Marcus relaxed and enjoyed himself more than he had in quite a long while. Finally, after dinner, the womenfolk left the room and Titus excused himself; then Quintus led Marcus out into the peristyle, where they sat down on a marble bench and talked.

"I hope the dinner and company were to your satisfaction," Quintus said.

"Absolutely!" Marcus replied. "The food was delicious and your family was very gracious."

"Did you take notice of my daughters?" asked Quintus.

"Beautiful ladies both!" said Marcus. "Where on earth did Antonia come by her hair and eye color?"

"My mother," said the senator. "She was of Gallic blood, and redheads are not uncommon in her line. Lucretia's hair is coppery in the sunlight, but Antonia's blazes like a bonfire!"

"And her eyes are like emeralds," Marcus said. "I am surprised she is still living at home."

"She is widowed," Quintus explained. "She was married at seventeen, but her husband was one of those seduced by Messalina. He paid for his foolishness with his life, and Claudius was kind enough to spare Antonia from exile, since she had no knowledge of her husband's infidelity."

"Why would any man ever stray from such a beauty?" Marcus wondered out loud.

"Lucius Junius Quivirius was wealthy, but rather stupid," Quintus said. "It was a foolish match for me to make, but he was so attracted to Antonia, and made me offers of land and estates if I would agree to the marriage. She found him unattractive and boring, and he tired of her almost right away—I think that he was one of those men who found the hunt more exciting than the kill, if you take my meaning. So he left her alone in his magnificent villa and took to chasing married women, and wound up in bed with the emperor's wife."

Marcus shook his head. "I was there the day Messalina met her end," he said. "She was a foolish and selfish girl."

Quintus nodded. "Her promiscuity left many men dead," he said. "I understand Claudius' decision—how could any emperor leave the men who cuckolded him still breathing! But it left my daughter a widow at age nineteen, and now very few men have expressed an interest in her because of her past."

"I find that hard to believe," Marcus said. "She is Venus personified, and obviously very intelligent!"

"Some men are threatened by intelligent women," Quintus replied.

"Some men are idiots!" Marcus snapped back. "A pleasing body lasts as long as it takes to bear a baby or two, but a sharp mind and a pleasant attitude make a companion one can grow old with!" He was thinking about his Uncle Mencius and Aunt Claudia, whose love had only been sharpened by her tempestuous personality.

"So you would not be turned away by her past?" Quintus said.

"I would count myself lucky if such a one as her would have me!" Marcus replied.

"Excellent!" Quintus said. "When can I announce your betrothal?"

"What?" Marcus said, feeling as if he had been hit between the eyes with the hammer used to sacrifice the Apis bull.

"That's what this evening was all about!" Quintus said. "I have admired you ever since the day I heard you argue Lucius Hortensius' case in court so brilliantly that I found myself agreeing with you and dropping the suit! And your conduct in the provinces has earned you the respect of all Rome. Antonia is quite taken with you, and I would love to see our two families united by marriage. Your uncle thought you might be receptive to such an alliance, so I decided to bring you into my home and see how you and Antonia interacted in person."

Marcus swallowed hard. He had figured that some proposals might be coming his way, given his rise in the world, but had not really anticipated one coming his way quite so soon. And, upon reflection, he found he could not imagine a bride lovelier than the red-haired Antonia. But what on earth would she want with him?

"I think that, before I commit to anything, I should like to speak to your daughter in person," he said. "We barely conversed at all during dinner."

"Of course!" said Quintus. "In fact, that was a test I had laid out for you. If you had agreed, based on a few exchanged remarks over dinner, she was prepared to reject you."

Marcus was quite flummoxed. No wonder she had been shooting him those cool, appraising glances over dinner! And the fact that Quintus was willing to give his daughter veto power over prospective suitors was a testament to the faith her *paterfamilias* had in her judgment.

His host had already scurried off, and moments later the tall, beautiful redhead emerged into the peristyle and stood before him, smiling. Marcus rose and bowed.

"*Ave,* Antonia!" he said. "Your father says you seem to fancy me for some reason, although I cannot fathom why."

"Come now, Marcus Quintus!" she said. "Surely you cannot be ignorant of the fact that you are now the most eligible widower in Rome?"

"I figured that I would, perhaps, be a more acceptable suitor now than I was when I left," he said. "But I think that you exaggerate!"

"I was watching the maidens of Rome as they watched you during your triumph," she said. "Believe me when I say you could have your pick of them! Empty-headed geese, for the most part, but many of them quite comely."

"I find none of them as lovely as you," Marcus said.

She smiled. "You do not think me to be damaged goods?" she asked him.

"Your father told me your story," he said. "Your husband was a fool, but that is no fault of yours."

"You don't think I should have hung on his every word, wide-eyed and eager, as if he was the wisest and bravest man on earth?" she asked.

"If you thought him truly wise and brave, of course," Marcus said. "But if he was an idiot you would have merely been encouraging his delusions."

"Are you wise and brave, Marcus Quintus?" she asked him.

"For some reason, people seem to think so," he said. "I simply do what I believe is right."

"That is what I admire about you," she said. "Any man who claims to be brave or wise probably isn't. The truly brave man knows what fear is, and the truly wise man is one who knows how little he knows."

"Do you truly wish to be my wife?" Marcus said.

She kissed him then, a long and lingering kiss that spoke of passions yet untouched, of want and loss and love whose depths she had yet to plumb. Marcus was gasping when she pulled away.

"Yes, Marcus Quintus Publius, nothing would satisfy me more!" she said.

"Then let us speak to your father!" he replied. "But first—"

He returned her kiss, and the loneliness and longing that had welled up in him ever since the death of Drusilla so many long ages ago, it seemed, at last found expression. It was her turn to gasp when he was done.

"My father chose well, for both of us, I think," she said after a moment.

"There is one thing," he said. "You should know this before we commit. I no longer follow the gods of Rome."

She paused. "I am no friend to the gods," she said, "but neither am I their foe. What has taken their place in your life?"

"A new God, one who manifested Himself as a man," Marcus said. "I am still learning His ways, but I know He is real. Have you heard of the Christians?"

"Only the name," she said. "But I am content to let you teach me."

"You would abandon the religion of Rome as easily as that?" he said.

"Any god that can command your allegiance is a god I should have no trouble respecting," she replied. And with that, they went to discuss their betrothal with her father.

Cadius was a bit dismayed when Marcus came home and told him that he had decided to take a bride, but the following day he took his adopted son to meet Antonia and the visit eased the lad's fears considerably. He was instantly taken in by Antonia's kind voice and lovely face, and when Marcus explained how he had come to adopt his former slave, she embraced the boy fondly.

"Had you not acted as you did," she said, "my betrothed might never have returned to Rome, and I would still be a lonely widow in my father's house instead of a prospective bride."

"I barely remember what happened," Cadius said truthfully. "They say I was nearly killed, but everything from the time that legionary charged my master until John and Paul healed me is a blur."

"I would like to hear more of this miraculous healing," she said. "Were you really run through?"

Shyly, Cadius pulled his toga aside to show here the white scar on his belly, and the one on his back that matched it. She studied the long-healed wound closely from both sides, and then shook her head.

"*Ecastor!*" she exclaimed. "I do not see how you survived such a wound!"

"He should not have," Marcus said. "His healing was a miracle of God, no less!"

"Is this why you decided to begin worshipping the God of the Christians?" she asked Marcus.

"Yes," he said, "that was the moment that convinced me that Jesus was indeed the Christ his followers claimed him to be."

"Now I am more eager than ever to learn more about him," she said.

"As am I," Marcus replied. "I did not have time for much instruction in His teachings. Now that I have returned to the city, I hope to find a community of Christians who can teach me more about Him."

They spent an hour conversing in the garden, and then Marcus presented his betrothed with a lovely necklace of pearls and rubies he had purchased in the exclusive market on the Palatine Hill. It had cost him more than the most expensive slave he had ever bought, but the way the red gems matched her flowing locks made it worth every sestercius. Antonia fussed a bit about how much such a piece of jewelry must have cost, but he could tell by the flush of her cheeks that she was pleased. Finally, he and Cadius parted company with her and headed back to Marcus' villa on foot.

"Well, what do you think, lad?" Marcus asked.

Cadius sighed. "She's beautiful!" he said. "I hope she makes you very happy!"

"I think she will, my son," Marcus said. "She certainly seems to be as sensible and kind as she is beautiful. I was relieved to see how willing she was to accept you."

"What if she had balked at having a former slave as your son and heir?" Cadius asked.

Marcus looked at him. "Well, engagements can be broken as easily as they are made," he said. The boy gave a sigh of relief.

The next few weeks passed in a blur. Every morning Marcus met with his clients and afternoons were spent either arguing cases in the Forum or making preparations for his Uncle Mencius' wedding—and for his own. After talking things over, Marcus had decided to schedule his own nuptials about two weeks after those of his uncle. He wanted to be able to congratulate Mencius and celebrate with him, without being worried about his own ceremony coming too soon thereafter.

He also wanted to have some time to see if he could find a Christian leader to conduct a ceremony. The new faith had arrived in Rome some time in the previous decade, but fear of persecution from Rome's large Jewish population, as well as the Roman government—after all, was it not a Roman prefect that sent Jesus to the cross?—caused most followers of the new faith to keep their heads down and mouths shut in public.

Finally, after a week of subtle inquiries, one afternoon he found a merchant dressed in traditional Jewish clothes standing outside his door after the morning cluster of clients had departed.

"How may I help you, sir?" Marcus asked him.

"I was told the master of this house was seeking to meet with a follower of Jesus the Nazarene," the stranger said.

Marcus smiled. "Indeed, I am! I wish you peace in His name, my brother!"

The man's eyes widened. "You too follow our Master?" he asked.

"I am trying to do so," Marcus said, "but my knowledge of Him is yet small. Would you please enter my home?"

The merchant bowed deeply. "I am Simeon, son of Jepthah," he said. "I was a follower of Jesus briefly, during the last year of his time with us, and I was one of some five hundred brethren who saw him after his Resurrection," he said.

Marcus directed his guest to the peristyle, where they sat down on a bench together. Over the next hour, Marcus explained to Simeon how he had become a follower of Jesus during his time in the provinces, and described the miraculous healing of Cadius, as well as the time he had spent with Paul, John, and Peter.

"You know the pillars of our faith as well as I do, then," the man said. "I was never one of the Apostles, and only followed Jesus from a distance after he healed my brother, Caleb, who was lame in his feet from birth."

"I hope to see one of the Apostles again one day," Marcus said. "I promised Paul that he could baptize me when we met again."

"I do not know Paul well, but my friends in Corinth say that he dreams of coming to Rome to instruct and strengthen the Church here," Simeon told him.

"It still surprises me that the original—what did he call them?—'Apostles' of Jesus are willing to accept Paul as one of their own," Marcus said. "Didn't he persecute the Church greatly at one time?"

"Indeed, he did," replied Simeon. "We named him 'the Sanhedrin's Scourge.' Yet the Lord saw fit to call and choose him to bear the name of Christ to the Gentiles, and has confirmed that choice repeatedly by the wonders He has given Paul the power to perform, as well as by dreams and visions sent to Peter and the others."

Marcus nodded, filing this bit of information in his growing stock of knowledge about his new faith. He visited with Simeon for a while longer before finally broaching the subject he wished to address.

"I am getting married soon," he said. "I want my bride and I to honor God in our vows, but I do not know how Christians celebrate their nuptials. Can you help me?"

Simeon furrowed his bushy brows. "Most of the brothers I know come from the sons of Israel," he said. "We celebrate our weddings according to our own Jewish traditions, but also voice a prayer to Jesus to bless our union. There is not a special ritual or ceremony that Christ ordered—I only heard him mention marriage twice."

"What did He say?" Marcus asked eagerly.

"He condemned the Pharisees for the frequency and callousness with which they set aside their wives," he said. "He said divorce for any cause other than adultery was wicked, and that any man who divorces his wife for any reason other than adultery is breaking his vows."

"I have no intention of divorcing my new bride," Marcus said, "and both of us are widowed, so I think our union should be considered honorable in God's eyes."

"Nearly all the disciples are married," Simeon told him, "as are the Lord's brothers. Peter also had a first wife who died, and he remarried just a few years ago, so I certainly think your intended marriage is honorable."

"What else did Jesus say about marriage?" Marcus asked.

"He quoted the Torah, the ancient Scriptures of the Jews," Simeon said. "It says: 'And God saw that it was not good for man to be alone, and so he made for him a woman, taken from his side. So then shall a man leave his father and mother, and cleave unto his wife, and the two shall be one flesh.' Those verses are quoted at every

Jewish wedding. To this he added one thing: 'Therefore what God has joined together, let no man put asunder.'"

"I like that," Marcus said. He walked into his office and retrieved a quill and parchment. "Can you say it for me again?"

Because Antonia was a widow, the wedding ceremony was much simpler than if she had been a virgin bride embarking on her first marriage. Marcus did not have to symbolically wrestle her from her mother's arms, commemorating the seizure of the Sabine women by Romulus and Remus in the age of myths. Instead, Marcus led a procession of his closest friends and relatives, including Cadius, Mencius, Rufus, and Cassius Claudius, across town to her doorway. He had already given her the traditional iron ring to acknowledge their engagement. Antonia met him at the door of her parents' home, bearing a torch lit from their hearth, as well as a spindle and distaff, symbolizing her assumption of the role of matron in her new home. Her face was veiled in the beautiful, flame-colored saffron veil known as the *flammeum.*

Quintus Africanus placed her hand in Marcus' own right hand, and with his left hand Marcus lifted the veil from her face. Smiling, Antonia spoke the ancient Latin phrase: *"Ubi tu Gaius, ego Gaia"*—"Where thou art Gaius, then and there shall I be Gaia." Once the words were spoken, the veil was lowered and the procession left the home of the bride's parents. Her sister and mother stood at the door, weeping as tradition required—although Marcus noticed out the corner of his eye that young Lucretia stuck her tongue out at her sister once her back was turned, doubtless a bit jealous of all the attention Antonia was getting. Antonia could not see, but her mother did and gave Lucretia a sharp jerk on the ear, so fast Marcus barely saw it. The young girl's tears became much more sincere after that.

Once more according to tradition, the procession split in two—Marcus had to be present at his *domus* in order to welcome his new bride. He arrived about ten minutes before her and stood just inside his doorway as she and the others approached.

Antonia discarded the burning brand, symbolizing her break with the house of her parents, and then gave the spindle and distaff to her maid. She rubbed the doorposts with fat and oil and wreathed them in wool, thus taking on the domestic duties of her new home. Marcus then removed her *flammeum,* and she spoke the Latin vow for a second time. At this point he swept her up in his arms and boldly stepped across the threshold into his villa. This deed was closely watched by all the witnesses, since the slightest misstep or stumble in carrying the bride into the new house was considered a disastrous omen. Marcus, however, was sure-footed, and Antonia was slim and light of weight; he deposited her in the atrium without missing a beat. The crowd threw up a great cheer, and bawdy songs and poems were shouted at the new couple. Marcus stepped out onto the porch once more and bowed to the assembled guests, then paid each of the attendants a denarius for their troubles.

Inside the home, Quintus Africanus, in his role as pontiff, tied their hands together at the wrist with a silken chord and passed them over three bowls—one filled with water, one with salt, and the final one containing a lit candle. These stood for life, prosperity, and the warmth of home. Here Marcus and Antonia parted from tradition—instead of making the traditional offering to Vesta and the household gods, or *lares,* Marcus knelt before the altar he had prepared to Christ. Not knowing what image would honor his new deity, he had, on Simeon's advice, etched the Greek letters *chi* and *ro* (for Christos) into the wall above a single lit candle. There, in the presence of Quintus and the Roman priestess called the *pronuba,* Marcus and Antonia repeated the simple phrase he had memorized:

"And God saw that it was not good for man to be alone, and so He created woman out of man's side. For this reason, a man shall leave his father and mother, and cleave unto his wife, and the two shall be one flesh. Therefore, what God hath joined together, let no man put asunder."

After the vow was spoken, the *pronuba* untied the silken chord and led Marcus and Antonia to the hallway, where they each laid a wreath of flowers and a walnut on the small, ceremonial bed called a *lectus genialis,* which had been set up there for the occasion. Antonia then bowed deeply to her new husband, and the *pronuba* led her to their bedchamber to prepare her for her husband's arrival, while Marcus went to the dining room, where his personal guests awaited. The feast for the bride's female guests had been held the night before, and the following evening a combined party would be thrown for both their friends and families.

He looked around the room at the familiar faces: his uncle Mencius, Cadius (who would be spending the night with his old friend Arnulf, the cooper's boy), Quintus Africanus and his son Titus, Rufus—who looked particularly sharp in his new lictor's uniform—Cassius Claudius, several of his most prominent clients, and finally a mark of favor from Claudius himself in the person of the emperor's two sons, Nero and Britannicus. Marcus had not seen Britannicus since the lad was a small boy. Now he was thirteen, and stood tall and strong beside his adoptive brother. Nero was all charm for the occasion, but Marcus could not help but note the cool, speculative glances he gave the others when he thought they were not looking.

The guests raised three cheers for the bridegroom when he stepped into the room, and Marcus drained his wine goblet in celebration, but made sure that the next two cups were thoroughly watered—he did not want to come to his marriage bed with his wits dulled! By now the bawdy jokes and suggestions were flowing thick and fast, and Marcus—always a rather private person where his love life was concerned—was beginning to get a bit red around the ears. After a particularly explicit verse by young Nero—Marcus did not think a fifteen-year-old should even be aware of some of the acts the poem described!—he stood and raised his glass one last time.

"I thank you for your gifts and good wishes, and I invite you all to come to the great feast tomorrow eve, when we celebrate this union with all our family and friends in attendance! But now it is time for me to go and finish this nuptial ceremony in *private,*" he told them. There were good-natured boos and catcalls, and requests for him to take one more drink with the group. However, no one really blamed Marcus for rushing this part of the ceremony, considering how lovely his new bride was, and how long he had been widowed.

One by one, his guests filtered out, offering final wishes and bits of naughty advice as they filed by. Marcus watched them go, and after the last of them filed out, he summoned Phidias and told him to make sure that the family slaves stayed away from the bedchamber for the evening, unless summoned. The old slave bowed, winked, and headed toward the rear of the house, where the servants were quartered.

The *pronuba* met Marcus in the hallway, frowning. She gave him a polite bow before speaking.

"Your bride awaits you, Excellency, but I feel that I must speak to you a moment," she said.

"By all means, Priestess," Marcus said. "What is your name?"

"I am called Lydia," she said. "I have served at many such ceremonies, but never one like yours!"

"What do you mean?" he said.

"You make no offering to Vesta, or to the *lares*!" she said. "This invites all manner of woes into your union!"

Marcus smiled. "I am a recent convert to a new faith," he said. "We have prayed to our God to bless our house and protect our marriage."

"But this is Rome!" she said. "The gods of Rome must be honored!"

Marcus shrugged. "If you wish to make an offering to them on my behalf," he said, "by all means do so. But I no longer hold with such things when I have any choice in the matter."

"Very well then," she said, "I will rest easier if I know the gods of Rome have been honored at your wedding."

"Do what you must, then leave," Marcus said as politely as he could. She bowed again, and he headed down the hallway to his bedchamber.

Antonia had removed her mantle and cloak, and stood before him clad in a simple white shift, knotted at the waist with a complex chord tied by her mother and sister. The knot was an ancient tradition, to keep evil, defiling spirits at bay.

"I began to wonder if you had changed your mind, husband," she said.

"No danger of that!" Marcus replied, drinking in her beauty. Her hair, which had been carefully braided in six plaits according to tradition, was now undone and hanging luxuriously about her shoulders, copper on cream. He knelt before her and began deftly untying the knot. He had been practicing all week; it was considered bad luck to have to fumble. Complex though it was, the chords flew apart under his fingers, and moments later the white shift slid to the floor.

"There is one good thing about this being your second wedding," he said when he could take a breath. Her loveliness was dazzling him.

"What is that, my husband?" she asked, stepping toward the bed.

"You do not have to play the role of the shrieking, reluctant virgin for me!" he said.

"What if that is what I want to do?" she asked with a sly smile.

"Is it?" he responded, trying to keep the dismay out of his voice.

"No," she said, and drew him into her arms.

CHAPTER XIX

"*Pater,* wake up!" Cadius' voice echoed through Marcus' dreams. They were rather pleasant dreams that he had no wish to let go of; he rolled closer to Antonia's side and away from the annoying light that was cutting into his brain.

"Wake up!" Cadius said again, and the urgency in his voice dispelled sleep once and for all. Marcus sat up abruptly, rubbing his eyes and trying to sort out what time it was. Antonia stirred beside him, pulling up the sheet to cover herself and opening one eye.

"What is it, my son?" he asked Cadius. The gangly youth, now nearly seventeen, was pale and obviously upset.

"The emperor is dying, Father," he said. "He is calling for you."

Marcus leaped out of bed, calling for his manservant to help him dress. He took a swig of cold water from the pitcher on the table in the atrium and swished it in his mouth, dispelling the sour taste of last night's wine.

A year and a half had passed since his return from the provinces. Marcus had indeed been elected as tribune that fall, and had served under the fifteen-year-old consul, Nero, for most of a year before resigning from the college of tribunes. He had wearied of cleaning up the impulsive Nero's messes—the boy was headstrong and emotional, and frequently made rulings based more on his whims and sympathies than on any sound legal footing or logic. Nero was intelligent and showed some promise, but he did not take being vetoed kindly, and Marcus was ready to spend some travel time with his bride. Claudius agreed to appoint another senator to the office of tribune in his place—the position was one of great honor, a high step on the *cursus honorum,* and there was no shortage of candidates, even for a suffect term of a couple of months.

Marcus and Antonia had spent several months in the lovely city of Pompeii, enjoying the beautiful villa the emperor had given Marcus upon his returned from Parthia. He frequently admired the steaming cone of Vesuvius that overshadowed the vineyards behind the villa. Occasionally the volcano emitted clouds of black smoke, and the well water sometimes had a slight taste of sulfur, but there had been no eruption in recorded history, and Marcus felt safe enough. Having time alone with his beautiful bride made the risk well worth it.

Antonia was everything a Roman wife should be—kind and loving, passionate in private, but always discreet and proper in public. She made Marcus feel twenty years younger, and she in turn respected and admired him. She told him once that every woman's desire was to be loved by a man she admired. Most men, he thought to himself, wanted the opposite—to be admired by a woman they loved. He was ashamed to admit it, but there were days that he had a hard time recalling his dear Drusilla's face, so completely was his grief healed. Cadius had quickly won Antonia's heart, and she spoke of the boy as if he were her natural son, even though that was a chronological impossibility. However, they were happy to leave him at their *domus* in Rome, from which he traveled every afternoon to train with the sword and spear on the Campus Martius. His pedagogue was impressed with the boy's quick wit and speaking ability, although he despaired of getting Cadius to read the Greek classics except under compulsion. Soon it would be time for Marcus' son to serve in Rome's legions, as a junior legate under an experienced officer. Marcus found himself simultaneously dreading his son's departure and wanting him to excel on the battlefield as a leader of men.

The pleasant interlude at Pompeii had drawn to a close about six weeks previous, when Claudius had asked Marcus to return to Rome and help him move some legislation through the Senate. The emperor had taken on the responsibility of censor a few months previous, and had purged the Senate of several members who could no longer meet the property qualifications for office—although he spared their *dignitas* whenever he could by giving them the private option to resign. He had then appointed many new members to take their place and enlarge the legislative body. What with all the turnover, experienced hands were more needed than ever, he explained when Marcus returned to Rome.

Marcus was troubled by what he saw of Claudius during those few weeks in which he was in and out of the palace on a regular basis. The emperor tired easily, and his old stammer returned more often. Sometimes he would drool a bit without noticing, although he was always quick to wipe his chin when he realized what was happening. Agrippina, still a beautiful woman on the outside but radiating subtle menace, was at his elbow every moment, scolding, wheedling, making suggestions, and whispering threats and promises. Claudius occasionally tired of her meddling and ordered her out of the room, but she was always back the next day, continuing to bend his ear.

Two other councilors attended Marcus and Claudius during those sessions: the new Praetorian prefect, Sextus Afranius Burrus, and Nero's pedagogue and advisor, Lucius Annaeus Seneca. Burrus barely concealed his contempt for the aging emperor, while Seneca was at least outwardly respectful. He was a noted stoic philosopher as well as an excellent rhetorician; he repeatedly made flattering comments about young Nero's genius, and what a remarkable emperor the lad would make. Burrus also flattered Nero, primarily when Agrippina was in the room. If they thought no one was watching, he and the empress would sometimes exchange glances that looked downright lustful to Marcus. But all three were trying to convince the emperor that Nero was Augustus reborn.

Claudius was having none of it. It seemed that the more he saw of his adopted son, the less he liked him. On the rare occasions that he and Marcus were alone, he began referring to the boy as Lucius Ahenobarbus rather than by his adoptive name. He also began to spend more and more time with his younger son, Britannicus, measuring the boy's intelligence and temperament, and finding that Nero did not profit from the comparison.

"You see, when the accursed Messalina met her end, my boy was very young," Claudius explained to Marcus in a whisper. "There were rumbles of discontent—what if I died and left only a child as my heir? Lucius Domitius was older; he was a nephew of Caligula and a direct descendant of Augustus. And, I must admit, his mother went out of her way to be appealing and pleasing to me for several years. Now her mask has slipped, and I recognize that I was duped. But Nero is married to my blood daughter, Britannicus' sister, and has gone to great length to make himself popular with the people. He is nearly seventeen now."

The emperor had looked around to make sure no one was listening. "Britannicus is very precocious for his age," he said. "He has the makings of a true Caesar, in the best sense of the word! I swear that the blood of the *Divus Julius* flows undiluted in his veins. When he turns fourteen in a few months, I can divorce Agrippina and send Nero and Octavia off to govern a province together, and train my true son to be an emperor who will make Rome proud!"

Marcus was interested and worried at the same time. He did not believe Agrippina would let her darling be set aside so easily, and told the emperor that.

"I know, my old friend," said Claudius. "That is why both boys are currently listed as my heirs. I have done my best to make them friends, which is no mean task—Britannicus despises Nero's cruelty, and Nero regards the lad as a threat. But all will be settled as soon as my boy comes of age. That is why I recalled you to Rome—I want you by my side when all of this comes to a head!"

That had been one week ago. Britannicus' fourteenth birthday was still four months off, and now it looked as if Claudius might not live to see it. Marcus pulled on his sandals and headed for the door, gesturing for Cadius to follow. The groom was standing in the street holding the reins of two horses, and father and son set off together.

"What has happened?" Marcus said once they were clattering along the cobblestones, speaking as softly as he could. Cadius had become friends with Britannicus as they trained together on the Campus Martius, and frequently knew more palace gossip than Marcus did.

"Claudius collapsed after dinner," Cadius replied, his face grim. "The cook says that someone brought in fresh mushrooms this very afternoon, and swears that they were good—but the merchant hung around the kitchens all evening, watching them being prepared. It would have been very easy to substitute or add something when the cook's back was turned."

Marcus sighed, and said: "Son, I want you to return to the barracks as soon as I am inside the palace. The death of an emperor is always a very uncertain time. I do not know how Nero regards me; it may well be that I face exile or worse in the next week."

"Surely not!" Cadius exclaimed. "You are one of the emperor's closest advisors!"

"That is what imperils me," Marcus said. By now they were making their way up the Palatine Hill, and he could see the torches blazing outside the palace. "Just do as I say!"

He dismounted and strode through the tall oak doors. Cassius Claudius met him in the hallway, his eyes red with tears.

"Does our master still live?" Marcus asked.

"Barely," the freedman replied. "His breath is growing shorter by the minute. But he is eager to see you one last time."'

Marcus strode down the corridor, his outline reflecting in the polished marble. Cassius guided him through the ornate doors that led to Claudius' bedchamber, a room Marcus had never seen. The walls were decorated with frescoes depicting the history of the Julio-Claudian family, as well as scenes from Roman mythology.

The emperor lay on his bed, his wheezing breath audible even before they entered the room. He was holding a linen kerchief to his mouth, and it was stained pink. His face was pale, and his hand trembled as it wiped the bloodstained drool from his mouth. There were huge black circles under his eyes, and sweat poured from his body. But his eyes flickered with awareness as he saw Marcus step into the room, and he gestured him to come closer.

The emperor's two sons stood at the foot of the bed, both of them looking nervous. Britannicus was weeping openly, while Nero looked torn between grief and nervous excitement. Agrippina stood at the head of the bed, across from Marcus. Her every movement and expression showed grief and deep concern for her husband, but Marcus thought there was a gleam of triumph in her eyes.

"Marcus, my faithful agent and friend," said Claudius. His voice was so faint that Publius had to lean close in order to hear.

"I come at your command, Excellency," Marcus replied.

A ghost of a smile flickered at the emperor's lips. "How many times," he wheezed, "must I tell you to call me Claudius?"

Marcus opened his mouth to reply, but the emperor held up his hand.

"My sons!" he called as loudly as he could. The two boys, Nero nearly seventeen and Britannicus a strapping thirteen, stepped forward. Now both of them were sobbing.

"I have left my powers divided between you," Claudius told them. "Whatever arrangements might have been made in the future, that is the state of things now. I go to take my place among the lions of our blood, and can no longer guide or guard you. By all the gods of Rome, I command you to respect and love one another from this moment forward, strive to rule well and be just. I would ask that you take my friend and faithful councilor Marcus to be your guide, and to be your advisor in all situations. Please . . ." His voice failed, but with a mighty effort he struggled to finish his thoughts. "Be kind to each other," he said at the last.

His eyes turned to Marcus, who could see the glaze of death slowly spreading across the pupils. With a supreme effort, the emperor of Rome spoke to his friend again. "Look after my boys," he said.

Marcus took the hand of this man who had ruled the world for thirteen years, and who had done so much to elevate him and restore the fortunes of his family. His own tears were flowing now.

"I shall regard them as my own sons," he said.

Claudius nodded, and a mighty spasm shook his body. His eyes widened in surprise. "Oh dear," he said. "I fear I have soiled myself." Then his breath gave out, and the portly body slumped and lay still.

Tiberius Claudius Caesar Augustus Germanicus, Princeps and Imperator of Rome, was dead.

Marcus released the hand that had gripped his so tightly moments before, and ignoring the foul smell that rose from beneath the sheets, kissed his old friend on the forehead. Agrippina followed suit, and then the two sons of Claudius did the same. They all looked at each other for a moment, and then filed out of the bedchamber. Agrippina turned to the servants.

"Wash him, and call the embalmers!" she snapped. "Burn the bedding! I would have no one know of the final indignity my husband endured."

Marcus nodded approvingly. He did not trust her for a moment—in fact, it would not surprise him at all to learn that she was the one who had poisoned his old friend—but at least, she was acting to preserve the dead emperor's *dignitas,* as any Roman matron should. It saddened him to think that a man who had overcome such great odds to rise so high had been forced to such an end.

The two brothers stood facing one another in the hallway. Marcus watched them, curious to see what would transpire next. It seemed as if the whole house fell silent as Nero and Britannicus studied each other in silence. Finally, it was Nero who extended his hand.

"Britannicus," he said, "I know that we have not always gotten on well. But I accept you as my co-emperor and partner, as our father wished. Let the thoughts that once divided us be put aside, and let us strive to fulfill his dying wish!"

Britannicus smiled, but there was still fear in his eyes. He knew that his life now hung by a thread, completely dependent on the goodwill of a mercurial seventeen-year-old whose reputation was not one of kindness.

"Son by adoption, son by blood, brothers by choice!" he finally said. "Let no harsh words ever divide us again, and let us govern Rome with the same wisdom and competence that our noble father modeled for us." He stepped forward and clasped Nero's hand.

Now the two brothers turned and surveyed Marcus, who looked back at them with a respect that was partly sincere and partly self-interested. The fate of the empire—and of his entire family—was in the hands of two teenaged boys! Although, looking at Nero's taller, muscular form, he realized that the real power lay with the elder, at least for now. It was Nero who spoke to him first.

"My father praised you in many ways, Marcus Quintus Publius," he said. "He told me you had more common sense and *virtus* about you than any member of the Senate, and always said that he was lucky to have you as a friend and advisor. Will you be our councilor and guide, as he requested?"

Marcus bowed deeply. "It would be my honor to offer what small wisdom I have to you and your brother," he said, "for the good of the Republic—and in honor of my dear friend's memory."

"Marcus Quintus," said Agrippina, "it was good of you to come so swiftly, in the middle of the night, to my husband's bedside. I know you must be weary, and like all of us, deeply worn with grief. Why don't you return to your home now? Call on the emperors tomorrow afternoon and we shall discuss my husband's funeral arrangements."

Marcus was being dismissed by a woman, and he knew it, but now was not the time to protest her presumption of power. He bowed to the two young rulers of Rome, then to Agrippina, and walked back down the corridor with a heavy heart. A Praetorian guard brought him his horse, and he rode back to his home, deep in thought. As he rode across the city, dawn was breaking, but storm clouds loomed in the western sky, with flickers of lightning running across them. He wondered if it was some kind of omen.

Antonia was awake when he returned, a mantle thrown over the shift she slept in. There was a fire burning in the brazier, for the autumn mornings were already turning cold. She met him at the door with a warm embrace and steered him toward the fire, pouring him a cup of fresh-squeezed fruit juice.

"Is he gone, then?" she asked.

"Yes," Marcus replied. "I was holding his hand when the life left his body."

"I did not know our emperor well," she said, "but I know he was your friend, and for that reason alone I would grieve, much less for the future of our Republic. What happens next? Who is his heir—Nero or Britannicus?"

"For the moment, both of them," Marcus said. "Claudius charged them to share power, and to be kind to each other. He charged me to be their advisor, mentor, and friend."

"A dangerous bequest, husband!" she said with a shiver.

"I know!" he replied. "But what can I do? I owe Claudius everything. He found me as a junior magistrate and pulled me up the *cursus honorum.* He showered me with favor, high office, and his friendship. How can I do less than to try and be the mentor he has asked me to be?"

She sighed, stood behind him, and rubbed his shoulders, trying to work out some of the tension that had built up there since he had left their bed two hours before. Marcus leaned his head back and rested it against her belly, enjoying her warmth and concern.

"Do you think that the two boys will be able to rule together?" she asked.

"Not really," he said. "Nero might share power with his brother for a while, if it were purely up to him. But Agrippina wants him to be sole ruler—or, truth be told, I think she wants to rule through him! I would not care to be in Britannicus' shoes right now."

"Maybe you can help Nero free himself from his mother's control," she said. "It is natural for boys his age to want to assert their independence."

"Agrippina is a viper of the most dangerous sort," he said. "I have a feeling the next year is going to be exceptionally difficult. No matter how I tread, I fear I will make some powerful enemies."

"I am by your side, no matter what," she said. "You are a good man and a good husband. Nero would do well to take you as his advisor."

"Thank you, Antonia. I need all the support I can get right now," he said.

"You must be exhausted. Why don't you drink a cup of mulled wine and try to sleep for a while?"

"I don't know that I can sleep," he said. "My mind is all awhirl. But I do think that I might lie down for a bit."

"Pray to Christ for guidance, Marcus. Surely, He will help you know what to do," she said.

Marcus nodded. He still had not heard from any of the Apostles he met during his travels, although a few members of Rome's small Christian community dropped by from time to time. He still did not know as much as he would have liked about the teachings of Jesus or the full story of His life, but that did not stop him from praying to his new God for guidance and help. He rose from the table to the small shrine in the corner, where the Greek letters Chi and Ro were carved into the wall. He lit the candle there and knelt.

"Jesus, Christos," he said, "hear the prayer of your grateful and humble servant. I do not know You as well as I would like, but I wish to honor and please You, in gratitude for your sacrifice on the cross—and for the gift of my son, whom You healed and restored to me. I do not know what course to take in this current dilemma, for it seems no matter which way I step the path is perilous. Guide me, I pray, that I may serve You and render some return for all that You have done for me."

He was not sure if Jesus heard his prayers or not, but the act of saying them always left his heart feeling a bit lighter. Antonia had come and knelt beside him. She did not articulate her prayers, but he could see her lips moving out of the corner of his eye. He had told her all that he had learned of Jesus and His teachings, and His miraculous resurrection from the dead, shortly after their wedding. She had listened carefully and questioned him closely. Some of her questions he knew the answers to, and some others forced him to confess his ignorance. After a week or two, she had raised the topic one evening, as they lay in one another's arms after lovemaking.

"I do not understand everything about your faith," she said, "but I can see how it affects your life. This Christ of yours has made you an even better and more decent man than you were before, by your own testimony. I would like to know more about Him someday—but for now, what you have told me is enough. Your god is my God, Marcus, just as you are my husband."

Ever since then she had joined him in his prayers, and when their Christian brothers came by to visit, she sat and listened attentively as they shared their own knowledge of Jesus' teachings. Some of the gaps in their knowledge had been filled, but Marcus still hungered for more and longed for the day that Peter's prophecy would be fulfilled and he could render some great service to God.

For now, he finished his cup of mulled wine—even though it was growing cold—and returned to his bedchamber. Slipping out of his robes, he lay down, staring at the mural on the ceiling. Sleep seemed like a distant memory, but Antonia followed him in and pulled his head onto her lap. She gently stroked his forehead, and before long the worries and tensions of the night melted away, and he closed his eyes.

It was noon when he finally woke, and he remembered his promise to Agrippina. He rose from his bed and called for some hot water, and quickly washed his face and shaved with a short, sharp knife. He chose a black robe, trimmed with the scarlet of his Senate rank, and stepped out of his home into the bright fall day. Rufus, now a full-fledged member of the College of Lictors, led the four-man escort that accompanied Publius on all official business. The city was strangely quiet; the common people huddled in groups, whispering among themselves, while the shops were hung with floral arrangements and black muslin cloth in mourning for the departed Claudius.

"It's always a bad business when an emperor dies," said Rufus. "No one knows what to expect, and everyone fears the worst, if you take my meaning."

"Truly spoken," Marcus said. "And it is just as true for us in the Senate as it is for the plebs living in the Aventine."

"Do you know what is going to happen, Senator Publius?" Rufus asked. He was always careful to refer to Marcus by his proper title in front of the other lictors.

"I know that we are going to hold a funeral," Marcus said. "After that, you know as much as I do."

He hated to be short with his old friend, but the streets were no place for a senator of Rome to speculate on the future right now. Everyone was listening, straining their ears for a bit of gossip, and Marcus had no desire to pour fuel on the fire.

Agrippina and Nero greeted him at the doors of the palace; there was no sign of Britannicus. But mother and son both seemed glad to see him, Marcus noted. Surely that must count for something.

"Marcus Publius," Agrippina purred, taking him by the hands and kissing his cheek in greeting. "It is good of you to come and offer guidance to my son. We need to plan the funeral rites for my husband."

"Tomorrow I will address the Senate," Nero said confidently. "I would see my noble father deified, as our forefathers Julius and Augustus were."

"That is an appropriate gesture," Marcus said, although he privately thought that Claudius would have been amused by the thought of such a sudden apotheosis.

"My brother and I would like for you to give a funeral oration before our father's pyre," Nero continued. "We will speak first, of course, as family, but we would like for you to represent the Senate."

"It would be my honor," Marcus said. "Claudius Caesar was not just a great ruler, he was a great man. It was a privilege for me to be his friend." He noted Nero's mention of Britannicus, and was glad to hear that Nero's adoptive brother had not been shunted aside yet. "Where is Britannicus?" he asked.

"He hasn't been up for long," Nero said. "After such an exhausting night, we all slept for several hours. He is helping the embalmers choose my father's burial raiment."

"The *Pontifex Maximus* is waiting," Agrippina said. "Let us go and meet him."

Marcus joined the family of Claudius Caesar to help plan the funeral of his longtime friend and patron. As they walked down the polished marble corridors of the imperial palace, Nero turned to his father's friend.

"Senator, I will probably need your advice very soon on how to deal with the Parthians. They were not pleased when my father refused Vologases' request to hand over Armenia, and I fear war is brewing."

Marcus began to talk to Nero about his impressions of Vologases, and for the moment it seemed that Rome's new co-emperor was hanging on his every word. Perhaps, he thought, his fears were needless.

CHAPTER XX

"Marcus Publius!" the voice echoed across the Forum. Marcus looked up from the bench, where he was conferring with one of his clients. The trial was scheduled to begin in less than an hour.

"What now?" he groaned. Ever since Claudius' funeral two months before, it seemed as if the government was lurching from one crisis to another. Every quarrel or sharp word between the two adoptive brothers was regarded as the prelude to civil war, and Agrippina had been relentless in her efforts to govern the empire through her son. As for Nero, he had begun shunting aside his younger brother more and more often, acting as if he were the sole ruler of Rome instead of co-emperor. On top of that, he was ignoring his lovely young wife, Octavia, who was the natural daughter of Claudius and the sister of Britannicus, and openly sporting with a beautiful former slave girl named Acte. Agrippina was furious with him for publicly shaming his father's house, but Nero stubbornly refused to put away his mistress or go near his wife's bedroom.

Burrus and Seneca had both enlisted Marcus' aid repeatedly. For whatever reason, young Nero seemed more likely to listen to them if his father's old friend lent his weight to their requests, and Agrippina also seemed inclined to give ear to Marcus' voice. The result of this increase to his *arctoritas* within the Principate was that Marcus rarely had time to get anything done for his clients; hence his irritation.

"You have to stop her, Marcus Quintus!" Lucius Anneaus Seneca wailed. "She is determined to attend, and it will be a diplomatic disaster!"

Marcus straightened up and patted his client, a Greek shopkeeper named Antigonus Pericles, on the shoulder. "Tell the Praetor I have been called to the palace again," he said. "If I am not back by our scheduled start time, ask him to move one of the other cases ahead in the queue. Rufus, inform the other advocates so they can summon their witnesses and be ready. Then get the other lictors and bring them quickly!" He turned then and spoke to his client. "I am sorry, my friend, but I will recover the damages for you if I have to pay them out of my own pocket!"

"It's all right, Excellency," the stooped, balding Antigonus replied. "I am proud to be represented by such an important person!"

Marcus took Seneca by the elbow and led him toward a colonnade where they could speak without a hundred prying eyes following them. Ducking behind a large pillar, he looked at Nero's tutor with exasperation.

"Now, please tell me what is going on!" he said.

He did not care much for Seneca. The man was a widely regarded Stoic philosopher, but his personal lifestyle did not live up to the austere philosophy he taught. Attached to Nero as a pedagogue for several years, he had exploited the boy's affections and been showered with gifts and lands, both by the imperial family and by sycophants hoping to buy influence with the young emperor. That being said, however, the old man was still a moderating influence on the temperamental Nero. He also had considerable respect for Marcus' political instincts.

"The king of Armenia has sent his grand vizier to Rome to beg our help against the Parthians, and Agrippina wants to sit on the *bema* seat during his interview," Seneca said hurriedly. "That is completely against Rome's *mos maorum,* and the Armenians will take it as a deadly insult!"

Marcus shook his head. Whatever one thought of the justice of women's subordinate place in society, it was the way of the world, and all Agrippina's scheming and maneuvering could not change it. He thought of how women were treated in the Eastern world, and recognized the truth of Seneca's words—having the empress on the throne when the delegation entered would be taken as an insult, even if Nero were seated beside her. But how could he dissuade her?

"Where is Britannicus?" he asked.

"In the courtyard with his friend Titus," said Seneca.

"We'll fetch him on the way," he said. "Let me handle Agrippina."

They quickly covered the distance to the Palatine—Rufus and his fellow lictors were excellent at clearing pathways through the crowded streets—and Marcus first cut through the corridors to the open courtyard, where he found young Britannicus practicing swordplay with a stocky youth about his own age. Nero's son was glad to see him.

"Marcus Publius!" he said. "It is good of you to come and visit!"

"I am afraid that today's visit is more business than pleasure," Marcus responded. "You need to go wash off and put on your dress toga. The Armenians will want to see both of our emperors today!"

"But Marcus, Nero said that I—" the boy began.

"Let me handle Nero!" Marcus said. "You go and get ready."

"Come on, Britannicus," said his companion. "I'll help you get ready."

There was something very familiar about the voice, and Marcus looked closely at the youth who had been sparring with the young emperor.

"Do I know you?" he said. There was something strikingly familiar about the lad.

"I am Flavius Titus," he said. "You met my father in Britannia."

"You're Vespasian's boy!" Marcus said. "You are the spitting image of your father!"

"So everyone says," the boy replied. "I suppose there are worse fates."

"Your father is a good man and a great general," Marcus said. "Give him my greetings when next you see him."

With that he headed down to the emperor's audience chamber. He heard the raised voices before he ever turned the corner. Nero and his mother were facing each other over the *bema* seat, a more ornate version of the curule bench used by Roman magistrates. This seat had been built for Augustus in the latter years of his reign, when he began receiving foreign diplomats in his own home rather than going to the Senate every time some foreign potentate wanted an audience. Burrus stood behind them, watching, his mouth set in a grim line from keeping his silence.

"You are still a pigheaded child!" Agrippina snapped at her son. "An adult should occupy the *bema* seat as a sign that our empire is not governed by adolescent whims!"

"You want to give the impression it is governed by women instead?" Nero shot back.

"I have the blood of the Caesars in my veins, and of Marcus Antonius as well!" shrieked Agrippina. "I could run this empire as well as any man!"

"If I were an Armenian diplomat, my impression would be that the empire is not governed by anyone at the moment," Marcus said. "Is that what you wish to project to our client kings?"

Both heads swiveled around to see Marcus' tanned, balding form standing in the doorway, his toga reflecting the sunlight from outside. Nero broke into a smile.

"Marcus," he said. "I was planning to send for you until Mother distracted me. I would have your counsel on how to answer the Armenian embassy."

Marcus nodded and entered the chamber. "Eastern potentates," he said, "set great store by appearances. Madam, I know this is hard for you to accept, but if you are visible at all during this embassy, the Armenians will take it as a grave insult. Their culture regards women as toys and child-bearers, not as counselors in matters of state. If you must listen in, then you must do so from a vantage point where you will be invisible. Now, Nero, you know that the Armenians are aware that you and Britannicus are officially co-emperors. If you receive them without him being present, they will take it as a sign that our government is divided against itself and weak. You must both receive them to show our unity and strength as Romans."

Nero frowned. He disliked sharing power with his brother, but he also had a fairly sharp understanding of the importance of appearances. Finally, he nodded and turned to Burrus.

"Fetch Britannicus!" he said curtly.

Burrus nodded and strode from the chamber. Agrippina shot Marcus a venomous look and made for a side door. Marcus knew that there was a small window on one side of the chamber, covered by a tapestry, which provided an ideal listening point for all that transpired in the audience room. Nero straightened his toga and placed himself on the *bema* seat, squaring his shoulders and facing forward. He erased all emotion from his features and placed his right foot slightly in front of his left, the classic pose of a Roman magistrate. In such moments, Marcus had to admit, the young man assumed a *dignitas* far beyond his years.

Nero turned his head to face the older man. "Britannicus will be seated on my right, as befits my co-emperor," he said. "I would have you stand on my left, in the position of trusted counselor. If I have any doubts, I shall confer with you. If you see me about to commit some grave breach of diplomatic protocol, give a cough and I'll pause for a moment. Then you can lean down and let me know how I have erred."

Marcus nodded and gave a small sigh. At times Nero showed great promise, he thought. But at other times he could be mean, petty, and self-indulgent. He hoped that, with maturity, Nero's virtues would trump his faults, but it was hard to see at this point which side of the lad's personality would win out. Power was such a strong narcotic, Marcus thought. Few grown men handled it well, much less a boy of seventeen!

Moments later Britannicus came striding into the audience chamber, clad in a white toga with the purple trim and scarlet cape that marked him as *Princeps*—in fact, his attire was identical to that of his brother, although Nero's colors were a trifle brighter and louder. A second curule chair had been built by Claudius' order a few years before, when he began having his boys sit in on his audiences. It was identical to Caesar's *bema* seat, except that it was two inches shorter. Britannicus approached it, then paused and extended his hand.

"*Ave, Frater!*" he exclaimed. "I thank you for the opportunity to take part in such an important audience."

"Of course you will take part!" snapped Nero churlishly. "You are my co-emperor after all, as everyone keeps reminding me!"

Within a few moments, the two brothers had seated themselves and Marcus took his place at Nero's left hand. Then the doors of the audience room were opened and the grand vizier of Armenia entered the room with his attendants. Marcus had never met this particular satrap before, and he had to choke back a laugh as the man approached the throne.

Nicomedes Bithynias was ancient, somewhere between seventy and eighty, but insisted on wearing a very obvious wig of bright red hair. His eyebrows had long since fallen out, but two very large and prominent ones had been drawn onto his forehead with *stibium* that almost but not quite matched the shade of his wig. He wore gold rings on every finger of each hand, and was very tall, although the effect of his height was somewhat diminished by his considerable stoop. His robes were gold, scarlet, and black, and two ornate earrings of gold, with ruby and emerald pendants, dangled from earlobes that had been stretched so far by their weight that they reached the bottom of his jawline. To make matters worse, he spoke with a slight lisp that caused both teenaged boys to smile whenever he opened his mouth. Fortunately, the news he bore was slightly more promising than the last few bulletins from Armenia.

"Noble Thaesarth," he said. "Ath you know, the king of the Parthianth, Vologatheth the Firtht—Hadeth take him for the mithery he hath cauthed!—invaded my homewand two yearth ago. He inthtalled hith howwible brother, Tiridates, as our new king, removing the noble monarch Rhamadistas, a fwiend and ally of the Thenate and People of Wome."

Nero was biting his lip very hard to keep from laughing, while Britannicus was looking at the ground intently. Finally, the older brother spoke.

"We are aware of Vologases' treachery," he said. "But is it not true that he was forced to withdraw his armies from Armenia due to a rebellion in Parthia?"

"Yeth!" said the old man. "And Rhamadistas has been reinsthalled as the king. He hath gone to gweat length to theek out and punish thothe who joined themthelveth to the Parthianth during hith exile. But now the people have dethided that they would wather be ruled by Tiridates inthtead, and are in open webellion againtht my thovereign lord, Rhamadistas, who callth upon the Thenate and People of Wome to aid him in hith hour of need."

Nero nodded. "It is high time that Rome taught the high king of the Parthians a lesson in respect," he said. "Return to us tomorrow and you will hear our reply at length."

"On behalf of King Rhamadistas, I thank Your Excellenthieth for thith audienth," the old man lisped before turning and slowly walking out of the chamber, so stooped that his head crossed the threshold well ahead of the rest of him. The doors swung shut, and the two brothers looked at each other and collapsed with laughter.

"How on earth did someone who speaks so poorly wind up appointed as ambassador?" Britannicus said.

Nero tried to imitate the Armenian. "I am motht thure that he ith a man of conthidewable talent and wemarkable abilitieth!" he said, and laughed even more.

Marcus allowed himself a chuckle or two—the grand vizier was indeed a ridiculous figure—and reminded himself that, for all the power they wielded, he was, after all, dealing with two teenage boys. Then he spoke.

"There are two ways, young Caesars, for a man to survive in a court full of dangerous, strong, and ambitious men," he said. "One is to be more dangerous, strong, and ambitious than all those around you. Unless you are a demigod, that path is fraught with risk. The other—the safer way—is to be so ridiculous, so harmless, that no one sees you as a threat. Let yourself be ridiculed and laughed at, all the while gaining the trust and goodwill of those who are doing the laughing. That was how your esteemed father Claudius Caesar survived the cruelty of Tiberius and the madness of Caligula. I daresay that our Armenian ambassador is a far more dangerous and capable man than his ridiculous appearance would lead anyone to believe. He uses his outrageousness as a cloak to hide his true abilities. Now that we have had our laugh, it is time to contemplate the tidings he brought us."

The two young emperors wiped the smiles from their faces as they reflected on what Marcus had just said. At that moment, they looked more like brothers to him than they ever had before. If only such moments could be preserved, he thought.

"What do you think we should do, Marcus Quintus?" Nero asked.

"We need to reinforce Armenia," he said. "While Rhamadistas is not the best client king in the world, he is Rome's client king nonetheless, and we are obligated to support him. Isn't Gnaeus Domitius Corbulo the governor of Asia Province right now?"

Nero nodded. "He is a capable general, according to all who know him."

"He should be sent to Armenia with several legions, in my opinion, and if the Parthians decide to push there, we must push back—hard!" Marcus said.

"I think you should go with him," Nero said.

"There are many others more capable—" Marcus began.

"Nonsense! You are the only living winner of the Grass Crown, and also the only Roman of rank who has personally met Vologases. You will be Corbulo's senior legate and second in command—and I will instruct him to defer to you in political matters," Nero replied.

"As always, I serve at the emperor's pleasure," Marcus said. Inwardly he was wincing—he had no desire to leave Rome so soon after finding true happiness in his new marriage. "May I ask that my son Cadius be assigned as my *conterburnalis*?"

"Why not?" Nero said. "He is of age for his first military assignment."

"Thank you, Your Excellencies. When do you wish me to depart?" Marcus asked.

"It will take some time for Corbulo to move his legions from Asia to Armenia," said Nero. "Take a few weeks to set your affairs in order. I have not forgotten how long you were away in service to my noble father. I doubt this assignment will prove to be as long, or as difficult. With you and Corbulo in command, I should not care to be a general in the armies of the high king of Parthia!"

Marcus smiled. "I thank you for your kind words, Caesar," he said.

"Come back tomorrow," Nero told him. "I want you to be present when I send dear old Nicomedes back with our reply!"

Marcus bowed. "I thank you for your trust, Caesar," he said.

Britannicus had been listening with a frown. He looked at Nero, who acknowledged him with a curt nod.

"Marcus Quintus, before you leave the city, would you send your son, Cadius, to see me?" he asked.

"Certainly, Britannicus," he said. "He told me that the two of you had been training together."

"He's been helping me improve with the *gladius* and *pilum*," the young co-emperor said. "He has been a good teacher and companion to Titus and me. I would like a chance to say my farewells to him."

"Then you shall have it," Marcus said. "Now, as you said, Nero, I have many things to set in order before I leave Rome."

Marcus dreaded telling Antonia about his orders, but she bore the news better than he expected.

"Separation is a woe all Roman women must endure," she said. "Especially those with highborn husbands. All I ask is that you return to me safely."

"I shall," he said. "It has been foretold that I will return to Rome."

She embraced him and laid her head on his shoulder. "You are a good man, and a good husband, Marcus Quintus," she said. "I have found greater happiness with you than I ever thought possible."

"And I with you, dear wife," he said. "As long as you draw breath, no other woman will exist for me."

She pulled away from him and studied his eyes. "You really mean it," she finally said.

"Of course I do," he replied. "I am no Julius Caesar! One woman has always been enough for me."

Adultery by men carried no stigma in Roman law or tradition, unless it was with another man's wife. Roman women were supposed to be held to higher standards, although having intimate relations with slaves was not thought of as adultery. However, Marcus knew that the Christians placed a very high premium on marital fidelity, and truthfully, he was so enamored of his young bride that the thought of sleeping with another woman was not even tempting.

"You need have no fear of me straying while you are away," she said. "No other man could measure up to you in my eyes."

Old Phidias was leaning on his cane in the doorway, and Marcus turned to him. "Send a runner and find Cadius on the Campus Martius," he said. "Tell him Britannicus wants to see him at the palace, and then have him return here."

"Aye, master," the old Greek said. "I am sorry to see you leave again, and even sorrier that I am too old to travel with you."

Marcus patted the old slave on his shoulder. "I will be depending on you to take care of my wife and keep my house in order," he said. "That means you are not allowed to die while I am gone!"

Phidias rolled his eyes and gave a snort. "I shall remind Hades of that when he comes to claim me!" he said.

He stumped off to find a messenger, and Marcus watched him go with some sadness. It was quite likely, he thought, that he might never see the old man again.

"Well, wife, we have the house to ourselves for the moment!" he said, looking at Antonia with a gleam in his eye.

"I was thinking that a sweet baby to care for might make our separation easier for me to bear," she said.

"We've been trying to make one for some time," he said, covering her forehead with kisses.

"Perhaps we should try again?" she asked.

"Every day from now until I leave," he said, reaching for the ties of her gown.

"*Dominus*," said old Phidias' voice from the door, "I am truly sorry to disturb you—"

"Then don't!" Marcus snapped.

"But a messenger from the Forum is here," the old slave continued. "The Praetor wants to know if you are ready to argue your client's case yet."

Marcus gave a long, exasperated sigh, but Antonia simply giggled.

"Well, husband," she said, "take this as an incentive to argue brilliantly—and quickly!"

She hugged him hard, pressing her body as tight as she could against his, and kissed him with such passion he forgot to breathe for a moment. When he recovered his wits, he looked at the red-haired Venus he had married and shook his head.

"I don't know that poor Antigonus is going to get my best efforts this afternoon," he finally said.

"Of course he will," she laughed. "You are too conscientious to do otherwise. And then you can put your best efforts into something else."

Marcus won twice that afternoon.

CHAPTER XXI

Marcus had figured that the new assignment might call him away from Rome for a year or two, but it was now well past two years and there was no sign that he would be headed home anytime soon. He was currently inside his legate's tent, taking refuge from the noonday sun and trying to catch up on his correspondence from home. Frustrated with his increasingly thinning locks, he had ordered his body servant Perseus—a new slave he had purchased before leaving Rome—to shave his head completely the year before and begin waxing it nightly. The straggling few hairs left had given up the struggle; now Marcus had to wear his helm whenever he left the tent by daylight or suffer the agonies of a sunburned scalp. But he was cooler and didn't have to worry about lice, or how to comb his increasingly scant locks, anymore.

Here inside the tent, helm and cuirass were set aside, and he surveyed the pile of scrolls the courier had dropped off an hour or so before. He yearned to read them, and was afraid to at the same time. So much had happened in two years!

Antonia had indeed conceived a child before he left Rome, but the baby—a little girl—had only lived for a month or two. The child was scrawny and underweight, and Antonia said that she had never learned to nurse properly, and had simply wasted away.

"It seems that many children born to our old patrician families are unhealthy," she had written him a month later. "However, while I grieve the loss of our tiny daughter, I am confident we will have better success the second time around. My mother gave birth to a son first who barely lived for a month, then bore my father two healthy daughters in a row. When you come home, my love, I will give you a healthy child, God willing. All I ask is that you stay safe from harm, and do all you can to speed that day! My books and weaving are a poor replacement for your company."

Marcus had saved that letter; he reread it often when he was feeling lonely. He had also instructed Uncle Mencius and his new wife to make sure that Antonia was a frequent guest, and had arranged for her to be given a couple of young kittens, for which he had received a grateful letter. She had named them Peter and Paul, which gave Marcus a chuckle.

Other news from home was not so good. Britannicus was dead; he had survived Marcus' departure from Rome by barely a month. According to his brother, Nero, the boy had suffered from occasional seizures throughout his adolescence and had suffered a particularly severe episode during a dinner party that caused him to choke to death. Mencius, in a letter that Marcus had burned after reading, stated that the lad had been poisoned by his brother after Agrippina had threatened to abandon her support for Nero and throw her lot in with his co-heir. She had been upset with her son over Nero's dismissal of one of her favorite freedmen, but her threat seemed to have cost Claudius' favorite son his life. While there was no solid proof of poison, Mencius noted that Titus, Britannicus' young friend, had drunk from the same cup at the supper and fallen gravely ill, taking three weeks to fully recover.

Agrippina had been exiled from Rome to her country estate at Misenum. Nero would go to see her from time to time, but the formerly close relationship between them was severed. Mencius had passed on a salacious bit of palace gossip: that the empress had been forced into exile after she had tried and failed to seduce her own son! In his occasional letters to Marcus, Nero rarely referred to his mother at all, so Marcus had no way of knowing if the sordid tale was true or not. Knowing Agrippina, it would not surprise him if it were.

The war against the Parthians was an exercise in frustration. Vologases had invaded Armenia right around the time Claudius died and installed his younger brother Tiridates on the throne, only to be forced by a harsh winter and rebellions in other parts of the Parthian empire to withdraw most of his armies. The Roman client king Rhamadistas had been restored to the throne, but had proven to be so obsessed with avenging himself on those who supported the Parthians that his own people had risen up against him and tossed him out. Now Tiridates was with his brother Vologases, waiting for a chance to regain control of the province.

That was the situation that greeted Gnaeus Corbulo and Marcus when they arrived in the province together. Corbulo had been placed in command of two provinces, Cappadocia and Galatia, with *proconsular imperium* to draft troops from neighboring provinces if necessary. He had quickly assembled three full-strength legions and two auxiliary units of cavalry—a force of some twenty thousand, all told—and driven the remaining Parthian garrisons out of Armenia in a fairly quick campaign. However, Marcus knew that Vologases was unlikely to give up his dream of ruling Armenia so easily, and that had proven to be the case. Parthian forces raided the border regions constantly, sacking and burning towns and occasionally destroying small Roman units that were caught out on patrol. Corbulo was waiting for his chance to engage the enemy in a full-scale battle and drive them back from Armenia once and for all.

Marcus liked Gnaeus Domitius Corbulo quite well. Corbulo reminded him of the blunt, competent Vespasian who had made such a favorable impression on him in Britannia. Marcus had no desire to steal any glory or credit from Corbulo, and the plainspoken legate made it clear that he was here to do a job and secure the province for Rome. He was indifferent to politics except when they promoted or inhibited his work. The two men frequently ate dinner together and discussed strategy; Corbulo was particularly interested in Marcus' battles in Pannonia and in his meetings with Vologases.

"Knowing your enemy is the most important aspect of warfare," he said. "That's how Augustus was able to defeat Anthony, you know. They had worked for and against each other, off and on, for the better part of a decade, and Augustus simply had his measure. He realized that Anthony's military reputation was overly inflated, while he himself, although he didn't revel in the battlefield the way Julius Caesar did, had acquired a sound grasp of strategy from his great-uncle. Not to mention he was a far better politician than Mark Anthony!"

"You seem to know a great deal about events from a century ago," Marcus had replied.

Corbulo laughed. "When I was a young *conterburnalis* I was posted to the Isle of Capri as a Praetorian guard," he said. "I stood in attendance over many a dinner while old Tiberius got drunk and regaled us with stories of his famous family. He was a funny old cuss—all the power in the world, and yet I don't know that I ever once saw him really happy. The closest he got was when he had the little children from the area around Neapolis come up and dance for him."

"There are rumors that he did more than watch the children dance," Marcus commented.

"Lies spread by that snake Caligula!" Corbulo exclaimed. "The worst thing I ever saw Tiberius do was lose his temper once and slap a little girl who had knocked his wine cup over. She started to cry, and he actually got on his knees and apologized, and plied her with sweetmeats until she would smile for him. He was a mean-tempered old recluse much of the time, but he did have a genuine soft spot for little children."

"Interesting," Marcus said. "Did you ever know Pontius Pilate?"

"Indeed!" Corbulo said. "I was on the island the day Caligula raped his little girl, and Pilate damn near killed him! Indeed, if he hadn't been determined to geld the boy first, he might have done so. But Sejanus arrived just in time and knocked Pilate out cold. That was the one time I saw old Tiberius genuinely grieve over a friend. He was terribly fond of Pilate, but Caligula was his only heir, and so the emperor had to exile his best friend to protect him from the vengeance of a psychotic teenager!"

Marcus shook his head and dismissed the memories of the conversation, looking at his stack of correspondence. Business before pleasure, he decided, and picked up the scroll from Nero.

Nero Claudius Caesar Augustus Germanicus, Princeps and Imperator of Rome, to Senator Marcus Quintus Publius, Triumphator, Tribune, Quaestor, and Deputy Proconsul of the Eastern Provinces,

How goes the war, old friend? Has Vologases come out to play yet? Are the Armenian nobles coming back to our camp, or do their sympathies still lie with the East? What of Rhamadistas? Can he still be relied on? Corbulo is a great general, but he has no head for politics, and I have not heard from you for some weeks. I am not trying to badger you, and I know that letters take time to make the long trip from Armenia to Rome, but I am anxious to know how things are going! I know that you would not deliberately leave your emperor in the dark. Hopefully your next missive will inform me of a smashing victory against Vologases. I pray the gods grant you good health and a swift return home. Write to me soon, old man!

Marcus rolled his eyes as he set the letter aside. It was Nero all over—trying so hard to be chummy and ingratiating, yet retain his *dignitas* at the same time—and with just the tiniest hint of a veiled threat. If only the lad would grow up some day, Marcus thought, he might make a capable emperor yet. As it was, Seneca and Burrus were able to rein in his worst impulses and keep the machinery of the empire running with some efficiency.

Next came several scrolls from Marcus' more important clients. Even halfway across the world, they still demanded for his patronage, his interest. Could he please ask the Senate for this tax exemption, or that bit of legislation, or perhaps interpose his *arctoritas* with a stubborn magistrate. He sighed and set those aside. They would get an answer tomorrow, perhaps, but not tonight.

Next he reached for a scroll from Mencius. He unrolled it with some anticipation, since his uncle always had the best gossip of anyone in Rome. This letter proved no exception.

Mencius Quintus Publius, Censor of Rome, Senator, and certified curmudgeon, to my nephew Marcus Quintus Publius, Triumphator, Tribune, and whatever other honors you may have won while I was not looking,

Greetings, young scamp! I trust this finds you safe and well, with the Parthian king's head in your saddlebag and wagons full of plunder trailing behind you as you prepare to return to Rome in triumph! Otherwise, I hope you are at least not clapped in irons or hanging from the city walls of Ecbatana!

The city is abuzz with rumors that Nero may actually be planning to do away with his own mother. They have been estranged ever since the death of Britannicus, and as Nero grows older, he becomes less and less restrained in his passions. Seneca is beside himself; he had envisioned Nero as a second Augustus, but what is emerging is closer to a second Caligula. Perhaps it's not as bad as all that—Seneca was always a pessimist—but the boy could certainly use your wise counsel right now. He has a cruel streak that is unnerving—rumor has it that he ordered a servant cut to pieces and fed to his pet lions for overcooking his supper!

Your young bride and my own dear Tertia have become fast friends, visiting the markets together twice a week and weaving in the afternoons. I am not entirely sure how you did it, nephew, but that young lady is convinced the sun rises and sets in your toga. She is a truly devoted wife, and I hope you have many happy years together.

The Christian cult which you have all but joined is becoming more widespread in Rome. There are a lot of ugly rumors about them, which are believed by the lower class of citizens—stories of cannibalism and orgies and other bizarre practices which bear no resemblance to the doctrines you told me about. Perhaps when you return you can do something to educate the masses. Your name is still held in high regard with the public, along with that of Corbulo. Everyone expects you shall trounce the Parthians in short order, so don't disappoint! Roma victor!

Smiling at that last bit, Marcus laid aside the scroll. Surely Nero was not so demented as to order his own mother's death, was he? He certainly did not sound that deranged in his letters.

Next, Marcus picked up the scroll from his wife. He held the cool papyrus to his cheek, wishing that it was her hand instead. He sniffed the letter, hoping perhaps that some trace of her sweet fragrance might be clinging to it. Alas, it only smelled of ink and the dried fibers it was made from. He broke the seal and read it.

My dearest husband, Antonia began, dispensing with all formalities, *in the midst of Rome's million and more people, I am alone without you. Your uncle and aunt are kind, and they are good company, but every evening my bed seems cold and empty. I am so proud of the trust that our emperor and the Senate and People of Rome have placed in you, and know that you will prove worthy of them all—but my selfish woman's heart simply wants her husband to be home again. Peter and Paul are a delight to me—I love to watch them chase each other through the house, and I have a feather tied to the end of a string that I use to set them playing when I am bored. This morning I woke up with one cat draped over my head and another lying across my feet. I could not bear to disturb them, so I simply lay there and enjoyed their soft purring for a while. They were a most kind gift, dear Marcus, but nothing can take the place of you in my arms. May the Christ we serve grant you and Corbulo a swift victory and a safe return, and if I ever let you out of my sight again, it will be against my will. Having found your love, I do not want to relinquish it again, not even for a season. Your lonely and love-struck wife, Antonia.*

Marcus read the letter three times, and then carefully folded it and put it in a leather pouch with Antonia's other letters. He would read it again, many times.

The last scroll was an enigma. It was sealed with a blob of red wax, and the Greek letters *chi* and *ro* were pressed into it—the universal sign that Christians used to recognize one another. But it bore no name other than the city it had been sent from—Caesarea, in the province of Judea. But who could have sent it? Marcus broke the seal and unrolled it.

Loukas Antigonus, physician and companion to Paul of Tarsus, to Marcus Quintus Publius, Senator of Rome, Deputy Proconsul, and Lover of God, it began.

I do not know who else to send this to, but Silvanus, another of Paul's companions, suggested that you might be able to help our friend. Even though he has committed no offense against Roman or Jewish law, Paul has been arrested in Jerusalem and taken to the governor's residence in Caesarea, where he is currently being held in custody. The leaders of the Sanhedrin, who have never forgiven him for surrendering to the service of Our Master, falsely accused him of profaning the Temple, and then instigated a riot when he tried to defend himself against their charges. The local centurion was going to interrogate him under the whip until Paul informed him of his Roman citizenship. The Jews said that they wanted to interrogate Paul further at the Temple the next day, but secretly they were forming a mob and planning to kill Paul in the streets. Hearing of their plans, the centurion sent Paul under armed guard to the governor, Antonius Felix. Felix has listened to Paul, and to his accusers, but steadfastly refuses to make a decision, and so my friend, and a beloved Apostle of our Lord Jesus, remains in prison despite the fact that he has committed no crime. Felix has indicated that he might be amenable to a bribe, but Paul donated all the gold in his possession to support the saints at Jerusalem. Frankly, even if he had the coin, I do not think he would bribe his way out of custody—it would not be worthy of his high calling as an Apostle of Christ to engage in such corruption!

You once told Paul that if it was ever in your power to aid him, you would be glad to do so. Your influence could surely help in this case, if you would use it in his favor, and earn the gratitude of all followers of the Way of Christ, as well as the blessing of our Lord. I implore you by the mercies of God to help secure Paul's release, for he longs to travel to Rome and preach the Gospel there. He has already written to the Roman church and they are expecting him to arrive soon. May grace and mercy be multiplied to you in the name of God the Father and our Lord Jesus Christ.

Marcus rolled the scroll back up and then sent Demetrius to find the courier who had delivered the day's mail. Moments later the weather-beaten legionary entered Marcus' tent.

"Where did you pick up this scroll, my friend?" he asked.

"In Rome, sir!" the man replied. "Your wife said that it had come to your villa over a month ago, and that I should forward it to you along with her letter and all the others in that bundle, except for the one from Caesar. I picked that up from him at Ravenna, where he was out hunting for wild boar."

Marcus frowned. It frequently took letters from the east end of the *Mare Nostrum* six months or more to reach Rome, and now this one had been sent back down the length of the sea and hundreds of miles overland to catch up with him. Paul may well have been in captivity for over a year at this point.

He picked up his helmet, stepped outside the tent, and strapped it on.

"I need to speak to Corbulo," he told Perseus.

CHAPTER XXII

Unfortunately for Marcus and for Paul, the arrival of the letter from Loukas coincided with Vologases' biggest military effort since the Roman legions arrived in Armenia. Marcus had gone to Corbulo's tent intending to ask for a leave of absence to go to Caesarea and secure Paul's release, only to find the headquarters all abuzz with reports that Tiridates had occupied the Armenian capital city of Artaxata and was building a line of forts to protect it. Corbulo, having spent two years training and grooming his legions for this campaign, was finally ready to teach the Parthians a lesson they would not soon forget. He called all his officers to meet with him the next morning.

"There are three massive forts protecting the route to Artaxata," Corbulo informed the gathered officers. "I will take the one to the north, at Arabacula. From there I can swing south to support either of you if things go afoul. Antiochus, I want you to take your own army and two of my legions and go after this southernmost fort at Baculites." The client king of Commagene nodded; he had been a loyal ally to Rome and was hoping to enlarge his territory at Vologases' expense. Corbulo turned and looked at his second in command.

"Marcus, you will take two legions and some Judean slingers and go for their jugular: the huge fort at Volandum. We go in fast and hard, if possible without warning, and the garrisons are to be put to the sword. Vologases needs to learn the price of defying Rome!" There were nods of agreement, and the men dispersed.

Marcus went back to his tent and wrote a brief letter to Paul and Loukas before donning his gear and mustering his legions.

Marcus Quintus Publius, Senator of Rome and Senior Legate to Gnaeus Corbulo, to Paul of Tarsus, Apostle of Jesus, and his companion Loukas Antigonus: I had intended to ride to Caesarea to secure Paul's release as soon as I received your letter earlier today. I am deeply sorry that my response has been so long delayed; your letter made its way to my house in Rome and then had to find its way to me on the Parthian frontier. It is my fond hope that your situation has already been favorably resolved, but if not, I gladly offer my services as your advocate. I will write a letter to the proconsul and urge your release, offering my personal pledge of your good behavior. If this fails, then I shall come as soon as my circumstances allow. Write to me as quickly as possible and let me know the current situation, and with Christ's blessing I shall see you soon.

Next, he quickly wrote a second letter to Antonius Felix, urging him to release Paul, whose good intentions and conduct he offered to vouch for. Then he entrusted both letters to a fast courier and dispatched him westward to Caesarea. Having done all he could do for Paul at the moment, he then strapped on his helm and stepped out of his tent. He had a campaign to fight, finally!

Marcus had never thought of himself as one who would relish battle—his days as a *conterburnalis* certainly were not marked by any great military promise—but ever since his experience in Pannonia, he found that he looked forward to the clarity of combat. It wasn't that he longed for bloodshed—violent death still made him feel sad and a bit sick at heart—but there was something about the idea of a supreme test of sinew and will that would settle an issue once and for all that appealed to him. There was also the undeniable fact that, if this battle went in his favor, he would be one long step closer to home.

His legionaries set out the next morning, covering the six hundred miles from Tigranocerta to Artaxata in a matter of a few weeks. The terrain was dry and dusty, and the days very hot, but the men were encouraged by the fact that they encountered no opposition, increasing their odds of surprise. Finally, one bright morning, the scouts Marcus had sent out came riding back with the report that the great fort was only a few miles away, over the next rise. Marcus ordered his men to halt and erect their portable fortifications. There was a small spring-fed stream winding down from the rocks, and he wanted his men rested and well-watered before they launched their attack. He set sentries out to watch for enemy scouts and monitor the fort. It was an impressive structure, built on the ruins of an ancient Babylonian city, whose stone walls had been expanded with massive wooden ramparts and a gate nearly thirty feet tall.

"We wait for dark," he told his officers. "An hour after sunset we set out. No torches or lights of any sort; nothing that will make any noise. I want to be at their gates before they know we are there. Marcus Licinius, I want you to take one of the uniforms we stripped from that Parthian cavalry officer you killed last spring and garb yourself in it. With any luck, we will trick them into opening the gate for us. If they do, we rush it and force our way in. If not, we'll use archers to take down the sentries and grappling hooks and ropes to scale the walls. Are we clear?"

The centurions nodded and went to spread the word to their men. Every century visited the stream, drank their fill, and replenished their canteens. The legionaries ate dried fruit and meat; no one wanted to risk a fire under the clear desert sky, where the smoke would announce their presence for miles. The day dragged on endlessly; Marcus could have sworn a week passed before the sun finally dropped below the horizon. All the long day, only one Parthian scouting party rode their way; a group of archers led by Cadius dropped each man from the saddle, killing all but one, and the horses were captured without much effort.

"Excellent!" said Marcus. "Now we have fresh uniforms and mounts; we can simply pretend to be this patrol coming in late."

"They will demand a password," Licinius said.

"Then we will have to get it," Marcus replied. "Isn't one of the Parthians still alive?"

The wounded cavalryman was brought into the Roman commander's tent, and Marcus knelt before him, questioning him in Greek.

"You know we will break you if we have to," he said. "All I need is the watchword to get the gates to open for us and I will spare your life."

"Rot in Hades, Roman dog!" the Parthian snapped. "I will never tell you, no matter how I am tortured."

Marcus gave a long sigh. "It doesn't matter how brave you think you are," he said. "You will break and tell us. The human body can only endure so much pain. But I despise the necessity of such things. You know I have been to your capital and spoken to your king. I can probably guess the password with little effort."

"Liar!" the man said. "No Roman is allowed to enter our great city and leave alive. Our password is the name of King Vologases' most prized possession, and of his worst enemy. You would never guess it in a million years!"

Marcus smiled. He remembered how proudly the high king had shown off the great speartooth cat so many years ago.

"Thank you, soldier," he said, patting the man on the shoulder. "You may take him away now, men. Leave him bound until the fortress is ours," he told the puzzled legionaries.

The Parthian looked bewildered. "I told you nothing!" he snapped.

"Actually, you did," Marcus said. "The watchword is 'Caesar.'"

The man's gaping expression told him all he needed to know.

Not long after dark, the bored sentry in command of the gate at the great fort at Volandum saw a cavalry patrol riding straight toward him out of the dark. As they came into the torchlight, he noticed a couple of the cloaks were bloodstained. The riders reined their horses in outside the gate, and he called out to them: "You boys have a little fun tonight?"

One of the cloaked riders nodded and replied to him in Greek, the common language of Vologases' polyglot army. "We ran into a large group of bandits, and a couple of the men are wounded," the man said. "Open the gates and let us in!"

"Give the watchword and I will!" the sentry replied.

"It's Caesar, you oaf!" said the rider. "Now let us in—I need some wine and my men need a physician."

The gates swung open, and the six riders passed through. The sentry thought it was odd that they still had their crossbows out, and odder still when the bows were suddenly leveled at him and his companions on the wall. Then a bolt skewered his heart, and he thought of nothing else for the seconds of life that were left to him.

Marcus, Cadius, and their four companions made sure that the watchmen were indeed dead, and then let out a loud whistle. An entire legion ran toward the walls, one century at a time. There were two sentries standing on the wall about a hundred feet or more from the gate; they gave the alarm as the Romans surged forward, but it was too late.

Years of frustration with an elusive and arrogant enemy boiled over as Marcus' men rampaged through the camp. Few Parthian soldiers tried to surrender; none succeeded. A dozen legionaries were killed and perhaps twice that number were wounded in exchange for three thousand Parthians killed. In less than an hour, the entire camp was in Roman hands. Only the camp followers and prostitutes were spared; most of them were perfectly willing to go to work for the victorious enemy. The bodies were dragged outside the city walls and burned on Marcus' orders; he dispatched riders to carry news of the camp's fall to Corbulo and Antiochus, and then spent a most comfortable night in the command tent of a Parthian general while Cadius guarded the door. All in all, he reflected as he closed his eyes, it had been a good day's work.

The next morning the entire camp was plundered of its stores, and Marcus' men, who had been on short rations during the march through the desert, found themselves feasting and drinking in unaccustomed splendor. Marcus gave them a few days to enjoy the spoils while he waited to hear back from Corbulo, but made sure the walls were manned and scouts dispatched daily to watch for any Parthian reinforcements or counterattacks.

Four days after the fall of Volandum, Marcus was eating his noontime meal with Cadius and his other junior officers when his messenger returned with a note from Corbulo.

Gnaeus Domitius Corbulo, Proconsul of Cappadocia and Galatia, Senior Legatus, Commander of the Eastern legions, to Triumphator Marcus Quintus Publius, Senator of Rome and Deputy Legatus, Greetings!

What splendid news all around! Your seizure of Volandum capped off our efforts with another victory; I was able to take Arabacula by storm with relatively few losses, and Antiochus seized the camp at Baculites with little difficulty as well. Prepare your men to march and hold your position; since you are in the central location, I shall bring my legions south to join you and Antiochus will come north to meet us by the end of the week. Then we shall advance on Artaxata together—and I pray to the gods that Vologases and Tiridates bring their armies out to face us! Then we shall wrap this thing up once and for all and you can return to your beautiful red-haired wife, while I shall be free of hearing you moan about how badly you miss her. Well done again, my friend. The emperor's confidence in you is well placed; you are as fine a soldier as I have ever served with!

Marcus read the letter out loud to Cadius after the other officers had left. His adopted son, now taller and broader in the shoulders than Marcus was, laughed at Corbulo's last line.

"You do tend to go on about her, *Pater!*" he said when Marcus shot him an injured look.

"I do not 'moan'!" Marcus snapped.

"No, you do not," his son said. "I would term it more 'whining.'" He ducked as Marcus threw his helmet at him, but both of them were laughing.

"If you marry the love of your life someday, you will understand," Marcus said.

Cadius grinned. "There is your problem, *Pater,*" he said. "You only have one love in your life. Me, I fall in love two or three times a day on a good day. My heart can never be broken because it's always finding new love."

"You are confusing your heart with the thing you carry in your loincloth," Marcus said. "They are very different, and you will discover that one day. I refuse to believe that Christ brought you back from the brink of death so that you could become the living incarnation of Priapus!"

Cadius grew more solemn. "I know I have a purpose to play at some point," he said. "I just don't know what it is."

Marcus retrieved his helmet and prepared to go outside and address his centurions. "God will reveal it to you when the time comes, my son," he said as he walked by.

Three days later, Corbulo's legions approached from the north, and the victorious generals embraced each other. The buff old soldier was impressed at the size and strength of the Parthian camp.

"It's a good thing you were able to trick them into opening the gate for you," he said. "Taking this fort by storm would have been a tough proposition!"

"I released the Parthian soldier who inadvertently gave me the watchword," Marcus said. "He helped me save dozens, if not hundreds, of my men's lives."

"I'd have cut his throat," Corbulo said. "That's probably kinder than what Tiridates and Vologases will do to him!"

"I think he knows that," Marcus said. "He rode off due west as fast as he could, away from Parthian territory. Now, come and share a cup of wine with me."

"Very well," Corbulo said. "I had a rider from Antiochus this morning; he should be with us by nightfall. Tomorrow we march on Artaxata! I figure that Tiridates and Vologases will have to defend it. The Armenian nobles are already sending delegations offering hostages and pledges if Rome will accept their allegiance once more. If we take the capital, the Parthians are done here."

Marcus grinned. "Then let's take it!" he said.

That night the three commanders gathered around a table in Marcus' headquarters and studied the map closely. They were now only a few days' march from the capital of Artaxata, so if battle was going to be offered by the Parthians, it would be coming soon.

"They will rely on their mounted archers, as they always do," said Corbulo. "They will try to make us break formation so the cataphracts can pick us off in detail. The Judean archers and slingers will help us in that department, but we will still probably suffer some losses. As soon as we sight the enemy, we'll need to form a hollow square. I'll need every centurion ready to give the order to form the turtle anytime the archers get close! We will hold our ground, and we will make them pay for each charge. Am I clear?"

The two generals and the junior officers all nodded. This would not be a sneak attack to capture a sleeping fort, but rather an all-out battle for the possession of Armenia, and for Rome's control of the East.

"Make sure that we have loaded all supplies and food we need, and set this place to the torch when we march out," Corbulo said. "We don't have sufficient legions to garrison the fort and advance on Artaxata, and we certainly don't want the enemy to occupy it and have a fortified base across our line of retreat."

"We've picked up about two hundred whores and camp followers," Marcus said. "They are earning their keep by cooking and laundering for the men, as well as their more traditional occupations. I'm going to suggest that we take them along—it will make the legionaries happy, and if we leave them in a burned-out fort they will starve."

"And spill our plans to any Parthian cavalry patrol that picks them up," Corbulo said. "Tell them they march with the baggage wagon and that if we lose, they will probably die."

"Make it so," Marcus told one of his junior legates. "Anything else, sir?"

Corbulo shook his head. "I suggest you try to get some sleep," he said. "Tomorrow we march!"

The next morning a huge column of smoke marked the site of the former Parthian fortress of Volandum as Corbulo's legions, reinforced by part of the Tenth Legion that had arrived after the fall of the frontier forts, made their way forward. It was thirty miles from the fort to the city of Artaxata, and the legions had barely left the burning fort behind when Parthian patrols began attacking their flanks. All day long the harassing attacks continued, with arrows raining down on the legionaries, who held their shields over their heads and cursed all things Parthian. Then the slingers and archers from Judea returned fire as the horse archers retreated, and their well-placed shots tumbled more of the enemy archers each time they made a pass. Two or three times the Parthian forces feigned retreat, hoping to lure the Romans out of formation, but Corbulo reminded his men—with blistering profanities in four languages—to stay in their ranks and not take the bait. Finally, the sun set and the Romans erected their portable fortifications; the walls were patrolled by triple the strength of the usual watch.

The Parthians tried to attack with fire arrows and light catapults during the night, but the Roman legionaries were so weary most of them slept through the harassing attack, while those on the wall returned fire with enough accuracy and effect that the enemy withdrew. The legions had covered nearly twenty miles that day, despite the opposition. When they broke camp the next morning and headed eastward, the Parthians launched one last attack, this time with the massive armed horsemen known as cataphracts.

In the past, these juggernauts had wreaked havoc on the legions of Crassus and Marc Anthony, but one of Anthony's legates had figured out that the deadly slingshot used by Jewish and Skenite warriors, if armed with lead shot, packed enough punch to knock the heavily armored warriors off their horses—and, if the horse was moving at full speed, the fall itself was often fatal to the rider, considering the weight of the iron and bronze armor they wore. Corbulo let the massive warriors close to within thirty yards before the slingers opened up; their deadly missiles sent cataphracts tumbling, and their horses stampeding in panic. A handful of the Parthian juggernauts reached the Roman ranks, which closed around them as the legionaries used their *gladii* to hamstring the horses, and then methodically pulled down, stripped, and killed their riders.

That was the end. The remaining cataphracts withdrew in disorder, with mounted archers sweeping in to cover their retreat. It was then that Marcus gained his first-ever battle wound; an arrow streaked over the heads of the legionaries and grazed his bicep just above his leather gauntlets. Blood flowed freely from the wound, but it was not deep, so Marcus pulled a strip of linen from his saddlebag, tied it with his free hand and his teeth, then remounted and rode on. Corbulo looked at the bloody bandage with a raised eyebrow when Marcus rode up to him moments later.

"I thought I told you to keep your distance from the enemy," he said. "I can't afford to lose such a good soldier, not to mention a friend of our emperor!"

"You should have told the enemy to keep his distance from me!" Marcus said. "It's just a scratch from an arrow; a parting gift from Tiridates, I hope!"

"Tend to the wounded and prepare to advance," Corbulo said. "We're only a few miles from Artaxata now!"

Marcus discovered, to his distress, that Cadius was also among the wounded. A Parthian arrow had caught him in the shoulder, penetrating his leather cuirass several inches. The *medicus* was using an arrow extractor to remove the iron point when Marcus arrived, while Cadius bit down on a leather strap to keep from screaming. Once the arrowhead was pulled free, the physician poured warm wine and salt into the wound, and then bound the young officer's arm into a sling. Cadius was pale, but managed a smile.

"Well, I'm out of commission for a few days at least," he said.

"There is no shortage of camp followers to tend to your wound," said Marcus. "Just save your strength and get better." He picked up the arrow and looked at the wicked barbed point. Taking a penknife, he cut away the wooden shaft and dropped the point into the leather pouch he carried at his belt.

"Why are you saving that?" Cadius asked.

"For you," Marcus said. "It will bring you luck. They say that Julius Caesar carried an arrowhead from the siege of Alesia on a leather thong around his neck for the rest of his life, and never suffered another scratch in battle. Ironically, he gave it to his great-nephew Octavian when the lad left Rome to wait for Caesar with his armies to invade Parthia. One week later, the *divus Julius* was stabbed to death on his way to the Forum. So make sure you keep this one with you at all times!"

The next ridge they mounted revealed the capital of northern Armenia looming in the distance. Not a single Parthian soldier lay between the city and them, and as they advanced, they realized that the city was strangely quiet. When they finally reached the gates, they were standing wide open, and a wrinkled vizier led a delegation of eunuchs, women, and old men to greet them.

"Noble sons of Rome," he said, "our high king has decreed that the city is indefensible, and has left us to your mercies. We entreat you to spare our lives, and use our city as you see fit."

"Your lives are your own," Corbulo said, "but the city will burn. We do not have the troops to garrison it, but I will not leave it here for Tiridates to snatch back the minute my back is turned. You may leave with us and make your lives in Roman territory, or you may flee to the east to join your master. Artaxata will be a smoking ruin when I leave it a week from now."

There was weeping and wailing from the delegation, but Corbulo would not be swayed. That night he and his officers stayed in the palace once occupied by Tiridates, while the legionaries fanned throughout the city, under the direction of their centurions, stripping away every bit of gold, silver, bronze, Greek statuary, or anything else that might conceivably fetch a decent price in the markets of Rome.

After dinner, Corbulo called Marcus into the royal bedchamber where the victorious general would be sleeping that night. Two of Tiridates' concubines stood in the corner, looking rather nervous. Corbulo shot them a wink and then turned to Marcus.

"I want you and your son to get some fast horses and a strong escort and head to Rome tomorrow," he said. "You will deliver a full report to Nero about the campaign. I am hoping we are done for now, but with the Parthians there is no telling. I am going to take my legions and do a slow retreat across the disputed territory, destroying all military fortifications and daring the enemy to come after me. If he does, I'll destroy him. If he doesn't, I think we may truly be done fighting for now. At any rate, you have earned your salt on this campaign, and I know that you are aching for home. Your boy has also served bravely. Is he well enough to ride?"

"I think so," Marcus said, "as long as we don't travel too fast. I need to swing down to Caesarea in Judea; I will just catch a ship from there bound for Rome."

"Judea?" Corbulo asked. "Why in the name of all the gods do you want to visit that cesspit of a province?"

Marcus grinned. "I have to spring a friend from jail," he replied.

CHAPTER XXIII

The next morning Cadius mounted up on his horse, still a bit pale but determined to ride rather than be carried in a litter—he said once was enough for that sort of thing. Marcus rode alongside him, along with a centurion named Antonius Gracchus. They were escorted by a full century of legionaries and twenty mounted auxiliaries. The men were in high spirits, relieved that the fighting was over and excited about the possibility of going home. Between the plunder from the three forts and the wealth looted from Artaxata, they would be mustered out with a handsome reward for their service once the war was done.

Marcus said a fond farewell to Corbulo, and then turned his face to the south and west, across the forbidding desert, toward the distant land of Judea. The men were in top condition, and well supplied; they rolled along at a brisk pace, pausing twice a day for food and a short rest, and making about fifteen miles per day. It was hot, but as they moved out of the desert and into the mountains, the temperatures cooled somewhat and there was more vegetation, and their pace picked up.

It took them the better part of a month to reach the regions around Cilicia, from where Marcus intended to turn southward for the last leg of the journey, toward Judea. As they made camp that night, a rider caught up with them, bearing a letter from Loukas. Marcus rewarded the courier and retired to his tent with Cadius to read the message.

Loukas Antigonus, Physician and Companion of Paul, an Apostle of Jesus Christ, to Marcus Quintus Publius, Senator, Triumphator, Legate of Rome, and Lover of God—

Grace and peace be with you always in the name of our Father and of the Lord Jesus Christ. I had despaired of ever hearing from you when your letter finally arrived last month. Paul is still imprisoned here at Caesarea, but events have taken an unexpected turn since I last wrote you. Felix's term as governor came to an end without Paul's case ever being resolved—

he still insisted on a bribe before he would grant Paul his freedom, while Paul, being innocent of any crime, refused to be extorted. God has used this captivity to his glory, however—Paul used his time in captivity to write many letters of instruction to the churches he has founded throughout the empire, and has received many visitors from those congregations. He has also preached the Gospel of the Kingdom of Christ among his guards, so that many of them have become followers of our Way.

Not long before your letter arrived, our new proconsul, Porcius Festus, arrived from Rome. He quickly visited Jerusalem in order to acquaint himself with the chief priests and scribes, who filled his ears with accusations against Paul. The passage of two years had not diminished their hatred in the least. They persuaded the governor to return Paul to Jerusalem under the guise of a new trial; however, what they really planned was an ambush by paid ruffians to kill Paul before he ever arrived. Advised of this plot by secret allies in the Sanhedrin—the Senate of the Sons of Israel—Paul protested against being removed from Caesarea. When the proconsul would not be dissuaded, Paul exercised the most sacred right of every citizen—he appealed his case to Caesar.

Once that was done, a trial in Jerusalem was out of the question. About a week after Paul's appeal, King Herod Agrippa and his wife Berenice came to pay their respects to Festus. Because his understanding of Jewish customs was rather limited, Festus did not grasp why the Jews were so angry with Paul. Therefore, he asked King Agrippa to hear Paul speak and perhaps clarify the issue. Paul gave a spirited defense of his faith in Jesus, so much so that Agrippa remarked that Paul had almost persuaded him to become a Christian. About the same time your earlier letter, addressed to Felix, arrived at the governor's palace. After reading it and conferring with Agrippa, Festus remarked, "This man might have been freed, had he not appealed to Caesar."

This brings me to my newest concern, Paul's impending trial in Rome. While there is a small community of Christians there, most of the people know nothing about our faith and the Roman church has been the subject of vicious slander. I fear that Paul may be sentenced to die based only on the common misperceptions about our Way. Therefore, your services as an advocate are more needed than ever. Yet, according to your letter, you are waging war on the Parthian frontier. What can we do in your absence to defend Paul against the charges that have been laid at his feet? Please reply to me soon. Yours in the service of Christ, Loukas Antigonus.

Marcus looked at his son. "It seems we are just in time," he said. "I hope Paul is still in Caesarea when we get there. Would you go fetch the courier for me?"

The rider entered Marcus' tent moments later. "How long ago did you leave Caesarea?" Marcus asked him.

"Just a few days ago," the man replied. "I had a good fresh horse and the weather was cool as I rode through Lebanon."

"Do you know if Saul of Tarsus was about to be shipped to Rome in the next few days?" Marcus queried.

"Luke—the fellow that gave me the letter—said that he figured they would probably be in Caesarea for at least another month," he replied. "Old Porcius Festus was going to wait for a big enough cargo ship to hold an escort of soldiers. Seems there are a lot of people who want this Paul or Saul or whatever his name is dead!"

Marcus nodded. "Do me a favor," he said. "I want you to convey this message to Proconsul Festus as quickly as you can. I am an advocate and Paul of Tarsus is my client. I would like a chance to confer with him and Loukas both before they head out to Rome."

"As you wish, Senator," the courier said.

Marcus sat at his desk for a moment and composed a few quick lines, then poured sand on the papyrus and blew it off—a quick way to dry the ink. He rolled up the scroll, poured a blob of sealing wax onto it, and pressed his ring into the seal. He dropped a sestercius into the man's hand.

"As quick as you can, my friend, and I'll buy you a drink when I see you in Caesarea. We should be there in a week or less!" he said.

Over the next few days they picked up the pace, moving through the rugged highlands of Syria and the beautiful green hills of Lebanon. Soon they could see the looming precipice of Mount Carmel, the tallest mountain in Judea, far off to the south. It took another two days of hard riding and marching, but finally they came riding into Caesarea from the north on the Ides of March in the sixth year of Nero's reign.

Marcus took an hour to get his legionaries situated in the large barracks where the governor's legion was housed, and to change out of his dusty traveling robes and don his military uniform—he thought it more appropriate than a toga, since he was coming straight from the battlefield. Then he headed for the governor's residence, built by Herod the Great as a guest house for Roman dignitaries a century before. The walls were polished white, and there was a Roman temple next to it. He paused to read the cornerstone and realized that the building had been constructed by order of none other than Pontius Pilate, some thirty years before, and dedicated to Tiberius Caesar. In his mind, he saw the face of Procula Porcia, and was again struck by how well she had aged. She must be at least in her mid-fifties, he thought, but she looked at least a decade younger.

Shaking away the memories, he mounted the steps and asked the legionaries guarding the door to announce him. Moments later, Porcius Festus came out of the audience room to greet him. Marcus had met Porcius during his tenure in the Senate under Claudius. Festus was a middle-aged, portly, affable Roman of impeccable lineage and moderate talents. He had a reputation as a capable, if unimaginative, administrator and a gifted compromiser. Many hoped that these abilities would help calm the perpetually troubled province of Judea.

"My dear Senator Publius!" The proconsul beamed. "I do believe the battlefield agrees with you—you are as trim and fit as I have ever seen you!"

"Weeks in the saddle and short rations will definitely work off any extra pounds one carries," Marcus replied. "How are you liking Judea?"

The governor scowled. "I am still not sure what I did to make Nero send me to this pestilential province!" he said. "It has provided me with one headache after another since I arrived!"

"Tell me about this Paul of Tarsus," Marcus said.

"I would assume you already know him, since you are his advocate," replied the proconsul.

"I do—he did me a huge favor a number of years ago," Marcus explained. "But I would like to hear your perspective on his case."

Festus furrowed his brow. "Well, I met briefly with Felix, my predecessor, when I got off the ship," he said. "He told me that there was a Roman citizen in custody who had appealed his case to Caesar. I asked why he had not been forwarded to Rome, and Felix hemmed and hawed and finally said that the local religious leaders had a strong interest in keeping him imprisoned as long as possible. Knowing Felix as I do, I assume that meant they bribed him to keep Paul in chains for as long as his term lasted. The man is insufferably venal!"

Marcus nodded. "I spent nearly three years chasing men like him out of office, but the empire seems to produce a never-ending supply of them," he said.

Festus nodded. "Rome has conquered so much territory that the opportunity for governors to start a nice profitable war has largely faded away. So now those with an appetite for wealth have to indulge in obscene levels of graft. I tell you, it is no wonder these locals hate us!"

He led Marcus up a stone staircase to his private quarters, which were comfortable but not ostentatious. A Greek slave poured them each a cup of wine, and Festus waved for him to leave, and then continued his story.

"Once I settled into my new quarters, I headed to Jerusalem to meet the high priest and the local leaders. They were friendly enough, but immediately started in with their demands about Paul." He took a sip of wine.

"As badly as they seem to want this man dead, you would think he was some sort of vile murderer or master criminal," Festus commented. "But the whole basis of their charges against him was related to his religious teachings. Apparently, there was some question about a Galilean rabbi named Jesus, whom they said was a dead heretic, and Paul said was a living son of God. The Jewish God,

I suppose, although I'm not entirely clear on that. I've never paid a lot of attention to Eastern religious cults. Isn't the Jewish God supposed to be invisible or something? What's he doing having children? That seems like something a Greek god would do! Anyway, I couldn't make head or tail of their accusations, except that they really wanted me to put this man to death, or let them do the deed themselves. Of course, he is a Roman citizen who has appealed his case to Caesar, so that is out of the question. I told them that they could send envoys to Rome to argue their case before Nero himself, and they got very huffy after that, and I headed back here more confused than I was before I left."

"So what happened when King Agrippa came to visit?" Marcus asked.

"You are well informed," Festus said. "Agrippa, as you know, is the oldest son of Herod Antipas. He was raised in Rome and named after Marcus Agrippa, old Augustus' bosom companion. But he has also never forgotten his roots, and is very well versed in the Jewish faith and the history of his people. I asked him to hear what Paul had to say, and the next day I brought the prisoner out before the entire court." He chucked before continuing. "I will say this much about Paul—the man is brilliant! I have never heard anyone who could quote so many ancient sources so freely. Mostly Jewish scriptures, which I didn't really understand—predictions about a deliverer they call the Messiah—but then he also was able to throw in references from Virgil and Homer to keep us Romans interested. But then he started in on this Jesus of Nazareth, the one the Christians worship."

Festus took another sip of wine and sighed. "I am confused by this whole thing," he said. "This Jesus was apparently a teacher and miracle worker, but he was also a descendant of one of their old kings—David, I think?—who was supposed to have an heir who would rule forever. But the priests and Pharisees—that's a sect of Jews—got together with old Pontius Pilate and had this Jesus fellow crucified. I'm not entirely sure what the charges were—I mean, heresy against a foreign god is not a capital offense! But this Jesus either wasn't really killed or else he came back to life, because next thing you know he's telling his disciples to go and preach and heal in his name. I had heard enough at this point, and I told Paul that his great learning had driven him mad!

"But Agrippa had been listening intently the whole time and seemed to be very interested in what Paul was saying. In fact, he even said that Paul had almost persuaded him to become a Christian! Well, he said he would like to hear more from Paul later on, and I had the prisoner returned to his cell. I asked him what he thought afterwards, and Agrippa told me that the Christians have gained a huge following now, not just in Judea but all over the empire, and that Nero should be careful how he treats Paul when the case goes on to Rome. It gave me a lot to think about, I can tell you that! I was glad when your letter arrived, because I am hoping that you can help me sort this out."

Marcus gave him a smile. "That is what I came here to do," he said. "I owe Paul a great debt, and I hope I can have him freed."

"That's the second time you have said that," Festus said. "If you don't mind my asking, what did Paul do for you?"

Marcus told him the story of the attempt on his life and the grievous wound that Cadius had suffered, and how Paul and John had healed the boy by praying to Jesus. Festus listened in indulgent disbelief, obviously thinking that Marcus was half mad or else pulling his leg. But as the tale wound up, he saw that the famous senator was entirely serious, and shook his head.

"Do you think there really is something to all this Jesus stuff then?" he asked.

"Indeed, I do," Marcus said. "In fact, I lack only being baptized before I can call myself a Christian."

The proconsul's eyes widened. "I didn't think any man of reason could possibly believe such nonsense," he said. "But I guess I was wrong. Well, you have my leave to spend as much time with Paul as you wish. I'm going to send him to Rome on a grain ship next month."

Marcus narrowed his eyes. "That's rather late in the year," he said. "I could take Paul with me when I sail in a few days and the journey might be safer."

Festus shrugged. "Paul is the one who asked me to wait," he said. "He is waiting for some messengers from Ephesus and Antioch."

Marcus stood. "I thank you for your time, Proconsul," he said. "I will go and see Paul now."

Festus stood and saluted. "Give my greetings to the emperor," he replied, "and tell him I will try to settle things down here."

"I will," said Marcus, "and I wish you luck! This is a difficult province to govern."

Festus gave a barking laugh and waved him away. Marcus turned to a nearby centurion. "What is your name, soldier?" he asked him.

"I am called Julius Macro, *Triumphator* Publius," the man replied. "I am *Primipilus* centurion of the Augustan Legion."

"Well, Macro," said Marcus, "I want you to go and find the prisoner Paul of Tarsus, and his companion, Loukas Antigonus, and bring them to me. I'll be in the commander's quarters in the barracks."

The man nodded and smiled. "Luke will be glad to see you," he said. "He and Paul have been hoping you would arrive before they left for Rome."

Marcus looked at him and recalled Loukas' letter. "Are you a follower of the Way, Centurion?" he asked.

Julius Macro looked both ways, and gave a quick nod. Marcus smiled. "May the grace of our Lord Jesus Christ be with you," he said.

The man's eyes widened, and he returned the smile. "And also with you," he said before he turned away.

The barracks commander had insisted that Marcus use his office and quarters while he was in Caesarea, and Marcus was glad of it. The office was large enough to conduct business with several people at once, and was on the second floor above the barracks and stables, which meant that no one could listen at the windows. Marcus called for some wine and papyrus, in case he needed to write anything down. There was a fair-sized table on one side of the room, with comfortable dining couches on either side of it. He decided to receive Paul and Loukas there, as equals, rather than while seated behind the legate's command desk.

Moments after he moved the pitcher and goblets there, the door opened and Julius Macro entered, followed by Paul, who was more scarred and stooped than he had been the last time Marcus saw him, and a tall, deeply tanned Greek who could only be Loukas Antigonus. Both of them smiled when they saw Marcus standing there.

"And so we meet a second time," he told Paul.

"I am glad that God has allowed it," Paul said. "There is a purpose to every meeting, and I know that God sent me to you eight years ago so that you would be here now, when I am in chains for the Gospel of Jesus Christ."

"I intend to have you out of those chains as soon as I can," Marcus said. "It should be a mere formality to have your case dismissed by Caesar. I only regret that it is necessary for you to make the long journey to Rome at such a perilous time of the year."

"It has been my heart's desire to visit Rome and preach the Gospel there for many years," Paul said. "I did not know I would arrive as a prisoner, but our Scriptures say that the Lord works in mysterious ways, his wonders to perform." He closed his eyes for a moment, and his lips moved, although Marcus could not hear anything he was saying. But then he opened them again, and his smile grew wider.

"But I have been remiss," he said, "in not introducing my companion. This is Loukas Antigonus, or Luke as we call him since he became a believer. He is my physician and my faithful companion."

The tall Greek looked at Marcus with keen interest. "I have heard many tales of the Roman senator who is sympathetic to the Way of Christ," he said. "It is a joy to finally meet you."

They seated themselves on the couches, and Marcus poured a goblet of wine for himself and Loukas, but Paul refused. "I only drink watered wine in the evenings, for my stomach's sake," he said. "I preach against drunkenness, so it is important that I not indulge in it."

Marcus nodded. "I always water mine after the first glass," he said. "I like to have my wits about me when I do business. Now, I am leaving for Rome in the next few days. I would rather you accompanied me, because in a month's time *Mare Nostrum* will not be safe for ships."

Paul shook his head. "I am not yet fit for a sea voyage," he said. "I have been ill for some time—I have a recurring fever and weakness that strikes me every year or two, and saps my strength. I have asked God to take it from me, but He has revealed to me that even in my weakness, He is strong enough to be sufficient for my needs. But I must recover my strength before I can undertake so long a sea voyage. I am not afraid—the Spirit has revealed to me that I will preach the Gospel in Rome and beyond before I am taken to my reward."

Marcus looked at Luke, who nodded in agreement.

"Well, then," he said, "in that case, we need to discuss the particulars of your case. Frankly, your being held in custody so long is an abomination of justice. You are a citizen of Rome and have committed no crime under Roman law! It should be a simple matter for me to persuade Nero to release you once you arrive in Rome."

"I don't know if that is true or not," Paul said. "Nero's current mistress is sympathetic to the Jews, and I know that the high priest and his cronies have written her about me."

"Not only that," Luke said, "but we have letters from Rome that talk about how the Way of Christ is blasphemed among the people there. There may well be pressure on Nero to put Paul to death to atone for the so-called crimes and sacrilege of the Christians."

"I have some standing in Rome," Marcus said. "Perhaps I can use that stature to influence how the people feel about our Way. But there is one problem—one that I hope the two of you can help me with. My knowledge of the teachings of Jesus is far from complete. I need to be better instructed in the tenets of our faith so that I can defend them against the false accusations being made in Rome."

Paul and Luke looked at one another.

"I think I can be of some help there," Luke finally said. "I have something I will send to you tomorrow."

Marcus raised an eyebrow. "What would that be?" he asked.

Paul answered. "Just before I was arrested, I met with the surviving Apostles of Jesus in Jerusalem," he said. "There were eight of us present. We were concerned because our numbers were dwindling, and the living memories of Jesus' time with us were in danger of being lost. After some discussion, James the brother of our Lord suggested that some of us write down our accounts of Jesus' life and ministry. Matthew, one of the original disciples, had already composed a preliminary account in Hebrew; while John Mark, a young kinsman of my friend Barnabas, had copied down many of the stories told by Simon Peter about the Lord Jesus. He made his account available to us, as did Matthew with his Hebrew *evangelion.* Brother Luke here had already been researching the life of our Lord for several years—neither he nor I were followers of Jesus during His time among us, so we were anxious to know as much as we could of what He said and did. Using Mark's writings, and Matthew's, and adding his own extensive research, Luke has composed a magnificent account of the things that Jesus said and did in the presence of His disciples. We were planning on taking it to Rome with us, but even as you spoke, the Spirit has revealed to me that it is you who must carry it there. But do not publish it until we have arrived."

Marcus nodded. "I will honor your instructions to the letter," he said. "I cannot wait to read this written version of the Gospel of our Lord!"

Luke smiled. "I have gone to great lengths to be as factual as possible," he said. "I am already working on an account of the things that Peter, Paul, and the other disciples have done since the Lord Jesus returned to His kingdom. I hope to have that account ready by the time we arrive in Rome."

"Then there is only one more thing we need to take care of," Marcus said. "Paul of Tarsus, will you baptize me?"

Paul took Marcus by the hand, and again his eyes closed and he moved his lips silently. When he opened them again, there was a touch of sadness in his expression.

"I will baptize you indeed, Lover of God," he said. "But it will happen in Rome, not here. The Spirit has told me that you must delay making this final step until after our appeal to Caesar has been made."

"I am not one to argue with the Spirit of God," Marcus said, "But I do not understand why."

"God does not always explain Himself," Paul said. "But I think that it may have something to do with your appearing before Nero. There is an evil spirit that hovers over the imperial throne—I have seen it in my visions. It despises our faith and whispers poison in the emperor's ear. Its influence is yet weak, but it will grow stronger over time. If Nero knows that you are a true Christian, he may reject your testimony altogether. If you can say, with perfect truth, that you are a sympathizer to our faith, but not yet a full member, he may be more inclined to listen to you. This much I do know—Nero will do great harm to the followers of Christ before his rule has ended, myself chief among them. But that time is not yet. It may be that, through your influence, I may be granted one more season of restraint, to bring a greater harvest into the Lord's House before my race is run."

Marcus looked at the scar-seamed, weather-beaten face of Saul of Tarsus. There was great sadness there, but there was, beneath it all, a powerful, welling spirit of unspeakable joy and majestic force. He knew that he was in the presence of a greatness that was far different, and more powerful, than that of any earthly ruler he had ever known.

"I know my service can never equal yours," he said. "But I hope I can play some part in the Lord's great work, if only to help you continue in it."

Paul smiled, and the force of the joyful spirit within him dispelled every shadow from the room. "One thing the Spirit has revealed to me, my friend, is that your name will be linked with mine to the end of the age."

Not long after that they left, and Marcus pondered what Paul had said. Was it truly his destiny to be a part of a movement that would live on till the world itself died? It was a sobering thought.

There was a swift trireme leaving for Rome in two days' time, and Marcus booked passage on it for himself, Cadius, and his military escort. Marcus finished writing up all his official reports to Nero about the Parthian campaign and his evaluation of Corbulo's performance—which was altogether positive. He enjoyed a final dinner with Festus, and reminded him to make sure Paul was embarked on a large, sturdy, and safe vessel when he left for Rome the next month. The day before his departure, he sent Cadius with a purse full of money and letters of introduction for Paul, so that the Apostle would be treated with courtesy and respect anywhere the name of Marcus Quintus Publius was known. He also wanted to make sure that Cadius got a chance to see and thank the man who had saved his life.

When Marcus' adopted son returned, he was bearing a large, thick scroll that was sealed with a blob of red wax. On the outer roll, next to the seal, a firm clear hand had written: "From Luke." As busy as he was preparing for departure, Marcus decided to read it once the ship had gotten underway. The next morning, he and Cadius boarded the ship, and sailors carried their luggage to the largest and most comfortable passenger cabin. It was no bigger than a typical bedroom in a country inn, but compared to the quarters Marcus had endured ten years before, when he first set out from Rome to tour the provinces, it was downright opulent. A small desk was bolted to the floor, and two hammocks were strung so that father and son could be rocked to sleep at night by the motion of the ship.

Within a few moments, the rest of the passengers had embarked, and the lines were cast off. The rowers hit their pace quickly, and the lumbering ship cleared the harbor and raised its sails, which quickly caught the wind and began propelling the ship forward faster than the oarsmen could row. The huge expanse of the Mediterranean stretched before them, glittering a brilliant shade of blue in the morning sun. Marcus watched as the huge artificial harbor of Caesarea faded in the distance and then went to his cabin, with

Cadius in tow. He retrieved Luke's scroll from his trunk and sat down at the desk, breaking the seal with a small paring knife. He had promised his son that he would read Luke's story out loud—the visit with Paul had set Cadius on fire with curiosity about the God who had saved his life.

Luke's handwriting was clear, precise, and fastidious; his Greek smooth, flowing, and impeccable. Marcus scanned the first paragraph and began to read.

"Inasmuch as many have undertaken to compile an account of the things accomplished among us, just as they were handed down to us by those who were from the beginning servants and eyewitnesses of the Word, it seemed fitting for me as well, having investigated everything carefully from the beginning, to write it out for you in order, most Excellent Theophilus, so that you may know the exact truth of the things you have been taught."

"Who on earth is Theophilus?" Cadius interrupted.

"That's me," Marcus told him with a smile. "That's the Greek for what Paul has called me since we met—it means 'Lover of God.' Now listen!"

CHAPTER XXIV

Marcus read Luke's Gospel from start to finish several times during that long sea voyage. It captivated him like no other written work ever had. Sweeping in its scope, poetic in its language, majestic in its message, it took root in his heart and turned his unrefined devotion to a God he had barely understood to a profound relationship with a Master whose presence shone from every word. At night, by the flickering light of the oil lamp in their quarters, he and Cadius discussed its content over and over—the remarkable circumstances of Jesus' birth, His wonderful stories that caused eternal truth to shine from everyday events, and the miracles that He performed wherever He went. The story of Jesus' trial and execution was so starkly told and so deeply moving that Marcus wept the first time he read it, and afterward found it impossible to read aloud without tearing up. The more Marcus read the book, the more eager he was to share it with Antonia when he returned home.

The voyage was comfortable enough for the first month or so, but then the summer winds began to fade. Several storms swept over them; none too violent, but enough to render some of the weaker stomachs on board incapable of holding food down. Marcus worried about Paul, who would be setting sail even further into the stormy season than he had. He prayed that God would bring the aging Apostle safely to Rome, and that his efforts to free Paul from captivity would succeed.

Despite the storms and contrary winds, the ship made good time. They sailed around the toe of the Italian boot with no further incident, and as Sicily passed by to the west, Marcus knew they were almost home. The last couple of days he spent most of his time on deck, watching the coastline slide by. Finally, one fine day at the cusp of summer and autumn, the port of Ostia came into view.

As soon as the lines were cast ashore and the gangplank lowered, Marcus and Cadius shouldered their bags and carried their lone trunk with them to the docks. There was a stable nearby, and they rented two sturdy horses and a pack mule to make the ride from the busy seaport to Rome itself. It was less than twenty miles, and the Ostian way was wide and traffic relatively light, so they were able to make a decent rate of speed and enter the city gates just before dark that evening.

Marcus' villa in the Quirinale was not far from the Ostian gate, so he and Cadius relinquished their horses at the local stable and grabbed the handles of their trunk, quickly making their way through the streets despite the crowds.

"You will need your lictors to get you through the streets tomorrow," Cadius told him.

"Indeed," Marcus said. "After we get home, would you mind going to the College of Lictors and making the arrangements? I'd like to get Rufus if he is available."

"Certainly," said his son. "And after that, I might see if I can find Arnulf and go have supper with his family—that would give you and Antonia an evening to yourselves."

Marcus raised an eyebrow. "Surely you are ready to come home by now?" he said.

The boy gave him a grin. The shoulder had healed completely during the long sea voyage, and his usual mischievous nature had reasserted itself. "I'll have plenty of time at home," he said, "but the way you have pined after her, I figure the least I owe you is one private evening with your wife. I don't know that I could sleep with the two of you together down the hall from me anyway!"

Marcus swatted him across the head good-naturedly. "You are incorrigible, boy!" he said. "But you might also be correct this once. Thank you for the gift of privacy, my son." He thought for a moment. "Be here before the second hour," he said. "I want you with me when I appear before Nero."

Cadius nodded with a wry expression. He had disliked Nero from the moment they met, and nothing the emperor had done served to change that opinion. They walked on up the street and turned the corner, coming to the front doorway of Marcus' villa moments later. Cadius sat down his end of the trunk, embraced his father, and trotted off in search of his old friends. Marcus watched him go with an affectionate smile, and then pulled the rope above the door, sounding a bell in the slaves' quarters. He heard a tapping sound in the front hallway, then the door opened and the wizened old face of Phidias peered out into the gloom. His eyes had grown milky with cataracts, Marcus noted.

"Mistress is at dinner!" the old Greek snapped. "Come back in the morning!"

"Now is that any way to greet your master after three long years?" Marcus said.

"*Dominus!*" the old Greek said with excitement. "By the gods, sir, I had no idea you were so close to home. It is good to see you again, sir—if I could see you clearly, that is. My old eyes are just about useless these days! I'll call Demetrius to have your bags brought in. I am so glad you are home!"

"You said my wife is at dinner?" Marcus asked.

Phidias scowled. "Yes," he said. "That no-good client of yours, Marcus Fabricius, has come around every day for the last three weeks, pestering her for news of you. I'll be honest with you, sir, I think he is up to mischief—or at least, he would like to be! *Domina* is a good woman, though—she listens patiently and sends him on his way every time."

Marcus scowled. He had prosecuted Fabricius in one of his first cases, for stealing another man's wife. Apparently, the rake had been impressed with Marcus' oratorical skills, because after Marcus returned from his tour of the provinces, Fabricius had hired his former prosecutor to help him recoup some debts he was owed by the tenants of one of his country villas. Marcus had taken the case but never warmed to the man, who was known as a serial seducer. Now he was sniffing around Antonia? Marcus strode angrily toward the dining room, and then paused at the door when he heard Fabricius speaking.

"My dear Antonia, your loyalty to your husband is commendable, but foolish. Do you really think Marcus has not warmed his bed with some Parthian whore at some point during these three long years? All I offer is a little affection and companionship during his absence. I assure you I am the soul of discretion."

The contempt in Antonia's voice warmed Marcus' heart as he listened.

"Marcus Fabricius, you obviously do not know my husband or me!" she snapped. "Three times you have come here under the pretense of business and made thinly veiled attempts to talk me into your bed. Now you drop all your masks aside and show yourself for what you are: a shameless seducer of married women! I must ask you to leave, sir, and not return. Rest assured my husband will hear of this!"

"Your husband has been gone three years!" Fabricius sneered. "And you yourself said your last letter from him was over three months ago, and dated two months previous to that! For all you know he is a moldering corpse with a Parthian dagger between his ribs, or being nibbled on by fishes at the bottom of *Mare Nostrum*. What will you do if he never returns, you cold-hearted witch?"

"I will live my life knowing that I was married to a man that is superior to you in every way," she said.

"How dare you!" snapped Fabricius. Marcus stepped into the doorway and saw him approaching Antonia with his hand raised.

"How dare you, sir!" he roared, and both of them froze. He crossed the room in three strides and slapped Fabricius across the face as hard as he could. The stunned Roman rake stood there, blinking, his eyes watering and a red handprint forming on his cheek. Marcus fixed him with a steely gaze.

"You are fortunate, indeed, sir, that I am a follower of Jesus the Nazarene," he said. "By Roman law and custom I could kill you here and now and no jury would dare convict me. To enter the home of your patron, your advocate, and try to seduce his wife—that is a crime in the sight of God and men! Get out! I am done with you. Find yourself another advocate, if you can. But if you ever enter my home again, I may forget my religion and take the vengeance Roman law and custom allow!"

Fabricius turned pale and scurried out of the room, gathering the folds of his toga around himself. Antonia watched him go, and as soon as they were alone together, she threw herself into her husband's arms.

"Oh, Marcus!" she said. "How I have missed you! That loathsome creature has been pursuing me for weeks."

He kissed her long and hard, first her lips, then her forehead, eyes, and neck. "I suppose I cannot blame any man for wanting you," he said. "But to betray the trust of a patron is a grievous sin. He will not be represented by any friend of mine if I can help it!"

"Be careful, my love," she said. "He is a friend of Nero's, they say. His cousin, Poppaea Sabina, is Nero's mistress."

Marcus sighed. "I absolutely refuse to spoil my first evening at home in three years with a discussion of imperial politics, much less our noble emperor's love life!" he said.

She kissed him in turn, hugged him again, and said, "I am only concerned for your safety and happiness, Marcus. Now, you have returned from a long and wearying journey. Are you hungry?"

"Famished," he said, "and sweaty from a whole day on horseback."

She clapped her hands and two young Greek slaves entered through a curtain that led to the kitchen. They were virtually identical, except that one had a small scar high on his right cheek.

"Pericles and Heracles," she said, "this is your *dominus* and my husband, Marcus Quintus Publius. He has returned from a long and weary journey. Take these dishes away and have the cook prepare him a freshly roasted leg of lamb with mushrooms and chickpeas. While that is cooking, I want a hot bath drawn for him and clean clothes laid out in our bedchamber."

"Twin Greek slaves?" Marcus whispered after they left to carry out her bidding. "They must have cost a small fortune!"

"A gift from the emperor last year, in honor of your service in Parthia," she said. "I heard a rumor that he bought them for Poppaea, but didn't like how much attention she gave them! Still, they have been first-rate domestics the whole time I've had them."

Marcus stretched. "By God, my dear, it is so good to see you again," he said. "You know my needs very well. A long hot bath, a good home-cooked supper, and an evening with you—I have dreamed of such a reunion for three long years!"

"Please tell me you are not leaving me again," she said. "This separation tore my heart."

"My plan is to retire from politics for a while," he said, "perhaps even for good. I think I would like to take you down to Pompeii and spend a few months in that lovely villa Claudius gave me. I'll let Cadius live here while we're gone—it's high time he began ascending the *cursus honorum* himself, and he can do that more effectively if I am out of his way."

He headed down the marble hallway that led to the private bath he and Antonia shared. The tub was sunk into the floor, with hot water piped in from a cistern on the roof, heated by a pair of charcoal braziers placed underneath it. The water was not as warm as Marcus liked it yet, but after a hot autumn day in the saddle, he found he did not mind. Antonia helped him out of his cuirass and tunic, and then unbuckled his sandals.

"You are not my slave, dear," he protested mildly.

"I don't want to share you with anyone tonight, bond or free," she said, and took his hand to lead him to the tub. He lowered himself into the tepid water and emitted an enormous sigh as she began to massage his shoulders. He knew that other things would transpire later, but for the moment, her voice and her touch were all he wanted.

They chatted for a half hour or so as he scrubbed the grime of the journey from his feet, hands, and body. She poured a bowl of rose petals into the water, and as the bath grew hotter, released some cooler water from the sluicegate that fed the tub. Soon the room was filled with the sweet aroma. They talked of minor things, about sights Marcus had seen, about Cadius' adventures and battlefield exploits, and about the meeting with Paul in Caesarea. Marcus had written her about some of these events, but much was news to her, since no letter from Caesarea could have arrived ahead of him. Antonia was, as always, a perfect companion, listening to Marcus with interest, asking questions that showed understanding and discernment, and supplying amusing anecdotes of home and hearth when Marcus got tired of talking. After a half hour, the curtains to their bedroom parted, and two fat felines entered the bathroom cautiously, their curiosity overcoming their aversion to water and strangers. They both eyed Marcus with the combination of curiosity and contempt with which cats regarded all other species.

"So these are Peter and Paul, I take it?" he asked.

"Indeed," she said. "The black and white one is Paul and the grey tabby is Peter."

Marcus held out his hand, and Peter sniffed it disdainfully, while Paul hopped onto a dresser and gave a demanding meow. Antonia laughed.

"They are not used to sharing my attention," she said, "but they will have to learn to deal with disappointment from here on out."

Marcus rose to his feet. "I am becoming positively waterlogged," he said. "And the smell of that roasted lamb is reminding me that I have not eaten more than a bite of very dry bread since I got off the ship this morning!"

He stepped out of the tub and Antonia reached in and pulled the wooden plug to drain its contents, which would be gathered in a basin and used to water the plants in the atrium. She toweled him dry and handed him a worn, comfortable tunic that he loved to wear around the house, and then they returned to the dining room. The furniture had been rearranged—Fabricius had been dining separately, on a guest couch, while Antonia had been across the table from him on a small divan. But now the two were pushed together, so that she could rest her head on her husband's shoulder as they dined—an arrangement usually reserved for private evenings. She dismissed the young maid—another slave Marcus did not recognize—and insisted on serving every morsel to him personally, taking joy in his appetite and, if the truth be told, enjoying how much he was savoring her presence. Is there anything better, she thought to herself, than for a woman to admire the man she loves? Except, perhaps, for a man to love a woman who admires him? She thanked God again that her father had arranged such an excellent marriage to such a good and decent husband.

Marcus ate until he was full, and then sipped a chilled glass of unwatered wine to wash his supper down. After he was done, he took his wife by the hand and led her to their bedchamber, where they sweetly made up for lost time until both were too exhausted to make up any more. By then the sun had long set, and the young maidservant entered the room with oil lamps and candles. In their flickering light, Marcus looked at his wife, still as beautiful as the day they were wed. He wondered what on earth he had done to deserve such a lovely and virtuous bride. They held each other for a long time, and then finally he pulled away from her and sat up.

"I brought home something remarkable I want to share with you," he said. "We cannot read it all tonight, but I thought you might enjoy hearing the first couple of stories this evening before we sleep."

She smiled. "You know how I love to read," she said, "but hearing you read to me is even better! What is it? A new copy of Homer, or Virgil?"

"This is so much better," he said. "It is the story of Jesus Himself, as told by Loukas, Paul's companion." He crossed the room and opened the trunk Demetrius had brought in, removing the scroll he had carried from Caesarea. He pulled the lamp stand closer to the bed, unrolled Luke's *evangelion,* and then began to read.

The next morning, he rose in the first hour and stretched. After all his travels, it was hard to believe that he was finally back in his own *domus,* in his own bedchamber, with his lovely wife sleeping by his side. He pulled the sheet down a bit and kissed her on the shoulder. She rolled over and opened her eyes, then started and sat up abruptly, the sheet falling to her waist.

"I am so sorry, Marcus!" she said. "I should have been up before you, making sure your breakfast was ready."

Marcus looked lovingly at his wife, drinking in the glorious sight of her. "Seeing you by my side, in my bed, is all the breakfast I needed this morning, my beautiful Antonia," he said. "It is all I dreamed of every night while I was gone."

She shrugged into a tunic and gave him a gentle smack on the shoulder. "Surely that is not the ONLY thing you dreamed of," she said.

He cracked a grin. "Well, I did once dream that Nero came riding into our camp on the back of Vologases' mighty speartooth cat, dressed as Diana and waving a codfish over his head," he told her. "But that was after I had taken milk of the poppy to ease the pain in my arm."

She traced her finger over the still-red scar where the arrow had torn his skin. "I am glad that was the only injury you suffered," she said. "I do not think I could bear to lose you."

"I may suffer greater injury yet, if I delay reporting to my emperor too much longer," he said. "I need a loaf of bread and some olive oil to break my fast, and then I must go to the palace. Cadius is supposed to join me."

"The boy is already here, *Dominus,*" said Phidias from the doorway to their bedchamber. "He inquires if he needs to leave you two alone any longer."

Antonia and Marcus exchanged a look, and then laughed. "Tell the scamp we will join him in the dining room momentarily," Marcus said. Phidias nodded and stumped out on his cane, and the two of them got dressed quickly. A few moments later, they entered the dining room, where Cadius stood, still wearing the cuirass and sword of a *conterburnalis.* He turned when he saw them enter.

"Mater!" he exclaimed, and embraced Antonia. She returned his hug enthusiastically.

"My dear boy," she said. "Your father told me all about your injury, and I rejoice to see you come home safe and healed of your wounds."

"I am glad to see him with you again," Cadius replied. "The old man is an absolute bear when he is missing you!"

"Incorrigible brat!" Marcus said. "I may ship you off to Britannia if you keep up this impudence."

The family laughed together and enjoyed a hasty breakfast.

When they were done, Antonia pulled Marcus aside for a moment. "A word of caution, my husband," she said. "Nero is not the insecure boy you left in Rome over three years ago. He has changed, and not for the better. The palace is a more dangerous place than it has been since the last days of Caligula."

Marcus frowned. "That grieves me to hear," he said. "Nero had great potential for good, but also for wickedness. I could see that in him when he was only a lad. I hate to think that his propensity for wickedness has won out."

He turned to his son. "Let's go, then, lad," he said.

When Marcus and Cadius walked out the door, a familiar voice greeted them.

"Marcus Quintus Publius, as I live and breathe!" Rufus roared. "It is good to see you again, sir, begging your pardon! None of these other senators I escort around is as good to me as you was!"

"Rufus Licinius!" Marcus said. "It is good to see you again, too, my old friend. Being a lictor seems to agree with you—you're a bit bigger in the middle than you once were!"

"Benefits of marriage, sir!" the brawny lictor said. "My Sarah is a wonderful cook, make no mistake!"

"Sarah?" Marcus raised an eyebrow. "You married a Jewish girl?"

"Jewish by birth, Christian by choice," he said. "She is a great-niece of one of the Apostles—mayhap you've heard of Saul of Tarsus? Although he goes by his Roman name, Paul, more often nowadays. He even mentioned me in the letter he wrote to Rome!"

Marcus shook his head. It seemed that the world was even smaller than he imagined, he thought. "Well, Rufus, I would have you and her to dine with us one evening soon," he said. "But right now, we need to get to the emperor's palace as soon as possible."

"We'll clear your way, sir, make no mistake," Rufus said, and turned to the other lictors. "Now lads, this is Senator Marcus Quintus

Publius, and he is a special friend of mine. You will escort him with all due speed and courtesy or answer to me for it! Am I clear?"

"Yes, sir!" the five men echoed back, and the procession set forth to the Capitoline Hill.

The palace was larger and more luxurious than Marcus remembered, but there was also an aura of sleaziness and iniquity that had not been there when Claudius was emperor. While the human body was a constant theme in Roman art, the frescoes, paintings, and sculptures Nero had chosen to decorate his palace with were gaudy and erotic to the point of tastelessness. The servants were more scantily clad and sauntered about, displaying their bodies as if this were a brothel rather than the seat of the greatest empire on earth. A tall young Greek, his face painted gold to resemble Cupid's, stood at the door of the emperor's audience hall, wearing a loincloth and a bow over his shoulder and not much else. Marcus eyed him with distaste and gave his name and his mission. The Greek nodded, bowed, and entered the chamber. A few moments later, he emerged and spoke.

"His Excellency the Emperor Nero will see you now," he said.

If the palace had indeed changed for the worse, it had done so to reflect the changes that Nero had undergone since last Marcus saw him. The emperor of Rome was seated in a huge, ornately decorated curule chair that was more reminiscent of an Eastern potentate's throne than the judgment seat of the head of a Republic. A crowd of people stood before him, some private citizens in formal togas, come with petitions and requests, but far more of them appeared to be entertainers, acrobats, and prostitutes. In one corner a large tiger paced back and forth at the end of a leash, while across from him a dwarf juggled brightly painted wooden balls. Nero himself sprawled on the curule seat, his toga stained with wine here and there. His scraggly beard did not cover the angry red pimples that had sprouted around his mouth and neck. His hair had grown thicker and curlier, and he wore it down to his shoulders in the back. He had gained a good deal of weight, mainly around his middle, so that the stained toga was stretched tight in the front. Standing by his side was a lovely teenage girl with long, curly blond hair, wearing a shift that exposed far too much of her body, making her look more like a slave than a Roman noblewoman. This, Marcus guessed, must be Poppaea Sabina. She leaned forward and whispered something into Nero's ear. He laughed, then kissed her on the cheek and squeezed her leg.

Marcus saw Lucius Anneaus Seneca standing to one side, looking as miserable as could be. He gave Marcus a despairing glance, and nodded toward the emperor. Marcus squared his shoulders and strode forward until he stood ten feet in front of Nero.

"Hail Caesar!" he said. "I have returned bearing news from Armenia!"

The emperor stood, shaking off his courtesan's hands, and grinned widely. For a moment, Marcus saw the old Nero there, intelligent, curious, and desperately eager to please. But the other Nero, the hedonistic, lazy egotist, was there too, cast aside for the moment, but eager to regain the ascendancy. The ruler of Rome stepped forward and embraced his old mentor with something like genuine affection.

"Marcus, my old friend!" he said. "How wonderful to have you back in Rome! I have heard whispers that things went well for you on the frontier, but not much more. I wish you had come to me when you arrived last night, but I know you were eager to see your lovely bride again, and to wash off the dust of your travels. So what is the news from Legate Corbulo?"

Marcus returned his embrace, and then withdrew two scrolls from the sinus of his toga.

"Here is the general's official report, still sealed, which he bade me carry to you when I left him in Armenia," he said. "This second scroll is my own report, including my thoughts and impressions of Corbulo's conduct and abilities as a military commander and a diplomat."

Nero took both scrolls and studied them a moment. "Come with me to the library," he said. Turning to the room full of people, he raised his voice. "Get out, you pack of sycophants!" he shouted. "All of you go home. Come back tomorrow!"

A groan of protest went up, but they filed out the door anyway. Nero watched them go for a moment, and then shouted again. "Seneca!! Where are you going, man? You're still my advisor, are you not? Come to the library with Marcus and me!"

He led Marcus down the hallway, muttering to himself under his breath. A slave came towards them, bearing a tray full of wine cups. Nero deliberately ran into the man, knocking him over and sending goblets flying everywhere.

"Oaf!!" he roared. "Lick up every bit of that wine, then go tell the Praetorians to give you fifty lashes for being such a clumsy idiot!"

The wretched slave dropped to his knees and began lapping up the spilled wine. Nero cackled with laugher. "By all the gods, man, do you not know a joke when you hear it?" he asked. "Have someone mop that up, and here are two denarii for playing along!" He flung two coins at the man and started striding down the hall again, still muttering.

Marcus looked back at Sejanus, who shrugged his shoulders in resignation. Then he followed Nero to the library. This was one room that had changed very little, Marcus saw. Scrolls were still stuffed into niches all across the room, and the statue of Augustus that had dominated one corner was still there. One shelf was filled with codices instead of scrolls, and Marcus found himself more approving of their presence than he had been so many years before. They were definitely more durable than scrolls, and easier to read once you became used to turning pages instead of unrolling papyri.

Nero flopped down onto a comfortable couch. Marcus noted with a start that it was the same couch where he had sat with Claudius, waiting the news of Messalina's execution. The emperor gestured for him and Seneca to sit down, so they sat on the nearest couch to Nero and waited for him to speak.

The emperor broke the seal on Corbulo's scroll first, reading through it quickly, occasionally rolling back to a previous paragraph and then proceeding onward. At one point, he raised an eyebrow, looked sharply at Marcus, then shook his head and read on. When he was done, he deftly rolled the scroll back up and opened the one

Marcus had written. He finished it just as quickly, checking back in one or two places, and then referring back to Corbulo's scroll for a moment. Marcus watched him with interest. This was the Nero that Claudius, Seneca, and so many others admired—a quick intellect with the ability to absorb and process information almost instantly. A shame, Marcus thought, that the young man was allowing his baser instincts to overrule his sharp mind.

"Well, Marcus, it sounds as if things are proceeding quite well in the East, thanks to you and Corbulo," he said. "Indeed, the two of you seem to have formed a mutual admiration society. He says you are the most capable subordinate he has ever had, and you say that he is Rome's greatest general."

"I don't know every general in Rome, sir," Marcus said. "But Corbulo is the sharpest man I have ever served under. If anyone can defeat the Parthians once and for all, it is him."

"Or you," Nero said. "The capture of Volandum—Corbulo says it was the neatest bit of work he'd ever seen. You captured a stronghold and put its entire garrison to the sword with minimal losses! I'm going to have the Senate declare two weeks of games and celebrations to commemorate the victories of Corbulo and Publius!"

"If it pleases you, Caesar, I should certainly be honored and I know Corbulo would be too," Marcus said.

"It does please me, Marcus. You have honored me with your counsel and your loyalty, and a Caesar should always pay his debts," Nero said. "Now, tell me, old friend, what's this I hear about a dustup between you and Marcus Fabricius?"

Marcus sighed. He figured that was what Poppaea had whispered to Nero about as he entered to room. Honesty was the best policy, he thought.

"Sire, I returned from three years and more campaigning and fighting for Rome to find this blackguard brazenly trying to seduce my wife in my own home! He is frankly lucky I didn't run him through!" Marcus said.

"And was your lovely wife receptive to his attentions?" asked the emperor.

Marcus smiled. "I think if I had not entered when I did, she might well have killed him herself," he said. "She is ferociously loyal to me."

"Ah, virtuous women!" said Nero. "Gratifying for you, no doubt, but how boring they are! Like my lovely wife, Octavia, foisted on me by my dear old fool of a father. She's a prime breeding heifer and little else. I prefer my women with a strong dash of wickedness and a background of broken oaths and hearts in their wake! Messalina—now there was a woman! She knew how to have some fun. What a shame my father had to relieve her of her head—I would have enjoyed getting to know her, if you know what I mean! So much more interesting than a dull, loyal, obedient wife whose eyes never wander. My Poppaea is married to another man, my old drinking comrade Otho. Does that keep her from climbing into my bed, and sharing me with other girls? Of course not. She has a sense of adventure, that one! But, to each his own. I am glad you find your Antonia satisfactory. She is lovely, I give you that. And loyal, if you prefer your women that way."

"I do, sire," Marcus said, thinking that if Nero found Antonia boring, he must not really know her at all.

"Again, I am grateful for your service, Marcus my friend," the emperor said. "How can I repay you?"

"There is one small matter in which I would ask your help," Marcus told him. "It involves a client of mine, one Saul of Tarsus."

"Ah yes," Nero said. "Isn't he a leader of those Christians or Nazarenes or whatever they are called?"

"Indeed, he is," Marcus replied. "But he is also a freeborn Roman citizen who has been jailed for two years on the flimsiest of pretexts. He had to appeal his case to Rome in order to avoid being sent back to Jerusalem and certain assassination."

"My Poppaea is crazy about the Jews," Nero said. "I don't know what she sees in them, but I know their high priest has written to her, urging her to ask me for Saul or Paul or whatever his name is to be executed."

"Sire, he is a Roman citizen who has committed no crime," Marcus said. "I understand the complex dynamics of Judean politics as well as any man, but let's be honest. The Jews are always outraged about something. Killing Paul would make them happy for ten minutes, and then they would make some other unreasonable demand."

"A good point," Nero said. "Is this client of yours in Rome yet?"

"He was not well enough to travel," Marcus replied. "He should be here in a month or two."

"Approach me about his case again, when he is here to answer before me," Nero told him. "But I didn't ask how I could reward one of your clients. I asked how I could reward you. What does Marcus Quintus Publius desire from his emperor?"

"Retirement, sire," said Marcus. "At least for a year or two. Your noble father gifted me with a magnificent villa in Pompeii that I have not visited in many years. I should like to go there with my wife and rest from my labors for a time."

Nero nodded. "I need you back in the Senate eventually," he said. "But I understand the need for rest. Take your lovely Antonia and go to Pompeii. See if you can sire a pack of babies on her if that is your desire! Return to Rome when your man Paul arrives and I will hear his case. Until then, enjoy your leave of absence."

Marcus bowed and left the chamber, his heart lighter than it had been in many years.

CHAPTER XXV

Paul did not arrive in Rome that fall, or during the winter. It was late spring when the ship carrying him and his companions arrived in the capital city. Marcus and Antonia were in Pompeii when they received a letter from the Apostle, after spending most of the winter there. Marcus broke the seal and read the scroll with great relief.

Paul, called to be an Apostle by the grace of Jesus Christ our Lord, to Theophilus, my brother in Christ and advocate in law, Grace and peace be unto you in the name of our Father and the Lord Jesus, who is our eternal advocate before the throne of Almighty God.

I had hoped to arrive in Rome much sooner, but it pleased God that our journey should be interrupted, although our passing inconvenience proved to the greater glory of His kingdom on earth. The vessel we took from Caesarea was not equal to the fierce storms of the autumnal season, so at Lycia we boarded a grain ship from Alexandria that was bound for Rome. Though the seas grew steadily rougher, we made good progress until we arrived at Fair Havens in Crete. That harbor was unsuitable to winter in, but the Spirit warned me that we should not go any further. I tried to persuade my companions to remain there till spring, but Julius the Centurion was persuaded by the captain to seek better harbor at the town of Phoenix, further up the Cretan coast. When a gentle south wind began to blow, he seized the opportunity to set sail again despite my warnings. We were well out to sea when a fierce nor'easter began to blow, driving us helplessly before it. The sailors and passengers alike began to despair of their lives, but the Holy Spirit spoke to me and promised that not a life would be lost if they would only follow my guidance. After fourteen days, the ship ran aground off the shores of Malta, and having partaken of some food, we came safely to shore by clinging to bits of wreckage as the waves broke our ship to pieces. Two hundred and twenty-six of us, passengers, crew, soldiers, and prisoners like me, all were delivered from death by the power of God, and many souls were won over as I proclaimed the word of Christ to them on the beach, not only of the ship's company but also of the islanders who came to our aid. So once more the Spirit of God bends the plans of man to serve a greater purpose! We spent the winter there, and the following spring we embarked for Rome aboard another vessel from Alexandria, that had wintered on the south side of Malta. We made landfall in the town of Rhegium and spent a week encouraging the brethren there while Julius reported to his superiors, then set out for Rome along the Appian Way. Last night we arrived at the Forum of Appius and stayed in the town of Three Taverns, where I had the opportunity to pen these lines to you. I am sending them to your house in Rome, and I hope in the Lord that your duties have not taken you away from home again. A company of the saints from Rome has come hither to meet me, and it is one of them, Trophimus, who bears this letter. May the grace of our Lord be with you, Lover of God, and guide you speedily to meet me, for I long to see your face once more.

Marcus gave Antonia a wry look.

"Well, back into the stews once again!" he said. "I suppose our idyllic spring had to come to an end eventually."

She hugged him with one arm, patting her swelling belly with her other hand. She had conceived not long after his return, and her face glowed with that special warmth that only a new life growing within could bring.

"It was a winter well spent, husband," she said, "but that does not mean you have my leave to go haring off across the world again! Do you wish me to return to Rome with you, or wait here for your return? I am not so far along that a voyage will endanger my health."

Marcus considered. "Let me proceed alone," he said. "Cadius is away with the legions again, so our house is available. If it looks as if I shall be detained, I will send for you."

She kissed him again. "Be wary of Nero, my love!" she said. "He is as changeable as the tides. For now, you are his esteemed counselor. But he might well cast you aside as easily as he has forsaken Seneca—or Agrippina."

She shuddered lightly upon saying the name of the emperor's mother. Seneca was in disfavor at the moment, banished from the palace—but Agrippina was dead. Not long after Marcus returned to Rome—he and Antonia had been in Pompeii for a couple of weeks—

he had received the shocking news that Nero had ordered his own mother's execution. The two had become more and more estranged after her return from exile. Rumors about exactly how she died varied, but most agreed that Nero had rigged a collapsible boat that would carry her far out into the waters of the Bay of Puteoli, then fold up and sink with her aboard. The plot nearly succeeded, but the collapsing lead roof opened a hole in the hull of the ship that she and her maid were able to escape through. Nero had reportedly panicked upon hearing of her survival, ordering his guards to go and finish her. Agrippina had apparently thought the boat's sinking accidental until a band of armed Praetorians confronted her, crossbows leveled. According to one particularly lurid rumor, at that point she had ripped open her robes and slapped her stomach, crying "Strike here! Aim your arrows at the womb that gave birth to such a monster!" Knowing Agrippina's penchant for drama, Marcus thought she might well have said such a thing. Her body had been carried to the palace in a covered litter, leaving a trail of blood drops across the Capitoline Hill. Nero had allegedly laid her body out on a dining couch, walking around her with a giggly Poppaea Sabina at his side, lifting his mother's limbs and commenting on her fine physical qualities. Marcus found such a tale difficult to believe, but many in Rome swore it was true. One thing was certain—Nero was no longer the boy he had once entertained some high hopes for. Marcus was only too glad to spend the winter in Pompeii and avoid the scandals and wickedness of the imperial court.

The villa that Claudius had given him was quite a luxurious affair, covering most of a city block. It had a beautiful peristyle, with a reflecting pond that caught the rainwater, and a lovely herb garden enclosed by a ten-foot wall behind the house proper. The dining hall was expansive enough to entertain twenty or thirty guests at a time, and there were several guest bedrooms as well as a lovely master bedroom with a private bathroom and dressing chamber adjoining. The entryway featured a beautiful fresco of Romulus and Remus being suckled by the she-wolf of legend, and the murals decorating the walls were tasteful and gorgeously executed. The statues were mostly first-rate copies of famous works of antiquity. The aesthetic refinement of the place was proof, commented Antonia, that Nero had never set foot there. From the garden, one could see over the wall the looming slopes of Vesuvius, with its smoke-belching cone reaching toward the sky.

Their time together had indeed been idyllic—tended by a small, loyal handful of servants (Marcus had left the twins in Rome, suspecting they might be spies for Nero), they had enjoyed more time with each other than they had at any point since their marriage. They went for long walks in their orchard outside the city walls that had come with the villa. They would pick ripe fruit from the trees and eat it as they walked; they had gone swimming in the clear waters of the Bay of Neapolis, and bought fish and crabs fresh from the market and grilled them for dinner over a driftwood fire on the beach. After the fiery passion of their initial reunion had died down to a more somber enjoyment of precious hours together, they spent long hours reading, dissecting, and meditating on Luke's wonderful book. Marcus had three copies made—one for himself, one for Antonia, and one that was kept in a cupboard at his Roman *domus,* so that the precious gospel would not be lost if his villa in Pompeii burned down. But he kept his promise and waited for Paul's arrival before sharing it outside his family.

Now, he thought as he packed his formal toga and donned his riding gear, the "Apostle to the Gentiles" had finally come to Rome! Paul's messenger Trophimus had agreed to wait until Marcus was ready to accompany him back to the city. Nero had two fast horses brought up from his stables so that they would be able to travel back to Rome quicker than the messenger had come on foot.

"We've been waiting for Paul to come and teach us for years," Trophimus said excitedly. "Aquila and Priscilla have done much good in sharing the words of Jesus with us, but Paul's letter on doctrine is so marvelously deep and inspired I cannot wait to sit and listen to him speak at length!"

"So you had never met him before this encounter?" Marcus asked him as they rode past the shadow of Mount Vesuvius. A single wisp of smoke hung over the cone, as it often did these days.

"No, sir, I am Roman born and bred. This is as far as I've ever been from home. I heard the story of Jesus last year from Aquila and Priscilla, when they arrived in Rome and began teaching in the Tentmaker's Square over in the Aventine district. I was there to purchase blankets for my wife when I heard them speaking and was totally caught up in the power of the Gospel. I brought my wife back the next day and we were both baptized not long after," the young man shared excitedly.

Marcus sighed. "I hope to be baptized soon myself," he said, "but Paul asked me to wait until his case was heard before Nero."

"You are a believer, then?" asked Trophimus.

"I saw the healing power of Christ demonstrated in a remarkable way a few years ago," Marcus told him. "I have believed in Jesus from that day to this, but I have not yet had the chance to be baptized in His name. I am confident that my heart already belongs to Him, but I look forward to the day I can call myself a true Christian!"

"I did not know there was anyone so high up that was a member of our Way," the young Roman told him. "You're a member of the Senate and a former tribune of the Plebs, aren't you?"

"Yes," said Marcus. "I was fortunate enough to call the Emperor Claudius my friend."

"Wait a minute!" Trophimus said excitedly. "You're THAT Marcus Publius? The one who won the Grass Crown in Pannonia?"

Marcus sighed again. "Yes, that was me," he said. "Although I do think that the men made too big an affair of what I did during that campaign. They were the heroes, not me. I saw a crisis, I took command, and I fixed things. That's what Roman officers are supposed to do. The legionaries did the rest."

"You rescued a legion from destruction and a province from being overrun by the Osterlings, is the way I heard it!" said Trophimus. "But I'd rather hear your version, sir, if you don't mind. It'll help pass the time on the road, don't you think?"

Marcus was a modest soul by nature, but he did rather enjoy telling stories, and Trophimus was so eager to hear him that he decided it could not do any harm. And it did indeed help eat up the miles as they galloped toward Rome.

It was late in the afternoon two days later when they entered the gates of the City of Romulus. They left their horses at a public stable outside the *pomerium,* and Trophimus guided them to a tavern that was favored by Christians, near the Tentmaker's Square in the Aventine district. It was a quiet place compared to most of the rowdy taverns and inns of the area. The gambling tables and whores that were a staple of Roman entertainment were largely absent, but the place was full of young children and their mothers. In one corner, a group of men and women were singing together, while across the room another group were all seated, facing Paul, who was standing with his back against the wall, smiling and preaching in a voice that was surprisingly loud for a man so short of stature.

"You see, my brothers, it is by grace we are saved through faith, not by our own works! If we could somehow earn our own salvation, the Lord of Glory would not have needed to go to the cross. But because none of us is righteous enough to stand before a Holy God, even as it is written—'there is none righteous, no, not one!'—God in his infinite mercy sacrificed His own Son to be the propitiation for our sins," he was explaining to them. He saw Marcus and waved him over, but did not interrupt his message.

"That is why there is no condemnation for those who are born again into the Kingdom of God," Paul continued. "Roman, Greek, Jew, Scythian, barbarian—our old selves are nailed to the cross with Christ and we are raised, as He was raised, to walk in newness of life. If any man is in Christ, he is a new creature! Old things have passed away, and behold, everything is made anew!"

There were appreciative murmurs from the cluster of listeners, and Marcus heard one or two of them say "Amen!"—which he knew from his time in Judea meant "So be it!" He found a place to sit on the end of one of the benches, next to a burly Greek with an enormous, shaggy beard and a surprisingly gentle smile. Paul held forth for another hour or so, and when he was done invited all those who wished to repent of their sins and find forgiveness in Christ to come and pray with him. A half dozen or so accepted the invitation, and Paul spoke earnestly with each of them before placing his hands on their heads and invoking the power of the Holy Spirit.

Afterward, a pretty teenage girl came forward, holding a baby in her arms. There were tears streaming down her cheeks, and glancing at the infant, Marcus saw why. The child had been born with a severe harelip that rendered her face almost inhuman. Such children were normally thrown over a steep wall near the Temple of Venus, which overlooked an ancient city dump. The fall would kill them and the hungry packs of dogs would dispose of their bodies before dawn. It was brutal, but it was the Roman way. Marcus was surprised that any *paterfamilias* would allow such a child to live, and edged a bit closer to hear what the woman had to say.

"Forgive me for daring to approach you, *Dominus*," she said to Paul. "I am not only a slave but a harlot—not by choice, but because that is the purpose for which my master bought me! I will understand if you are unwilling to speak to me at all."

The aged Apostle smiled, and his scarred, deeply lined face shone with a tenderness that caught Marcus by surprise, even though he had seen it once before. The man's compassion was a palpable force.

"My dear child, you did not embrace a life of wickedness, it was forced upon you," he said. "I too am a slave—a slave to the Master who redeemed me when I was the most wretched of men. While He walked among us, he reached out to the poor, the destitute, the broken, and yes, even to the harlots."

She began weeping even harder. "Sir, I ask nothing for myself," she said. "I am unworthy of God's love! But my poor child—she bears the price of my sin in her poor, scarred face! My master said she was a monster and beat me when I refused to throw her to the dogs, but the way her face looks is not her fault. It is mine. God is punishing her because of my sins!"

Paul took the tiny child in his weather-beaten hands. "My dear girl," he said. "Once when Jesus was in Jerusalem, he and his disciples came across a man who was born blind. They asked Him: 'Who sinned, this man, or his parents, that he should have been born this way?' Jesus set them straight—He said 'Neither this man, nor his parents, sinned that he should be born blind. He was born this way so that the glory of God might be seen in his life.' God does not smite the innocent for things they did not do. Even so it is with your baby. She was not born this way to punish you for a sin you did not choose, nor did she herself do anything to deserve this fate. Rather, God marked her for a time, that everyone might see His power manifested in her."

With that he leaned forward and kissed the baby on her brow, then placed his hand over her face and raised his eyes toward heaven. Something moved in the air around them—for a moment, all the lamps in the room glowed brighter, and the sweet scent of springtime roses filled the air. Paul moved his lips in silence for a brief time. Then he slumped, as if some power had gone forth from him. When he removed his hand, the little girl's face was as flawless and beautiful as any child's could possibly be. The mother gave a scream of shock and delight, and everyone in the room gathered around to behold the miracle that had just happened.

"God be praised!" said an excited voice, and Marcus recognized the tall form of Luke standing by his side. The girl's mother was still making tiny little mewing noises in the back of her throat, too overcome with emotion to speak. Finally, she cradled the baby in one arm, flung the other one around Paul's neck, and kissed the old man on the cheek—then pulled away abruptly, terrified at her presumption.

"I'm so sorry, sir!" she exclaimed. "It's just that—this is so much more than I had ever dared hope! You have performed a miracle!"

"Signs and wonders come from God, my dear child," he said. "Your daughter is whole now. But it is your broken spirit that truly needs healing. You hold yourself of no worth, yet God treasures you so much that He gave His only Son to purchase your forgiveness. Will you not accept His gift of salvation?"

"I want it more than anything in the world!" she said. "But what can I do? When I return to my master, he will order me into the bed of whoever gives him a denarius for my body. How can God save me when my life is so full of sin?"

"No sin you can imagine is stronger than His love," Paul said. "But if you are willing to seek forgiveness in Him, perhaps one of my brothers in Christ can help you out of your plight. There are some men here who are blessed with this world's goods; surely one of them can purchase you from the brothel where you toil against your will."

Marcus did not even wait for Paul to look his way. His heart was broken for this young woman, and he wanted more than anything to give her a better life.

"I am a member of the Senate of Rome," he said, "and my wife is expecting a child soon. She could use the assistance of a wet nurse. After I am done here, let me speak with your master and I shall purchase you from him."

For the second time that night the girl was rendered speechless. She fell to her knees and tried to kiss Marcus' feet—no easy deed when she was still holding her child in one arm—but he pulled her gently upright and looked her in the eye.

"No need for all that," he said. "What is your name, child?" he asked her.

"I am called Diana," she said. "It's sad for a slave girl to bear the name of a goddess, is it not?"

Marcus smiled. "It's a perfectly good name," he said. "Why don't you let one of these dear ladies tell you more about Jesus, while I speak with Paul for a few moments?"

"Yes, *Dominus!*" she said, and a tall woman that Marcus later learned was Priscilla took her by the hand and led her away. Paul spoke to a couple of others who had waited patiently to speak with him, and then gestured for Marcus and Luke to follow him. They went up the stairs to a small room with several beds, where Paul and his friends were staying. Paul sat on the end of one bed while Marcus sat across from him on another.

"By the grace of God, we meet again," Paul said. "It has been a long road, has it not, my friend?"

"Yours much harder than mine," Marcus told him. "But it is good to look upon your face. I am glad you survived all the hardships of your journey!"

Paul smiled, but his face was weary. "The Spirit revealed to me long ago that I would have the opportunity to preach the Gospel in Rome before I was called home," he said. "There are many times when I have longed to be absent from the body and present with the Lord, but I know that my purpose is not yet fulfilled. Already believers from all over Rome are flocking to hear me teach. There is much work for me to do here, but I need to know what my legal status will be. Have you had a chance to speak with the emperor about my case?"

"Only briefly, when I first returned to Rome—you were right," Marcus told him. "His mistress has been in communication with the priests in Jerusalem, and they want to see you put to death. But the emperor does not seem inclined to condemn a Roman citizen on the word of a group of subjects known for rebellion and disobedience. He told me to return to him when you had arrived in Rome, and I will do that as soon as I may."

Paul closed his eyes, and seemed to be listening to a voice no one else could hear. He nodded, and when he opened his eyes, he fixed Marcus with a penetrating gaze.

"You must go tonight," he said. "The Spirit holds open a door, but the dark force that hovers over Nero will try to shut it soon. Go now!"

"Very well," Marcus said. "If that is God's will, then that is what I will do. But first I have a slave to buy, apparently."

Paul leaned over and squeezed his shoulder affectionately. "That was a noble thing to do, Lover of God," he said. "I would not have asked it of you, but I am grateful that you volunteered."

"It is the least I could do," Marcus replied.

He returned to the common room of the inn, to see a cluster of women gathered around Diana. They were taking turns holding her baby while she stood there, smiling broadly and crying at the same time. Her hair and clothes were soaking wet, and Marcus realized that she must have been baptized while he was speaking with Paul. He felt a tiny surge of jealousy and hoped his own turn would come soon. One of the ladies draped a clean, warm mantle around Diana's shoulders, and she took her child back and came up to him, smiling shyly.

"I am ready to follow you, *Dominus,*" she said.

Marcus smiled. "I'm afraid I must follow you," he replied, "since I have no idea where your master lives."

"Oh, yes!" she exclaimed. "I am sorry to be such a simpleton—this is all so overwhelming! The brothel is just a few streets over. I will go in and fetch my master—you don't need to be setting foot in such a seedy place. Oh, I will be so glad to leave it forever!"

Marcus followed her lead, and five minutes later they were standing outside a truly disreputable-looking whorehouse. The burly guard standing at the door was trading bawdy remarks with the largest woman Marcus had ever seen, a middle-aged behemoth whose folds of fat spilled over her rather scanty garments.

"Diana, you slug!" she said. "Master's been calling for you! You are in for a beating if you don't have a good excuse for running off on a busy night. There are sailors lined up three deep at the bar waiting for girls to service them. You need to get to work!"

"I am sorry, Fatima," said Diana. "But I don't think I'll be much help. This gentleman is wanting to buy me outright!"

"What?" The huge woman glared at Marcus, her piggy eyes barely visible through the folds of fat bulging from her face. "Why would you want such a skinny little wench, my fine sir? I could show you what a real woman could do, and you'd never give her a second glance thereafter!"

She spoke crude Latin with a thick accent that Marcus placed almost immediately. He gave the enormous woman a wink. "Judea, is it?" he asked.

Her jaw dropped, and for a moment he got a clear look at her muddy brown eyes. Then she furrowed her brow and they disappeared again.

"Right you are, Excellency," she said. "A little town called Bethsaida originally, and then Caesarea, where the prefect, my darling Valerius, became absolutely entranced by my charms. He tried to leave me there when that awful Pontius Pilate replaced him, but I caught a ship for Rome and once he saw I was here, Valerius set me up in a nice little house, higher up on the Aventine. I was his mistress, and it was a good life!" she said.

"What happened?" Marcus replied.

Her voice took on a shuddering note, and her massive frame shook. He suddenly realized she was weeping.

"My dear old Valerius got himself stabbed in a riot at the Forum, right around the time Caligula was murdered," she said. "Those other hoity-toities couldn't appreciate the virtues of a big girl like me, and I slowly slid down the Aventine until I finally would up here, helping Diocrates run this place. But I was a fine courtesan once, and could be again if anyone gave me the chance!"

"I'm sure you could," Marcus said, privately thinking that would only be the case if there were a very lonesome and desperate whale looking for love along the Roman coastline. "But I do not want Diana for a concubine—I am looking for a wet nurse and she has a child at her teat."

"A monster is more like it!" snapped Fatima. "I told her to kill that poor miserable little thing. What kind of future can a girl with that face have?"

She obviously had not glanced at the sleeping baby's face, and Marcus decided not to enlighten her. He was spared any further conversation with the unpleasant behemoth because the door of the brothel swung open at that moment, and a heavyset, seedy-looking

Gaul emerged. Diana followed closely behind, clutching her baby tightly. There was a red spot on her cheek, illuminated by the torchlight on the porch.

"What's this nonsense about someone purchasing this worthless whore?" he bellowed.

"It is not nonsense. I require her as a wet nurse for my child, and am willing to pay fair market value," Marcus said.

"Fair market value?" the man sneered. "What does a fancy Forum-frequenting dandy like you know about 'fair market value' for Aventine prostitutes?"

Marcus tried to control his temper. "I have traveled from one end of this empire to the other," he said. "I know the price of slaves quite well. I am a busy and important man, on my way to the Palatine to see Nero himself! Now, here are thirty sesterces, and another ten to make up for the short notice. That's twice what you paid for her, I'll warrant. Take it and I will be on my way."

The man's eyes narrowed and his jaw clenched. "No one makes demands on me!" he snarled. "This girl is my property, and I don't care if Nero himself wants her, I will not be ordered around!"

Despite his faith in the Prince of Peace, Marcus was just about fed up with this seedy pimp. He covered the distance between them in three quick strides, grabbed the man by his tunic, and jerked him forward and down, off the porch face-first—and straight into Marcus' knee, which he snapped upward to catch the villain in his nose. The man tried to get up, and Marcus gave him a wicked kick to the solar plexus which doubled him over. Fatima screamed and ran inside, while the burly guard stepped down into the street, ready to defend his master. Marcus gave him no time to make a move—he stepped forward and brought his elbow straight up under the man's chin as hard as he could. The guard's head snapped backward, and he collapsed like a sack of flour. The pimp was slowly getting to his feet, eyeing Marcus warily.

"Forty sesterces," Marcus said, tossing a bag of coins at the man's feet. "And she never looks upon your face again."

"Fine!" snapped the angry Gaul. "She's a no-account whore anyway! Always whining and crying—no one wants to couple with someone like that. Good riddance!"

Marcus turned on his heel, with Diana walking closely behind.

"That was the bravest thing I ever saw!" she said. "You're a hero, just like that senator that won the Grass Crown in Pannonia!"

"Really?" Marcus asked her in amusement.

"Yes, sir. I went to his triumph, you know! Such a grand occasion. Why, you even look a little bit like—" Suddenly she quit speaking for a moment, and he turned and gave her a smile.

"Oh! Oh my!" she exclaimed, and did not talk anymore all the way to Marcus' *domus* in the Quirinale district.

CHAPTER XXVI

Marcus left the grateful Diana at his home, astonishing Phidias, who had stumped to the door on his cane ready to chase off whoever was ringing the bell after dark. The old man was glad to see Marcus, and was surprisingly gentle with Diana, considering his gruff nature. Marcus stayed there long enough to don a toga and summon a litter and some lictors to escort him to the Palatine, even in his district; Rome was becoming an unsafe place for men of wealth to be on the streets at night. Gangs of young thugs roamed the streets, robbing, raping, and assaulting at will. Gossip had it that the leader of one of the more prominent gangs bore a striking resemblance to the emperor himself.

To his surprise, the detail of lictors was led by none other than his old friend Rufus, who was so glad to see Marcus he gave him one of the bone-crushing hugs that he reserved for his closest friends.

"Well, Senator, it's a joy to see you and no mistake! This lictor business earns me some good coin, but it's no stroll in the garden, I can tell you! Cut-throats and scoundrels abound in the streets these days, and things are getting worse instead of better. Six of my lads were attacked while escorting a Praetor home the other night, and two of them were killed outright, and another one is still abed with his injuries," he told Marcus.

"Terrible!" said Marcus. "I am glad you were free to lead my detail, then—there is no one I'd rather have by my side in a tight spot!"

"I have given standing orders to my men, that if Senator Publius calls for lictors, they are to summon me, no matter what the hour or where I am," Rufus replied. "You gave me a shot at the good life, Your Excellency, and I am forever in your debt for it!"

Marcus clapped him on his shoulder, which was not unlike smacking one of the marble columns at the Forum. "You have paid that debt many times over, my friend," he said, "but it is always good to see you. Now get me to the palace as quick as you may!"

Marcus climbed into the litter, and the bearers started forward at a good clip, Rufus and his six lictors striding on either side and ahead, clearing the way by sheer force of presence—and, occasionally, a swat with a cudgel. Looking through the curtains, Marcus could see that the streets were unusually clear, especially of women and children. At one point a group of young men, bundled in mantles that hid their faces, paused at the entrance of an alley and watched the litter go by, obviously weighing their chances at plunder. One of their number shook his head, and they all melted into the shadows.

They arrived at the palace in short order, and Marcus disembarked, asking the bearers and Rufus to wait outside for him. He approached the tall wooden door and spoke to the black-armored Praetorians who were standing guard there.

"Senator Marcus Quintus Publius, *triumphator* and holder of the Grass Crown, requests an audience with the *Princeps*, the most excellent Nero Claudius Caesar Augustus Germanicus," he said, drawing himself up to his full height.

The two guards snapped to attention, and one of them spoke.

"The emperor is hosting a feast tonight," he said. "You may enter, but good luck getting his attention."

Marcus walked into the huge marble corridor beyond the doors and turned. He didn't have to ask where the feast was—the cacophony of sound echoed throughout the entire palace. He followed his ears to the great dining hall which had been built, but never used, by Tiberius twenty years before. When he stepped through the arch into the room, the sight that met his eyes gave him pause.

Nero reclined on a couch at the head of the room, his toga half off, with Poppaea Sabina sitting on his lap, her arms around his neck. A serving girl, bare to the waist, stood behind him, running her fingers through his thick curly hair and feeding him grapes. In the center of the dining hall a bed had been set up, where several female slaves were crawling all over two young men as the dinner guests watched and applauded drunkenly. Along the wall, a whipping post had been set up, and another slave was enthusiastically beating a young man, whose screams at each stroke of the lash made Nero giggle and point. Some of the guests were groping at serving girls or each other, while two women were fighting on the floor, rolling back and forth, tearing clothes and skin, and gouging at each other's eyes while the nearby spectators shouted encouragement and placed bets as to who would win. Marcus groaned to himself as he realized that many of the guests at this bacchanalia were members of the Senate of Rome.

Marcus was too young to have ever been a guest at the court of Augustus, but he remembered his father describing the simplicity and *dignitas* with which Rome's first emperor had conducted his business, and how humble and plain the imperial home was. He wondered what the Republic had come to. Vologases' court was more dignified than this! Shaking his head at the sad decline of his country, Marcus stepped across the threshold and entered Nero's great hall.

At first no one noticed him, but then the emperor spied his old mentor and stood, his disarranged toga sliding to his waist, revealing a belly grown fat with indulgence. Nero belched and tugged his garment back over his shoulders, and then helped Poppaea to her feet. His sudden rise had sent her tumbling, but her giggles showed she was unhurt and still ready to play.

"Marcus Quintus Publius!" shouted the emperor of Rome. "How good to see you, my old friend! If I had known you were in town, I would have invited you to join my banquet. Isn't this terrific fun?"

Marcus surveyed the debauchery around him with a raised eyebrow. "If you say so, Highness," he replied. "My tastes run to simpler evenings and less riotous company."

"You old bore!" said Nero. "The most competent man in Rome, a lion on the battlefield, and a mouse in your own home! Come forward and have a seat. I'm composing a new song—it's a tribute to my rival Vologases of Parthia. Come, have a listen!"

Marcus protested, but Nero would not take no for an answer, so he chose a seat near the emperor's dais, shoved a slumbering, drunken senator out of the way, and reclined at the table. A half-naked slave girl tried to sit on his lap, but Marcus pushed her aside.

In Rome, sexual relations with slaves were the norm for many men and some women. Such coupling was not even considered adultery, but Marcus' fierce love for his wife was compounded by his own strong sense of *dignitas.* Intimate relations were for private moments, not for party entertainment. Even the *Divus Julius,* whose affairs were legendary, never once did the deed in front of witnesses that Marcus heard of. He found the raw sexuality of Nero's court repulsive.

The emperor had grabbed a lyre from under the table, and suddenly a hush fell over the entire hall. Even the catfight between the two women stopped after a bystander gave one of them a sharp kick. As they separated, Marcus was astonished to see that they were actually the wives of two senators he knew, rather than slave girls brawling for the crowd's entertainment. What was Rome turning into?

Nero struck a few off-key chords on the lyre, then began belting out a tune in a voice that was not quite singing or shouting but some awful combination of the two. About the kindest thing that Marcus could think of about the emperor's singing voice was that it detracted from just how terrible his playing was. The lyrics were at least somewhat clever, if rather crude. The song began with:

Vologases, Vologases, Parthia's high king,
Wants a bigger empire because he has such a small thing!
He keeps big lions and tigers, and even a speartooth cat,
And two enormous crocodiles, with hungry dragon eyes.
You have to wonder about a man
Who is so obsessed with size!

On and on it went, verses piled upon verses, all questioning the endowment and stamina of Rome's great rival. Performed by a true bard, the song would have merited much bawdy laughter and a shower of coins. Nero was not a true bard—but his guests sat rapt, their eyes never leaving the emperor's face, as if they were hearing Homer himself declaim *The Iliad* set to music. After a half hour or so, the lyrics became first boringly repetitive, and then more and more obscene. Marcus could tell many in the audience were straining to maintain their focus, and finally one elderly senator, whose red face bespoke an excess of wine, slumped face first onto the table, sound asleep.

Nero did not notice at first—he was halfway through a verse in which Vologases had a slave girl whipped to death for laughing when she saw him naked—but suddenly he stopped in mid-song when he noticed the slumbering senator. Marcus glanced down the couches and saw boredom and amusement replaced by stark terror on every face there. What was going on?

"INGRATE!" Nero roared at the top of his lungs. "Pig! *Mentula!* I compose an epic for the ages, a masterpiece that will make poets weep for a thousand years, and lavish you with my wine and my hospitality, and this is how you repay me! You dog!!"

Someone poked the senator, who opened his eyes, shook his head, and looked up at the emperor. Suddenly the flush of alcohol deserted his face, and he went stark pale.

"Forgive me, Excellency!" he said. "I am an old man, and I have been sick. It was only out of reverence for your person that I dragged myself out of bed to come here tonight, but my illness must have been more severe than I thought!"

"LIAR!!" Nero yelled again. "You've been in attendance at the Senate every day this week! You come to my home, drink my wine, insult my art, and then lie to me in the bargain? Praetorians! Here, now!!"

Six black-clad guards approached from their stations at the doors and seized the gibbering senator. He struggled for a moment, then slumped and burst into tears. Nero smirked at the assembled guests.

"Take him outside and flog him!" ordered the emperor of Rome. "Then expel him from the city gates and tell him that he may not enjoy fire, water, or bed within five hundred leagues of the city as long as I shall live. His family can join him in exile, and count me merciful!"

"Great Caesar!" a trembling voice said from the foot of the table. Marcus was surprised to see Lucius Anneaus Seneca standing there, looking even more miserable than usual.

"Oh, what is it, old man?" Nero snarled, his voice full of contempt.

His former tutor gathered his courage and met the emperor's gaze. "It is customary to allow a man twenty-four hours to set his affairs in order before sending him into exile," he said. "And a vote of the Senate is required to confirm any sentence of exile from Rome."

Nero's eyes narrowed, and his already-red face grew even darker. "You are fortunate, old man, that I am fond of you!" he snapped. "Otherwise you would be joining Antonius Fabius in exile! A vote of the Senate? Hah!! What is the Senate of Rome but a collection of dull politicians who are unworthy to lick the boots of a living god, the last descendant of the *Divus Augustus*? Fabius is lucky that I let him live after the insult he gave me under my own roof!"

Seneca quailed under the emperor's fierce glare and sank back into his seat. Nero watched his victim dragged from the room, and then slumped into his seat. Poppaea shoved the slave girl aside and began massaging the emperor's brow. Nero's anger faded, and was replaced by a profound sadness. For a moment, Marcus thought that the ruler of the world was about to weep. The guests sat, silent, at their couches, afraid to make a sound. The emperor's mistress nodded to the musicians after a few minutes, and they began softly playing on the flute and lyre.

It was a mistake. Nero raised his head, and his anger returned. "Get out, all of you!" he snapped. "You are not worthy of my genius! Leave my house, and do not return until you are invited back!"

The guests streamed toward the doors, but Marcus held his place for a moment. Nero saw him and smiled sadly—and for just a moment, Marcus saw the boy he had once hoped might be a good ruler. Nero was a lost child, he thought, deserving of scorn but also of pity.

"You stay, my old friend," he said. "You are the only one I can trust around here. It is good to have you back. Let's go down to the library. This place stinks!" He rose and swayed on his feet for a minute, then watched as the last of the guests fled. The naked slaves on the bed at the center of the room froze, unsure of what they were supposed to be doing.

"Go on, all of you!" he said. "Get yourselves some food from the table and go back to your quarters. You, too, Poppaea," he said to his mistress, who had been following behind him closely. "I'll join you shortly. Bring Andrea and Porcia to my bedchamber, and wait for me."

Marcus followed the emperor to the library, where Nero collapsed on a couch and motioned for Marcus to sit across from him. The emperor gave a long sigh.

"So what did you think of my song, old friend?" he asked.

Marcus swallowed hard and prayed for guidance. He had promised to always tell the emperor the truth, he thought to himself. It was time to keep that promise.

"Your Excellency, while the lyrics were somewhat clever at first, the musical quality resembled that of two alley cats being slowly disemboweled with a dull knife and calling their friends for help," he said.

Nero's eyes narrowed for a moment, then suddenly his face relaxed and he laughed, a long, hearty laugh that was more wholesome-sounding than anything that had come out of his mouth all evening. His whole frame shook, and tears rolled down his cheeks. It was a long time before he could speak.

"By all the gods, Marcus, was it as bad as all that?" he finally asked when he could breathe. When Marcus nodded, the emperor of Rome collapsed into laughter again. When he finally grew quiet, he looked at his old mentor with eyes that were clear and calm.

"You are perhaps the only man in Rome who would ever speak so bluntly to me," he said. "Seneca might have done so, once upon a time, but he has become an old woman of late. You're a good man, Marcus, a Roman of the Romans. Now tell me, what brings you to the palace at such a late hour? I know you don't care much for parties!"

Marcus swallowed. "When I returned to Rome from Armenia, Your Excellency, I advised you of the plight of a client of mine, a citizen of Rome from Tarsus in Cilicia named Paul."

"Ah, yes" Nero said. "He's the one the Jews are so angry with! They keep writing letters to my sweet Poppaea, urging her to use her influence with me to have him executed."

Marcus nodded. "Sir, I've known Paul for several years. He is innocent of any crime against the Senate and People of Rome. They simply bear him a grudge because he teaches a new version of their old faith, one which denies the power the priests wield over the people. It's a harmless cult, sir, and Paul is a harmless man."

Nero nodded, looking more bored than concerned. "Well, I can't release him without hearing their side of the story," he said. "But so far not a one of them has journeyed to Rome to make their case! Sending letters to a woman, as if Poppaea rules over me! It's insulting, if you want to know the truth, and presumptuous on her part to encourage it. Still, she is dear to me, and I do not wish to make her unhappy without cause. Nor do I wish to do an injustice to an innocent Roman citizen." He thought for a moment, looking at the shelves full of scrolls and codices as if seeking inspiration.

"Here is my verdict!" he said so suddenly it caught Marcus by surprise. "Your friend Paul is placed under house arrest. He may move around Rome with a guard, but he cannot stray across the *pomerium* on pain of death. His accusers will have two years in which to travel to Rome and make their case against him. If they do not show up by the end of that time, all charges will be dropped, and Paul will be a free man. If they do come here, I will hear the case in person and judge it on its merits. There! That does justice to all concerned, don't you think?"

Marcus thought. It wasn't entirely fair, but it was probably the best deal he would get from Nero, now or later. He nodded.

"I think Paul will be more than satisfied," he said. "He has wanted to come to Rome for many years, and has only just arrived. He would probably plan on staying here at least a year anyway."

"He may choose a house to rent within the city," Nero said, "and I will assign Praetorians to guard him."

"I thank you for your wisdom and justice, great Caesar," Marcus said.

Nero scoffed. "Don't flatter me, Marcus. Your honesty is your greatest virtue!" he said. "Now, go on home to your lovely bride, and give her my greetings."

"Antonia is with child," Marcus said. "She remained in Pompeii."

"Well, have her come here now!" Nero snapped, suddenly sounding irritated. "I need you back in the Senate, not lounging in your villa under the shadow of Vesuvius."

"As you wish," Marcus said.

"Take one of my slave girls home with you," Nero said. "They are highly skilled, and I know you must be tired and lonely after a swift road trip."

"That will not be necessary," Marcus said. "I purchased a new slave girl this evening."

Nero grinned and slapped Marcus on the shoulder. "That's more like it, old man!" he said. Marcus did not see fit to explain the situation, and took his leave before Nero's mercurial moods could change again. After he left the library, he heaved a sigh of relief and thought about how wise Paul was to tell him to come tonight. A surly, hungover Nero might not have been nearly so agreeable.

As he rode back to the Quirinale in his litter, Marcus reflected on what Paul had said earlier. Was there a dark spirit hovering over the emperor of Rome? It certainly seemed so at times. Nero's mood swings and wanton cruelty were not the patterns of a well-ordered mind. But was that evidence of demonic possession, or simple, encroaching madness? Marcus did not know and did not care to find out. When he arrived at his *domus,* he paid off the bearers and gave Rufus and his men a handsome tip for their services, and then retired to his bedchamber, shrugging out of his toga before Phidias could even lend a hand, and collapsed into his bed. He was asleep before the old Greek slave finished folding his garments and putting them away.

The next morning, he rose, bathed, and put on some comfortable robes. He called Pericles to bring him a quill and papyrus and penned a quick, affectionate letter to his wife, bidding her to pack up the bags and close up the house in Pompeii, since their presence was required in Rome. The handsome Greek twin assured Marcus the letter would be in Pompeii in two days' time.

That being done, Marcus pulled on his sandals and sent a runner to fetch Rufus and his six lictors. He did not send for a litter, believing that if a senator of Rome could not walk the streets safely with an armed escort in broad daylight, then the city was in even worse shape than he had guessed. Rufus seemed to agree; when Marcus told him they were headed to the stews of the Aventine, he scowled slightly but nodded. Then they set out across the great city.

Rome was aging badly, Marcus thought. The City of Romulus had grown in fits and starts over the eight centuries since it was founded, and that mixed legacy showed in its architecture. Magnificent marble homes stood cheek by jowl with shabby wooden *insulae*; some temples were sumptuously appointed with statues of the gods painted in lifelike colors standing outside, while others were in severe disrepair, their statues faded and peeling dried paint, and their roofs missing tiles. The Quirinale, his own district, was not as bad, but when they crossed through the Shepherd's Gate into the Aventine, the quality and condition of the buildings grew worse and worse. By the time they reached the inn at the edge of the Tentmaker's Square, the buildings were mostly squat hovels, or rickety, multi-story wooden *insulae* with hundreds of tenants and thatched roofs, firetraps waiting to happen. Incredibly enough, the *Divus Julius* had been raised by his mother, Aurelia Cotta, in this, the worst district of Rome—albeit higher up on the hill, where things were not quite as decrepit. Still, it amused Marcus to think of the greatest of all the Romans running through these streets as a barefoot boy.

Paul was not inside the inn, although Luke was there. Marcus took a moment to compliment him on the wonderful book he had written, and then followed the Greek doctor's directions to find Paul working in the Tentmaker's Square. The square was crowded with merchants and customers, but one corner was crowded with people who were not jostling, bidding, or looking at cloth. As he approached the dense knot of humanity, he heard Paul's unmistakable voice rolling across the square toward him.

"I tell you, my dear brothers; that in Christ circumcision and uncircumcision no longer matter!" Paul was saying. "The work of hands, cutting upon the flesh, cannot erase the stain of sin that is in the heart of every man! The blood of lambs and bulls cannot wash it away, nor can offerings made to idols, shaped by human hands, so-called gods who cannot see, feel, speak, or think! It is in Christ that we find our righteousness, our hope, our salvation! If any man could have been saved by the Law alone, then our Lord died for nothing! The Law cannot save, but it points us to the one who can. That is why there is no condemnation for those who are set free in Christ Jesus. The perfect law of love has set us free from bondage to the law of sin and of death!"

Marcus had heard Paul speak before, but the man's voice radiated such power that he simply stood for a while and listened to the great Apostle preach. He thanked Jesus for sending him to find this man, so many years before, during that frantic race to Antioch. Finally, Paul's message wound up, and he invited all who had trusted Christ to meet him at the public baths that evening to receive baptism as a symbol of their new faith. The crowd began to disperse, although a few who were sick or crippled remained behind, hoping that Paul would heal them. Several who had come limping up on crutches walked away carrying them, and one man whose eyes had been covered with bloody bandages ran about the square, praising God that his sight had been restored.

Paul prayed with the last unfortunate, and then pulled a large square of fabric into his lap and began deftly sewing it onto another square, his hands fairly flying as he worked.

"You are a skilled tentmaker," Marcus said, coming up and kneeling beside him. Paul greeted him with a warm smile.

"All members of my sect of Judaism, the Pharisees, are required to learn a trade, so that we can support ourselves as we study the laws of Moses," he explained.

"That is a worthy tradition," said Marcus.

"How went your audience with Nero?" Paul asked him.

Marcus explained in detail the horrible banquet, and finally his interview with the emperor. Paul nodded, and smiled again when Marcus was done.

"They will not come," he said. "The high priest and his cronies do not care if I preach the Gospel in Rome, as long as I am gone from Jerusalem. Two years is not a very long time—I will need that long to preach the Gospel to all the brothers here, and to train them in the commandments of the Lord. When my house arrest is ended, I will travel west. I long to preach the Gospel to Spain, and Gaul, and perhaps even in Britannia before my race is run."

Marcus nodded. "I have kept my end of the bargain, my friend," he said. "Now I would ask a favor of you."

"What is it that you wish, Lover of God?" asked Paul.

"Baptize me tonight with the others," Marcus said, his tone pleading.

Paul's smile rivaled the sun in its brightness. "It will be my greatest pleasure, dear brother!" he said.

CHAPTER XXVII

Being back in Rome was a difficult transition at first. Pompeii had been perfect for Marcus and Antonia—his campaigns and careful investments had made him enough money that he could, if he chose, never work as an advocate again. That leisure had given them time to enjoy each other's company and that of a few friends, in a town that was known as a haven of rest for Rome's busy upper classes. The pace of life in Pompeii had been relaxed and fulfilling, while Rome never seemed to rest.

Serving in the Senate was now a trial to Marcus. The senior legislative body of the Republic had become a pointless debating society that wound up approving whatever Nero wanted done. When the emperor came in to speak, the senators fell all over themselves to endorse his policies; when he stayed away, as he frequently did, only the most innocuous of bills were introduced, and everyone was afraid to take a stand until they found out how the emperor felt about the issue. It soon became apparent that the emperor's request for Marcus' return was not motivated by any desire to see the Senate run more efficiently. Nero just seemed to want his old mentor around again. That being said, he rarely called on Marcus for advice. When an invitation did arrive from the palace, it was usually to a dinner with Nero alone, occasionally with one or two others in attendance. The emperor wanted to hear gossip and stories about old times, not discuss policy, on those occasions.

As Marcus got to know the adult Nero better, he recognized a pattern. Nero thrived on sensation—he was an Epicurean gone amok; trying to enjoy every pleasure life had to offer until he became so jaded he enjoyed nothing. But after going on a binge, the emperor would send away all of his prostitutes, dwarves, freaks, and hangers-on, and then he would call on Marcus, Seneca, and a few other friends from his youth and try for a while to recapture his ambitions of being a wise and competent ruler. He would draft legislation, review reports from governors, order the legions to one post or another, and meet with the Senate. While his enthusiasm was undeniable, many of his proposals were impractical or prohibitively expensive. Marcus and Seneca would invariably point this out, and Nero would argue, protest, pout for a while, and move onto his next scheme. After a week or so of trying to rule the empire, he would weary of the effort and announce a banquet at the Palace, beginning the whole process over again. Marcus attended the dinners, avoided the parties, and tried to do what he could to keep the damage done by Nero's bipolar rule to a minimum.

On the brighter side, the Christian movement in Rome was growing rapidly thanks to the influence of Paul. More and more people came to the Tentmaker's Square, or to Paul's rented house, to hear the great Apostle hold forth on doctrine. He preached with two Praetorian guards standing on either side of him, but not even the dreaded black uniforms could keep the crowds at bay—and, over time, a number of Praetorians converted to Christianity as well. With Paul's permission, Marcus commissioned a publishing house to distribute copies of Luke's Gospel, and more and more Roman subjects and citizens were reading the words of Jesus and converting to the new faith. Marcus even managed to introduce Seneca to Paul and the two men conversed for the better part of an afternoon. The Stoic philosopher was impressed with the Christian Apostle and vice versa, but whether anything further came of the conversation Marcus was not able to find out.

A few months after Marcus returned to Rome, Antonia presented him with a beautiful daughter. With her blessing, Marcus named the girl after his first wife, Drusilla. One of the things that he loved so much about his scarlet-haired bride was that she never resented his fond memories of the long-lost love of his youth. The child was healthy and loud, with a strong appetite. Diana, the slave girl Marcus had rescued from prostitution, was a devoted nurse and attendant to the baby and to Antonia as well. Freed from her horrid past, she blossomed into a sweet-natured and confident girl, as well as a radiant follower of Christ. Marcus, having never had a child of his own before, was fascinated and occasionally exhausted by the demands of parenting. Roman fathers by tradition had little to do with the raising of their young offspring, but he was fascinated by the baby and loved watching her play in the nursery. He frequently brought home baubles from the market for the child's entertainment.

One of the props to Nero's stability passed from the scene that year—Sextus Burrus, commander of the Praetorian Guard, died after a brief illness. There were the usual rumors of poisoning, but Nero seemed to be so grief-stricken by the loss of his trusted palace guard that Marcus paid scant heed to them. Burrus was given a state funeral, and Seneca gave the oration as his body was committed to the pyre. The old philosopher was looking sadder and sadder these days—he had hitched his fortunes to Nero's rising star, only to watch his pupil become an unstable and tyrannical debauchee. He frequently spoke privately to Marcus of how he wished Britannicus had become emperor instead—a wish Marcus shared but was too wise to state openly.

Paul was proven correct in his prediction—not a single representative from Jerusalem showed up to make any charges before Nero. Whether this was because the high priest knew his case against Paul was too flimsy to bear weight in a Roman court, or because of the growing unrest in Judea, no one knew. But Paul regularly received letters from Peter, John, and James the brother of Jesus, which he shared with Marcus. Jews were growing more and more restive under Roman taxation, and tensions between Greek merchants in Caesarea and Decapolis were growing. Paul wanted Peter to come to Rome and help him nurture the church there; Peter had initially been reluctant but was more and more leaning toward making the journey.

Near the end of Paul's two-year house arrest, Luke came to have dinner with Marcus and Antonia, bringing Priscilla and Aquila with him. Paul, suffering from a relapse of his old ailment, had begged off that night. Technically, he was only allowed to go from the marketplace to his rented house and back again, but the Praetorians allowed him to travel freely about the city as long as he told them where he was going and allowed his escort to accompany him. Marcus regretted his friend's absence, but enjoyed the dinner with the other three nonetheless. He noticed that Luke periodically shared a knowing glance with the other two, and seemed unusually cheerful all evening. It was as if they were sharing a private joke at his expense.

Finally, Marcus had enough. As the last of the food was taken away and glasses of pomegranate juice were poured, he confronted his friends.

"All right, out with it, someone!" he said. "You've been glancing at me and chuckling all evening. If I'm going to be the butt of a joke, I'd at least like to know what it is about!"

Luke shook his head, but his smile widened. "Not a joke, my dear friend!" he said. "It's just that, well, I have brought you a gift. I showed it to Priscilla and Aquila earlier, but I didn't want to get it out till the table was cleared."

"A gift?" Marcus said. "Now I am indeed curious!"

The lanky Greek went to the front hallway, where he had left a shoulder bag full of various knickknacks that he carried with him everywhere. He reached into it and drew forth a large, fat scroll.

"I am hoping you will use your influence to distribute it, as you did my first book," the physician said, "but I wanted you to have the very first copy. It is, in fact, the only one in existence, although I still have all my notes."

Marcus' eyes widened. "This is a magnificent gift!" he said. "But you have already written about the deeds of Jesus. What is this book about?"

"The acts of his Apostles," Luke said. "I traced the history of the Way from the day Jesus returned to His Kingdom until Paul's arrival in Rome. It doesn't include everything that befell us, but it does give a broad picture of how our faith spread from Jerusalem to the furthest corners of the Empire."

Marcus rose and bowed. "A princely gift indeed!" he said. "You are a fine author, my friend, and if this is anywhere near as good as your first effort, I predict that it will be read from now until the day Christ returns for us!"

Luke and the other two guests also rose.

"I hope you will enjoy it and learn from it," he said. "We must return early, so that I may monitor Paul's symptoms. This fever that plagues him cannot be cured, but I know some herbs that will keep the outbreak from becoming too severe. He should be on his feet in a few more days—these relapses rarely last very long. Enjoy the book—read it at your leisure, then you can turn it over to the copyists and we can begin sending it to all the churches in the empire."

Marcus realized that most of the followers of Jesus were quite poor, and he enjoyed being in a position to act as the church's patron and benefactor in Rome. It would cost a tidy sum to send copies of Luke's book throughout the empire, but he counted it as money well spent, advancing the Kingdom of Christ on earth and educating His followers. He thanked God for the chain of events that had given him the wealth to help Paul advance the Gospel.

After they left, Marcus curled up on his couch with Antonia beside him and began reading out loud: "The first account I composed, O Theophilos, about all that Jesus began to do and teach, until the day He was taken up to heaven, after He had, by the Holy Spirit, given orders to the Apostles whom He had chosen. To these He also presented Himself alive after His suffering, by many convincing proofs, appearing to them over a period of forty days . . ."

By the time Marcus read the last lines of the scroll, it was far past midnight and the house was still. Antonia had finally dozed off with her head on his shoulder as the story reached the point where Paul was arrested in Jerusalem, but he kept reading out loud anyway, savoring the words even as he lowered his voice to keep from disturbing her. The book was magnificent! The eloquence of Peter on the day of Pentecost, his miraculous delivery from jail on the eve of his would-be execution, the dramatic conversion of Paul, confrontations with Jews and pagans alike as the Gospel spread throughout the eastern half of the empire—Marcus was swept away in the story just as surely as Paul's ship had been swept up in the ferocious storm that bore the Apostle and his companions to Malta.

He reflected on the story as he carefully rolled the scroll back up and slipped it back inside its calf-skin cover. He wanted to read it for himself at least one more time before taking it to the copyist, he thought, but he did not want to waste too much time. This was a message the world needed to hear! He carefully lifted Antonia in his arms—despite his slight build, Marcus was strong as an ox, a strength born of years in the saddle and on the road. He carried his beautiful wife to bed without waking her, and slipped out of his tunic into bed next to her. Sleep came quickly.

In his dreams, he saw a congregation of the faithful gathered together. Paul and Peter were there, as well as John, Barnabas, Priscilla, Aquila, and many other figures—some he knew and some he did not. They glowed with an unearthly light, flickering tongues of fire that shone with no earthly color hovering over their heads. Then he saw Nero, a huge, towering colossus with iron feet and shoulders that brushed the clouds. The giant emperor's face was twisted with rage and madness, and crouching on his shoulders, Marcus could see a black, serpentine form with glowing red eyes and a forked tongue that dripped acid on Nero's tunic as it whispered in his ear. Nero hoisted a huge amphora on his shoulders and dumped its contents onto the assembly of believers. But instead of wine, raging red flames poured out of the jar, landing in the midst of the disciples of Jesus. A few of the pale lights were extinguished by the blast of hellfire, but most of the disciples were simply borne away by the red wave, and wherever they landed, the pale light spread and grew. Gradually, Marcus felt himself rising in the air, higher and higher, until he could see all of the city of Rome, then all of Italy itself, and then Africa to the south and Gaul and Spain and Britannia to the north. Higher and higher he rose, until he saw landmasses that resembled no place he had ever heard of, across vast expanses of water that dwarfed *Mare Nostrum* in size. And everywhere he looked, the pale light of faith kindled and took fire, even as Nero's scarlet blaze burned itself out and dwindled. A voice whispered in his ear: "And this is not yet the end." Then his eyes opened, and he beheld the morning sun blazing outside his window, and realized he had slept very late indeed.

Marcus did read Luke's "book of acts" again—twice more, in fact—and Antonia read the entire story as well, before he took it to the house of Polycrates and Sons, one of Rome's largest publishers and copyists. He left careful instructions to send a copy of the book to the twenty largest cities in the empire, addressed to names on a list that Paul and Luke had given him the day after the dinner party, the leaders of the Christian movement in every major city. Once the copies were commissioned and sent out, however, he took care to destroy the list. Opposition to the Christian movement was growing in many corners of the empire, and he had no desire to help the enemies of the Cross of Christ find their prey.

Once he was done, Marcus walked across town to the Aventine, accompanied by his usual escort of lictors, to see how Paul was doing. Even though the fever had abated, he was still concerned for his friend's health—the aged Apostle had been pale and wan when Marcus called on him the day before. He arrived at Paul's rented home and was shocked to hear the sound of loud sobs coming from the courtyard. Fearing the worst, he rushed across the threshold, but before he could even see him, the sound of Paul's voice carrying over the sobs reassured him that his worst fear was unfounded.

"Brothers, do not weep!" Paul said. "Rejoice rather that our beloved brother has been reunited with his master and family. Did he not write you, while he lived, telling you to count it all joy when various trials come your way?"

"I know what you mean, Brother Paul, but this was not a trial, it was an execution!" said a familiar voice. Barnabas was standing in front of Paul, who was holding a short letter in his hand.

"The Lord Jesus said that the world would hate us all the more because we love Him," Paul replied.

"What has happened?" Marcus asked.

"Oh, my dear friend!" Paul said. "Forgive us for not noticing your arrival. Our hearts are heavy with grief, even as we rejoice that one of our number stands in the presence of the Lord. James, the brother of Jesus, has been killed."

Marcus was stunned. He had only met James once, briefly, in Jerusalem, but the story of "the Lord's brother" was well known to the church. Born to Joseph and Mary two years after Jesus' miraculous birth, James and his other siblings had never believed that their older brother was sent from God. To them, He was an embarrassment, a black sheep who had deserted his mother and young siblings to pursue a calling they all doubted. They had scolded Jesus, harassed Him, and tried to get Him arrested on at least one occasion. Then came the crucifixion, and a broken-hearted James had fled Jerusalem, believing that his hostility and skepticism had goaded his brother into the disastrous confrontation with the authorities. But somewhere on the road back to Galilee, the risen Christ had appeared to James. From that point on, James had never once doubted that his earthly brother was indeed the Son of God. He had become a fearless leader in the Jerusalem church, known far and wide for his justice and piety—indeed, his friends and enemies alike called him "James the Just."

Paul handed Marcus the scroll, and Marcus saw that, despite Paul's brave and reassuring words, the parchment was stained with fresh tears. He swallowed hard and read the short epistle.

Simon Peter, bond-servant of our Lord Jesus Christ, to our beloved brother Paul: grace, peace, and the comfort of the Holy Spirit be with you. It grieves me to inform you, dear brother, that our beloved James, the Lord's brother, has passed into eternity. As you know, James and I have remained in Jerusalem over the years, even as our fellow Apostles have scattered across the Empire bearing the Gospel to the uttermost parts of the earth. We stayed for two reasons: so that there would always be living witnesses of our Lord Jesus' words and deeds here in the city where He was glorified, and also in order to preach the Gospel among our own people, the descendants of Abraham.

James has always enjoyed the respect and esteem of the Jews for his great piety and love of our law and traditions, even though he has clashed many times with the High Priest and his cronies over the message of the Gospel. When the prefect, Porcius Festus, died suddenly, the new High Priest Ananus, who is an enemy of Christ, quickly assembled the Sanhedrin before the new governor could arrive. He ordered James arrested and brought before the Council, accusing him of flouting our laws and traditions and of blasphemy for proclaiming that Jesus was the Christ. Before passing sentence, he asked if James would offer any defense of his actions.

James, being filled with the Holy Spirit, looked at the High Priest and said unto him: "Rightly did my Lord call you people whited sepulchers, outwardly pure but inwardly full of wickedness and corruption! You place your faith in this great temple, made with the hands of men, but as my brother prophesied, so I now also proclaim: Not one stone shall be left on another of this edifice to your pride and arrogance! For it is not God you worship here, but your own foolish traditions, which have no power to save. Many of you who hear my voice shall live to see this place in flames, and the enemies of Israel plundering its treasures!"

At these words Ananus was filled with great wrath, and ordered the Temple guards to seize James and take him to the pinnacle of the Temple and cast him off. But despite the great distance of the fall, James was not killed; instead, he sat up and began prophesying further disasters upon the people of Jerusalem and their priests, who had rejected the living God for the traditions of men. So the members of the Sanhedrin seized cobblestones and began to stone James, but even as his body was broken by the stones, he continued to preach with words of fire, proclaiming the wrath of God on this wicked and perverse generation. Finally, one of the Temple guards grabbed a fuller's pole and swung it so hard that James' head was crushed by the blow, and he gave up the ghost.

We buried him outside the city walls, in a cave not far from where our Lord Himself was laid. But the High Priest's actions have outraged many in the city, and not only those of the followers of the Way. A deputation has been sent to the new prefect, Albinus, complaining of these actions, and the new prefect has relieved Ananus as High Priest.

As for me, the Lord has revealed that it is time for me, too, to leave Jerusalem. The wickedness of this city and its rulers stinks in the nostrils of our God, and judgment must fall on them soon. I must join you in Rome, to strengthen the body of Christ that is there, and so I will leave within the fortnight. May the grace of our Lord Jesus Christ be with you all. God willing, I shall see you soon.

Three weeks after the letter arrived in Rome, Peter followed. Marcus was on hand as Paul and the rest of the Jerusalem church greeted the "Big Fisherman" from Galilee. Peter's hair was white with age, and he was more stooped than Marcus remembered him, but he was still a head taller than the average Roman. He smiled at Marcus when he saw him.

"Greetings, Lover of God!" he said. "Your name is known and loved by all those who follow the Christ."

Marcus bowed deeply. There was something majestic about this big man, he thought. He had once attributed it to Peter's innate *dignitas,* but now he realized that what he was seeing was a reflection of Christ himself in the eyes of a man who had forsaken all to answer the call to God's service. John had told him once that, ever since the Risen Christ had appeared to Peter, the Galilean's voice and face had subtly changed.

"It took me a while to understand what the difference was," John had said. "But I finally realized I was hearing echoes of the voice of Jesus every time Peter spoke."

Now Peter was looking at Marcus with a gaze that bespoke joy and sadness at the same time. "I told you we would meet, ere the end came," he said. "That end is nearer now than ever before. Prepare yourself, Lover of God, for difficult times lie ahead."

Two months later Nero's deadline for the Jews to press charges against Paul passed, and not one denizen of Jerusalem had arrived in Rome to denounce the former Pharisee. Marcus caught Nero in one of his serious, industrious moods, denouncing the squalor of the city of Rome and wishing he could rebuild it all.

"The city is old and rotten!" Nero exclaimed. "Wooden buildings, marble, brick, and mud hovels stand cheek by jowl! We need to level the city, one block at a time, and rebuild it with uniform architecture and materials throughout!"

"Such a project would be ruinously expensive, Excellency," said Seneca, who still tried to exercise some restraint on his former student.

"Only if we do it all at once," Nero countered. "If we do one block at a time, paying for the labor and material, and don't start another until the treasury is replenished, we can gradually remake the entire city into a worthy capital for the civilized world!"

Seneca, surprised at the emperor's thoughtfulness, nodded in agreement, and Nero beamed. Marcus saw his moment and seized it.

"Caesar," he said, "if I may change the subject for just a moment?"

"By all means!" Nero said. "Before Seneca finds yet another reason that my wishes should be thwarted."

"Two years ago, I approached you about one of my clients, Paul of Tarsus," Marcus said.

"Ah, yes, the leader of the Christians," Nero replied. "Those rascally Jews have never sent a single messenger to explain whatever it was they had against him."

"That is true, sire, and his two years of house arrest are up," Marcus told him. "According to your decree, may I tell him his liberties are restored?"

"Yes, yes!" Nero said. "It would be good to have him out of the city in any case. Even my own Praetorians are quoting this sage from Galilee Paul prattles about! Now come, Marcus, and look at this design I have drawn for a new palace. I am so tired of living in that dump on the Palatine. Here is a home worthy of my genius!"

Marcus looked at the emperor's design for a monstrous mansion that would cover most of the Palatine Hill, consuming dozens of other villas, and tried to look impressed. But he was already looking forward to giving Paul the good news, and so when Nero finally tired of building plans and rumors of a renewed war with Parthia, Marcus asked for the emperor to sign Paul's release, and then took his leave and headed down to the Aventine to the Apostle's house. He carried with him the decree he had drafted and gotten Nero to sign before he left. Finally, he would be able to dismiss the two Praetorians who shadowed Paul everywhere.

He could hear the Apostle's strong voice preaching a familiar sermon as he entered the Tentmaker's Square. He had heard the words many times before, but Marcus still paused a moment to soak them up.

"What then shall separate us from the love of Christ?" Paul asked the crowd. "Shall death? Life? Principalities and powers? Events in the here and now? Events yet to come? What can separate us from Christ's love? Neither height, nor depth, nor any other created thing, can break the firm hold that God's love has on us through our Lord Jesus Christ!"

People were nodding, and many were saying the Hebrew word that Marcus had learned so long ago: "Amen!"

Paul paused for a few moments to take a drink of water, and Marcus pressed through the crowd to make his announcement. The Apostle smiled to see his friend, and Marcus unrolled the proclamation.

"By order of Nero Claudius Caesar Augustus Germanicus, *Princeps* and *Imperator* of Rome," he read, "let it be known to all and sundry that Paul of Tarsus, also known as Saul, is hereby released from house arrest. His full rights of citizenship are hereby restored, and his right to travel freely wherever the name of Caesar is acknowledged, and beyond if he so chooses. In the name of the Senate and People of Rome, signed this day, on the Ides of September in the tenth year of his reign, by the Emperor Nero himself."

A cheer went up from the square, and Paul embraced Marcus fondly.

"Praise be to Christ, our advocate before the Father," Paul said, "and to Marcus Quintus Publius, our advocate before Caesar—and a true Lover of God!"

That night Marcus sat at a table in the familiar tavern where Rome's Christians gathered, with Peter, Luke, Priscilla, and Aquila joining him and Paul. He finally asked the question that had been forming in his mind all day.

"Where will you go now?" he asked.

Paul smiled. "Peter has agreed to stay on in Rome until I can return," he said. "I plan to travel through Gaul and Spain, and finally to Britannia if I can, to spread the Word to those who have not yet heard it. The Spirit has revealed to me that I have little time left. But if I am to be poured out like a drink offering, I would like to die in the service of my Redeemer, spreading His Word until the very end."

Not long after that, Paul and Luke left the city. Peter continued to preach to the crowds in the Tentmaker's Square every day, although his poor Latin led him to rely on the services of John Mark, a young half-Jew from Jerusalem, to translate his words into Latin for the crowds. Peter's Greek was quite passable, but here in the capital city, many of the plebs had never learned the Greek language. John Mark had composed a short Gospel of his own, transcribed from Peter's stories about Jesus, and copies of it were now circulating through the city alongside of Luke's more eloquent and expanded story of Jesus' life.

Nero continued to degenerate into cruelty and madness. His dinners and planning sessions with Marcus became fewer and fewer, and his wild orgies lasted for days, and then weeks. Seneca became involved in a plot to assassinate the emperor, and when it became evident the plot had failed, he opened his veins in a tub full of hot water and ended his life.

A few weeks later, it was Poppaea Sabina's turn. She had become pregnant with Nero's child, and the emperor had ordered her husband, Otho, to divorce her so he could marry Poppaea himself. Initially Nero doted on his bride, and even more on the unborn son whom he said would become the greatest emperor Rome had ever known. But Poppaea's pregnancy was not an easy one, and she was becoming quite heavy as her term drew near, and less able to take part in Nero's nightly debaucheries. This caused the emperor to go wild, seducing or raping any woman he could get his hands on. Marcus became so concerned he sent Antonia and their daughter, Drusilla, back to the villa in Pompeii.

Three days after they left, according to palace gossip, Poppaea had lit into Nero about his constant carrying on with other women. Nero had just returned from the chariot races where he had drunk heavily all day. He flew into a towering rage and threw her to the floor, kicking and stomping her until Poppaea's head was crushed and their half-formed child was aborted from her dying body. Then the emperor came to his senses and wept uncontrollably, but it was too late to undo what had been done. Devastated by his own deeds, Nero locked himself in his rooms and refused to see anyone for several weeks.

Marcus was beginning to wonder if Nero was going to abdicate the throne altogether. Missing his wife and child, Marcus also wondered if Nero would even notice if he simply left the city and returned to his villa in Pompeii. But he feared Nero's mercurial moods so much he decided to wait until the next day, then go and personally ask Nero's permission to permanently retire from the Senate. Relieved at having made his decision, Marcus went to bed early that night, a copy of Luke's gospel next to his bed, open to the story of the lost son.

It was still dark when Demetrius shook him awake. There was a heavy smell of smoke in the air, and Marcus could hear screams and cries in the streets outside.

"What is going on?" he demanded.

"Rome is burning, *Dominus*," his steward told him. "We must flee!"

CHAPTER XXVIII

"I will speak for them!" Marcus exclaimed, as every head in the Senate swiveled to stare at him.

Nero shook his head and sighed. "Marcus Publius! I might have known," he said.

Six weeks had passed since the Great Fire, but Rome was still uncovering and burying its dead. Marcus had been fortunate—his own home had been spared, but Rufus and his family were burned out. Over half the Aventine was destroyed, and many of the Christian community rendered homeless. Marcus had dug deep in his own pockets, buying food and renting rooms for the displaced faithful, as well as trying to help some of his more destitute clients. The poorer districts of Rome had been hardest hit by the fire—the huddled *insulae* and crossroads colleges in the Aventine and the other low-rent areas had been consumed, many of them with their inhabitants trapped inside, screaming and choking with smoke as they burned alive.

And now the emperor was trying to blame the fire on the one community that had been most devastated by it? Marcus was furious—as angry as he had ever been. Nero was fixing him with an angry stare, but Marcus met it with a glare that was just as intense and not diffused with madness or evil. Instead, it was a righteous indignation that stirred within him as he stepped out into the aisle to face the emperor of Rome.

Nero watched in astonishment. It had been years since anyone stood up to him in public, and the sight of his old mentor standing on the Senate floor, his eyes blazing with fury, was not something he was prepared to deal with. He opened his mouth to speak, but nothing came out. Marcus seized the moment and spoke before the emperor could cut him off.

"LIAR!!" he roared. "How could you? There is no group in Rome less likely to commit such an outrage than those whom you would seek to blame for this blaze. Virtually all of Rome's Christians live in the poorest districts, the regions hardest hit by the fire. Many of them perished in the blaze, and many more are now homeless and destitute! Are you so desperate to deflect blame that you deliberately seek out the least likely suspects, simply because they are poor and unpopular? Shame on you, son of Claudius! Your noble father would be revolted by such crass fraud!"

The members of the Senate looked at one another in shock. For all his military honors, Marcus was widely known as a soft-spoken, affable man who rarely raised his voice in debate. For him to confront the emperor seemed totally out of character. A few who could remember his youth recalled his fiercely argued legal cases and saw the eloquence of the man they had called "Young Cicero" on display once again. But they held their peace. Silence reigned in the Curia Julia as Nero stared at his accuser.

"I might have known," Nero repeated. "Did you think I was unaware? Did you think your emperor was a fool? You are one of them! I know you were baptized into the cult of the Christians years ago. Tell me, Publius, you who are too self-righteous to attend my parties—how many Christian orgies have you attended? How many babies' blood have you drunk?"

Marcus' reaction caught Nero and the entire Senate by surprise. He did not try to answer the charges—not with words, at least. Instead, he threw back his head and laughed. He laughed long and hard, a clean pure laugh of pure amusement. Nero grew even more angry and perplexed at this, but words failed him for the second time. The senators did not say a word, but watched with wide eyes. Finally, Marcus caught his breath and spoke again.

"I will not insult your intelligence, Sire, by presuming to think you believe the words that just came out of your mouth. Does anyone believe that Christians do these things? Honestly, we might be more welcome here in Rome if we did. The wickedness of this city is so great that orgies and blood-drinking would fit in perfectly. But that is not our way! Do any of you have any idea what Christians actually believe? NO? I will tell you!"

Marcus reached into his pocket and unrolled a small scroll in which he had copied parts of Luke's *evangelion.* In the presence of the emperor and Senate of Rome, he read out loud the words of Christ Himself:

But I say to you who hear: Love your enemies, do good to those who hate you, bless those who curse you, and pray for those who spitefully use you. To him who strikes you on the one cheek, offer the other also. And from him who takes away your cloak, do not withhold your tunic either. Give to everyone who asks of you. And from him who takes away your goods do not ask them back. And just as you want men to do to you, you also do to them likewise. But if you love those who love you, what credit is that to you? For even sinners love those who love them. And if you do good to those who do good to you, what credit is that to you? For even sinners do the same. And if you lend to those from whom you hope to receive back, what credit is that to you? For even sinners lend to sinners to receive as much back. But love your enemies, do good, and lend, hoping for nothing in return; and your reward will be great, and you will be sons of the Most High, for He is kind to the unthankful and evil. Therefore be merciful, just as your Father also is merciful.

The senators stared at him as the words rolled from his lips. His voice took on power and authority as he spoke, and for a moment, time stood still. Nero tried to open his mouth two or three times, but each time it snapped shut again. Marcus, in his mind's eye, could imagine an angel clapping its hand across the emperor's mouth to keep him from interrupting the words of Jesus. It was funny, he thought—here he was signing his own death warrant in front of the emperor himself, and the thought of fear did not even occur to him.

"This is our creed," Marcus said. "These are the words of our God Himself, when He walked among us as a man. We do not hate, we do not retaliate against those who hurt us, and above all, we do not kill! No one who follows the teachings of Jesus would dare lift his hand to harm any of the people of Rome, much less burn down half the city and kill tens of thousands! I say here in the presence of you, the *Imperator* himself, and in the presence of the Senate and People of Rome, that the Christians of Rome are not guilty of this heinous crime! *Absolvo,* I say! There is no fault in them!"

Nero's face had gone from red to purple, and at these last words he found his voice and shouted, descending the dais and confronting Marcus from only a few feet away.

"*Tacete!*" he roared. "Shut up, Marcus Quintus Publius!" The emperor swallowed hard, and glared at Publius with venom in his gaze. Something not quite human slavered from behind his eyes, and for just a moment Marcus thought he saw something black, foul, and clawed clinging to the shoulders of the emperor of Rome. Nero's voice dropped in volume, but the sheer malice in his words made Marcus step back.

"Do you think you are the only Christian I have talked to?" he sneered. "Do you forget that many of my Praetorians guarded your *friend*—" he fairly spat the word out—"Paul the so-called Apostle? Do you remember that some of them were seduced by his poisonous words into embracing the cult of the Nazarene? I interrogated them for days until they confessed their guilt! They were the ones who told me that Paul and that big oaf from Galilee, the fisherman Peter, ordered them to help set the fires!"

"And how long did you have to torture them to extract such falsehoods?" Marcus said. "You and I both know that if you inflict enough pain, men will say whatever you wish to hear!"

"SHUT UP!" roared Nero. "You are unworthy to speak in this hall!"

Fast as lightning, he strode up to Marcus and ripped the Grass Crown from his head, throwing it to the ground and grinding his heel on it. A collective gasp went up from the Senate. The *Corona Granicus* was the highest military honor Rome could confer, given out less than a dozen times in the history of the Republic. To treat it with such disrespect was sacrilege, but none of them dared say a word.

"Your Grass Crown is hereby revoked, Marcus Quintus Publius. Your membership in the Senate is likewise revoked, as is your Roman citizenship. I banish you from Rome for the remainder of your days. The only thing that preserves your life is the affection I once had for you. Leave this city forever! Go to Pompeii, if you wish, but if I ever look upon your face again, I will take your life or perish in the attempt. Do you understand me? Get out, old man! Out of Rome, and out of my life!" Nero was breathing heavily, his cheeks flushed.

"Great Caesar!" a voice exclaimed. Antonia's father, Quintus Africanus, his hair white and leaning on a cane, stepped into the aisle. "This is an outrage! The emperor does not have authority to revoke a Grass Crown, and only the Senate may strip a man of his citizenship!"

Nero looked past Africanus, at one of his Praetorians, and gave a curt nod. The guard stepped up behind Quintus Africanus and ran him through with his *gladius.* Quintus stared down at the blade's point, emerging from his chest, and then looked at his son-in-law. A look of shock spread across his features, and he opened his mouth as if to speak, but only bloody froth came from his lips. He slowly collapsed forward, leaving the black-clad Praetorian holding a stained blade. Marcus caught him as he fell. He looked from Quintus' face, now peaceful in death, to the twisted features of the emperor of Rome. Rage and grief overwhelmed him. He slowly lowered Africanus to the floor and then stood, his toga stained with his father-in-law's blood.

"I wish your adopted father had lived long enough to disown you, as he planned!" Marcus finally said. His words seemed woefully inadequate.

Nero laughed. "I made sure he did not!" he barked. "Now go, Publius, before I change my mind. Because if I do change my mind, I will see your naked infant daughter nailed to a cross and your wife ravaged by all my Praetorians before she joins her child—and you! Go while I yet offer you life!"

Martyrdom was one thing Marcus did not fear, but the threat to his wife and daughter broke his spirit. Without a word, he turned and fled. Even as the doors of the Curia Julia swung shut behind him, he heard Nero's voice echoing from the marble walls: "Now does anyone want to follow him, or is the Senate of Rome ready to vote on my proposal?"

It was with a heavy heart that Marcus retrieved his wife and child from their home in the Quirinale and gathered their personal effects. He swung by the inn where many of Rome's Christians had taken up residence since the fire and warned Peter of the emperor's decree.

"Fear not, my brother," the Big Fisherman said calmly. "We have a place prepared where we can evade detection for a time. Many of us will perish, but the Word of the Lord will endure, as will His church. You have fulfilled your destiny, and rendered the service I foretold. Thanks to you, generations yet unborn will read the magnificent Gospel Luke wrote. Now the Spirit stirs me once more, and I can tell you with confidence that your time has not yet come. Go to Pompeii with your wife, where years of peace will await you before our Lord calls you home."

Marcus embraced the old Galilean, weeping openly. "Will you not go with me?" he asked Peter.

"No," the disciple of Jesus said. "This is now my place. I have known for many years that Rome would become my tomb."

Heartbroken, Marcus and his family—joined by Rufus and his wife, since the big man had been expelled from the College of Lictors—took their leave of Rome and headed south, down the Via Appia, toward Pompeii. Rufus took his setback in stride, as he tended to do with everything.

"Easy come, easy go, says I!" he commented. "I never asked to be a lictor, much less a chief lictor. But I enjoyed it while I did the job, and was rather good at it, too! But here's the thing, Senator—er, I mean, Marcus—I'm going to have to get used to that, you know. You've always been one of the high and mighty, ever since I knew ye! That's why I was so surprised when you took notice of me."

"You were going to tell me what 'the thing' was," Marcus commented drily. He enjoyed the big man's company, but Rufus' banter was not cheering him up as it normally did.

"Begging your pardon, sir!" Rufus said. "My mind is like an old maid's trunk—all sorts of stuff buried up in there, with no telling what's liable to surface at any moment. Now, where was I? Oh, yes, irony, that was it! What's ironic about this whole mess is that I never became a Christian. I mean, I thought about it a few times, but honestly, no disrespect intended, I like killing people too much to be a good Christian. Always thought I'd've made a good legionary, you know. But with Sarah being one of the faithful, and her being Paul's niece as she is, I figured that away from Rome would be the best place for her—and me! Especially after they drummed me out of the lictor's college, just because I spoke up for you."

Marcus patted the big man on the arm. It still felt like he was whacking a sturdy young oak tree, he thought. Good old Rufus! Loyal to a fault, strong as an ox, and just simple enough not to worry about the complexities of life.

"For what it's worth, Rufus," he said, "I'm glad our paths lie together. You're a good man, and I'm glad I was able to help you rise in the world for a while."

"Bless your kind heart, Marcus! I would have wound up with a dagger between my ribs in some Aventine alley if it weren't for you," the big man replied. "If you are going to fall from power, I'll fall right by your side—all the way to the very bottom, if need be!"

"Let's hope it doesn't come to that," Marcus said.

It didn't, although it came pretty close. Marcus arrived safely in Pompeii and moved back into his villa. Many of his newer servants remained in Rome, since he had given them the choice to accompany him into exile or stay and be granted their freedom. The twins Pericles and Heracles were gone, as was Demetrius—albeit with many tears of regret. But the man had a family to look out for, and an offer of employment in another household. Old Phidias, faithful to the end, came along with Marcus' family, blind as a bat now and hobbled with arthritis, but still barking orders to the other household staff. Diana remained also, refusing to even consider leaving Marcus' service.

The villa at Pompeii was large and comfortable, with room for many guests. Marcus made sure that any fugitive Christians, fleeing Nero's holocaust of persecution in Rome, received shelter and coin for the road when they sought refuge under his roof. Dozens passed through his house, and somehow, he managed to help them all financially, despite his vastly reduced fortune.

Those who remained in Rome paid a heavy price. Nero's decree declared all Christians to be *hostis*, their lives forfeit upon capture. Hundreds were rounded up daily by the black-clad Praetorians who swept through the poorer districts of Rome searching for them. The means of identifying Christians was simple, and relied on the faithfulness of believers to betray themselves. The Praetorians carried with them a portable altar with statues of Jupiter Optimus Maximus, Romulus, and the *Divus Julius.* All who were arrested were given a choice: sacrifice and pray to the gods of Rome, or face execution. Thousands of Christians bravely refused to betray their God, and were thrown into the dungeons. After a month of this, Nero staged a spectacular show of barbarity: over twenty thousand Christians were crucified in one day, their crosses placed on either side of the road every hundred feet or so, from the *pomerium* of Rome all the way to Nero's country villa, nearly twenty miles away. Their bodies were smeared with pitch, and as night fell the Praetorians rode ahead of the emperor, lighting the writhing bodies on fire one by one, until Nero could ride from the capital to his villa by the light of their martyrdom. So perished Simeon, the son of Jepthah, Marcus' first Christian mentor in Rome, and the earnest young Trophimus, who had so enjoyed Marcus' stories. Other Christians were carried to amphitheaters and fed to wild beasts as cheering crowds watched the slaughter. It was the greatest mass execution Rome had seen since the defeat of the *Spartacanii* by Crassus over a hundred years before.

But still Peter and Paul eluded capture. Peter was somewhere in Rome, Marcus knew, but neither he nor the Praetorians knew where.

Paul was somewhere in Spain, the last Marcus heard, preparing to take ship to Britannia, with Luke, the beloved physician, by his side. As the months passed since the fire, Marcus began to pray that perhaps his two friends might be spared the fate of so many believers.

Cadius was dismissed from the legions because of his relationship to Marcus not long after this, but his commander, who had come to have a great affection for the young officer, ignored Nero's order to execute the lad and sent him home to Pompeii instead. Marcus' adopted son had greatly enjoyed the army, and was rather bitter for a time, but his faith in the God who had healed him as a teen gradually assuaged his disappointment. The fact that he took notice of Diana almost right away may have had something to do with his restored equilibrium as well—he fell head over heels for the slave girl, leaving Marcus little choice but to set her free. She came to see him not long after Cadius took notice of her, deeply upset.

"*Dominus,*" she said, "as grateful as I am for your kindness, you must send me away. Send me back to Rome, or to another household. It isn't right that your son and heir should become entangled with me, a slave—and a former whore at that! I'm not good enough for him!"

Marcus took her aside and put his arm around her shoulders. "My dear girl," he said. "You were good enough for our Lord and Master to go to the cross to save you from your sins, before you were even born! You were good enough that I purchased you from slavery and whoredom, because I could look in your eyes and see the true innocence in your heart. You are certainly good enough for my son."

"But he is a high-born Roman and I am only a slave girl!" she said.

Marcus laughed for the first time since leaving Rome. He laughed until tears rolled down his cheeks, which caused Diana no small amount of frustration and confusion. Cadius came into the peristyle and saw her hurt and his father's mirth and started to grow angry.

"*Pater,*" he said sternly, "why are you laughing at the woman I love? Such cruelty is unlike you!"

Marcus caught his breath. "You see, my dear boy, she thinks she is unworthy of you because you are 'a high-born Roman' and she is a slave!"

Cadius' eyes widened, and he too began laughing. Diana looked from father to son as if they had both gone mad. Finally, Cadius caught her in his arms and kissed her passionately.

"I was going to tell you, my darling, truly I was," he said. "The moment didn't seem right yet. You see, before I was adopted by Marcus Quintus Publius, I was purchased by his uncle and given to him as a gift."

Her eyebrows shot up in shock. "You mean— " she said.

"That's right!" Cadius replied. "I, too, was once a slave."

"If a slave is good enough to be my son, then a slave is good enough to become my daughter-in-law!" Marcus said. "Now let me get your manumission papers drawn up, dear girl, so we can begin planning a wedding!"

Cadius and Diana were married a month later, in a simple Christian ceremony presided over by one of Paul's young disciples, an earnest young Christian named Timothy. Marcus and Antonia watched in joy as their adopted son embraced his bride, and Marcus was glad that the villa Claudius had given him so long ago was big enough for two couples to live in comfortably. While the Praetorians still swept Italy in search of Christians to be crucified or fed to the lions, they continued to give Marcus' estate a wide berth. In this, at least, Nero kept his word.

Almost two years after Marcus was expelled from the Senate, an urgent letter from Rome arrived. It was carried by none other than John Mark, Peter's interpreter, who rode into Pompeii in the middle of the night on a horse that was as sweaty and exhausted as its rider. The letter was from Paul to Timothy, but Timothy was no longer in Pompeii, having left for Ephesus to take over as pastor of one of the churches there. There was no letter for Marcus himself, but an oral message from the church in Rome.

"Peter and Paul have been arrested," Mark told him. "Peter has been in hiding since shortly after the Great Fire, along with many of the other followers of Christ, in the catacombs below the city. But as the initial purge faded, some of us began to come topside again, in order to purchase food and earn some coin. We have some friends and sympathizers who have never forsaken us—indeed, without them we should have perished in those awful months when so many died. These last few months there have been very few arrests, and Peter, who hated the dank underground passages, decided to come topside and begin preaching in the Tentmaker's Square again, not every day, but once or twice a week, in the evenings. Two weeks ago, the Praetorians took him into custody, and he is locked up in the old Tullianum. Nero intends to execute him soon."

"Horrible!" said Marcus. "What about Paul?"

"Paul had been preaching for the last year in Spain," said Mark. "He was planning to take the Gospel to Britannia, but his old fever came back with a vengeance and laid him low the day before he was to take ship. He was barely able to get out of bed when the Praetorians finally caught up with him. He's been conveyed back to Rome for a formal trial. Nero knows that the Senate is increasingly discontented with his rule, and he can't afford to simply kill Paul, as much as he would like to. Nearly everybody now knows that the charges against our Church were nothing but rubbish from the start—and the bravery with which so many of our brothers and sisters have faced death has swung some public sympathy back to us."

"I must try to save Paul," Marcus said. "I owe him more than my life."

Antonia began weeping. "Please, my husband, you know Nero will kill you if he finds you! I love Paul, too, and I love Jesus, but I don't think I can survive losing you!"

Marcus kissed his wife fiercely. "I have no intention of dying, my dear," he said. "I've been planning for some time how I might return to Rome undetected. Tell me, how would you describe me to one who does not know me?"

"My husband is the kindest, bravest, and best man on earth!" she said.

Marcus scoffed. "I thank you for the sentiment, dear wife!" he said. "But I meant my physical appearance, not your rather distorted view of my personality."

"Ah!" she said. "Well, let's see—my husband is of average stature, clear of eye, strong of build, and has a head so perfect that God has seen fit to remove every single hair that might disguise its proportions."

"Exactly!" said Marcus. "Now excuse me!"

He vanished from the room for a few moments, retreating into his study. As John Mark, Cadius, and Antonia waited impatiently, they heard some sounds of rummaging and fabric swishing. Finally, a stranger appeared in the door. He was at least two inches taller than Marcus, with long, curly black hair and a thick beard, and one shoulder that stood a good bit higher than the other.

"Who are you?" shrieked Antonia. "Where is my husband?"

"Right in front of you, my dear," the stranger said in flawless Greek.

"Jupiter!" exclaimed Cadius. "I never would have known you, *Pater*!"

Antonia blinked and then embraced Marcus. "How on earth did you do this?" she said.

"I've thought for some time that I might need to return to Rome to rescue some of our brethren," he said. "So I began quietly accumulating these articles of disguise. The wig and beard are woven from real hair, and are made to be as realistic as possible. The hunched shoulder is simply a roll of padding placed inside the tunic, while the shoes have special thickened soles to make me look taller.

They say that when Augustus was a young lad, trying to capitalize on his resemblance to Julius Caesar, he had a similar pair of shoes made, so that he would come closer to matching his uncle's height. Now I think I can safely travel to Rome undetected. Perhaps I can deliver Paul or Peter or both from captivity. John Mark, will you accompany me?"

The disciple sighed. "I really should," he said. "Did you know that I was in Jerusalem the night Jesus was arrested? I saw the mob as it went by my house, and got out of bed to follow them. I didn't even have time to throw on a tunic—I simply wrapped a linen sheet around myself and went after them. But in the struggle and confusion when Jesus was arrested, one of the temple guards grabbed at me and I ran home stark naked—with him holding one of my mother's good sheets! I've spent a good part of my life living that down."

Marcus nodded. "So that was you!" he said. "I read that passage in your Gospel and wondered who it could have been."

John Mark gave a wry grin. "Yes, it was me. That was my only brush with Jesus before He was crucified, although I was part of a large group that saw Him after He rose again. At any rate, I promised Paul that I would deliver this letter to Timothy. If he is in Ephesus, then I need to take a ship there right away. I will ride for Neapolis in the morning."

Marcus pressed a purse full of coins into his hand. "This will pay for your passage," he said, "and God speed your journey! I will try and keep Paul alive until you return, one way or another. It will be best, I think, if I travel alone. Farewell!"

Rufus would not hear of allowing Marcus to return to Rome unescorted, though. Finally, Marcus extracted a promise from him that he would wait outside the city wall. Too many people knew of the close association between them, and Rufus' face was well known in Rome. His presence might tip someone off as to the identity of his bearded companion.

The journey was uneventful, and it was near dusk when Marcus arrived outside the city wall. Rufus took a room in the inn next to the stables, just outside the *pomerium,* while Marcus slipped through the gate and into the stews of the Aventine, where many Christians still operated businesses secretly. He found the inn Mark had told him of, with a clever design carved on the wall next to the door—an anchor and a fish, representing the cross and the Greek word for Christ.

He slipped inside and sat down at a bench, ordering a glass of wine and scanning the crowd for a familiar face. He was rewarded nearly an hour later when the door opened and Luke stepped inside. He waited for the author of the Gospel to take a seat, then quietly crossed the room and sat down across the table from him.

"Hello, old friend," he said.

Luke looked at him with a puzzled expression. "Do I know you?" he asked.

"You should!" the bearded stranger said. "You dedicated two of your books to me!"

"Marcus?" the Greek asked incredulously.

"Better to call me by the name that you gave me long ago," the former senator said. "Theophilus I am from now on."

"Of course!" Luke said. "But why are you here? Nero has descended into the blackest pits of madness and evil. He will kill you if he finds you."

"I want to see Peter and Paul," Marcus said, "and rescue them if I can."

Luke smiled. "Seeing them will not be hard," he said. "Both have been allowed visitors. But freeing them? I don't think it can happen. They are closely guarded at all times. Peter is to be executed very soon. Paul will at least be afforded the courtesy of a trial, since he is a Roman citizen."

"Can I see Peter tonight?" Marcus asked.

"Probably," said Luke. "Let's go now, before the changing of the guard. One of the evening shift guards is sympathetic to our cause, although he is not a believer. He has let me bring food and blankets to Peter on more than one occasion."

They slipped out of the inn and headed to the lower edge of the Capitoline Hill, where Rome's ancient prison, the Tullianum, was located. Luke whispered something to the guards, and they parted to let the two men through. Peter was chained to the wall inside, wide awake, singing softly under his breath. His brow furrowed when he saw Marcus, but then his eyebrows rose and he smiled.

"Well done, my friend," he said. "I think your own mother might have passed you in the street as a stranger!"

Marcus knelt by his side and took him by the hand. The Apostle was gaunt, but his expression was full of peace.

"Simon Peter, let me get you out of here," he said. "I know the city well, and I brought gold to bribe the guards."

Peter's brow furrowed again but this time in anger. "Get thee behind me, Satan!" he snapped, causing Marcus to recoil. The anger faded almost right away, however, and the Big Fisherman reached out and took Marcus by the hand.

"That's what Jesus said to me, nearly thirty-five years ago, when I tried to stop him from going to Jerusalem," he said. "It was God's will for him to die there, just as it is God's will for me to die here. After He rose from the dead, Jesus took a walk with me, along the shores of the Sea of Galilee. Three times he asked me if I loved him, and three times I told him that I did. The last time, he looked at me and said: 'When you were young, you girded yourself and went wherever you wished. But when you are old, another will gird you and bind you and take you to a place you do not wish to go.' Now that time is at hand, my friend. I am seventy-five years old. Nearly forty years ago, a stranger passed by my boat and said 'Follow me, and I will make you to fish for men.' I have caught my share for His kingdom, and now it is time for me to lay aside this earthly garment. God has spared me again and again, that I might live to see this time and this place. If I were to run away from Rome, Jesus Himself might have to come down from heaven and be crucified yet again. I ran away from Him once. I will never do so again."

Marcus nodded, blinking back the tears. He embraced the elderly Apostle once more, and they prayed together, then he left with Luke.

Without Marcus even asking, Luke took him next to Rome's other prison, the Mamertine, where the Praetorians guarded the emperor's personal captives. There Paul was waiting, pacing back and forth in a cell that was chilly in the evening dew. He too took a moment to recognize Marcus, but embraced him once he did.

Once again, Marcus tried to persuade a disciple of Jesus to flee the city with him. Paul was just as stubborn.

"It has been revealed to me that I will have a chance to proclaim the Gospel before Nero himself before the end. I do not know if I can overcome the dark spirit that drives him, but I look forward to the contest!" the Apostle to the Gentiles said. "And if it is indeed time for me to lay aside my burdens, so be it! I have fought the good fight, I have run the race, I have finished my course. Henceforth is laid up for me in heaven a crown of riches—and not for me only. You, too, my friend, have earned a reward from our Savior. Go, and continue to live in exile. Teach all who will listen about the Lord Jesus, and proclaim His suffering and His triumph until He calls you home, or returns for His church—although I see now with the eyes of death that many ages will pass before the trumpet sounds and the dead in Christ shall rise. I am content, Theophilus. Do not think to save me, for I was saved long ago. But take Luke with you. He is not under arrest, but if he continues to stay by my side he may yet share my fate. Go now, and may my God supply all your needs through his riches in Christ Jesus."

Frustrated in his purpose but strangely at peace, Marcus returned to the inn where he was staying. He spent several days trying to persuade Luke to come to Pompeii with him, but the physician would not be swayed. Paul needed him more than ever now, he said, and he was determined to stand by his friend through the very end. Finally, Marcus gave up in frustration and left the city, full of sorrow but still glad he had made the journey.

As he exited the city gate, he saw a group of prisoners being led outside the *pomerium* for execution. To his enduring grief, he realized that one of them was Simon Peter. Despite his years and his emaciated condition, the Big Fisherman carried the heavy crossbeam on his shoulders without stumbling. Tears streaming down his cheeks, Marcus followed them to a rugged hill overlooking the Appian Way. He saw Peter whisper something to his guard, and then watched in wonder as the upright beam was lifted out of the ground, reversed, and put back in its shaft. Peter's arms were tied to the crossbeam and his wrists nailed to the wood. Deep groans were the only sound he made as he was lifted, feet first, into the air. His ankles were tied around the upright shaft, and then a spike was driven through them as well. Head down, the old Galilean hung there. His end came quickly—unable to breathe, Peter asphyxiated within the hour.

Marcus cautiously approached the young legionary who led the execution detail. He tried to hide his grief under a mask of casual curiosity.

"I've never seen anyone crucified quite like that before," he said.

"And I've never crucified anyone upside down before!" the man replied. "But he asked for it. He said he wanted to be crucified upside down because he wasn't worthy to die in the same way his master did. These Christians! They are all half mad, if you ask me!"

EPILOGUE

Paul did indeed bear witness in front of the emperor himself, if only briefly. He was charged with inciting arson in connection with the Great Fire, but the only evidence was from the converted Praetorians that Nero had tortured to death. Prosecutors were unable to produce any living witnesses who could connect Paul with the fires, and the great Apostle defended himself and his fellow Christians so vigorously that Nero stomped angrily out of the court, and the jury returned a verdict of *absolvo* at the end of the day.

But arson was not the only charge. Nero had also accused Paul of "introducing new and dangerous doctrines" and being a follower of a proscribed faith. Paul pleaded guilty to being a Christian, but gave a ringing defense of his faith, saying that it was neither new nor dangerous. But the jury was afraid to cross the emperor a second time, at the end of the day voted *condemno.* Paul was led outside Rome a few days later, far beyond the *pomerium,* and was beheaded within sight of the hill where Peter had been crucified. His faithful disciple Luke stayed by his side the whole time, and saw to it that Paul was given a decent burial. The authorities made no attempt to prosecute him—the death of Christ's two greatest followers seemed to have satisfied the people's bloodlust, if not Nero's. Luke decided to fulfill Paul's lifelong dream and make the journey to Britannia as a missionary. He spent ten years there, spreading the Gospel among the Celts and the Picts, before dying at the hands of a Pictish chieftain who despised the new religion.

Marcus and Antonia stayed on in Pompeii, enjoying their beautiful villa and walking along the beach with Drusilla, Cadius, and Diana. A year after Marcus returned from Rome, Diana bore Cadius a strong, sturdy son whom they named Paul. Diana's firstborn, Vorena, whose ruined face Paul had healed, was growing into a beautiful and mischievous little girl. She and Drusilla were closer than sisters, and played together every day.

Nero's behavior grew more tyrannical and bizarre year by year. He built an enormous palace that covered half of the Palatine Hill, and erected a statue of himself that stood nearly eighty feet high—the "Colossus of Nero," they called it.

The war with Parthia had flared again after Marcus left, and after one severe defeat Corbulo had mauled the Parthians so badly that they withdrew to their own territory once more. However, the praise for Rome's greatest general suddenly fired a terrible jealousy in Nero, and he imagined that Corbulo was going to lead his legions to Rome and proclaim himself emperor. In a drunken panic, the emperor had written a letter declaring Corbulo a traitor and demanding that he return to Rome for trial, or else end his life honorably. The buff old Roman had accepted his fate with his usual aplomb, saying of Nero: "He is worthy!" before falling on his sword. Marcus was horrified when he heard the story, but there was nothing he could do about it except say a prayer for the soul of his friend and former commander.

Finally, the Senate sickened of Nero's cruelty and madness and voted to strip him of the Principate and all his other titles. Legionaries were sent to arrest the emperor and bring him to Rome for trial on charges of treason and corruption. Rather than face the disgrace of being publicly executed and his body thrown from the Tarpian rock, Nero stabbed himself in the neck as the soldiers closed in. His last words were: "What a great artist the world loses in me!"

Three emperors vied for the throne after Nero died. Otho, Galba, and Vitellius each ruled for a matter of weeks or months before being cast down and killed. Finally, Marcus' old friend Vespasian, who had been putting down a fierce rebellion in Judea, came to Rome at the head of his army and was declared emperor, first by his legions and then by the Senate. He restored a great deal of dignity and respect to the imperial throne over the next decade, and as James had prophesied, his armies laid waste the city of Jerusalem and tore Herod's great temple apart until not one stone remained on another.

Not long after Vespasian became emperor, Marcus received a letter informing him that his citizenship had been reinstated, and that he could reclaim his seat in the Senate if he would sacrifice to the gods of Rome upon arriving in the city. He never answered the letter, nor did he ever return to Rome. In time, the name and accomplishments of Marcus Quintus Publius were forgotten by the people of Rome, but the name of Theophilus—"Lover of God"—was spoken with honor by Christians the world over from that day to this.

POMPEII, ITALY
2014 AD

The tourists walked through the ancient Roman city, looking at the structures that had been encased in ash since 79 AD. Magnificent villas, open-air markets, statues, colorful frescoes, and, of course, the plaster casts of the victims of Vesuvius' wrath were all a part of the tour.

A married couple from the United States—actually, he was from the USA, while his bride hailed from Italy—were supposed to be there as tourists. But since both of them were archeologists by trade, they actually knew more about the site than their tour guide. Their English was also better than his, so he decided to let them answer the questions at the end of the tour.

A minister from Texas raised his hand, and the young archeologist called on him.

"Josh, isn't it?" he said, and the man nodded. "Has there ever been any evidence found to support the contention that there were Christian families living here in Pompeii?"

"Funny you should ask," the scientist replied. "Just recently, archeologists uncovered the remains of a beautiful villa on the edge of town. The artwork and statuary were pretty standard, with one exception: none of the statues or inscriptions depict the traditional gods of Rome. In the room where the shrine to the household gods should have stood, the simple outline of a cross has been carved into the wall."

"That's amazing!" the man said. "I wonder who owned the villa."

"Their names are not recorded in any of the inscriptions," Josh told him. "But they did find the remains of a man and woman just inside the gate of the home. They poured plaster into the cavities left by the bodies, as they have done here since the 1800s. What they found were the bodies of a man and a woman, who appear to have collapsed as they tried to escape. They were still holding hands."

CAST OF CHARACTERS

(in order of appearance)

Nero Claudius Caesar Augustus Germanicus—Fifth Emperor of Rome, known for his corruption and cruelty, suspected by many of setting the Great Fire

Laecenius Bassus—consul during the year of the Great Fire

Licinius Crassus—co-consul during the year of the Great Fire

Marcus Quintus Publius—newly elected senator, defender of Christians, hired as an advocate to represent Paul of Tarsus

Mencius Quintus Publius—Marcus' uncle and patron, friend of Claudius Caesar

Quintus Hortensius—a consular and senior senator, defender of the Jews

Porcius Antonius—the *Princeps Senatus* during the reign of Claudius

Demetrius—Marcus' household steward

Drusilla—Marcus' deceased wife

Phidias— Marcus' elderly body servant and attendant

Vitellius Scribonius—Roman businessman, Marcus' first senatorial client

Gaius Antillus—Roman businessman, trainer of gladiators

Lucius Berettus—pleb seeking legal help from Marcus

Rufus Licinius—street brawler who became Marcus' bodyguard

Phillipus—Mencius' steward

Claudia Publius—Mencius' wife and Marcus' aunt

Cadius—slave boy given to Marcus by his uncle, later Marcus' adopted son

Lucius Hortensius—Marcus' legal client; plaintiff in a property case

Gnaeus Sempronius—Praetor who served as a judge in the trial

Fabius Ahenobarbus—Marcus' old friend and rival in the courts

Quintus Africanus—defendant who purchased Lucius' villa

Valeria Messalina—the wife of Claudius, executed for adultery

Fulvius Gracchus—Roman merchant, legal client of Marcus'

Marcus Fabricius—Roman dandy who stole Gracchus' wife

Cassius Claudius—freedman of Emperor Claudius; accompanied Marcus on his inspection tour

Armenius—lictor who accompanied Marcus and Cassius on the tour

Titus Granicus—corrupt governor of Tarraconensis

Ambrosius Pullo—centurion in Tarraconensis

Maximus Crassus—deputy who replaces Titus Granicus

Hylia—local girl whipped for refusing to bed Titus Granicus

Ardelia—Hylia's sister, offers herself to Marcus

Porcius Masigius—proconsul of Lusitania

Gaius Bibulus—prefect of Tingitana

Octavius—freedman who runs the province for Bibulus

Lucius Numidicus—prefect of Mauretania

Julia Agrippina Minor—wife of Claudius, mother of Nero

Pyronius—Greek tutor who helped Claudius overcome his speech defect

Titus Flavius Vespasian—Roman general, acting governor of Britain, future emperor

Varus Marius—prefect of Germania Inferior, blackmailed by his legate

Cardixa—German barmaid who provided Marcus with information

Dragox—innkeeper and pimp for Maxentius

Lucius Maxentius—corrupt prefect running Germania Inferior

Sergius Paulus—centurion promoted to replace Maxentius

Lucas Amelius—proconsul of Germania Superior

Quintus Ambrosius—proconsul of Raetia

Democles—Ambrosius' corrupt steward

Titus Andronicus—retired proconsul, ran the colony in Pannonia

Eleazar ben Mosche—Jewish merchant interviewed by Marcus

Antonius Lycenus—prefect of Lycia and Pamphylia

Phillipus Acro—corrupt prefect of Galatia

Marcus Amelius—his legate and partner in crime

Cornelius Cinna—Christian centurion, converted by Peter's preaching

Paul (Saul) of Tarsus—Apostle, leader of Christian efforts to evangelize the Gentiles

John—an Apostle of Jesus who prayed for Cadius to be healed

Silas—disciple of Jesus and a companion of Paul and John

Naomi—formerly Procula Porcia, widow of Pontius Pilate, now a Christian

Miriam—the sister of Jesus of Nazareth; John's wife

Joseph Barnabas—traveling companion of Paul and John

Gaius—formerly Decimus Pontius Pilate, son of the Roman prefect

John Mark—disciple of Jesus, companion of Paul and John

Ventidius Cumanus—prefect of Judea

Simon Peter—leader of the Apostles, encounters Marcus at Jerusalem

Manlius Hortensius—centurion who escorts Marcus to Parthia

Ventularia—Parthian officer who escorts Marcus to Ecbatana

Vologases—newly minted king of Parthia, challenges Rome's control of Armenia

Perseus Democritus—vizier to the Parthian king

Antonius Corbulus—commander of the *XIX Legion Pannonia,* appointed by Marcus

Tertia Livilla—Mencius' second wife, widow of one of his old friends

Decimus Meridius—*Primipilus* centurion of the Pannonian Legion, who recommended Marcus for the Grass Crown

Simeon bar Jepthah—a Jewish Christian who befriends Marcus in Rome

Antonia Minor Africanus—Marcus' second wife

Lucretia Africanus—Antonia's younger sister

Sextus Afranius Burrus—prefect of Nero's Praetorian guard and advisor to the young emperor

Lucius Annaeus Seneca—a well-known Stoic philosopher who was Nero's tutor, and later, a key advisor to the young emperor

Gnaeus Domitius Corbulo—commander of the Roman army in the war against Parthia

Perseus—Greek slave acquired by Marcus for his second expedition

Loukas Antigonus— AKA St. Luke, physician and traveling companion of Paul

Antiochus of Commagene—client king of Rome who commanded soldiers during the Parthian war

Antonius Gracchus—centurion who escorted Marcus back to Rome from the Parthian War

Pericles and Heracles—twin slaves gifted to Marcus by Nero

Poppaea Sabina—mistress, wife, and ultimate victim of Nero

Trophimus—a Roman Christian who carries Paul's letters to Marcus

Diana—a slave girl purchased out of harlotry by Marcus

Fat Fatima—a huge prostitute from Judea who wound up in Rome

GLOSSARY OF LATIN TERMS

Absolvo: a verdict of "Not Guilty" declared by a Roman judge or jury

Agrodatio: the Roman adoption ceremony by which a grown man was adopted into a new family, frequently necessary when a noble family produced too many sons for the father to be able to afford their ascension of the *cursus honorum*

Amuensis: a scribe or secretary who penned letters dictated by another

Arctoritas: the circle of influence and prestige enjoyed by a member of the Roman aristocracy—it was measured by the number of clients one had, the respect one commanded from his peers, and one's public reputation

Armillae: a golden armband awarded to legionaries who slew an enemy in hand-to-hand combat

Ave: "Greetings!"—a common Latin salutation, "Hello" in English

Balneator: the proprietor of a public bathhouse

Cacat: Latin slang for human feces; sometimes also used as an expletive

Calvarium: the skull

Centurion: a noncommissioned officer in a Roman legion who commanded 100 legionaries and around 20 auxiliaries

Cognomen: the first part of a Roman's name. Typical Romans had three names; although members of important families might add more. To address someone by their *cognomen* was a sign of friendship and familiarity

College—in ancient Rome, this term signified a guild or a club rather than an educational facility

Comitia: the assemblies of Roman citizens that voted on election days

Condemno: a verdict of "Guilty" from a Roman court or magistrate

Consul: The chief executives of the Roman Republic; two in number, they were elected by the citizens of Rome and served a one-year term. Under the emperors, the office held less power, but still carried great prestige

Conterburnalis: a junior officer in the Roman military, equivalent to an ensign or field cadet

Corona Civitas: the Civic Crown, Rome's second highest military decoration. It was awarded to any soldier who saved the life of a comrade, held his ground throughout the battle, and personally killed at least one of the enemy

Corona Granicus: Rome's highest decoration, a simple crown woven from the grass of the battlefield where it was won. This award was given to any soldier who single-handedly saved an entire legion from destruction

Culus: slang term for the anus

Curia Julia: the Court of Julia, a public building erected by Gaius Julius Caesar in honor of his daughter Julia, which became the customary meeting place of the Roman Senate in Augustus' time

Cursus Honorum: the "ladder of honors"—the succession of offices that a successful Roman was expected to occupy on his way to the highest elected position, that of consul

Denarius: a common Roman coin made of silver, which represented one day's wage for an average laborer

Divus Augustus: the "Divine Augustus"—the title granted to Caesar Augustus after his death and deification

Divus Julius: the "Divine Julius"—the title granted to Gaius Julius Caesar after his death and deification

Dominus: "Master," the customary honorific used by Roman slaves. *Domina* is the feminine

Domus: "home," one's personal residence

Ecastor: "By Castor!"—a mild expletive used by Roman men and women in polite conversation to express dismay or disbelief

Edepol: "By Pollux!" a companion expletive used more often by Roman men than women

Fermia balnea: a public hot bathhouse. Rome featured a number of these; places where a man could soak in hot water, socialize with companions, and enjoy a massage before going home

Fortuna: the Roman Goddess of Luck, believed to favor certain individuals

Gens humana: the human race; mankind

Gladius: a Roman short sword. The blade was double-edged, and typically sixteen to eighteen inches in length

Hostis: a declared enemy of the state, whose life and property were forfeit upon capture

Hubris: (actually Greek rather than Latin) a pride so great that it offends the gods

Imagio: a wax funeral mask of one's most famous ancestors, worn by actors during family funeral processions

Imperator: literally "conqueror," this was the designation normally given to any Roman commander who vanquished an enemy army on the field. Later, it became the title of Rome's rulers, and passed into English as the word "emperor"

Imperium: the right to command; conferred by the Senate and People of Rome, or later by the emperor. There were different levels of *imperium,* according to one's rank

Imperium mais: the authority to pass judgment on Roman citizens, regardless of their rank

Insula: The Roman equivalent of an apartment complex; usually a three- or four-story building with several small apartments all facing onto an inner courtyard

Kalends: the first day of a Roman month, which traditionally fell on the new moon (prior to the adoption of the Julian calendar in 44 BC)

Lares: the household gods that guarded every Roman family

Latifundium: a large Italian plantation, employing the labor of hundreds of slaves

Legate (also Legatus): the commander of a Roman army, while a junior legate commanded individual legions within the army

Lictors: the honor guards assigned to Roman officials—the greater the number of lictors, the higher the rank. The senior lictor would carry the *fasces* which represented the official's *imperium*

Ludus: a training school for gladiators

Ludus Magnus: Rome's largest gladiator training facility

Mare Nostrum: "Our Sea," the Romans' nickname for the Mediterranean

Mater—formal address for one's mother

Medicus: slang term for a physician

Mortis Collegia: an organization that carried out all necessary services and rituals for the dead of Rome, from cremation to the building of crypts and monuments

Mos Maorum: the traditions of the Roman Republic, the way things had always been done, similar to the Biblical "traditions of our elders"

Pater: formal address for one's father

Paterfamilias: "Head of the Family"' the formal position of the father in a Roman home. As head, he literally had the power of life and death over family members

Patria potestas: literally "the possession of the father," referring to a Roman father's power of life and death over the members of his family

Pax Romana: the "Peace of Rome," begun during the reign of Augustus, which would last for nearly 200 years without large-scale wars

Pedarii: (singular ***pedarius***) a "backbencher"' junior members of the Roman Senate who generally did not speak unless called upon

Phalerae: a disc worn on the breastplate; could be gold, silver, or bronze according to the valor of the act it was awarded for

Pilae (singular ***pilus***): the standard spear used by Roman legionaries, about five feet in length, with a forged iron head. They were designed to be thrown, although they could also be useful in short-range combat as a thrusting lance

Plebeian: the historically "common" classes of the Roman Republic, although by Pilate's time plebs were eligible to hold any political office, and comprised more than half the membership of the Senate.

Podex: the part of the anatomy one sits on; the buttocks

Pomerium: the sacred boundary of the city of Rome. By tradition, no military commander could cross it without laying down his *imperium*

Praetor: a local magistrate, elected by the citizens of Rome. The Urban Praetors were in charge of maintaining the city of Rome's infrastructure, including roads, aqueducts, and sewers, as well as public buildings

Praetorian Guard: the personal bodyguards of the emperor of Rome

Prefect: a Roman official who was appointed by the Senate or emperor rather than elected; there were both military and civilian prefects

Primus Pilus (also ***Primipilus):*** literally "First Spear," the highest ranking centurion in a legion of Roman soldiers

Princeps: one of the emperor's official titles, loosely translated to "First Citizen"

Princeps Senatus: The senior member and leader of the Roman Senate

Principate: the office of emperor

Proconsul: a Roman governor who has held the rank of consul before being sent to his province

Publicani: also called tax farmers, they were usually local residents who contracted to collect taxes from the native population. Called "Publicans" in the New Testament, they were universally despised

Quaestor: an elected magistrate of the Roman Republic, whose members automatically qualified for a seat in the Senate

Quirites: "Citizen"; Roman society had three divisions—citizens, subjects, and slaves. Citizens of Rome had legal privileges that its foreign subjects did not, including the right to vote in Rome's elections and the right to appeal their case to Caesar himself

Retarius: a gladiator who fought with a net and a trident as his weapons

Rudis: a wooden sword used for training purposes

Sagum: a leather cloak worn by soldiers on campaign; it was oiled to keep it supple and waterproof

Secutor: a gladiator who fought with the sword and shield

Spartacanii: the army of slaves that followed Spartacus in his rebellion against Rome in 70 BC

Stadia: a unit of measurement, approximately 600 feet

Stibium: makeup favored by prostitutes and older women in the East; believed to have been invented in Egypt; also the reddish makeup worn by a *Triumphator*

Tacete: "Silence!"—a rude way to tell someone to be quiet

Tata: childish name for one's father, equivalent to "Daddy"

Tetrarch: one who governs one-fifth of a kingdom—a title given to Herod the Great's sons after their father's kingdom was split between them

Toga virilis: the solid white, formal garment a Roman man donned upon reaching manhood at age 16

Torcs: a golden necklet awarded for valor in combat

Tribune: an elected official who represents the interests of the electorate. Military tribunes acted as liaisons between the soldiers and their commander; Tribune of the Plebs was a very important political office that automatically enrolled its members in the Senate. Historically, Tribunes of the Plebs could introduce legislation and veto any proposal from the consuls or the Senate. Although their powers were reduced under the principate, the office still carried great honor and was highly sought after.

Triumph: a victory parade through the streets of Rome for a successful general. Triumphs had to be approved by the Senate, and were rarely awarded in the first century

Triumphator: a Roman general who has been granted a triumph

Triumvir: "One of three"; the Triumvirates were alliances between powerful statesmen in the Roman Republic in order to govern public affairs. The First Triumvirate was between Caesar, Crassus, and Pompey; the Second Triumvirate was between Octavian, Marc Anthony, and Lepidus

Vestal Virgins: the ten priestesses of Vesta, the goddesses of hearth and home, bound for the duration of their office to remain pure. They were usually pledged to Vesta at age 8 and released from their vows at the age of 35

Virtus: virtue, decent and honorable standards in one's dealings

ABOUT THE AUTHOR

LEWIS BEN SMITH is a pastor, schoolteacher, historian, and enthusiastic Indian artifact collector. A lifetime of studying New Testament and Roman history inspired his deep interest in the origins of our New Testament. One day in 2012, he began writing notes during a chapel service that became the outline of his first novel, *The Testimonium,* published in August 2014. Since then, he has written three more novels, including the prequel to this work, *The Redemption of Pontius Pilate,* and a sequel to *The Testimonium* titled *Matthew's Autograph.* He lives with his wife, Patricia, and a small menagerie of miscellaneous animals in Greenville, Texas, where he hopes that he will one day sell enough books to buy a lake house, retire from teaching, and spend his golden years hunting arrowheads and writing more books like this one. Your purchase will greatly help expedite that process!

CPSIA information can be obtained
at www.ICGtesting.com
Printed in the USA
LVHW091727110319
610227LV00002B/418/P